To Ben,

with every good wish

from

The
Disciple,

Whom he has Promised

to Sponsor.

Michael Mallm

14 . X . 2021

Philadelphia

The Disciple

A NOVEL

Michael Mallon

ZULEIKA

First published 2021

by Zuleika Books & Publishing

Thomas House, 84 Eccleston Square
London, SW1V 1PX

British Library Cataloguing in Publication Data

A catalogue record for this book is
available from the British Library

ISBN: 978-1-9161977-1-8

Designed by Euan Monaghan
Printed in England

ACKNOWLEDGEMENTS

Faber & Faber Limited: W.H. Auden, *The Orators: An
English Study* (1932); W.H. Auden, 'The Quest' from
Collected Poems, ed. E. Mendelson (1976); T.S. Eliot,
'Gerontion' from *Collected Poems*, 1909–1935 (1947).

The Belknap Press of Harvard University Press:
Henry James, from *Letters*, Volume III,
1883–1895, ed. L. Edel (1980).

IN MEMORIAM

J. P-H.
1913–1994

If any man *come to me, and hate not his father,
and mother, and wife, and children,
and brethren, and sisters, yea,
and his own life also,
he cannot be my
disciple.*

St Luke

Contents

BOOK FIRST

CHAPTER I

Rogation Days

'FOLLOW ME, AND I will show you the view from the loggia,' Sir
Christopher Noble-Nolan said.

'Yes, I'd love to see it,' the 24-year-old John Forde said to the
distinguished art historian – nearly half a century older than himself – whom he trailed after.

Once they had climbed a steep staircase and a forbidding-look-
ing door was unbolted, they passed into a vaulted, open-air room,
jutting out toward the Arno, with expansive views of Florence on
three sides, each one neatly framed by a pair of Doric columns, as
if to demarcate precisely the spot from which one should stand and
behold the monumental vista: the cupola of the Duomo, the spire of
the Palazzo Vecchio, the colonnade of the Uffizi and the *campanili*
of one imposing Renaissance church after another, all encircled by
the poetically undulating hills of Tuscany.

In that summer of 1983, it was both thrilling and terrifying for
John Forde, on this his first trip to Europe, to stand in such prox-
imity to the city of his dreams, for he had, from the time that
he began to study art history as an undergraduate, harboured an
especial devotion to Florence. *And thou, his Florence, to thy trust /
Receive and keep*, he quoted silently as he gaped at the sight before
himself, praying, as one might for a good harvest or an increase in
vocations, that his burning desire of escape – escape from the eternal struggle of scrimping and saving and scholarshipping, escape,
even more, from the parched landscape of his middle, middle-class
childhood in Providence, Rhode Island – should be realised here,
in Florence, the 'City of Flowers', as she has been known for century upon century *upon* century.

'Well, there you have Florence – all within touching distance,' Sir

3

Christopher Noble-Nolan said, waving his hand in a proprietary gesture.

Have it? If only I did have *it,* John sighed to himself. Aloud, he merely said, 'Spectacular.'

'It *is* nicely positioned, isn't it?' Sir Christopher asked with a rhetorical flourish.

'I suppose it's even better than the view from Belcanto,' John said, referring to the villa, just outside of Florence, where he had heard Sir Christopher speak on Botticelli's illustrations for the *Divine Comedy* less than one week ago, a lecture round which he had organised his entire summer travel plans.

Ever since he had come across the name – that, to him, magical-sounding name: Christopher Noble-Nolan – when idling round the art and archæology library on a lonely Friday night during his freshman year at the University of Chicago in 1977, John had convinced himself of a mystical union with the illustrious scholar. In the years that had elapsed since, he made himself obsessively familiar with every aspect (professional *and* personal) of Sir Christopher's life: the relations he bore; the schools he had attended; the clubs he belonged to; the societies he was a fellow of; the decorations he had been awarded; and, most important, the books he had written – from the first monograph he published, in 1937, when he was twenty-three years old, right up through the volume of collected essays that came out just this spring. Thus was it but little wonder that John should have felt utterly transported when, last week, on 23 June, the Vigil of the Baptist, he beheld the tall, thin, beautifully groomed art historian ascend the dais with aristocratic aplomb. To John, Sir Christopher presented an urbane image of Olympian detachment – elegant, without being dandified; unusually refined, rather than conventionally handsome – in whom intellectual attainment was indissolubly wedded to social distinction. Mesmerised by the commanding timbre of the voice holding forth on Botticelli's illustrations for the *Divine Comedy*, John felt that he could, at last, see the advantage of *the long study and the great love that had made* him search volumes. As if overcome by a vision, John was convinced that he finally beheld his *master and author.*

'Oh, but this view is infinitely superior,' Sir Christopher declared. 'To begin with, it is just the right height, so that one doesn't see any of the suburban sprawl that one does from Fiesole. From here, one has the illusion that there is just the historic centre of Florence and the surrounding hills. And one doesn't really want anything more than the illusion, does one?'

But John did want more than an illusion – much more. He wanted to be firmly planted *at the foot of a noble castle, seven times encircled by high walls, a sweet brook flowing round.* And so it was that, on the very day following the lecture at Villa Belcanto, he had made a pilgrimage to Palazzo Vespucci – where, tradition says, Dante often dined with the Ospizio de' Pelegrini after hearing Mass at the adjoining church – and deposited with the surly portress a cal-culatedly sincere letter of admiration, addressed to Sir Christopher Noble-Nolan, KCVO, CBE, FBA, FSA, FRSL.

'Now, you mentioned in your letter,' Sir Christopher continued, sitting down on a cushionless wicker chair, as he motioned for John to do the same, 'that you've done some work on Botticelli.'

'Well no, I mean yes, but, uh, I've just begun, really,' John stam-mered, as eager to establish himself as he was anxious not to stake false claims he might have later to recant. 'I only started a little while ago, but I have pretty much decided that I want to write about a group of Botticelli's followers. I am particularly interested in Bartolomeo di Giovanni and the Master of San Miniato. Of course, Botticelli comes into that, though I wouldn't presume to deal with his work. I realise that's much too big a subject. My real aim is to try to reconstruct the actual workings of his studio from the point of view of the artists who were trained therein.'

'What a frightfully good subject.'

'Unfortunately, my dissertation adviser, Professor Isner, doesn't share your enthusiasm.'

'Oh, old Milton Isner, you mean? I've known him since he was a graduate student himself, and, believe me, I wouldn't worry too much about what *he* thinks,' Sir Christopher said with a dismissive chuckle.

'Hmm.' John smiled, secretly thrilled to collude in such denigra-tion. Though he could not deny that his professor was a perfectly able dissertation adviser, and always a conscientious one, John knew in his heart that Milton Isner – he of the shiny polyester suits; he of the thinning grey hair (parted just slightly above ear level); he of the flat Middle Western twang and the altogether unforthcoming manner;

he, the married suburban commuter; he, the Jewish atheist – bore no relation to the etiolated æsthete whom he had envisaged, before he came to graduate school, acting as his mentor, his Mantuan guide. Romantic egotist that he was, John's intellectual vanity demanded that he picture himself safely escorted on the back of Geryon by someone such as Sir Christopher Noble-Nolan – he of the Oxbridge education (and attendant accent); he of the doctorates of honoris causa; he of the knighthood and the altogether patrician demeanour; he, the celibate expatriate; he, the Roman Catholic ritualist – which is why, in searching for a dissertation topic, John had been determined to find a subject that would relate to (without seeming to impinge on) Sir Christopher's Botticelli work, a long-standing project that he had already heard talked about in New York.

Though the grant that had made possible John's summer trip to Europe was specifically intended to help a graduate student define his dissertation proposal, he had resolutely decided, *before* he set foot abroad, to commit himself to a group of obscure followers of Botticelli. He knew that much study (and a good deal of speculation) had been devoted to reconstructing the young Botticelli's training in the studio of Fra Filippo Lippi, but that little work had been done on the constitution of the large *bottega* he himself eventually founded, and John hoped that, by addressing this question, he would be able firmly to ally himself to Sir Christopher Noble-Nolan. That he might, at the same time, incur the wrath of Professor Isner, whose supposedly steadfast assistant he had been all of the last year, excited him more than it intimidated him.

'As you know from the lecture the other day,' Sir Christopher continued, 'I am now engaged on a full-scale monograph on Botticelli, so I think I'm in a much better position than old Milton Isner to pronounce on the matter. And it's not,' he added, 'as if he's a connoisseur. I mean, Isner's attribution of a picture – positive *or* negative – is not about to change its value. He knows about documents, not works of art. And I always say that if a document contradicts *my* eye, I assume that the document is at fault.'

'That's a nice way to put it,' John said, trying not too blatantly to reveal the admiration he felt for the power that a connoisseur like Christopher Noble-Nolan can wield, for he realised that Sir Christopher, with his stellar reputation – never the slightest hint of any truck with the marketplace – could, with but the flick of a footnote, alter the value of a work of art by millions, indeed many millions, of dollars.

'That's really, you see, why one has retired from all positions in London and moved out here, so that one can devote one's self entirely to scholarly writing.'

'I suppose that it must be a relief to be free of all that administration?'

'To be honest, I rather liked the administration, or administering people at any rate. But yes, I am happy to have returned to the fold of pure scholarship. And now that one has done so, *nothing* must get in the way of the Botticelli work. First, I am to finish the book on Botticelli's illustrations for the *Divine Comedy*, which has been commissioned under a beautiful contract – they are planning to produce not so much a coffee-table book as a billiard-table one – then, I will return to the full-scale monograph – the catalogue raisonné is nearly complete – and finally, when that is done, I plan a comprehensive study of the Botticelli shop. So, I greatly look forward to your work. It should dovetail neatly with what I am engaged on.

'Do you know *Hamamelis*?' Sir Christopher asked, reaching out to caress the branch of one of the many plants growing in terracotta pots on the loggia. He indicated the abrupt change in subject by briefly, though markedly, raising the pitch of his voice.

John stood up and, simulating interest, inspected the spindly and, to him, far from prepossessing shrub. There was a pot of rather unusual green flowers that he liked, but he didn't dare draw attention to them, as he had no idea what they were.

'It comes from the Himalayas, *Hamamelis* does. Very rare. One had to be taken to a nursery garden near Volterra to find it. It flowers on Epiphany, you know.'

John didn't know, but he nodded vaguely, for he wanted to please without appearing *intent* on doing so. When, on Tuesday of this week, he had received a terse postcard from Sir Christopher, acknowledging his letter and inviting him to turn up – any day he chose – at his apartment at five o'clock, John had been torn by the temptation instantly to gratify his desire to meet the object of his fascination and the belief that his own cause would be best served by a show of disinterested restraint. He reasoned that it would be advisable to come on the Thursday – neither too soon nor too late – but, in the end, unable to curb his ardour, he rang Sir Christopher's bell at one minute past five on the Wednesday, 29 June. Impatient as he had been to penetrate Sir Christopher's lair, he did not, however, once there, intend to stay long, for he thought that a short visit held greater promise of future invitations. He was pleased that Sir Christopher seemed genuinely reluctant to let him go when, after having been there for three quarters of an hour, he made a motion to leave. He insisted that he did not want to impose but said that he would like to come back soon, giving precise details of his dates, for he very much wanted to impress on Sir Christopher the fact of his limited presence in Florence. Nonetheless, as he descended the staircase from the loggia and followed Sir Christopher through the majestic hallway, he began to think that perhaps he had been too hasty in taking his departure.

Just as they arrived at the confluence of the L-shaped hall – the front door of departure now staring him in the face – John turned round and, pointing in the other direction to a set of closed double doors, asked, in quiet desperation, 'Is that your study?'

'It is, but I'm afraid that it is hardly visitable, as it is in the most frightful muddle. And I imagine it will have to stay that way, now that summer is upon us, till one can find someone to arrange it in the autumn.'

'I'd be happy to help you sort things out,' John said unhesitatingly.

'Oh, in *that* case!' Sir Christopher said, striking another high note.

'I would certainly do whatever I could, though I'm not, I mean, here much longer, as I already said.' John had flown from New York to Milan at the beginning of June and come straight to Florence, having arranged, in advance, to sublet from a fellow graduate student a small, fetid flat in via Sant'Agostino through the end of August. He planned to use this apartment as a base, whilst travelling the length and breadth of Italy throughout the summer, to see in the original all those works of art that he had only ever known from books, photographs and slides.

'You'd better come and have a look before you make any rash promises,' Sir Christopher said as he pushed open the double doors to his study. 'You see what one means.'

John *did* see. He stood in a long rectangular room with a French

window at the north end, providing a broad view of the Arno, in front
of which loomed a grand refectory table and an even grander chair
– worthy of, at the very *least*, a cardinal – whilst a smaller window
on the east wall provided a lyrical vision of San Miniato al Monte.
Immediately to the right of the entry was a piano, upon which sat a
large armillary sphere, reminding John of the one that Botticelli had
depicted in the fresco of St Augustine in *his* study; above hung a picture of the *Lamentation*, which was, John thought, late fifteenth-century Lombard, though any precise attribution escaped him.

Otherwise, the walls were covered with bookcases, wrapping
round the corners of the room, right up to the windows. Though
the shelves were already full to the point of overflowing, box upon
half-opened box of more books lay scattered about the room. Inter-
spersed with them was an avalanche of photographs (of works of
art, not of people), slides, periodicals, off-prints, a rolled carpet, a
pair of chairs still covered in plastic packing, two good old trunks
and several cheap modern suitcases that appeared to be bulging
with papers. Towering over the scene, like a group of misplaced
sentries, stood five metal filing cabinets, all of a slightly different,
drab hue. Looking round, John thought of the bookless rooms of
his childhood and exhaled, not discontentedly, but almost with an
air of relieved satisfaction, as if to say that he had finally, after years
of wandering, reached his true port of entry.

Unlike a bibliophile, who values each volume individually, he was
aroused by the abundance of books. He felt that he learnt something,
indeed became something, just from the very profusion; the sight of
all these books, the smell of them, the touch of them excited him.
And this was a sensation that no institutional library could inspirit,
for he found that, just as pearls, even if they be carefully kept, will
lose their lustre if they are not worn, so too is it necessary that books
be owned and handled for their magic to be ignited. That so many
of these volumes were battered or mis-shelved only added to his
sense of awe, confirming his conviction that the books by which he
was surrounded were not distraction for the rich but tools for the
knowledgeable. He walked up to the altar of a writing-table and
piously ran his fingers along its book-laden, paper-strewn surface.

'I'm afraid that I wasn't exaggerating,' Sir Christopher broke in
on John's reverie.

'No, you weren't.'

'A veritable Augean stable it is,' Sir Christopher said. 'Of course,' he continued, 'Peter did the best he could. He really worked wonders in the short time he was here. It was he who hung all the pictures and organised the plants. But now that he's gone back to London – well, I don't see how things will ever be put right.'

Peter? John thought but refrained from asking, for he imagined that it would be better for him, as is often the case when learning a new language, to try to piece things together from context, rather than to interrupt the flow of conversation in pursuit of precise definitions. Instead, he said, 'If you think it would help, I could come back tomorrow afternoon and try to make a start at organising some of these books.'

'But that would be *too* marvellous.'

'I could call first, if you want – but, I'm sorry, you said in your note that your telephone is broken. I mean, uh, that's why you told me just to turn up like this.'

'It's not broken, the telephone. The wretched thing has never been turned on, or whatever they're meant to do to it. There's a number, and there's a telephone, but there's no sound when one picks it up,' Sir Christopher said with unconcealed exasperation.

'I wonder what can be done?' John said, thinking aloud.

'If you could find out, I should be more than grateful.'

'How long have you been living here?' John asked.

'Actually *in* this apartment, just over a fortnight. I stayed in an *hôtel* for the first month, whilst the worst of things was being straightened out. I must say that I never imagined that it would be quite so difficult to get settled. And this does *so* interrupt one's work. Not,' Sir Christopher stopped himself, 'that one wasn't perfectly right to move out here; it's what one's always dreamt of, so when Antonia Vespucci told me that this flat in their palace was available to let – well, I thought one really had to nab it at once. It's just that, perhaps, one should have waited to move till the autumn, as many people suggested.'

'I've been told that everything really closes up here in summer, particularly during the month of August.'

'Does it not! Which means that one has only another few weeks to get this flat organised, before things come to a complete standstill. In the past, I admit, I've always rather liked the idea that Florence should be almost hermetically sealed during the month of August. Lord knows, I've spent every summer here for nearly the past fifty years – excepting the war, of course – and I always found it immensely conducive to work, what with all that intense heat and everything tight shut. But then, one had never before been responsible for organising a household. For the summer, one had always taken furnished flats, which came provided with servants, and where everything was done for one. *Frightfully* fussing, this is!' Sir Christopher said, agitatedly twirling his hand in the air, whilst raising his voice an octave – maybe two.

John was as struck by Sir Christopher's frequent reference to himself as 'one' as he was by his habit of stridulously contorting his voice, to the point of a near choking sound, over a selected word or two. To say, however, that he broke into a high-pitched tone would be misleading, in that the effect produced, at least on John, was one not of effeminacy but of unassailable authority. Grasping for a subject to dispel the discontent that Sir Christopher's voice betokened, John said, as he clutched the edge of the refectory table and looked down at a small pink manual typewriter, out of which fluttered a crinkled sheet of paper, 'Well, it looks as if your work has not been *completely* interrupted.'

'Oh, yes, that's a review I'm writing about several new monographs on early quattrocento painters, but even that has been going on for much longer than usual.'

'I don't think it will be all that difficult to get things settled. Should I come by a little earlier tomorrow, say round four? Though I don't want to interrupt you at teatime,' John said, not because he was so naïf as to imagine that all English people religiously took tea at four o'clock, but because he wanted to get as clear a picture as possible of Sir Christopher's habits.

'You don't have to worry about interrupting tea, I can assure you, as there is no one to make it. The servants don't live in, you see, which is probably why things seem so strange to one. Anyway, yes, why don't you come at four tomorrow.'

✝

John held his hand over the spout, trying to judge from the force of the steam if the water had boiled, for he didn't think it likely that such a battered kettle would produce a whistle. And as he had taken such trouble in procuring the tea, he wanted that it be perfectly brewed. After having visited several shops this morning, he finally settled on a tin of Russian tea, made by an émigré firm in Paris, which he found in a dark, but welcoming, shop in via de' Tornabuoni. At first, he wondered if he shouldn't choose some obviously English brand of tea, but he preferred the canister of the Russian one and, as it was more expensive than any other, thought it would make the greater impression. Sir Christopher's cry of delight with the offering, verging on euphoria when John explained that he could actually *make* the tea, had more than justified his choice.

'Do you have everything you need?' Sir Christopher asked, peering irresolutely into the kitchen.

'I think so. I found this nice strainer,' John said, holding up an elaborate piece of Victorian silver. 'But I don't know if that's the teapot you use,' he continued, pointing to a coarse earthenware vessel.

'I suppose that it will do, though there *is* a proper Georgian one, but Lord only knows where that Indian has put it.'

'Indian?' John asked.

'Rita, the maid. She insists she's only half Indian; the other half is Neapolitan, *if* you please. What a combination!'

'Has she been with you for a long time?'

'No, it was Peter who found her, when I arrived here. She was very highly recommended, or so Peter says. But I don't like the look of her. Very shifty. In London, I had a lovely Portuguese couple who lived in the basement of my house and looked after one beautifully, but I am told that it is quite impossible to find that sort of thing here.'

Peter – again, John said to himself as, aware that he was being observed, he manœuvred deftly round the kitchen, warming the pot, measuring the tea and slicing the lemon.

'My, how capable you are,' Sir Christopher said, being as proud of the humble tasks he himself had never performed (make tea or slice lemon) as he was of the impressive ones (write books or direct museums) that he had.

'Hmm.' John smiled, mistaking the remark for an unmitigated compliment. 'Shall I bring the tea back to your study?'

'I think we've done enough in there for today. Why don't we go to the drawing room? Or, better yet, why don't we go up to the loggia – if that tray isn't too heavy for you?'

'No, I'm sure that I can manage,' John said obligingly, even though he would have preferred to remain inside, with the works of art, of which he had caught but a glimpse, rather than outside, with nature.

'How nice,' Sir Christopher said, leading the way.

'Oh, I forgot.' John stopped. 'Do you take milk?'

'I'm afraid I do, generally, but I doubt that the Indian has thought to lay any in.'

'No, there is some,' John said, putting down the tray. 'I saw it in the refrigerator, only I couldn't find a pitcher.'

'There *is* a perfectly decent jug for the milk, though I haven't the foggiest notion if Rita has unpacked the silver chest. Let's just have a look,' Sir Christopher said, opening the door of a cabinet at random. 'You see' – he pointed at an assortment of ill-stacked china – 'what a slut she is. It's in the refrigerator, you said?'

'The milk? Um, ah, yes,' John stumbled, taken aback by what he misinterpreted as the uncharacteristic vehemence of Sir Christopher's remark. 'Here it is,' he said, hesitantly retrieving a cardboard container.

'I think it's too squalid without a proper silver jug,' Sir Christopher said, recoiling from the commercial packaging. 'Let's just forget about the milk.'

And once they were installed under the loggia, Sir Christopher did seem to forget any cares that might lour his horizon – whether it be a misplaced milk jug or an unfinished review – and to settle down contentedly. 'Too, too delicious,' he said, sipping his tea.

John smiled, happy to have been able to please Sir Christopher, for, though they had spent little more than one hour together this afternoon arranging the books, he could already see that the art of placating him would require much skill. It was not that Sir Christopher had been in the least rude to him but that the older man could not conceal his impatience with anything that kept him from his work. Sensing that his most effectual contribution would be to establish a climate propitious to Sir Christopher's writing, John fortified himself with another sip of tea and said, 'I've just had an idea about arranging the books which, well, I mean, I don't want in any way to appear forward—'

'No, don't worry about that,' Sir Christopher broke in, eager to encourage anyone in looking after his practical affairs.

'It's just that it seems to me that the books are so confused – biography and history, even some fiction, mixed in with the art history – that we have to take some of the books off the shelves first, in order to create any sort of general filing system.'

'I don't know, that seems terribly like backpedalling,' Sir Christopher, who only wanted to be finished with the matter, said.

'Well, you see,' John spoke quickly, hoping that his plan, seen in its entirety, would convince, 'I think that if I could establish an order first, I could then move ahead with great speed. To be honest, it's the sort of thing that is best done by one person. So, I was wondering, what would you think of my setting up a desk for you, just a temporary sort of thing, somewhere else? You said there was a spare room, I think. I could put everything you need for the review you're working on at the moment – typewriter, necessary books and anything else you can think of – together. This would leave you free to write in peace. Then, I bet within a week or two, I could have your study in perfect order, and you could move back in there and work just the way you always have.'

'But that is more than one has the right to ask! Do you *really* think it possible?'

'I do, though I'd better start right away – tomorrow morning that is – as I won't be in Florence *that* much longer,' John said, returning to a familiar theme.

'Of course, tomorrow,' Sir Christopher said, missing (or choosing to miss) John's emphasis.

'Perfect.'

'Oh, but blast, isn't tomorrow the first of July, Friday?' Sir Christopher asked.

'Yes, it is,' John, who had haggled over each day of the calendar, answered assuredly.

'Well, I'm afraid that there's nothing to be done about that. I've got Dodo Delfington for the whole day tomorrow – I'm meant to be taking her to Arezzo and Borgo San Sepolcro, for which she will certainly have laid on a car – and there's no chucking *her*.'

'Oh,' John whispered, unable to mask his disappointment.

'Of course, if you didn't mind, you could stay here by yourself tomorrow,' Sir Christopher said.

'No, I wouldn't mind that,' John, who was thrilled at the prospect of an entire day, an entire day *alone*, in Sir Christopher's apartment, said with a smile. 'It might even be easier that way to set up your provisional study.'

'The Indian, Rita, can, of course, give you luncheon; it won't be very good – it will probably even be thoroughly nasty – but it will be something.'

'That sounds fine.'

'Right you are. Why don't you come at nine tomorrow morning, as I don't imagine Dodo will want to set off before half past? Thank goodness you're here or one might have quite forgot about the whole thing. And what's more, Alice Varrow is giving a dinner in Dodo's honour tonight, and, believe me, she'd make no end of trouble if one failed to turn up. I don't know if you've come across old Alice?'

'No, I'm afraid I haven't met her,' John said flatly, so as not to disclose the fact that he had no idea of whom Sir Christopher was speaking.

'Oh well, I'm sure you will. No foreigner in Florence escapes her grasp. Alice Varrow has lived here forever, up the hill at Bellosguardo, in a misshapen little cottage, surrounded by what *could* be quite a pretty garden – if only poor old Alice didn't have such appallingly suburban taste in plants. But she is something of an institution – albeit a crumbling one – but an institution nonetheless. She used once to write rather decent biographies – of a purely popular sort, mind you – but she now seems reduced to churning out nothing but books about decapitated ladies.'

John laughed and then, in what he hoped sounded a spontaneous fashion, added, 'On the other hand, I really did admire your mother's book on the Princesse de Lamballe.'

'Oh, but, Mamma's book,' Sir Christopher said, glibly accepting that his family's accomplishments should be common knowledge, 'was a *serious* piece of work, and, then again, the poor *princesse* was not so much beheaded as dismembered. Whereas old Alice – well, you know, it's Marie Antoinette one year and Madame du Barry the next. Still, one can't *not* dine with her, though I do feel that I ought to be taking you out, after you've given up so much of your time. I don't suppose you would be free to dine with one tomorrow night, after I get back from Arezzo?'

'Um, yes, I'd be able to, of course,' John murmured. Fearful of betraying even a fraction of the emotion he felt, he changed the subject and, pointing at the plants, asked, 'How do you water them all?'

'There's a derelict lavatory off that room to the left there. I imagine they rather want watering now.'

'Do you want me to do it?'

'Perhaps we could do it together. It's the one practical thing I like doing, though I must say that it takes rather a time, filling and refilling the can with water.'

'Why don't you get a hose?' John couldn't help asking.

'I never thought of *that*!'

'Actually, I noticed that there's a shop on the ground floor of the building where I'm staying in via Sant'Agostino that sells all sorts of gardening supplies. If you wanted, I could pick up a hose there and bring it along tomorrow.'

'What a frightfully good idea. Here,' Sir Christopher said, extracting a square black leather wallet with gilt-metal corners from his coat and proffering a large banknote. 'You'd better take this for now, and then we can settle other business matters later. You mustn't forget about that.'

John pressed the money into a pocket without looking at it, whilst thinking that there was little chance that *he* would forget about what Sir Christopher called 'business matters'. Lying awake in bed last night, he had repeatedly asked himself if he were not being foolish to offer his services without an overt promise of remuneration and, even more so, to sacrifice his days, during which he was meant to be studying works of art. But as he paced round the loggia this afternoon, handing cans of water to Sir Christopher and admiring, when bidden, some straggly branch or minuscule bud, it was impossible for him not to feel that he was following his properly ordained path. With all the fervour of the neophyte, he told himself, as he watched the, to him, entirely beautiful, tall, silver-haired man clip, trim and soak the myriad plants, that he had entered into an intimately shared communion.

Professions of faith notwithstanding, he passed another uneasy night, frequently wondering why Sir Christopher did not want to accompany *him* to Arezzo and Borgo San Sepolcro. He would, of course, have declined any such invitation, pointing to all the work he had to do, but he still would like to have been asked.

CHAPTER II

Providence

THE FOLLOWING MORNING, John set out deliberately early. He wanted slowly to savour the entire world of Oltrarno – that little sliver of Florence, on the south side of the river, where Sir Christopher Noble-Nolan's empyrean realm was to be found. He headed straight for Piazza Santo Spirito, washed his already clean hands in the square's central fountain and then entered the church. He knew that Vasari had written that, if only Brunelleschi's plans had been followed, this would have been 'the most perfect temple in Christendom'. As it was, John still found the building staggering – the complete antithesis of the cinder-block barrack that had been his childhood church in Providence. He genuflected, opened his red missal-like guidebook and began intently to study every altarpiece, decipher countless inscriptions, light several candles and, just generally, to bask in the golden glow of a magnificence that he had hardly thought possible. Finally, in a daze, he stumbled outside and proceeded to wander up the via Maggio, inspecting one sumptuous palace after another, till he found himself confronted by the profligate grandeur of Palazzo Pitti, which enchanted him, but not more so than a modest dwelling en face bearing a plaque announcing that it was here that Dostoevsky had completed *The Idiot* in 1869. It was not, however, till he turned in the most picturesque bend of the via de' Bardi and was confronted by the severe rusticated elevation of Palazzo Vespucci that he felt that he beheld not just a vision to be treasured but a salvific realm to be lived in; here, he discerned, not just a goal, but the way by which that goal was to be reached.

John entered the dark and, to him, wonderfully suggestive courtyard of Palazzo Vespucci – at the behest of a now smiling portress

– and stood in awe for several minutes. To his right, he beheld a fine Andrea della Robbia relief of the Virgin kneeling before the infant Christ, next to which was hung a large coat of arms, painted on leather, celebrating the alliance of the Vespucci and Cattaneo families, whilst ionic capitals danced all round him and uneven, presumably ancient, paving stones supported him.

After having caressed the neck of the marble sculpture of St John the Baptist at the foot of the staircase, he reverently began his ascent. On the first-floor landing, he halted again, staring at a genealogical tree of the Vespucci family frescoed on the far wall. This represented an enormous oak, from which dangled hundreds and hundreds of leaves, the inside of each one being filled with the name – an ever-recurring Amerigo or Buonamico marrying a predictable Cosima or Laudomia – and dates of Vespucci descend-ants. A distant view of Florence nestled at the bottom, whilst a large cartouche, bearing the inscription *Vespucci Guerrieri Pacifici* flew defiantly overhead.

John's thoughts turned, naturally, to the celebrated navigator who, having trailed in Columbus's wake, brazenly imposed his own name on the continent discovered by his predecessor. How utterly convinced, John thought to himself, must those such as the Vespucci, those who could trace their ancestry for hundreds and hundreds of years, be of their hereditary entitlement, how proud of their forefathers. He could but contrast them with himself: he, who had always been so keen to distance himself from his family in Providence; he, who had so often been embarrassed – embar-rassed to the point of repudiation – by his descent from a herd of immigrant labourers. Discountenanced by the shame he felt for the very blood coursing through his veins, John girded himself to walk whither he would and rang Sir Christopher's bell.

He was ushered in by an excited woman – undoubtedly, the much-maligned Rita, he thought – whose twittering manner and yammering voice would, John saw, instinctively rattle the stately Sir Christopher. He also had to admit that she *did* look as if she had just got off the last boat from Bombay, but he could see no harm in trying to make friends with her, and yet, before he could get very far, Sir Christopher came out to the hall himself and quashed any such possibility.

'You will *never* guess what happened this morning!' he said by way of greeting.

'I have no idea. Nothing bad, I hope,' John said, already feeling vaguely guilty.

'On the contrary. It's working now, it's really working – the telephone.' Sir Christopher beamed. 'At about a quarter past eight this morning, a disreputable man appeared at the front door—'

'*Si, un uomo molto bizzarro,*' Rita chimed in.

'*Prego,*' Sir Christopher said harshly, pointing the woman back to the kitchen. 'He said that he was sent here by Signor Masone.'

'Missoni?' John asked, clutching a bag with the, as yet unacknowledged, hose.

'Exactly my first reaction. But then, when he said Signor *Pietro* Masone, the penny dropped. Don't you see? It was Peter, Peter Mason, who sent the man here. He told me, before he went back to London, that he had met someone who works for the telephone company – Lord only knows *how* he met him – and that he asked him to come round here and see about the machine. Hence our new-found friend this morning. He was quite clever, I must say. He just twisted a few wires, climbed out on the roof for a moment, came back and played with a few more gadgets and then threw his hands up in the air joyfully, saying "*Ecco fatto!*" And by half past eight he was gone and the telephone was buzzing. It *is* strange this country, you know. All those people at Alice's dinner last night, all those Marchese and Contesse, were perfectly useless when one explained the predicament of the telephone. At least one has learnt that it is no use trying to put on high-level pressure in this country, certainly not where practical matters are concerned. One has to go right to the source.'

'Amazing,' John said distractedly.

'I've already rung up Peter to thank him. Woke him up, I dare say. Just as well. That's really what he needs – somebody to spur him on. But one shouldn't find fault, I suppose, as it is thanks to him that the telephone is actually working. Finally, one of these extraordinary creatures Peter's in the habit of picking up has paid off.'

John smiled and made appreciative noises but, all the while, was thinking that, once on his own, he must discover *who* this Peter Mason was and where he fit into Sir Christopher's life. Any such residual resentment he might have felt last night about not having been asked to come along to Arezzo and Borgo San Sepolcro instantly vanished.

The moment Sir Christopher left, John pounced on the address book he had noticed lying next to the telephone. He turned to the *M* section and found, the first name on the page, 'Peter Mason, Esq', with a London address that meant nothing to him and a telephone number. Unable to infer anything from this skeletal information, he went to Sir Christopher's study and randomly opened the drawers of the different filing cabinets but found only official-seeming correspondence and masses of photographs.

After only a few moments of frantic rifling, he stopped abruptly, walked over to the French window and leant his head against the glass. He realised that, in his excitement, he was wasting time, precious time – a characteristic mistake, he thought, and one which he now was determined to avoid. He drew in his breath, concentrated on the view for a few minutes and then decided his course of action. First, he would devote the entire morning to ordering the books and setting up the makeshift study for Sir Christopher – just as he had claimed he was going to do – for he saw that, no matter how preoccupied he was with unravelling the mystery of Peter Mason, it was still essential that he carry out the work he said he would. Only now, he planned to operate at breakneck speed, so as to have finished what would appear to be an entire day's work by lunchtime; then, he would have the afternoon, once the maid had gone, entirely to himself, to scour as he liked.

When he first stood in the via de' Bardi, glancing up at the façade of Palazzo Vespucci, John had imagined Sir Christopher living, appropriately he thought, in an enfilade of grand, tenebrous and distinctly uncomfortable Renaissance rooms. He was, therefore, surprised, when he did penetrate the inner sanctum, to come into a long, elegant L-shaped hall, lined with grisaille neo-classical *papier peint,* leading to a series of light-filled rooms with dazzling views across the city and on unto Fiesole.

The first door on the left opened into a rotunda-like room, which, with its object-filled vitrines, its excised illuminations and its trompe l'oeil decoration, looked more like a princely *Kunstkammer* than the dining room it was. Beyond this was the drawing room, as John already revelled in calling it, the lemon-yellow walls of which were hung with a few minor quattrocento pictures and several important Baroque ones, pride of place being given to a magnificent canvas of John the Evangelist by Domenichino, with a celebrated provenance, which hung between the two French windows that overlooked the river. After lunch, once Rita had finally departed, he stared hard at this picture, thinking that, even if John the Baptist was the patron saint of Florence, the city of his dreams, he would much rather identify himself with the disciple whom Christ loved than with the hair-shirted ascetic who had had his neck lopped off for devotion to his master.

The few art-filled houses that John had contrived to penetrate in the past – always on some scholarly pretext – invariably left him with a dispiriting impression of desiccated luxury, but here, in Sir Christopher's domain, he experienced art as the handmaiden of life – civilised life. There were no picture lights, no ostentatious frames, no little gilt name tags, nothing to call attention to itself – these works of art were not mere decoration but an ineffable element of the atmosphere. Such a seductive vision of an æsthetic and personal harmony was confirmed, for John, by an unusual, though restrained, juxtaposition – Italian bronzes and bindings next to oriental ceramics and textiles – such as he had never before seen. This afternoon, he wandered round, brushing his hand against one object after another, as a pilgrim might rub the surface of a relic in the hope of extracting some talismanic power, stopping finally in front of the fireplace.

He focused on a large, impressively stark bowl of bell metal, with scroll handles and lunar symbols cast in relief on the sides, which stood in the centre of the mantelshelf. He was woefully ignorant of, and not always very responsive to, non-Western art, but he found himself deeply struck by the delicacy and craftsmanship of this dish, the origin of which he could not divine. He also assumed, from its prominent position, that it must be quite important. Though he couldn't be sure, he imagined that such a receptacle was meant to have served some ritualistic function, the sort of thing in which one might place a burnt offering.

He picked it up gingerly and, almost overcome, clutched it to his breast. Not long ago, he had read in a novel that when a man becomes a Hindu ascetic all of his former belongings – his clothes, even his shaved hair – are burnt as a symbolic gesture of his severance with the past, as if to say that everything he has ever done, everything he has been, is expunged, forgotten. He pictured the ashes from just such a cremation being offered up in a vessel like this one. And as he clung to the object, he wished that he too could expel his past, to set it all on fire and reduce the twenty-four years of his life to a handful of dust which could be contained in an urn on Sir Christopher Noble-Nolan's chimney-piece. And yet, long though he might to reconfigure the contours of his life, he knew subliminally that, like the deposed king long before him, he could never forget what he has been or *not* remember what he must be now.

He thought it a particularly cruel trick of fate that he should have been born in a place called – of *all* things – Providence. Even as a schoolboy he had found it odd that there were so many American cities named after classical sites – Troy, Alexandria, Memphis, Syracuse – with which they had not the slightest connexion, but the idea of 'Providence' positively discomposed him. Though John had felt both intellectually and socially vindicated when, at the age of fifteen, he learnt that Roger Williams, the founder of Providence, should have taken Hebrew lessons from Milton at Cambridge, he could never bring himself to share Williams's conviction that it was 'God's merciful Providence' that had delivered him unto the shores of Narragansett Bay, leading him to found the new settlement as a refuge for persecuted dissenters, for refuge Providence had never been to John Forde.

The world all before him and Providence his guide? Had not, he thought, the world all been kept from him and Providence been his gaoler? There was no argument, great or small, that would allow him to *assert Eternal Providence, / And justify the ways of God to men.*

When he thought of his childhood in Providence, there was neither illumination nor support; that which was murky turned pitch dark, that which was low was forcefully spurned. Sometimes, he was perverse enough to imagine that he would actually have preferred to have been the son of overtly objectionable parents – a drunken father and a shrewish mother, say – in that he would, then, have been justified in shrugging off his origins; as it was, he still lacked the boldness to subject his benign (though aggressively conformist) parents and four uncomprehending (though passively hostile) brothers to the thoroughgoing renunciation of which he fantasised. And yet, abrogate though he might the assertion of both eternal Providence *and* the sway of natural birthright, the yearning that impelled him to cling to that empty metal bowl was born of a concomitant, though unacknowledged, belief that he could never, in any worthy sense of the word, be master of his own fate.

And so it was that, after having carefully returned the object to its proper place, he continued, *hand in hand with wand'ring steps*, and slowly took his way through Christopher Noble-Nolan's kingdom, grafting his own image onto its suggestive surface.

He passed back to the front hall, at the end of which loomed Sir Christopher's study, while to the right were two doors, one leading up to the loggia and another giving on, John thought, to Sir Christopher's bedroom. With doubtful and timorous steps, he pushed forward, till he found himself in the latter room.

Except for one gold ground picture, which John was pleased to be able to identify as being by the hand of the Master of Monte Oliveto, the walls were covered with red and black chalk Sienese Baroque drawings, but it was, above all, the seemingly common-place objects – the shoehorn, the hairbrushes, the clock – transformed into precious possessions by virtue of their dressing in ivory, silver and tortoiseshell, that seduced him. He was similarly dazzled by the long row of sombre suits he found hanging in a mahogany clothes press.

Leaning forward, he gently brushed his forehead against sleeve after coercive sleeve. He felt physically aroused by these clothes – richly textured, perfectly cut, utterly confident – but also deeply threatened by them. He was tempted to plunge himself into this mountain of enticing fabric, to writhe about in it, but, true to character, he continued merely to glide his head along the unrumpled surface.

Pulling himself back, he peeked into the small adjacent bathroom and caught an unwanted glimpse of himself in the mirror. Had he stopped to consider himself, he would have seen an ordinary-looking young man of slightly less than average height, whose studied sobriety did not sit entirely naturally with his wavy hair, green eyes and freckled skin. But as he was not so much interested in the figure of himself as in the shadow of that figure, he turned quickly, almost hostilely, away from the glass.

When a visitor entered this apartment, he was instinctively drawn to the left, in continuance with the grisaille decoration of the L-shaped hall. There was, however, a door on the right, which brought one to another, smaller corridor, leading to an enfilade of three rooms parallel to the façade of the palace. Though high-ceilinged and well proportioned, these chambers provided no view and fronted the much-traversed via de' Bardi, and it was clear from their disordered state that they were of secondary importance to their governor. And yet, it was precisely the indeterminate nature of these rooms that appealed to John's imagination. He had heard the first on the right referred to as the 'box room', which he took to mean a combination of office and storage; the middle one, where he had set up the writing-table for Sir Christopher was called simply the 'spare' – though John still thought of it as the 'guest room'; the third one, which contained a good deal of disassembled furniture had, so far, eluded labelling.

Dreamily, he wandered through this row of interconnecting rooms and began to imagine himself installed in this realm. Dream? Scheme? Where does the one (passive and harmless) leave off and the other (aggressive and nefarious) take root? In John's case, it would be difficult to say, and he certainly did not know himself, for his motives, like those of most people, were neither wholly corrupt nor wholly pure. And yet, he *did* actively eschew the flagrant opportunism of an Undine Spragg or the, to him even worse, corrupting venality of a Lucien de Rupembré, as he felt that an entrance obtained by means of obreption would poison any taste of success. His confusion stemmed from the fact that he did not want to intrude; he wanted to *belong*.

Downcast by his own aspirations, he went back to Sir Christopher's study and surveyed his own handiwork. He had, he thought, made a good show. Only three o'clock and it looked as if he had done a long day's work, and so he decided that he could freely begin to browse in the filing cabinets, but now he would approach the matter systematically. In this way, he did unearth some personal papers amongst the welter of professional material, including a bundle of letters written by the schoolboy Christopher Noble-Nolan to his mother, Dame Sophia – a distinguished biographer to whom her elder son, so John gathered, had been passionately devoted – letters which were, to John's surprise, addressed, 'Dearest, most preciousest, most belovedest Mamma', and signed, to John's near stupefaction, 'Your ever and always loving Tophereen'.

He also came across a packet of clippings and letters related to the violent death of Sir Christopher's younger brother, Christian, who, like his mother, was a celebrated biographer as well as an admired travel writer. Content though he was with his discoveries, he was still dismayed to have found no sign of the mysterious Peter Mason.

When it started to get on for four o'clock, he thought that he should resume work with the books, in case Sir Christopher were to come back early. He knelt down and, slitting open a box at random, was arrested by the cover of a little paperback: *Romanticism* by Peter Mason.

He picked up the skimpy book and, turning to the back cover, read: *Peter Mason was born in 1940. He is a recognised authority on eighteenth-century British art. He is also the author of* Neo-Palladianism *and* Fauvism *in this same series,* Style and Culture. *Mr Mason lives in London.*

John was momentarily rattled to have learnt that Peter Mason was an art historian, and a seemingly prolific one at that. Flipping through the pages of *Romanticism*, he was, however, pleased to note that this was a particularly short and superficial bit of work.

In the same box he found another little book by Peter Mason – *Post-Impressionism* – from the same collection, as well as quite a large one, with more illustrations than text, entitled *British Cabinet Makers and Furniture Designers.* John noted that none of these volumes was inscribed, though a card, on which was printed 'With the Compliments of the Author', was tucked inside each one. He put these books on a shelf of their own and, staring at them, recalled Sir Christopher's censure – *needs someone to spur him on* – with satisfaction. Clearly, he thought, an art historian working on the followers of Botticelli would be infinitely more valuable to Sir Christopher than a feckless dilettante living in London. He also did not fail to calculate his own age – nineteen years younger than Peter Mason – as a distinct advantage. Thus encouraged, he went on sorting books for another hour.

✝

When Sir Christopher returned from Arezzo, John jumped up and offered to make tea, though he suggested that, today, they remain in the study, rather than go up to the loggia, ostensibly so that he might explain the filing system he had devised; in truth, he wanted to probe the mystery of Peter Mason.

After having poured the tea, John began, 'I've blocked this long wall out for monographs. To be honest, I'm not sure if they'll all fit. They might have to be restricted to only those on Italian artists, but that we won't be able to tell till all the books are unpacked. In the corner, I've started to put books on iconography – Panofsky, Saxl, Gombrich et al. – and other works that should be arranged by author rather than subject.'

'That all seems highly sensible,' Sir Christopher said.

'I think that the biggest remaining cluster of books will be museum catalogues. I thought we might put them along the left-hand wall.'

Sir Christopher nodded approvingly.

'I suppose that there should also be a topographical section, though I am not sure exactly how much space that will require. And then, we have to find room for all the general books, history as well as art history, on the ah—' John stumbled before uttering the next word. After a moment's hesitation he blurted out, in what he hoped was a convincing accent, 'Ré-nay-ssänce.' Finding that his pronunciation elicited no discernible reaction – which he took as a favourable sign – he continued, 'But the real problem is what to do with all those art historical books not directly related to your work – not to mention the stacks of biography, fiction, poetry etc. My idea—'

'Yes?' Sir Christopher broke in encouragingly.

'Well, I thought that maybe the first room along the via de' Bardi, what you called the "box room", could be turned into a sort of office, with these filing cabinets lined against one wall and shelves put along the three other walls to house all the miscellaneous books – everything, that is, from the Goncourt on eighteenth-century French painting to surveys of Oriental art. That way, your study would be quite clear, with only the books you immediately needed to hand. I could even then unroll this nice-looking Aubusson carpet in here.'

'This seems to me a brilliant plan. If you really think it possible, that is.'

'Oh yes,' John said confidently. 'The only thing I wasn't sure about was what to do with the books with personal associations? I assumed that you would want to keep all of your mother's books together. I've arranged them chronologically, starting with her translation of Novalis's *The Disciples at Saïs* in 1903, right up through her studies of Madame de Staël, Queen Christina and so on,' he said, pointing to a long row of biographies and belles-lettres written by Dame Sophia Noble-Nolan. 'So far, I've only come across two of your brother's books. I put those next to your mother's.'

'Right you are.'

John found Sir Christopher disarmingly laconic on the subject of his younger brother but did not think it the moment to try to draw him out on the matter. Instead, he persevered in his plan – a plan, he hoped, so suitably dissimulative as not to arouse suspicion – for extracting information about Peter Mason. 'I see that you also have a number of signed first editions by Dame Lettice Brompton-Corlett, who is one of my favourite novelists,' John said, proud to know that this woman's given name was pronounced, not to rhyme with Matisse, but exactly like the vegetable. 'Do you want them filed here, in your study?'

'I am afraid that there won't be room for them in one's study, even if Lettice *is* frightfully clever. You know that it has been said that if Giacometti's sculptures could speak they would sound just like the characters in one of her novels.' Sir Christopher smiled. 'I should think her books might go in the spare room, something to impress the guests,' he said.

'Similarly, there are quite a number of books – all warmly inscribed – by the dance critic Jefferson Birstein. Should those also go in the spare room?'

'Yes, they should. And those books ought really to impress the guests. Jefferson is, perhaps, the only *true* genius one knows. Much more than just a dance critic, he's a genuine ballet impresario; one might call him the direct heir to Diaghilev.'

'Yes,' John said, disconcerted to hear Dame Lettice Brompton-Corlett described as merely 'frightfully clever', while Jefferson Birstein was extolled a '*true* genius'. Continuing cautiously, John added, 'And then, uh, I've grouped together all of these books – and there are rather a lot of them – both by and about the New Brutalist architect, Andrew Bruntisfield. They do, I must say, seem rather out of place here.'

'No, everything to do with Andrew Bruntisfield stays right here, in my study,' Sir Christopher said firmly. 'He can be filed right after Brunelleschi.'

'Yes,' John answered meekly, dismayed by the heated competition that, he feared, might be lurking in this corner. How else could he explain Sir Christopher's unlikely interest in this, to him, utterly repellent architect? 'Of course,' he continued, 'I know that you dedicated your book on Piero to Andrew Bruntisfield, back in 1965, so he must be a great friend of yours.'

'Yes, he was – a pillar of one's life, really.'

'*Was?*' John asked.

'But he died last spring. Didn't you see the obituaries? They were everywhere. Tremendously laudatory.'

'No, I'm afraid I didn't,' John said, reassured by the knowledge that a possible rival for Sir Christopher's affection was out of the way. 'But,' he continued, 'he must have been rather young to have died. Wasn't he? Not yet seventy?'

'More like not yet sixty. In fact, he was only fifty-four when he died. He was fifteen years younger than one. Terrible waste it was, his death. All on account of those ghastly cigarettes – his one vice. He was the only person whom I've ever known to smoke more than Crystal. In fact, that's how I met him.'

'Through your brother, Crystal?' John asked, titillated by his own use of this family nickname, which he had read of but never before dared to utter.

'Yes, you see, just before the war, Crystal had been taken ill at Saint-Malo, where he was busy with research for his book about Chateaubriand, and, sitting in a doctor's waiting-room there, he made friends with a hockey player from Amiens, of all places, who was so alarmed by Crystal's condition that he escorted him personally back to London. My gratitude to him was redoubled when, after the war, this same hockey player – Gilles or Jacques, something like that – put Crystal in touch with Andrew Bruntisfield who, he said, was a brilliant undergraduate at Cambridge, reading architecture. Needless to say, Andrew was much too serious for Crystal's fluttering tastes, and so he passed him on to one. One will never forget that first evening when he came to dine: we stayed up till dawn, delineating, in the most minute detail, the contrasting approaches to domestic architecture of Brunelleschi, Alberti and Palladio. A week later he moved in.'

'You lived together, then, you and Andrew Bruntisfield?' John asked, avid for background.

'Oh, *yes*,' Sir Christopher said, as if pronouncing a well-known historical fact that was too obvious to need verification.

'I hope you don't mind my asking?' John said, afraid to have overstepped the unstated bounds of decorum.

'On the contrary. It's nice that there is someone who is interested in one's past. Feel free to ask anything you like.'

'Did you,' John, emboldened by Sir Christopher's forthcomingness, asked, 'go on living together up until his death?'

'Goodness, no,' Sir Christopher said. 'First, he lived with one for a few months, in very cramped conditions, in a flat one rented in Ladbroke Grove, just above Crystal's. I had moved there after Mamma died, as her house in Holland Park was much too large for me on my own. Then, one took the leasehold on a very pretty, but not large, Georgian house in Bedford Gardens, and Andrew lived with me there for about two strained years. He would stay up all night, working in the dining room, and, when one came down to breakfast, one would find the table littered with paper and pens and pencils and ink – and cigarette ash absolutely everywhere! One morning, when I found him still up from the night before, I tossed a newspaper at him and said, "I think you will find a good number of advertisements in there for flats to rent." '

'Just like *that*?' John asked, feeling simultaneously chagrined for the victim of Sir Christopher's ruthlessness and comforted to have his dead rival summarily dismissed.

'Oh, but it was the kindest way.' Sir Christopher smirked. 'Of course, Andrew said that one was being terribly cruel, but I told him there was no other solution, no other means of salvaging our friendship. And, you see, young as he was then, he had already started to become quite successful. It was not long after that his career took off spectacularly. And he began winning all those prizes

– students writing dissertations about his work and commissions flying in left and right. He was, don't you know, colossally rich by the time he died.'

'Really?' John said; he wanted to ask but did not dare, pace Sir Christopher's invitation at openness, if Andrew Bruntisfield had left him any portion of his vast wealth.

'Of course,' Sir Christopher said, as if sensing John's curiosity, 'he left everything, every last farthing, to the RIBA, as well he should have. Still, it *is* funny to think that, when I first met Andrew, he didn't have a bean to his name. He'd finished at Cambridge, with a first naturally, but couldn't formally take his degree, as his ghastly father, a dentist in South Africa, refused to pay his university fees, so I stepped in and paid them myself. And jolly good investment it was – quite the best investment one has ever made.'

'And tell me,' John asked leadingly, 'do you admire his architecture?'

'I admire his *success*.' Sir Christopher smiled slyly. 'Of course, you couldn't pay me to live in one of his houses! All that wet-looking *béton brut* slathered on the walls. That was his great invention, you know, flinging about huge chunks of concrete where it was structurally unnecessary. Concrete as decoration. Those rich masochists couldn't get enough of it.'

'I had no idea of all that,' John said. 'Obviously, I'll make room for the books, make a little – or should I say large? – Bruntisfield shelf.'

'Good,' Sir Christopher said contentedly.

'And finally, uh, um, finally,' John faltered.

'Yes?' Sir Christopher asked.

'Well, I was just wondering—' John stopped himself, lacking the courage to pose the question that had possessed him all day. But as he knew, knew all too well, that he who will not lift the veil is no *true* disciple at Saïs, he compelled himself to press forward and enquire about that which he most feared. 'Wondering, um, ah, that is,' he said, 'about Peter Mason?'

'What about Peter?' Sir Christopher asked amiably.

'I wanted to ask you about his books. I've unpacked quite a number of them – all on such diverse subjects, I must say. Well, I was wondering if you wanted to keep Peter Mason's books together in your study?'

'In one's study? Poor Peter's books? In one's *study*!' Sir Christopher very nearly shrieked. 'You mean, all those pathetic little books he's penned for that appallingly vulgar series – *Style* and whatever it's called. Oh no, that wouldn't do, wouldn't do at all – fond as one is of him.'

'He does seem to be rather prolific,' John said, trying desperately to assume a bored tone of voice.

'Oh there's hardly a subject he won't write on – from Buddhist temples to Bauhaus thingumajigs – except, of course, what he is *meant* to write on.'

'The eighteenth century, you mean?' John asked.

'And Reynolds in particular. He started on him, I don't know how many years ago – fifteen, twenty even – and he's produced nothing but one measly little article in *Apollo*. And it's not as though it's a very difficult subject, not like the Renaissance. It is, after all, just simple *English* art.'

John smiled, more out of confusion than agreement.

'Come now,' Sir Christopher countered, 'you must admit that there is no comparison between the two subjects. With English eighteenth-century art, most pictures are signed and dated and the documents, if not already published, are easily available and present no problem of transcription. Whereas with the Renaissance, one needs a profound grasp of historical method, wide-ranging knowledge of original sources and, above all, an *eye*. No, Peter ought to have finished that book years ago. Instead, he's spent his time leading these ridiculous little tours to Japan and Thailand and Peru and every old place, when he should have been sitting at home in London and writing about Sir Joshua.'

'Perhaps he needed the money,' John said, surprised to find himself defending Peter Mason, for whom he felt a genuine (albeit fleeting) pang of sympathy.

'That's no excuse. I found job after job for him, only to have him booted out time and again. There is, I am afraid, nothing businesslike about Peter, nothing at all, but then, I suppose, that that's part of his charm.'

'Yes,' John said curtly, all sympathy spent.

'Consider the telephone! Who but Peter - Peter with all his extraordinary relations - could have arranged that?'

'Quite. Oh, and there's one last thing that I wanted to ask you about the books,' John said, eager to drop the subject he had gone in search of. 'I was wondering if I might borrow one of Joseph Leigh-Fiennes's diaries? I see that you have several volumes.'

'Fines, it's pronounced *Fines*,' Sir Christopher said.

'Sorry,' John said, blushing crimson.

'Goodness,' Sir Christopher said cheerfully, 'there is no reason why you should know how to pronounce his name. I think that you must be the only American who has ever even *heard* of poor old Jo Leigh-Fiennes, so entirely, so provincially English, is he.'

'Really?' John, who regarded Sir Christopher as quintessentially English, asked bemusedly.

'Oh, yes. One has all those volumes of his seemingly endless diary only because one is routinely sent them by the publisher, as he is forever going on about one's family. Do feel free to borrow as many as you like, though you must remember never to take him entirely seriously. Old Jo's writing, you know, is littered with opinions, but it is absolutely *devoid* of ideas.'

'That's strange, because, uh, not long ago I, um,' John floundered, 'read a review someplace, in the *TLS* I think, saying that he was one of the greatest diarists of all time, a sort of cross between Pepys and André Gide.'

'*Please!*' Sir Christopher guffawed. 'I don't think you can have read that in the *TLS*. Perhaps in one of those rubbishy English dailies, or maybe in that Waugh-run reactionary publication, whatever it's called, but not in a serious paper like the *TLS*. To tell you the truth, I shouldn't have thought Jo had ever read Pepys in his life, and as for Gide – well, I doubt that the silly old thing has even *heard* of him.'

'Well, in that case, I mean, um,' John stammered, 'if you think I shouldn't read—'

'No, go ahead. Read as much as you like,' Sir Christopher said. 'I suppose old Jo might provide you with a rather interesting picture of life in London, particularly during the war, as he did make a point of meeting a great many well-known people.'

'Maybe I'll just have a look at the first volume, the one that begins in 1942. Now,' John said more confidently, 'would you like to see how I've set up your temporary study? You have to tell me if I've forgotten anything.'

Far from finding anything lacking, Sir Christopher appeared to be delighted with the arrangement that John had devised. 'Yes, this should put one right back on track. Now I can really get on with that blasted review.'

'Well, that was the idea.'

'But what's this?' Sir Christopher asked, pointing to a receipt and a few Italian banknotes resting under a glass paperweight.

'That's your change. From the hose,' he explained.

'I don't think we need be so precise as that,' Sir Christopher said, scooping up the money and pressing it on John.

'No,' John protested, believing that, if he were not faithful in the *unrighteous mammon*, Sir Christopher would never commit to his trust the *true* riches. 'I don't think that would be right. Unless,' he suddenly recanted, 'unless, of course, there were some other household item you needed? I could pick that up with the change.'

'Oh!' Sir Christopher exclaimed. 'Well, there is the soap. I told that fool Rita to get some and she came back with a rectangular hunk of mint-green-I-don't-know-what.'

'What kind do you want?'

'I generally use that French soap – something and something – though it doesn't have to be exactly the same. It's just that it must be round – not oval, let alone rectangular – and of a pale colour and *œillet*-scented. Other than that, *any* type will do.'

'Right,' John said, seeing that Sir Christopher was perfectly in earnest.

'And did she give you luncheon, that Indian?'

'Yes, she—' John said, vainly hoping to defend poor Rita, for, inefficient and overly excitable though he could already see that she was, he felt sorry for her and found her nervous manner and shy smile endearing.

'Well, you see, then, how hopeless she is,' Sir Christopher broke in. 'I suppose that one will have to put up with her through the summer, as there's no question of finding anyone new for August. But come September – well, I mean, could you imagine giving Dodo Delfington – you know she threatens to come back in the autumn – whatever old Rita produced for you for luncheon today?'

'She might get better with time,' John tried.

'Doubt it. What's wanted is someone like Piera.'

'Piera?'

'The weekend maid. She's exactly the sort of stout, sensible Tuscan *contadina* who has always looked after one. You'll see.'

John liked the idea that he *would* see, as it implied, at least to him, that he had a future here, but he still felt unsure about how to apply this remark in any realistic sense. After a moment, he ventured, 'You said that Lady Charles Delfington's coming back to Florence?'

'You know her?' Sir Christopher asked, looking pleased.

'Just *of* her, I'm afraid,' John said. Having also glanced at the *D* page in Sir Christopher's address book this morning, he had found the name: Lady Charles (Dorothy) Delfington followed by addresses in London and Venice.

'Yes, of course you would, as she comes from your part of the world, though I don't think she's been back to Newport for years.'

My *part of the world!* John said ruefully to himself.

'What one will ever do about entertaining *her*, when she does come back, as she's bound to do sooner or later, I simply cannot think. And then,' Sir Christopher continued, 'there's Alice Varrow. She was already agitating last night about being invited to a meal. But one can always just take old Alice to a restaurant. Speaking of which, I should go and change so that we can go off to dine. I think it best if we go to Cammillo – much the most traditional restaurant left in Florence. Why don't you look out the vodka whilst I am in my bath? I think we both rather deserve a thimbleful.'

CHAPTER III

Fide Honor

THE FOLLOWING MORNING, Saturday, John arrived at Palazzo Vespucci at a quarter past eight, letting himself in with the precious latchkey – a, to him, wonderfully antiquated contraption – that Sir Christopher had entrusted to him when they dined together the night before. They breakfasted quickly, flipped through the newspapers that John had picked up on his way and then set about their respective tasks: John spent the morning arranging books, whilst Sir Christopher was locked up with his typewriter in the makeshift study; they broke for a brief lunch at one o'clock, each immediately returning afterward to his work, till about five o'clock, when they had tea on the loggia and attended to the plants; at six, John went out to buy one or another supply and to post (as he was already fond of saying) a stack of letters and then on to his own apartment to change; he reappeared at a quarter to eight for a drink, after which they dined at another local trattoria. John had instinctively understood that, when in a restaurant, he was meant to order exactly the same thing as Sir Christopher, for Christopher Noble-Nolan appeared to take it as a personal affront if someone chose to eat something he himself did not like, as much as if another declined something he *did* like. Sir Christopher could not, for example, support that anyone should defile salad with vinegar, which he loathed – it should only be dressed with oil and lemon – and tripe was simply beyond the pale, any more than he could abide that someone should *not* want *fraises des bois*, which he adored. From the night of that first dinner, routine was cast as ritual, and John flailed about desperately trying to decode the signals, so that when he arrived on Sunday morning and saw that Sir Christopher was wearing a white shirt, whereas he had, the other days, worn a striped one and only

changed into a white shirt for dinner – suit and tie remaining inviolable – he instantly sensed that the regimen was to be subjected,
slightly but nonetheless significantly, to variation.

'I'm told by Merry Vespucci,' Sir Christopher said, referring to his
landlord, Count Amerigo Vespucci, as John stepped into the front
hall, 'that there's a decent Mass in a chapel in Piazza Santissima
Annunziata at half past ten. We might try that.'

John was beginning to realise that his own propensity for secrecy
and half statement could actually prove a beneficence in his relations with Sir Christopher, who himself did not appear to like
posing direct questions. Inference and deduction, often leavened by
assumption, formed the ingredients of his conversation, so that it
would have been supererogatory, at best, for John to have offered to
attend Mass with him; the fact of the Mass having been announced
rendered John's presence there a fait accompli. His confession was
sealed. Nonetheless, John had been distinctly nonplussed when,
Friday evening, the first time they dined together, Sir Christopher
had flatly said to him toward the end of the meal, without the
slightest hint of an interrogative tone, 'You're a Catholic.'

'I, um, yes, I am,' John had replied hesitantly, reluctant to commit
himself on so personal a matter as religion. He knew that Sir Christopher – son of an Irish Catholic father and a convert English mother
– was born and raised Roman Catholic and that he had even been
given over for ten years of his youth to the hands of the Benedictines
before going up to Oxford, but he did not know to what extent he
was *pratiquant*; the many religious objects in his house – of, transparently, æsthetic rather than devotional interest – proved nothing.

'I assumed you must be,' Sir Christopher said contentedly. 'Otherwise, you wouldn't have understood so clearly what one meant by
the word "vocation".'

This was the only allusion Sir Christopher had yet made (and
would ever make) to John's original letter, in which he had admiringly quoted Sir Christopher for having written in the preface to
his recent book of collected essays that 'art history is a vocation, not
a profession in the conventional sense'. And oblique though the
reference was, John interpreted it as commendatory.

Still wading his way through the uncharted waters of Sir Christopher's thought patterns, John, with extreme caution, replied, 'Quite.'

'To tell you the truth,' Sir Christopher said, 'I've always felt sorry for those poor benighted souls who have had no religious education. Must be a terrible handicap for anyone wanting to study art history.'

'You can't imagine,' John said, gaining momentum, 'what it's like in New York. For instance, when I was in a seminar on Fra Angelico, last spring, most of my fellow graduate students were unable to comprehend why, when the Pope had just officially beatified Fra Angelico last year, he was not immediately declared a saint. I tried to explain to them – impossible though it proved – that two more miracles were still wanted for him to become a saint.'

'There are, of course, the works of art. What could be *more* miraculous than the paintings of Fra Angelico?' Sir Christopher said.

'True,' John, afraid that he had overreached himself, replied submissively.

'In any event, I'm happy to know, for sure, that you are a Catholic and not a lapsed Catholic; I would find it so common, so frightfully common, to be a *lapsed* Catholic,' Sir Christopher said, though John had, in fact, averred nothing as to the state of his beliefs. 'It makes things so much easier between us, your being a Catholic. That was Andrew Bruntisfield's only flaw – not being one of us – that and the cigarettes.'

'Yes, it does make things easier,' John, who was positively exultant at the thought of having his position allied to that of Andrew Bruntisfield's, said. Thus encouraged, he asked Sir Christopher, with uncharacteristic confidence, 'So, you quite *believe*, then, in all the tenets of the Church?'

'Oh, I can believe in anything that is depicted in a predella panel. In fact, it wouldn't surprise one in the least to see a saint come crashing through the ceiling of one's drawing room.'

'That's an appealing image,' John said with a smile, 'but it's not exactly what I meant. I was just wondering if, well, if all those years of Catholic education didn't leave you with any lingering sense of guilt?'

'Guilt? Guilt! What on earth would one feel guilty *about*?' Sir Christopher asked, genuinely shocked.

'Well, you know, um,' John havered, 'guilt about, ah, not following certain rules of the Church, certain codes of behaviour, shall we say.'

'But those rules do not apply to *one*,' Sir Christopher intoned in his most autocratic manner. 'Rules,' he continued, pointing to a particularly dreary, presumably married, couple seated in a far corner of the restaurant, 'are meant for the likes of them. *We* can just thank God – and I do thank Him every day – that we are cut from a quite different (infinitely superior, I daresay) cloth. How degrading it must be to be condemned for all one's life to reproductive mating. And as for guilt? Well, it's not as though we've broken a vow – not like a divorced husband and wife, now that would be a serious breach of faith – no, we simply lead a life apart and so are not subject to the statutes of the multitude, *we few, we happy few, we band of brothers*.'

'It's reassuring to hear you say that,' John said quietly, 'though I can't pretend I was raised according to such principles.'

'I'm sure you'll get over that. I, of course,' Sir Christopher said, 'never had to get over it. Mamma, you see, was absolutely adamant that neither my brother nor I should ever marry. Frightfully bad she thought marriage was for a writer's career, and there was obviously no question of either one of us *not* becoming a writer.'

John had not failed to notice that his own background appeared to be of little interest to Sir Christopher. But rather than feel slighted, he actually experienced a great sense of liberation: in the shadow of such indifference, he need feel no temptation, as he had often done in the past, to lie about, or even to edit, his familial legacy; he could simply occlude it. Lying, as he had already learnt to his peril, was such an effort – one could *so* easily be tripped up – whereas effacement seemed, to him, a passive stance, entailing no threat. Thus did John, at that first dinner, gleefully blot out his past and concentrate, instead, on the fact – the to him miraculous fact – that, without ever so much as having mentioned the word 'homosexuality', Sir Christopher let it be known that he assumed, with unerring limpidity, John's membership (along with his own) in a sacred sect, which, so far from being a curse, was a true calling, a 'vocation' of the highest order. And as he watched Sir Christopher prepare for Mass this morning, dressed in a superb black-on-black suit of the lightest twilled wool and clasping a beautifully worn missal – another one of which he confided unto him – John realised that their allegiance to the elect, this secret *band of brothers*, need be neither uttered nor abjured, but merely absorbed into the fabric of a recondite (and Roman) Catholicism.

As a young boy – eight or ten years old, say – John was in the habit of proudly announcing that he wanted to become a priest when he grew up. And though his brothers might tease him relentlessly for this, saying that he was only trying to court favour with the nuns at school and that he probably liked the idea of prancing about in a soutane, his aspirations were, in a twisted sort of way, sincere. Having been taught (and believed at that age) that the religious life was the highest station to which a mere mortal could aspire, he could not imagine setting his sights elsewhere. Why, he had asked himself at a tender age, content oneself with the lowliness of the laity when one could aspire to the princeliness of the hierarchy?

Tellingly, as the first disturbing glimmering of adolescent desire began to flaunt its irrepressible head, he was ever more drawn to the Church, hoping that, there, he had found the perfect place in which to hide, a safe haven where he would never be questioned about his celibate status. But as fifteen morphed into sixteen and sixteen into seventeen, and as his sights roamed wider and his vision of the world expanded, Catholicism, most particularly the Irish American Catholicism by which he found himself surrounded in Providence, came to represent a repressive and unimaginative force to him. At the Christian Brothers school he had been obliged to attend, John had developed an instant and intense loathing for the religious order by whom he was taught. So rebarbative did he find these red-faced, ignorant, bigoted bullies, extolling the brutal virtues of Irish chauvinism, whilst shamelessly indulging their unquenchable penchant for pædophilia, that John (who kept his head low and sedulously followed the rules, thereby avoiding any unwanted advances) was inspired to let his dawning Hibernophobia take root. How wonderfully appropriate, he had thought it, that the entry to purgatory was said to be located in Ireland, through a cave in County Donegal, discovered by St Patrick himself. And yet, the schoolboy John Forde would not allow the aversion he felt toward the coarse followers of Edmund Rice to influence his views on the Church or to affect the state of his own soul. He would not grant them that importance. These *soi-disant* 'Christian' Brothers might disgust John, but they had no power to offend him: he would cling to his faith in spite of, not because of, the education he received.

Now, having had it confirmed that Sir Christopher was not just a Roman Catholic but a practising one went far in diluting the shame John had felt about his Irish Catholic inheritance and the envy he had long harboured for the Protestant ascendancy. He remembered that he had experienced a curious pang of something approaching exoneration when, on first looking Sir Christopher Noble-Nolan up in *Who's Who*, during his undergraduate days, he learnt that the full name of this illustrious scholar was Christopher Anthony Edward Charles Henry George *et omnes sancti* Noble-Nolan, as that string of Christian names repudiated, for him, the supremacy he had long bestowed on a host of well-born Americans, bearing their mothers' maiden names as middle names. *Wasn't there something distinctly royal*, he had asked himself, *about all those Christian middle names?* Even so, he realised that John Patrick Forde was not a name ever likely to be confused with royal associations, and, though he had long since consigned his dreaded middle name to cold oblivion, he still found, even today, that it assuaged his ego to summon up the memory of Sir Christopher's full name.

As he sat this morning in the caliginous chapel of San Filippo Benizzi, which was tucked away in a corner of Piazza Santissima Annunziata, John admired the large picture of the assumptive Virgin, adored by Sts Jerome and Francis *poverino* – the titular saints of the confraternity that formed the presiding spirit here – as well as the parallel pews, the altar that had *not* been turned round to face the congregation and, above all, the general aura of crumbling poetic grandeur. He essayed to enact convincingly the motions of the Tridentine Mass, which had been abandoned with such amnesiac vigour by the American clergy that he, who had been born in 1959, was utterly unfamiliar with the ritual. Though he had studied Greek and Latin for four years at the school run by the detested Christian Brothers, he could not remember ever before having heard the Mass properly celebrated.

Casting round surreptitiously, he imitated the sparse congregation, crossing himself at the asperges, beating his breast during the Confiteor and genuflecting at the mention of the Incarnation, but, bemused by the order of the missal, he was incapable of intoning the responses. He just moved his lips and hoped that Sir Christopher – more than God – was taken in. Throughout the Mass he tried to keep his gaze focused on the priest, but it was difficult for him not to glance occasionally, both in gratitude and in emulation, at his imagined deliverer. When it came time for communion, and he saw that Sir Christopher made no approach toward the sanctuary, John followed suit and held back.

On their return from Mass, John assumed that the diurnal routine would proceed in its customary fashion, so he was surprised to see Sir Christopher settle himself on the loggia with the stack of English and Italian newspapers they had bought on the way home, and he was even more unnerved to learn that Sir Christopher would be out to lunch with Alice Varrow, for he did not like the idea of being left alone with the weekend maid, Piera. He only met her for the first time yesterday, but he had experienced an instant, and he feared reciprocal, antipathy. He imagined that she looked on him as an interloper and that she attributed some base, conniving motive to his presence. He could not think how Sir Christopher could profess to like this gruff, scowling, moustachioed woman, but, knowing that he did, John felt determined to conquer her. Unfortunately, he had the idea, ignorant as he was of servants in general and Tuscan peasants in particular, that he could triumph by lording it over her.

Piera, for her part, did not actually distrust the new arrival; she simply found him supernumerary and refused to waste her breath on him. So far as she was concerned, she was employed by the *Professore,* and it was from him alone that she would take orders. Unlike Rita, she produced a distinctly good meal for John, but she plopped the food down on the table so unceremoniously that he could not wait for her to be gone. And yet today, when he found himself alone in the apartment, he was consumed by no inclination to snoop, as he had been on Friday, for the suspicion that he imagined Piera imputed to him stung him fiendishly. Directly he finished lunch, he returned to the study and resumed the task of ordering the books with even more care than usual, until, with a sense of great abatement, he heard Sir Christopher turn the key in the door shortly before four.

'Did you have a nice luncheon?' John asked unnaturally.

'Not *too* bad. It was Alice's usual sort of thing,' Sir Christopher said, clearing a seat for himself in the still cluttered study. 'Always too many people squeezed into that little house. I suppose that it's some sort of Mitteleuropa thing taught her by her mother – writing off as many obligations for as little money as possible.'

'But I thought she was English?' John said, having looked Alice Varrow up in the course of the week.

'Though she was born in London, she's not really English, not at all. Her mother was a Serbian, Viennese, I-don't-know-what mixture. And quite charming she was, Mrs Varrow. Jewish, of course, everyone always said, though Alice would sooner die than admit that. And her father, though he tried to pass himself off as some sort of bogus Anglo-Irish colonel, was rumoured to be an escaped Russian convict, but no one ever knew for sure. Little wonder that Alice can be peculiar, what with a background like that.'

'Did your father know her father – I mean, as her father *claimed* to be Anglo-Irish and everything, I thought—'

'Goodness, no. My parents led quite serious lives, whilst Alice's – well, I think she and her dreadful sister spent their entire childhood in *hôtels*, moving with the seasons, staying at the most fashionable resorts imaginable, in the cheapest rooms possible. No connexion at all with my parents. And anyway, my father's family was not *Anglo*-Irish. Just straight Irish. Like yours – I imagine?' Sir Christopher smiled at John.

'Ah, um, yes, I've been told my name *can* be Irish,' John admitted. Actually, he *knew* that his father's family was of Irish extraction, but he had long been grateful that the name Forde should (unlike his mother's maiden name, O'Donnell) defy any obvious ethnic affiliation. As a young boy, John had found the name Forde terribly wanting in glamour; it seemed, when weighed on his childish scale of values, pathetically prosaic. In time, however, he came to treasure his surname *because* it was common. The name Forde could belong to anyone – even, he discovered, someone in the *Social Register* – so that he was now exceedingly reluctant to ally himself with any camp. It was all very well, he thought, for Sir Christopher Noble-Nolan to acknowledge his own ancestry, he with his knighthood, he whose eponymous paternal grandfather had also been so decorated, he with the British tag 'Noble', defying anyone to challenge the indignity of the transparently Irish surname, 'Nolan'. But for himself? For John Forde of Providence, Rhode Island? He feared that it would be fatal to reveal too much. Continuing cautiously, he said, 'Actually, I've always liked to imagine that I bore a direct connexion to the Caroline dramatist, my namesake, and *he* was born of an old Devonshire family.'

'But I didn't think the playwright had an *e* at the end of his name,' Sir Christopher said.

'True,' John conceded, 'but, John Ford added an *e*, you know, to the anagram that he made out of his own name: *Fide Honor*. It only works with the addition of an *e*. And it appears right there, the anagram *Fide Honor* – "Honour through Faith" – on the original title pages of *The Broken Heart* and *Perkin Warbeck*.'

'No, I don't know anything about that,' Sir Christopher answered, evincing not the least desire to be enlightened on the matter.

'And then,' John, in a desperate attempt at staking his claim, said, 'there is magnificent Forde Abbey in Dorset. That *is* spelt with an *e* at the end.'

'So it is,' Sir Christopher said in a transparently bored voice.

'I've also been told,' John said, thinking to redeem himself in Sir Christopher's eyes, 'that the name Forde, with an *e*, can sometimes be Welsh.'

'Mercy!' Sir Christopher exclaimed. 'You wouldn't want to be Welsh at *any* price. Such terrible swindlers and liars they are, the Welsh.'

'Really?' John asked, surprised, as he had always imagined that it was smarter to be Welsh than Irish.

'Oh yes, it's a well-known fact: you can never trust a Welshman. Where do you think the word "welsher" comes from? No, you're better off being Irish.'

'Yes,' John said, misunderstanding the implications of the state-ment to which he had just agreed, for he assumed that Sir Chris-topher was preaching the gospel of appropriation when, in fact, he was reading a lesson on acceptance.

'But I don't think one need bother too much about ancestors,' Sir Christopher said blithely. 'I certainly don't. In fact, I always thank God that one was born and educated in England. My moth-er's family were, of course, of pure, sensible English stock. How perfectly dreadful it would have been to be brought up an Irish intellectual. But in the end, the only thing that really matters is to be getting on. And that's a question of character, not of blood.'

'Hmm,' John agreed, happy to close the subject. 'Did you want me to reserve a table at Cammillo? I thought you might want to go back there again, as it's the last night.'

'What do you mean the *last* night?'

'Didn't you see the sign in the window, when we dined there on Friday, saying that, as of Monday, they would be closed?'

'Why didn't you tell me?' Sir Christopher asked, upset.

'I just thought—'

'But I don't see how it's possible that they can be closing already. We're not even in the middle of July. I think you must be mistaken. It must be *next* month that they are closing.'

'I thought,' John said apologetically, 'that the sign said that they would be closed for the next three weeks and that they would be open for the entire month of August, but maybe I misread it.'

'Well, I suppose that *is* possible. It might even be a blessing, as everything else will surely be shut during the month of August. What one will do then, I simply cannot think.'

'I saw there was a list in the *Nazione* this morning of all the res-taurants and shops which are to remain open during the month of August. I actually cut it out for you.'

'Shall we have a look at it?'

'Yes, of course, but, well, I was wondering, what you would think if I were to make dinner for you here, one night next week.'

'Make it *yourself*, you mean?'

'Yes, I just thought for a change.'

'But do you know how to make a dinner? I know that you pre-pare the tea beautifully, but, well, an entire meal, that would be frightfully complicated.'

'Yes,' John said and smiled, 'it *would* be more involved, but we might try it, at least once, even if I can't promise very much.'

✝

It was not till ten days later, a Tuesday evening, that John was granted the opportunity to display his culinary skills. He did not, in fact, know the first thing about the kitchen, but he thought

– particularly as he had already been overtaken on the matter of the telephone – that a show of competence in this domain would prove a useful way of ingratiating himself to Sir Christopher. After having fingered through several cookery books, which he found scattered amongst the boxes in Sir Christopher's study, he settled on the most complicated menu he could imagine, for he felt that such kudos as he might garner from this undertaking stood in direct proportion to the elaborateness of the food he was to present. A safe, decent little meal would, for his purposes, accomplish nothing.

Though he had never tasted, let alone made, a soufflé, Sir Christopher's several references to the delicious ones that his Portuguese servant used to make in London left John in no doubt as to how the dinner should begin. For the *plat principal*, that which he still thought of as the entrée, he decided on *cailles aux raisins*, the recipe for which he found in a little buff-coloured volume, *Lady Sysonby's Cookbook*, which was annotated in a hand that he now knew to be that of Sir Christopher's mother, Dame Sophia. To conclude, he made, from scratch, a raspberry sorbet that he packed into one of the many Victorian moulds he had found stored in the kitchen. For the soufflé he had the good (if wasteful) idea of going through a trial run at about six o'clock, with the result that the golden crown of the one he produced at half past eight, towering above its rim, gave, John was content to see, tremendous pleasure. The crisp, rather too crisp quail were not, he realised, equally successful, and the mushy wild rice that accompanied them did little to help his efforts, but the ice that followed secured his triumph.

'I do think it was clever of you to have known about those moulds. I don't suppose that they've been put to use since Mamma's day. She always ordered the most beautiful jellies and shapes,' Sir Christopher said, taking a large second helping of raspberry sorbet.

'Well that's what they're for,' John, making a concerted effort to sound off-hand, said.

'And when you think of that really rather nasty luncheon that Alice gave one last week. If only she were here now, wouldn't she be impressed!'

'I'd make dinner for her one night, if you like,' John said, having been waiting for an opportune moment to suggest this.

'Really?' Sir Christopher said.

'Yes, certainly.'

'But I am not sure that you should spend your time doing that sort of thing,' Sir Christopher said, genuinely hesitant.

'I wouldn't mind, but there's not, of course, all that much time, as I really do have to start travelling. Why, I mean, I haven't even yet been to Montepulciano!'

'It would, of course, be nice for you to meet Alice. In spite of all her faults, she is worth knowing,' Sir Christopher said, ignoring the issue of John's departure.

'I *would* be curious to meet her, and I really don't mind making the dinner.'

'I must confess that I never envisaged that the matter of entertaining would be such a problem here. Of course, in London, one never had people to dine at home. There were just lunch parties, but very splendid lunch parties they were, and then I could always take a fellow art historian to my club for dinner.'

'Brooks's?' John asked.

'Uh... yes,' Sir Christopher looked across the table with surprise. 'Goodness, you *do*,' he continued, staring straight at John, 'seem to know an awful lot about one.'

John blenched, afraid that, like a criminal under cross-examination, he had exposed himself by an inadvertent expression of familiarity, overfamiliarity. Did he know too much to be innocent? Desperate to retrieve the situation, he said honestly, if weakly, 'I suppose that it must be something I picked up from reading Jo Leigh-Fiennes's diaries. I remember that he says that he ran into you and your father at Brooks's one night. And I just assumed—'

'I do think,' Sir Christopher said in a markedly disapproving tone, 'that you seem to be wasting an awful lot of time on those silly old diaries, when you ought to be getting on with all the new books and catalogues that have come out for the Raphael quincentenary.'

'Yes, of course,' John said with mock repentance; in truth, he was utterly enthralled by the Leigh-Fiennes diaries, the tenth volume of which he was now edaciously devouring, for the depth of his longing to be included in Sir Christopher's future made him equally avid for any knowledge he could glean of his past. Thus was he held spellbound by this portrait of a world in which one lunched and teaed and dined with the Noble-Nolan family, and in which one went with them to concerts and to lectures and shared their recherché literary expeditions.

Jo Leigh-Fiennes, as John was now pleased to think of him, might well be, as Sir Christopher insisted, a provincial, reactionary bigot, burdened with limited imagination and endless umbrage, but he was also, to John, a dazzling magician, conjuring up a gallery of wonders: the redoubtable Dame Sophia Noble-Nolan, known here simply as 'the Dame', who seemed to think there was no greater honour in life than to be a member of the literary Noble-Nolan family; the young Christopher Noble-Nolan himself, already obsessively dedicated to his métier, banging away at his typewriter, whilst the guests chatted over tea in the next room; the younger brother, Christian, known as Crystal, by whom the diarist was besotted, who supped with duchesses, slept with rough trade, wrote with elegance and came to an unfortunate end; and, finally, the *non*-head of the household, Major-General S.P.H. Noble-Nolan, treated as an outcast – not coming up, not remotely so, to the elevated standards of the terrifying trinity that were his wife and two sons – who was thought so unpractical and wasteful that, not only was he not allowed to handle money, he was not even permitted to *carve*.

Over the years, Jo Leigh-Fiennes's multi-volume diary would assume the status of a sacred mantra for John – perused repeatedly, some passages actually learnt by heart – but for now, he merely said apologetically, 'I'm afraid that I was just curious about you and your family – *overly* curious you may think.'

Well respected and well known as he was in his field, Christopher Noble-Nolan was perfectly accustomed to people being desirous of his opinion on works of art. Indeed, it now seemed to him that scarcely a day passed when his judgment on some Renaissance picture or other was *not* solicited. He was not, however, used to being the subject of personal interest – that was a rôle that had been apportioned to his younger brother – and he was surprised to find that he liked the attention, liked it perhaps more than he cared to admit, so that he replied amiably to John, 'Nothing wrong with curiosity. Where would art history be without it?'

John felt confident enough to smile, but not so confident as to tell Sir Christopher that he himself had, that very morning, been inspired by Jo Leigh-Fiennes's example to buy a large marbled notebook at a printing press, right in via de' Bardi, in which to begin his own diary.

'Anyway, if you really want to meet old Alice,' Sir Christopher continued, 'I am happy to invite her.'

'Any night you like,' John said lightly, relieved by Sir Christopher's apparent lack of suspicion.

'Why don't I call her now? She *will* be taken aback. Could you just look her up in the book?'

'Do you think she's *listed* in the telephone book?' John asked in disbelief.

'I've never known Alice to turn down an opportunity to see her name in print.'

As Sir Christopher stood in the hall speaking on the telephone, John began to clear the table. By the time he finished rinsing and stacking the plates, he found Sir Christopher in the drawing room, listening to a recording of he-knew-not-what.

'You know the Köchel number?' Sir Christopher said over the music.

As if guided by divine providence – the presence of which John had so often doubted – he looked down at the record sleeve strewn on the low table before the fireplace and descried the numbers '551', which he nervously repeated.

'That's all right, then. One certainly wouldn't like to be associated with someone who *didn't* know the Köchel number of the *Jupiter Symphony*, or, indeed, all 626 Köchel numbers for the matter of that,' Sir Christopher said magisterially.

John nodded vaguely and sat down, thrilled by the idea that he should be thought of as being 'associated' with Sir Christopher, but he was still trembling from what he viewed to be a narrow escape. Until Sir Christopher had alluded to the question of Köchel numbers, John had not even been sure that he was listening to Mozart, let alone exactly which symphony. For a second, he closed his eyes and said to himself, *Oh God,* another *subject to master.* Opening his eyes, he said aloud, as if to regain his footing, 'There are now these new things, called compact discs, which are meant to put LPs quite to shame.'

'One wants *nothing* to do with any modern gadgets,' Sir Christopher said staunchly. 'The phonograph records have done quite nicely by one for decades and will, I am sure, go on doing so.'

'Of course,' John apologised and, slipping into what he already considered his usual armchair, shoved the offending volume of Jo Leigh-Fiennes's diary, which he had been reading before dinner, behind a cushion. He took an exhibition catalogue about Raphael as an architect from the table and opened it carefully. Assuming what he hoped was a suitably convincing air of lucubration, he did try to read, but the threat posed by the music impeded any real concentration.

'Alice jumped at the invitation, of course,' Sir Christopher said as soon as the record ended. 'We settled on Tuesday the nineteenth, exactly a week from today – I hope that's all right for you. The only problem is that her older sister, the dreaded Trixie, will be staying with her, and she's insisted on bringing her along.'

'Her sister's called Trixie?' John asked, amused.

'Short for Beatrix, I suppose. Rather ridiculous name, Trixie, I grant you, but I can only tell you that it is one of her *better* features. She's an aged, deaf, unregenerate fascist.'

'Is she stone deaf?'

'Alas, no. She hears *just* enough to interrupt the conversation.'

'And a fascist you said?'

'Yes. She spent the entire war in Italy. She was married to a prominent fascist called Giraldi, then the vice-mayor of Florence, but now long since dead. Thank God! When her husband was finally allowed back in the country – they had to hide out in Switzerland for years, mind you – they wisely decided that it would be best to stay away from the scene of so many of his wrongdoings, and so they settled up north. Lago di Garda or Lago di Como. Somewhere up there. Trixie Giraldi, she is. You'll see. Now, shall we listen to one more thing on the gramophone?'

'Yes, whatever you want,' John said.

'What a blessing,' Sir Christopher said, smiling broadly at John, 'that one is starting to establish a normal rhythm again. Yes, everything has begun to fall into place.'

CHAPTER IV

The Other Parish

'OF COURSE, CHRISTOPHER, your mother always had the most delicious food – even during the war. One never would have thought' – Alice Varrow turned to John – 'that Dame Sophia, ascetic blue-stocking that she was, would have been interested in something so mundane as mere *food*.'

John made a quick mental note that the name of Sir Christopher's mother was pronounced 'So-fī-a', not 'So-fē-a', which he never would have guessed on his own.

'She was terribly trouble-taking about her table, your mother. Wasn't she, Christopher?' Alice Varrow continued.

'She was just very trouble-taking about life in general,' Sir Christopher said stiffly.

'I remember those savouries,' Alice Varrow persisted.

'Savouries? Yes, that's quite true,' Sir Christopher said more warmly. 'Mamma always did order *the* most delicious savouries – particularly those marrowbones, wrapped in white damask. Funny, one's never given savouries anymore.'

Having imagined that the conversation this evening would be conducted on an intimidatingly elevated plane, John felt a mixture of relief and disappointment to find himself confronted by an onslaught of macaronic bantering, in which frenzied tales of sexual intrigue, money woes, alimentary obsessions and valetudinarian crotchets kept incongruous company with abstruse literary or historical allusions. He could see that Sir Christopher, if not exactly bored, was unwilling to make any effort, thus leaving it to Miss Varrow to direct the conversation whither she chose. John realised that she only turned to speak to him when she failed to elicit a response from Sir Christopher, but he was not in the least put out, for her manner implied a natural complicity that gave him a feeling of inclusion, so that it was with little hesitation that he thought of introducing himself in the conversation. 'Actually, I noticed that there's a whole chapter on savouries in Lady Sysonby's book,' he said.

'Lady Sysonby? Lady Sysonby! How do you know about Lady Sysonby, a good young American like yourself?' Alice Varrow asked.

'I just came across her cookery book the other day. It was mixed up with some of Sir Christopher's art history papers. And I thought I would try something from it,' John said, having decided, with Sir Christopher's full approval, to replicate (though refine) the meal he had made last Tuesday night.

'Well, this quail looks delicious, and the soufflé was perfection, but then I've always said that Christopher's the luckiest person in the world – wonderful at getting people to look after him. It's a real talent that. I wish I had it, instead of always having to fend for myself. Mind you, one does have a magic touch with the lower classes. They simply adore one! Mummy didn't give one her beautiful green eyes, but she did leave one something much more useful: the gift of finding, and what's more *keeping*, servants. But even they need a holiday, especially an Italian servant like my ancient Judita. So, there I'll be, stuck in Florence, all alone, over *ferragosto*. If anyone had ever told me, when I arrived, at the age of seven, in this manless town, that I'd still be living here, more than half a century later, I would have said he was mad.

'Do you know' – she veered back to John, happy to have a new face to subject to her familiar tale – 'it was snowing, positively hailing, when I got off the train that day I first arrived in Florence. And who was there to meet one but a fusty old Scotch spinster with a wheelbarrow? Yes, I'm not exaggerating, a *wheelbarrow*! Tears streaming down one's face, they were, as we struggled through the snow back to her dreary flat. I thought I had been sent to Siberia.'

'You weren't moved by your first sight of Brunelleschi's cupola?' Sir Christopher asked mockingly.

'Really, Christopher! One was a pampered little girl. What possible use could one have had for a heap of old stones? And one was accustomed to being brought up in the most luxurious of circumstances. But Daddy was dying in the south of France, and

Mummy didn't want one to witness it. Still, it was terribly hard on one, being sent out here, all alone, packed off to Miss Penrose's school every day of the week. And Trixie, being *so* much older, was allowed to stay behind with them – quite, *quite* unfair. It wasn't until three or four years later, after having tried every cure going, that Daddy died in Baden-Baden and Mummy came out here to join me, buying the villa at Settignano. Those first years, in the late twenties and early thirties, were pure bliss. The garden was a perfect paradise, the servants – not *one* Bolshevist amongst them, so unlike nowadays! – were as charming as they were plentiful and the villa was stuffed, positively chock-a-block, with *the* most amusing guests. Everyone so gay!

'You know, I remember that Crystal came to stay with us for an entire month in the spring of 1939 – right after he won the Hawthornden prize for his brilliant book on Chateaubriand. He was already, back then, thinking about writing on Edward VII, which, I am happy to say, I encouraged him to do, over a tête à tête dinner in town, in some little trattoria near San Niccolò. So engrossed were we in conversation, plotting the whole book – spilling the beans on Mrs Keppel and so on – that a passing couple, English of course, stopped at our table, saying they assumed, as we looked so besotted with each other, that we must be in Florence on our honeymoon. We both thought this so funny, so improbable – what with Crystal's taste for the underworld – that we broke into hysterical laughter. When we recounted the story to Mummy the following morning, she said – you simply won't believe it – "I can't think *which* one of you I would pity more!" '

'She was no fool your mother,' Sir Christopher interjected.

'But then the war came,' Alice, who was not to be deterred, continued, 'and we lost everything. I escaped with Mummy. We got the final, and I mean *final*, boat out of Saint-Jean-de-Luz. And that we almost missed, when Mummy caught a glimpse of a ravishing dress in the window of some shop. The sort of thing one only finds in France. Mummy said it was the last pretty dress one would see during the war, and she was going to have it. And have it she did. But I said that, in *that* case, I was going to have a bottle of scent. Who knew when one would find a lovely bottle of scent again? Well, by the time we finished bargaining, we nearly missed the boat.

Anyway, we made it to London, whilst Trixie remained behind with her husband, Pifi. What else could they have done?

'Directly the war was finished, Mummy came out to collect the pieces, such as they were. She tried to keep the villa on for a few years, taking in paying guests, but it was just too difficult, especially once she was run over by a Vespa – just as she was stepping out of Palazzo Portinari after lunching with Lulu – and had to have *both* her legs amputated. I remained in London for a bit after the war, coming out for holidays, but then, when my book on royal mistresses, *The Wages of Beauty*, became an absolute *runaway* best-seller in 1946, one was forced to move out here permanently to escape those bloody socialists and all their taxes. That criminal, and I mean *criminal,* Clement Attlee was responsible for it all! And here one has remained. Who would have thought it?'

'Goodness Alice, you should write your autobiography,' Sir Christopher said, stifling a yawn.

'Yes, people are always telling one that. But I don't see the point. I'm sure it wouldn't sell. After all, who wants to read about the upper classes nowadays? I'm much better off going on the way I am, with my biographies. The new one on my beloved Empress, Sisi, is bound to be a wild success. But still, in order to start writing it up, one needs to be looked after. I was meant to go and spend a lovely fortnight by the sea with Tommy Tornabuoni at Forte, right over *ferragosto,* but now he's gone off to Switzerland to have some little operation. Most inconsiderate! And then he's going to recover at the Beau-Rivage. Lord knows what that will cost. You'd think he might invite one to keep him company after his operation. Imagine how that might inspire one? It makes one shudder to think that it was just there, as Sisi set forth from the Beau-Rivage, that that filthy Italian anarchist drove a needle – not a knife, but a knitting needle – into her throat. Goodness, one can almost feel it oneself, that needle *plunging* right into one!'

'And so I gather, dear Alice,' Sir Christopher said mockingly, 'that you have forsaken decapitated ladies for stabbed ones.'

'Fun you might make of one, dear Christopher,' Alice said grandly, 'but I can assure you it was no laughing matter what Sisi had to bear. And if only Tommy would invite one to Lausanne over *ferragosto* I am sure that one could write up the most riveting scenario. But no, one has just to hear about that *quite* minor operation of his. You would have thought, from the way he drones on, that he was going in for quintuple bypass surgery.'

'And what actually is wrong with poor old Tommy?' Sir Christopher asked, obviously uninterested.

John was amused to hear the man whom he knew, by reputation, as Tommaso, Barone Tornabuoni referred to as 'poor old Tommy'. And he gathered that, though Barone Tornabuoni was often hailed as the final arbiter of artistic taste in Florence, he was, in fact, respected, not for his books – all written in English – but because he was known to be the richest man in the city. Sir Christopher, John clearly understood, did not share the general enthusiasm. Specialist that he was, Sir Christopher could not but be impressed by Barone Tornabuoni's collection – including a series of three mythological Botticellis, with the Tornabuoni escutcheon incised into their original frames, a Ghirlandajo altarpiece, a portrait attributed to the young Leonardo (which Sir Christopher resolutely gave to Verrocchio) and a host of important primitives – and he was *almost* awed by his pedigree, but he could not take the man quite seriously. Entirely too precious for his taste. Barone Tornabuoni called himself an æsthete; Sir Christopher labelled him a dilettante.

'Tommy's got the usual thing for a gentleman of that age – the prostate,' Alice explained.

'Did you say something about Tommy's estate?' Alice Varrow's sister, Trixie, asked in the undertone so frequently adopted by the near-deaf.

'No, no,' Alice Varrow raised her voice. 'His prostate. He's going to have it operated on in Lausanne, old Tommy.'

'Tommy, darling Tommy, an operation? Oh dear, is he dying?'

'No, Trixie, it's just a simple prostate operation.'

'What?'

'Prostate!' Alice snarled at her sister across the table.

'I can't understand you if you grit your teeth, dear Alice.'

'Oh, for God's sake, it's a prostate operation. He can't pee, don't you know.'

'And for an æsthete like Tommy,' Trixie Giraldi said, rubbing her temples. 'What a tragedy!'

'I fail to understand,' Alice, increasingly agitated, replied, 'how it is any more tragic for an æsthete than for a *carbonaio* not to be able to pee.'

'But for Tommy, above all, surrounded since birth by all those beautiful things – the quattrocento panels and the Renaissance furniture and tapestries – and not to be able to see any of them. Is he *completely* blind?'

'Oh my God! She must think I said see and not pee,' Alice said to Sir Christopher, who refused absolutely to register the exchange between the two sisters.

'Are you speaking to one?' Trixie Giraldi persisted.

'Not see, Trixie, pee. He can't *pee*,' Alice Varrow positively shouted, contorting her face into a hideous arrangement of warring wrinkles and distended flesh.

'What?'

'*Could* you make her understand?' Alice Varrow asked, grabbing hold of John's arm. 'It's a wonder one doesn't go mad with her staying in one's house. I must say that I would rather have my little problems of circulation, which occasionally make it a bit difficult for one to walk, than to be deaf as a post the way she is.'

'And I,' Trixie Giraldi, having, for once, heard perfectly, said, 'would rather be a little hard of hearing than be a cripple like you, dear Alice.'

Parallel to the intellectual conversation he had anticipated, John had conjured up an image of Miss Varrow, the professional biographer, as a thin, lithe, demure, scholarly-looking lady, with tightly coiled white hair and sensible shoes. Instead, he was confronted by a large, fleshy, heavily painted woman, with a mass of dyed curls, wrapped in pastel-coloured frills and flounces and bloated feet, rising – like his own beautifully puffed soufflé – high above the rims of her patent leather court shoes. Alice Varrow's sister – her much *older* sister, as she stressed repeatedly – conformed more closely to stereotypical refinement, yet there was a harshness in her handsome, but stony, visage which John found slightly repugnant, so that he instinctively turned back to Alice Varrow, once he had enlightened her sister.

'Of course, I might feel a bit more sympathy for old Tommy,' Alice, ignoring her sister, continued between bites of quail, 'if I hadn't had Lulu de' Portinari on the telephone all afternoon, telling me that it's definite – all settled – about Tommy's palace. They've even cooked up some enormous party in Palazzo Vecchio in December, so that they can celebrate the bequest. If you ask me, they're going to all this trouble just to make sure that he can't back out.'

'What about his palace?' Sir Christopher asked, evincing more interest now.

'That it's to go to Florence. The whole damned thing – the palace and *all* its contents – he's leaving to the city of Florence.'

'I don't see what else you could do with a patrimony like that, if you don't have any relatives. You wouldn't want it all to end up in some terrible muddle, the way things did with Bibino Salviati's palace, now would you?' Sir Christopher asked.

'Oh, darling Bibino – when I think of his pathetic life, my heart just sinks! He was positively enslaved to that mad – and I mean *raving* – Welsh witch mother of his, the Marchesa Gwendolina. He had, I tell you, to dine with her every night and *then* to tuck her in. Myself, I've always been absolutely terrified of lunatics, ever since I read *Jane Eyre* at the age of six. Why Mummy ever allowed one to be exposed to such a thing, at a tender age like that, I shall never know – but read Miss Brontë one did. One can only say that one thought Gwendolina would, like the first Mrs Rochester, never have the decency to die. Bibino himself was over eighty by the time his mother finally keeled over. No wonder that he wasn't as others are, dear Bibino.

'Do you know,' Alice Varrow said to John, who hadn't the slightest idea whom she was talking about, 'Bibino was longing, but absolutely *longing* to marry one before the war? But I was only sixteen and Mummy wouldn't hear of it. I'm sure that's why he never married: he never got over one. The nasty Florentines – you'd better beware of them, if you're planning to stay here, young man – all loved to snipe that he wasn't the marrying kind, *l'altra parrocchia* as they say here, but I am the one to testify that that is simply not true.

'Mind you.' She shifted back to Sir Christopher. 'It was all so long ago that one didn't expect him to leave one much in his will, but still, I do think that one deserved some lovely little *ricordo*.'

'But I thought Bibino didn't leave a will and that the *maggiordomo* forged one, in which, miraculously, everything was left to him. Wasn't that the problem?' Sir Christopher asked.

'The problem, if you want to know – the real nigger in the wood-pile,' Alice said, shocking John with the expression he had never before heard, 'was that Welsh relative who emigrated to New Zealand and had the cheek to turn up here and claim everything, but *every*thing, for herself. But that's neither here nor there. One hadn't seen much of Bibino for ages – he had gone a little funny himself after all those years of attending to his dreadful mother – but with Tommy, it's quite a different matter. There's no question of him not drafting a will. It's a done matter. I think it's simply shocking, wicked really, that he plans to leave everything to this bloody town.'

'Would you prefer that he leave it all to that, that what's-his-name – Woodsworth or Woodstock – who looks after him?' Sir Christopher said tauntingly.

'Looks after him? Looks after him!' Alice yelled. 'Looks out for *himself*, you mean – that Texan tart, that Woodstoke. I think he's a real Gaveston figure, the way he's insinuated himself. The worst sort of American. Not in the least *salonfähig*. Mind you,' she said to John, 'I am sure that you are an entirely different class of American altogether. Rhode Island, you said? Yes, *quite* a different matter – Newport and all that. I had lovely days there before the war when my book on Cleopatra came out – wild success it was – and one was being fussed up to no end. Dodo's father even gave a ball in one's honour, in that rather fantastic house of his overlooking the bay. But this Woodstoke from Texas – just the mention of his name!

'What' – Alice redirected her attention back to Sir Christopher – '*can* Tommy have been thinking of? Undoubtedly, it's that Woodstoke who's come up with this whole ridiculous scheme of leaving Palazzo Tornabuoni to the city of Florence. You can be sure that he stands to gain, *somehow*, from all of this. And as if Florence needed another museum. Why this town is nothing but a glorified clip joint nowadays. They can't even look after what they've got. Either they strip the places bare of every charming, personal association – the way they did with Lady Selina's villa at Fiesole, Belcanto – or they let them run to wrack and ruin. Everyone's always complaining that the galleries in this town are in a deplorable state – *when* there're open!'

'The museums were beautifully kept in Mussolini's time,' Trixie Giraldi, having caught a drift of the conversation, interposed.

'Palazzo Tornabuoni is an historical entity of unparalleled

significance – unique. And it is *imperative*,' Sir Christopher said with scornful severity, 'that it be kept together. It's quite a different matter to some villa at Fiesole, fitted up at the turn of the century, like Selina Watson's. Just think of all those magnificent Renaissance pictures, right there in via de' Tornabuoni, in the very palace for which they were painted.'

'Oh, I don't care a fig about those old *fondi d'oro*,' Alice said breez-ily. 'It's the *pretty* things I mind about – the eighteenth-century French fans and the Venetian lacquer and that trove of American silver. For, let's be honest, Christopher, you can go on till you're blue in the face about that blasted old Renaissance, but it's all that lovely *American* money from Tommy's mother and grandmother that's kept the place going for the past 150 years. And you'd think that Tommy might leave some of those personal things to his friends – and I am his oldest friend.

'You know,' she said to John, 'I shall never forget when I first laid eyes on Tommy. It wasn't in Florence, but on the shores of Lac Léman, where he was declaiming his poetry through a megaphone to a coterie of admirers, with the Château de Chillon as backdrop, just after the Great War. I thought I had never seen anything so romantic in my life. It was as though Byron himself had mate-rialised before one. Mind you, I am *much* younger than Tommy – scarcely out of the nursery one was at the time – but he picked me out of the entire crowd, much to my delight, I admit, and presented me with the white narcissus from his buttonhole. From that day forward, we were the closest of friends. But' – she swung back to Sir Christopher – 'what use does Tommy have for his old friends, now? Lulu de' Portinari told me – told me gloatingly, I might add – that it is all signed, sealed and delivered. She and Tommy share the same *notaio*. And – wouldn't you know it? – that little man told her this morning that there is no going back. He even showed her some stamped document. But then why should old Lulu care about the state grabbing all of Tommy's treasures – not one single bequest to me – when she's already inherited a fortune from her limp little husband, years ago?'

'I am afraid that the truth of the matter, dear Alice,' Sir Chris-topher said, 'is that, at *our* age, we're unlikely to inherit anything.'

John thought it generous of Sir Christopher to refer to 'our age' when speaking to Alice Varrow, who claimed to be two years older but looked, easily, ten years more. Her reply, however, did not imply much in the way of gratitude.

'Don't be irritating, Christopher! That's just what Lulu kept saying to one all afternoon. And you certainly don't want to be compared to *her*, do you?

'Have you any idea of what Lulu de' Portinari did during the war?' Alice Varrow asked John.

'No,' he replied with a smile, as he thought of the eponymous altarpiece by Hugo van der Goes, all the while exulting in the notion that there should still be people who rejoiced in the name Portinari.

'There, Mummy was in London with me, worried to death she was about Trixie and Pifi, who were stranded out here in Italy. And what do you think Lulu decided to do at the very height of the war? She went to the trouble of having an enormous, but I mean *enormous*, black-edged envelope sent to Mummy in London, sent via the Vatican by diplomatic immunity, if you please. As you can imagine, Mummy nearly fainted dead away at the sight of that envelope. She thought Trixie and Pifi might have been gunned down in Piazza della Signoria. Oh, how cross Mummy was when she opened it to read that it was with "*la più gran tristezza*" that Duchessa de' Portinari announced the death of her beloved husband, Pigello de' Duchi de' Portinari. I'll never forget the wording of the card: "*si è spento serenamente*". Well, no one ever imagined *he* would have died in combat.

'On top of which, it's a fact – a proven fact – that the marriage was never consummated. Mummy had it on the best authority: a maid. *No* better source of inside information than a servant, I can promise you! There she was this sweet little girl – Ornella or Ornetta, some such name – who used occasionally to do sewing for Mummy, but her real job, poor thing, was to be Lulu's evening *femme de chambre*. And she *swore* to Mummy that Lulu, every night of the entire first year of her marriage, would wander round the palace unto the wee hours of the morning stark naked – and I mean starkers – holding aloft an enormous gold crucifix by Cellini or Bellini, one of those frightfully valuable things that the Portinari have stashed in every cupboard, screaming, "*Vous allez faire votre devoir!*" (Lulu was stupid enough to think that, if she spoke French, none of the servants would understand her, but understand her they did, all too well.)

'This went on for an entire year. Every night found the naked Lulu – a sight I am happy to have been spared, believe me – slumped before the locked door of the Duke's *appartamento*, pounding on it, as she chanted her pathetic refrain: "*Vous allez faire votre DEVOIR!*" And every night that angelic little seamstress had to drag the naked Lulu across the freezing terracotta floor back to her own rooms.

'Then, on the first anniversary of their marriage, Gello opened the door after just one thump from Lulu. But rather than admit his wife, Gello began to hurl Italian banknotes at her, screaming, "*Soldi! Soldi!* That's what you want, isn't it? *Soldi!* You *putana!*" as he lunged for her neck.

'Fearing for her life, Lulu picked up her crucifix and positively ran back to her chambers. From then on, it was she who locked her door every night, whilst every day she lit a candle to the Virgin, praying for her husband's death. "*La più gran tristezza*", indeed!' Alice concluded her oration in a furore of clamorous indignation.

'*Please*, Alice!' Sir Christopher raised his hand as if to halt traffic.

'Well you must admit that it is rather provoking. There, Lulu had been praying, for years, *years* mind you, for her husband to die – and she only refused a divorce because she wanted that title *and* the money – but then, when he finally did up and die, she went round playing the bereaved widow, with black-edged envelopes into the bargain.'

'I can believe,' Sir Christopher said, 'that it might *once* have been rather provoking – forty years ago. But I hardly think that anyone much cares about the matter today.'

'Really, Christopher. There's no need to be rude,' Alice said, vainly trying to draw up her curved back. 'But if you prefer to be so terribly *au courant*, perhaps you can tell one about some art historian who's just written a book on Masuccio?'

'Do you mean Masaccio?'

'Yes, whatever. He's called Bentley-Gordon, the young man who wrote the book, or so Lulu said.'

'You mean Masolino then, not Masaccio,' Sir Christopher said.

'I was sure that it began with *M*, but that's neither here nor there,' Alice said. 'Do you know this Bentley-Gordon? What's he like?'

'I know that he did come to see me in my office in London a few years ago, but I can't really remember anything about him. And one certainly wouldn't have the slightest idea, were he to walk into the room right now, who he was. But why ever are you and Lulu interested in him? This is not, I assume, a newfound interest in art history for the two of you.'

'Believe it or not,' Alice said conspiratorially, 'Lulu's niece has married him. It all happened very mysteriously and very quickly. The Portinari had long since given up hope of marrying that girl off to anyone – not without reason, mind you, for she's as plain as the night is long and without so much as an *ounce* of charm – so they're quite happy, in a way, to have her off their hands, but, then again, if you ask me, I think they're rather worried. Must be a bit odd, you know, any man who would want to take up with such a girl. I think Lulu secretly fears that, like her own husband, he belongs to *l'altra parrocchia*, though she pretends, naturally, to be delighted. She insists that he comes from quite a good Scotch family, but I could only tell her that *I* had never heard the name before. Bailey-Gordon would be quite another matter – but *Bentley*-Gordon? And you don't know anything about him either, Christopher? Ha, sounds very dubious to one.'

'I didn't say,' Sir Christopher corrected Alice, 'that I didn't know anything about him, only that I didn't remember him – didn't remember him personally. But it so happens that I am reviewing his book on Masolino, working on it right now, as a matter of fact.'

'What? You're reviewing his book? I don't believe it. This is going to cause a *sensation*!' Alice cried as she plunged into the raspberry sorbet.

'Really, Alice, there's no need to jump to the third act,' Sir Christopher said loftily. 'It's not as though one doesn't normally write reviews of books about Renaissance art. This one is, though, I admit, a bit different. It's a sort of omnium gatherum, dealing with several different monographs on early Renaissance painters, of which Mr Bentley-Gordon's just happens to be one element. And, thank God, it is nearly finished. It's taken much longer to write than it ever should have.'

'I'll have to get on to Lulu at once. She'll want to know all about this. I do hope that you are going to be kind about the book.'

'I'm going to be truthful.'

'Oh please, Christopher, don't pull your *de haut en bas* face on one.

'You know' – Alice lurched back to John – 'it really is quite amazing that Christopher and I have remained such good friends all these years. He, ever the serious art critic, and I, well I quite admit to being frivolous. Mind you, I love to look at pretty things, and, Lord knows, I wish I owned a few,' she said, casting her eye covetously round the object-filled room, 'but I was never the type for running off to Empoli to ooh and aah over a few battered predella panels. I've always preferred people to things, but then I suppose that is why I am a biographer. Wildly curious one is to know about the secret lives of others. Now, you'll have to come up to see me some afternoon at my little house and tell me all about yourself. You'll be in Florence for some time, will you?'

John nodded ambiguously, all the while asking himself the same question. How much longer would he remain? How much longer *could* he remain? The month of July was more than half over, and he had hardly begun to penetrate the treasures of Florence, let alone to travel fervidly about Italy, as he had initially vowed to do. By rights – certainly by the terms of his grant – he should have ventured forth like a pilgrim, seeking out works of art, whereas he had elected to enclose himself like a drudge, filing books. In a sense, he felt privileged to have caught a glimpse of what, he realised, was the last gasp of the Anglo-Florentine colony – a world that he had read much about and dreamt even more of. But he also feared that, having once seen this world up close that he would, when separated from it, as inevitably he imagined he would be, feel all the more excluded.

He decided suddenly and, he thought, definitively, as he half listened to Alice Varrow recount yet another story of Florentine machination, that he must extricate himself from Sir Christopher, from the books and from the derailment of his plans. He would come back tomorrow morning, explain his system of filing and then politely absent himself. *This is just a useful contact,* nothing *more,* he repeated to himself forlornly as he looked over at Sir Christopher.

But when he did return the next morning, his resolve, though sharpened by a restless night, collapsed utterly. Finally, the following Tuesday, 26 July, the day after he had at last finished arranging Sir Christopher's study, John arrived earlier than usual, determined to announce his intention of leaving for Rome by the end of the month, only to find himself foiled again.

That morning, Sir Christopher presented him first thing with the manuscript of his review, saying, 'Here. You'd better read this and tell me what you think of it. I'm sure that one could never have finished it if you hadn't arranged things in the flat. To tell you the truth, one was beginning to get rather worried that one had lost one's touch, but then you turned up and put things right.'

John was immensely flattered to be told that he had 'put things right', but he was even more honoured to be asked to participate in what, he knew, Sir Christopher considered the sacred ritual of writing, so that, banishing all thoughts of excusing himself, he immediately sat down with the manuscript. He read with a concentration that he did not know he possessed – weighing each word, mulling over every phrase, sizing up the shape of one paragraph after another – till he had established an almost somatic contact with the pages. It was impossible for him not to be impressed by the fluency of a much-practised professional like Sir Christopher. Tentatively, he marked a few instances where he believed that a word, or even a comma, might profitably be changed, but he also saw that it would serve no purpose merely to bow obeisantly before the master. Thus did he decide to proffer, amidst a flourish of praise, *one* substantive suggestion.

Girding himself, as he stood before the now immaculately arranged refectory table in Sir Christopher's study, he said nervously, 'My only general point is about the Masolino frescoes at Castiglione d'Olona. I'm sure that it's my fault – as I don't know them in the original – but I have to say that I found your description a bit confusing. Not with the frescoes in the baptistery – that's all perfectly clear – but with those in the Collegiata. It's the part about the unusual arrangement of the cycle of the life of the Virgin being dictated by the uneven compartments of the crossed-ribbed vaulting.'

'Where?' Sir Christopher asked, grabbing the manuscript from John.

Afraid that he had overstepped himself, John obsequiously pointed to the passage that he found difficult to follow and, like an accused schoolboy waiting whilst the evidence against him is weighed, withdrew to one side.

After a remarkably short time, Sir Christopher looked up and said, 'You're right, quite right. That bit is rather muddled. Now, you've never been there, you say.'

'To Castiglione d'Olona?' John asked.

'Yes,' Sir Christopher said. 'You've been to Milan, of course.'

John hesitated, taking a few moments to grasp that, when Sir Christopher said 'Mill-en', he was referring to the place that most others called 'Mi-lan'. Finally, he bobbed his head and said, 'Yes, I did stop there briefly on my way to Florence. But no, I didn't make it to Castiglione d'Olona, much as I would have—'

'Do you drive a car?' Sir Christopher asked.

'Well,' John said, surprised at the succession of questions, 'I do have a licence, but I've never driven in Europe – if that's what you mean? – and I don't know how to drive a stick shift.'

'Myself, I was, long ago, strongly – *quite* strongly – advised against driving,' Sir Christopher smiled proudly. 'But it seems to me that, as you've made such a Her-cül-ē-an – or Her-cu-lē-an, as I imagine you would say – effort over putting the books in order, you deserve some special trip. In addition, of course, to what I shall pay you. Before I forget, here's a modest cheque for that.'

John took the cheque and, without looking at it, folded it into his pocket, thinking all the while about Sir Christopher's reference to his pronunciation. He wondered if the hours he had spent practicing the word 'Ré-nay-ssänce' had made any impact at all.

'What would you say,' Sir Christopher continued, 'if we made a trip to Castiglione d'Olona? We could go to Milan by train and then stay at that nice *hôtel* in via Manzoni, where they could arrange for a driver to take us for the day to see the Masolino frescoes at Castiglione d'Olona. I've, of course, been there several times before, though probably not for twenty years, and I think a visit now would put the final touch on this review. What is today, Tuesday, the twenty-sixth? I'm out to dine tomorrow night with Baba Braccio, but we could leave first thing Thursday morning, the twenty-eighth, spend two nights in Milan and be back here on Saturday, the thirty-first, before August descends upon us. And it is certainly not as if we have to worry about getting tickets for La Scala at this time of year.'

John assented at once, naturally. And yet, even in those first delirious minutes, he realised that he would now be absolutely obliged to postpone his departure. Though he worried that his air ticket could not be changed without incurring a substantial penalty, he was, nonetheless, sure that something momentous had just occurred. When he walked out of Palazzo Vespucci that night, after a leisurely dinner and a long stretch of *Figaro*, he looked, whilst standing under the first street light he came to, at the cheque that Sir Christopher had given to him. Any qualms he had harboured vanished instantly: the sum made out to him was exactly double the stipend he had been awarded for an entire summer of travel.

†

One of the first things that John bought with his unexpected windfall was a smart travelling case, as he would have been embarrassed to be seen with the decrepit luggage he had been carting about all summer. But when he placed his gleaming new acquisition on the platform early on Thursday morning, he was suddenly apprehensive that he might have gone too far, for, next to his bag, Sir Christopher's looked decidedly dowdy. Was there not, he wondered, something inherently vulgar about *new* luggage? But John could tell from Sir Christopher's demeanour that bags, whether dingy or dazzling, were the last thing on the scholar's mind. The train was late, and Sir Christopher appeared transparently agitated.

'I suppose that we just have to be patient,' John ventured to say, as yet another delay was announced.

'In her book on Christina of Sweden, Mamma cited one of the Queen's favourite maxims: *Patience is a virtue for those who lack courage or conviction*. It's a motto by which, from earliest childhood, one was taught to fashion one's life,' Sir Christopher said, turning away abruptly.

Feeling thoroughly admonished, John hung back, standing sentinel over the bags. Not knowing what to do, as Sir Christopher furiously paced the platform, he bent down, opened his new case and pulled out the copy of *La Prisonnière* that he had intermittently been struggling through, ever since he had boarded the plane back in New York over a month ago. In truth, he would have much preferred to go on reading the paperback of *Daniel Deronda* that he had bought in via de' Tornabuoni a few days ago, with which he was getting on splendidly, but he thought Sir Christopher would be more impressed by a French novel.

He opened the book, delighted that Albertine had finally moved in with the narrator – to the great distrust of the housekeeper – but, much as he would have liked to assume her position as a mirror image to his own, he realised that their roles were, in reality, reversed, as it was the narrator, the *maître de maison*, who sought to ensnare his beloved, not the interloper, that is himself, who longed to be introduced.

Wondering where he fit into the hierarchy, he let his eyes wander from the page and fixed his gaze on Sir Christopher. John was surprised, and not a little impressed, to see him striding up and down, brandishing a stack of newspapers and an Italian translation of Agatha Christie. How, he wondered, did Sir Christopher dare to present himself in public so self-confidently, yet unadorned by any of the requisite decorations of intellectual honour. *What message are those newspapers and cheap paperback meant to convey?* he asked himself.

He found it difficult to believe that anyone – any mildly self-respecting intellectual, that is to say – could read simply for pleasure. John often read with pleasure, sometimes great pleasure, but never *for* pleasure. Like the Underground Man, he was stirred, delighted and tormented by reading; but, unlike the Underground Man, he did not read in the hope of stifling the external sensations that were ceaselessly boiling up inside himself – on the contrary, he read in the hope of stimulating the tumult exploding behind his calm, composed façade. With age, and the aid of a quite exceptional memory – a memory that allowed him to learn many a verse by heart but that, at the same time, prevented him from ever forgetting a slight (real or imagined) – he would eventually arrive at a stage where it was often difficult for him to distinguish between the mysteries of life and the entelechies of literature, but now, as a young man of twenty-four, struggling in the heat of the July morning with his halting French and stealing covert glances at Sir Christopher, he was conscious only of the *absence* of pleasure that his reading afforded him.

When, after about three quarters of an hour, it was announced that the train would be arriving shortly, Sir Christopher came up to John and stood, smiling silently, next to him. He could see that

Sir Christopher was visibly mollified by the news, and John too felt calmed, as though he himself had somehow been responsible for the delay. He sensed that it would be misguided to say anything and returned to his book with easeful thoughts. But he quickly felt the stare of Sir Christopher over his shoulders and so turned round to meet his gaze. He closed the book and held up its title for inspection, which was, he imagined, what Sir Christopher was interested in.

Sir Christopher glanced at the spine of John's book and then, looking at the tracks, said, 'I suppose that one would be more likely to understand Proust, if one had *ever* been jealous oneself.'

John reeled back, as if struck. Was this, he wondered, some sort of rebuke? Did Sir Christopher already sense (and rebuff) John's possessive, cloying nature? And what exactly did Sir Christopher mean to imply by his own incomprehension of jealousy? Was it his way of emphasising the unimportance of John, or indeed of anyone, in his emotive life? Did he want to tell John that the welcome that had been accorded to him, the invitation to travel that had been extended to him, had been born of a mere velleity? That he could be as easily cast aside as he had been taken up? Or was he, John asked himself, being overly sensitive?

But he would not be answered so easily. Like the Moor before him, John was jealous, not for a cause, but because he *was* jealous. Glumly, he looked at Sir Christopher, who seemed, to him, the picture of sublime detachment, far removed from any hint of pretext. John would have liked to push the conversation further – just to be sure that there was no basis to his doubt – but he did not have the courage to speak. It was thus, for him, a great relief to witness the tentative approach of a gangly young man.

'Sir Christopher?' the stranger asked in a squeaky voice.

'Yes,' Sir Christopher said in his least forthcoming manner.

'I don't know if you remember me, but, um, I came to see you in your office some time ago about my work on Masolino. My name's Gordon Bentley-Gordon.'

'Quite,' Sir Christopher said.

'May I present my wife, Sabina?' the young man asked, pointing to a plump, moustachioed woman of indeterminate age. 'I think you know her aunt, Duchessa de' Portinari.'

'Indeed, I do,' Sir Christopher said, nodding but not offering his hand. 'We're just on our way to Milan,' he continued, pointing to John but making no introduction. 'Why don't you ring up my flat later in the month. We can't possibly talk now – what with the train about to arrive.'

Although he had already registered that any unexpected incursion into Sir Christopher's orbit, whether in his study or in a library or in a museum, even in a restaurant, would not be countenanced, John was, nonetheless, slightly startled by Sir Christopher's abruptness.

'I wonder what strange twist of fate blew *him* into our path so early in the morning?' Sir Christopher said, as soon as they were alone.

'It is an odd coincidence. And just as we are setting off to *Mill-en*,' John said, daring to imitate Sir Christopher's pronunciation.

'Unfortunately, it doesn't make one think any the better of his book. It really is a rather pedestrian piece of work. I hope that Alice won't be *too* cross with one about the review,' Sir Christopher said with a chuckle.

Wanting to allude to, but not specifically to mention, the distinctly epicene manner of Mr Bentley-Gordon, as well as the ungainly aspect of his bride, John said guardedly, 'Anyway, one can see why Alice Varrow was so surprised that he should have married Duchessa de' Portinari's niece.'

'Oh!' Sir Christopher exclaimed, 'I'm not in the least surprised that he should have married. After all, it's not as though he's a particularly *talented* art historian. I'd say that he may, by nature, come from what Alice would call *l'altra parrocchia* – he certainly looks as though he's from "the other parish" – but that he has, quite in keeping with his weaknesses, defected. To judge from his writing, I should say he lacks courage; but, then, not everyone has the strength of character to assume the higher calling. Many a second-rate art historian has thrown his hands up in despair and got married.'

When, a moment later, the train whistled, John chose to hear this screeching sound as a summons, an irrefutable summons, to his true apostolate.

CHAPTER V

A Forsaken Net

JOHN WAS AFRAID that Sir Christopher would, in his impatience, open the door before the train came to a complete stop and fall out, but he did not dare to say anything. Even before they arrived at Prato, Sir Christopher had been so fidgety that John understood immediately that he was meant to pile up the luggage in the cramped vestibule near the exit, thereby ensuring that no one could pass before them. Now that the train had clapped into Santa Maria Novella station, and whilst it was still jolting back and forth, Sir Christopher began frantically to rattle the door handle and to push and twist the red knob to its right. When, at last, the door did open – of its own accord – Sir Christopher bounded out of the carriage, nearly losing his footing in the process. John followed straightaway, offering his arm for support, but was brushed aside.

'*Facchino! Facchino!*' Sir Christopher began to shout, snapping his fingers and addressing no one in particular. When he saw a porter approaching, he turned to John and said, 'Here, you deal with the bags, and I'll go on to secure the taxi. Otherwise, we'll be stuck at the back of a frightful queue.' And with that he disappeared into the crowd.

John did manage to engage the porter, though he had more than a little trouble explaining that another bag and a stack of books still remained in the train. He tried to hurry the porter, who seemed as lackadaisical as he was jovial, but his injunctions produced nothing but a series of smiling shrugs. When, halfway up the platform, the man stopped to offer one of his fellow workers a cigarette, John spoke with such uncharacteristic sharpness that he did appear to make some impact. But the main hall of the station was so congested that John feared that any further entreaty to make

71

haste might actually be counterproductive; thus did he keep silent, whilst the porter dawdled and he himself was assailed by visions of a fumingly restive Sir Christopher Noble-Nolan. When he finally reached the taxi rank, which was pullulating with a disordered mass of tourists, gypsies and disgruntled locals, John looked round desperately, wondering how he would ever track down Sir Christopher. In the end, it was the porter who espied him.

'*Eccolo – suo padre!*' the porter, pointing to Sir Christopher at the front of the line, exclaimed.

John ran forward, counted the bags again, proffered an extravagant tip and slid into the taxi beside Sir Christopher, revelling all the while in the words the porter had just spoken: *suo padre. Your father,* he repeated to himself. Could anyone really think that Sir Christopher was his father?

John glanced at his own reflexion in the driver's rear-view mirror only to confirm what he already knew: he was himself shorter, softer, spottier than the angular and, to him, terribly impressive-looking art historian with flaring cheekbones, arched eyebrows and craning neck who was seated beside him. Altogether unlike. But even if he did not resemble Sir Christopher in a biological sense, he was pleased that he should appear, by virtue of placement and demeanour, to be the son of a man of such distinguished bearing.

As a child, John had often dreamt that he belonged to quite a different family from the one he had actually been born into; night after night, year after year, he had lulled himself to sleep by projecting himself into any number of grand, appealing settings, with appropriate parents and siblings to match. Even as an adult, he was not above dreaming that he was the scion of an illustrious family, proudly carrying on a noble tradition. The transparent illogicality of the matter – that he, John Forde, should have been born to different parents but remain physically the same person – did little to discourage his wide-ranging fantasy. That someone, even if just a porter, could be so easily duped by surface appearances encouraged John to believe all the more deeply in such genealogical delusions.

As soon as they entered the apartment, John went straight to Sir Christopher's newly organised study. He began methodically to unpack the stack of papers which their short trip had produced, as he imagined – correctly, he soon saw – that, in spite of the hour, Sir

Christopher would want immediately to go over the recent notes for his review, if only briefly. He hoped that, in thus anticipating the wants of his master, in sensing his habits, in cloaking his merest inclinations in the guise of urgent needs, he was able to demonstrate, not to explain, that he had no need of *bit and bridle* – that he was capable of being guided by the eye alone.

When he heard the first clacking of the typewriter keys, John withdrew and went in search of the things he had dropped in the front hall. He deposited Sir Christopher's bags in his bedroom and then occupied himself with dinner, most of which Piera had prepared in advance. After they had dined, he put *Figaro* on the phonograph for Sir Christopher, resuming at the exact point where they had left off on Tuesday evening, whilst he himself went back to the bedroom and set about the task of unpacking. He did so in a comparatively languid fashion, reflecting, as he sorted through dirty underclothes and extra (still fresh) white shirts, on the strangeness of his position, here in the heart of Sir Christopher's existence. And yet, he could hardly call the apparent intimacy he presently enjoyed unimaginable, for picture himself he had, over and over again, locked in the firmament of his would-be master's world. Listening to the distant hum of the music, he was tempted, but only for a moment, to congratulate himself on the realisation of his dream, for he was astute enough to grasp that his dream had been not realised but glimpsed.

He knew that the generous cheque Sir Christopher had given to him could, if he were careful – no more pigskin travelling cases, that is – see him through to Christmas. But what then? He had rented his one-room apartment in Florence only through the middle of August, but, though he supposed that the graduate student in New York from whom he had taken it would be only too happy to extend the lease, he saw clearly, all too clearly, that it was perfectly otiose to linger about Florence till his money ran out, for he might then find himself utterly bereft, having sacrificed a university affiliation without having secured a position in Sir Christopher's realm.

His brief exposure to Sir Christopher's enlightened (and enlightening) response to works of art made him dread ever more intensely the return to Professor Isner's sere and pedantic little domain of black-and-white photographs and digressive footnotes, but, unattractive though that prospect was, he knew that he did, at least, have a place in graduate school, whereas in Florence he could count only on a precariously tenuous existence. He needed, he felt, an incontrovertible guarantee of acceptance, that is to say a specific invitation from Sir Christopher, asking him to stay on in Florence, but he also feared that if he were to confront Sir Christopher outright – query his intention or demand an explanation of the apparent detainment he was fostering – that he might be sent packing at once. To assert? To insist? Surely, such a course would be fatal, the very contrary of the *rôle* he had striven so hard to play, and yet he did not feel that he had time, as the summer contracted more tightly and the future loomed less promisingly, to stand by patiently, waiting to see if his position would spread out or shrivel up. And the more did he fret, the less did he feel capable of taking action.

Alarmed by his own indecision, he took up one of the handsomely worn missals lined across the back of the dressing table, in the hope of falling upon some suitably auspicious feast day on which to confront Sir Christopher – a day on which he would ask him, ask him plainly, what was the future to be between them. *Was* there to be a future?

He knew that, whilst seeking divine guidance, Francis of Assisi was said to have thrice opened the Gospels at random and fallen, all three times, on the same passage, in which Christ exhorts His disciples to leave their earthly belongings and to follow Him. And he had a vague memory of another such scene of *sortes sanctorum* in Thomas Hardy, but he couldn't quite remember where. He did not know if such cleromancy would work with a missal rather than a bible, but, pressing its supple leather against his face and inhaling its seductive scent, he could but think of how different it was to the cheap paper ones, replaced each month, on which he had been reared in Providence. He read the inscription on the flyleaf of the missal, which he already knew well – 'To my most darling Tophereen, with deepest love from Mamma, St Christopher's Day, 25 July 1925' – causing him both to smile and to sigh, and then began to dip randomly into the book.

He was embarrassed to see that there were still so many formulations of which he remained utterly ignorant, but then he had been weaned on the butchered, post-Vatican II liturgical calendar, from which St Christopher himself had been expunged. He was, of course, familiar with all the major feast days and could follow the logical sequence of the season, but it would take him rather a time to work out why *Septuagesima* Sunday should mark the ninth, rather than the seventh, week before Easter. And what, he wondered, was the difference between a 'Double of the First Class with an Octave' and one which was known as a 'Greater Double' – not to mention a 'Semidouble'? As tomorrow would be the fourth successive Sunday that he accompanied Sir Christopher to the Tridentine Mass, he felt confident of steering himself from the asperges through the Salve Regina, though many of the ritualistic arcana still seemed foreign – and, therefore, alluring – to him.

He closed the missal again and forced himself immediately to reopen it at random. He landed upon 6 August, the Transfiguration. *What feast*, he asked himself, *could be more propitious? Exactly one week from today. My very own Mount Tabor.*

But just as he began to consider the implications of this date, he was shaken out of his fantastic imaginings by the distant music. As if drawn by a higher power, he let the missal drop, went back into the hall and into the rotunda of a dining room where the phonograph was hidden in a cabinet – only the speakers being exposed. Hardly able to believe himself, he surrendered to the rousing music as the entire cast chanted:

'*Suo padre?*'

'*Suo padre.*'

'*Tuo padre.*'

He stood in the embrasure of the door leading to the drawing room and smiled lovingly at a beatific vision of Sir Christopher, dozing in his armchair – the latest issue of *The Burlington Magazine* splayed across his lap. Soaking up the words of the opera, John felt sure that the divination he had sought would be realised. It was as if Mozart himself had set to music the very words that the porter had spoken to him at the railway station this afternoon.

He remained standing there through the Countess's next aria, reflecting that this was the first time in his life that he had ever genuinely been moved by opera. That night, he took the libretto of *Le nozze di Figaro* home and studied it carefully, the refrain *suo padre* resounding in his ears till the early hours.

✝

The following morning, Sunday, they went to Mass, naturally, but they came back directly – no dawdling over newspapers or cups of cappuccino – as Sir Christopher wanted to set straight to work on his review. On the Monday, John busied himself with laying in provisions for the month of closure that was upon them.

Re-entering the apartment after lunch, he was greeted with the familiar sound of Sir Christopher's furious clacking of the type-writer. Not sure what to do, now that he had the study arranged, he sat in the drawing room and waited, settling down with the paperback of *Far from the Madding Crowd* he had bought that morning. Without much difficulty, he found the vaguely recalled scene of bibliomancy.

Wondering to whom she will be betrothed, Bathsheba Everdene randomly opens the scriptures in the hope that the verse she falls upon will elucidate her future. She finds herself in the Book of Ruth and, misapplying the passage in question, thereby sets in motion her own series of uninterrupted troubles. In the notes to the edition John was reading, he found the following words of Ruth, words that he hoped would presage his own future, words that he longed to utter to Sir Christopher: *Whither thou goest, I will go; and where thou lodgest, I will lodge: thy people shall be my people, and thy God my God.* He had no idea how long he had been swooning over this passage when Sir Christopher surprised him.

'Oh, there you are,' Sir Christopher said, with *more* than a trace of disapproval on finding John in the shuttered drawing room, hovered over a novel at four o'clock in the afternoon. 'Why don't you have a look at this?' he said, extending the revised copy of his review.

'I was just checking something, uh, a reference, a—' John said fumblingly as he jumped up.

Sir Christopher, obviously uninterested in excuses (valid or oth-erwise), cut him off and said, 'Yes, well, let's concentrate on the matter at hand, shall we? And do let us hope that all that time spent going hither and thither to Castiglione d'Olona was time well invested. Now, tell me what you make of the review. I'm going to lie down in my room. One is quite exhausted after all that work.'

Turning to go, Sir Christopher looked down distastefully at the paperback John had distractedly left strewn on the chair and said, 'Never got on with him. He always makes one feel so emotionally inadequate, Hardy does.'

John clutched the bundle of papers to his breast and nodded to Sir Christopher, who retreated to his bedroom. He then went straight to Sir Christopher's study and, still breathing heavily from what he viewed as a narrow escape, laid out the papers that had been entrusted to him. The bulging pile of which he had assumed stewardship consisted of the original (now much crumpled) copy of the review, to which Sir Christopher had affixed a mass of small additions and corrections, typed on uneven strips of paper and stapled, higgledy-piggledy, onto the old sheets, plus two and a half entirely new pages, all of which was scored with a series of nearly indecipherable holograph corrections. He began by folding out and pressing down the various kinks and wrinkles, till he had modelled the semblance of an immaculate substance. Only then did he turn his mind to the appointed task.

Though he had been deeply impressed by the combination of fluent expression and commanding scholarship in the first draft of the review, John experienced a sense of amazement, bordering on fear, at the perfect concinnity that Sir Christopher had been able to introduce to his work in the time that he himself had been ineffectually fretting over a series of dates. After he had twice read and taken notes on this long review – it was now almost twenty-five pages of typescript, but the specialised periodical for which it was written would grant Christopher Noble-Nolan any length he liked – he turned the final page face down and let his head drop. How, he wondered, could he ever compete? (He did not, unfortunately for him, yet realise that he was not *meant* to compete.) What, he asked himself, was he doing here? Doubt assailed him on every side, but then doubt, if not exactly his strength, *was* the begetter of his ambitions, so that, anxious though he was, he was able to gather himself, along with the sheaf of papers, and to creep up to Sir Christopher's bedroom. He pressed his ear against the door and, hearing vague sounds of stirring, tapped timidly.

'Yes? Oh, yes, do come in,' Sir Christopher said welcomingly.

John found Sir Christopher – his coat and shoes removed but his tie and braces still in place – lying on his small four-poster bed amidst an array of newspapers and books. Without waiting for him to speak, or even to sit up, John immediately launched into a pæan of praise for the revised version of the review but, in the fear of sounding smarmy, stopped himself in mid-sentence and asked abruptly, 'Would you like me to retype it for you?'

'If you *could*!' Sir Christopher exclaimed, contorting his voice in the fashion with which John now felt himself thoroughly familiar.

'I'd be happy to,' John said. 'But as the review is now rather long, I think I will have to take it back to my apartment and type it there.'

'Why don't you bring your typewriter here and install yourself in the room that I had been using as the makeshift study. You could turn that into a sort of office for yourself,' Sir Christopher said.

'I suppose that would be the easiest way to go about it,' John said, straining to conceal his elation. 'The only thing,' he continued, 'is that I do need to ask a few questions about your handwriting. I could make out most of it, of course, but I did want to be absolutely sure.'

'Only a *few* questions? You must be even cleverer than I thought. I can't, goodness knows, read my own writing half the time,' Sir Christopher said, casting a smile and propping himself up higher on his pile of pillows.

John knew that, as a rule, Sir Christopher hated to repeat himself, even though the archness of his accent often led many people to ask him to do so, and that he hated, even more, to be obliged to justify anything – from his attribution of a picture to his dislike of the Welsh – which, to him, seemed perfectly self-evident. Having more than once witnessed the signs of Sir Christopher's burning impatience – the clenching of the teeth, the warping of the mouth, the exhalation of exasperation – that such requests could unleash, John had made a list of only the most egregious cases of indecipherability in the hope that, once these were clarified, the others might simply fall into place. But he was so encouraged by Sir Christopher's transparently good humour – a mood which, John did not understand, was the outcome of having successfully finished a piece of work – that he handed over the manuscript with but little of the anxiety he had anticipated and stood tranquilly at the side of the bed with his sheet of queries.

He gripped the corner post with his left hand and, leaning over Sir Christopher's shoulder, pointed out problem words or phrases with his right one. From his upright position, he took careful note of each explanation that was proffered, but in the pauses – sometimes long pauses – during which Sir Christopher puzzled over his own handwriting, he began covertly to survey the figure stretched out before him.

Christopher Noble-Nolan seemed, to John, like Milton's Adam, to have been expressly formed for *contemplation and valour*. As he observed Sir Christopher, he was suddenly reminded of a lecture that he had attended when an undergraduate, in which a celebrated French anthropologist recounted that a certain tribe of Indians – John had no idea which – have a single word for 'young and beautiful' and another for 'old and ugly', but the person before him, though old to John, was anything *but* ugly. In gazing on Sir Christopher, he saw decades of uninterrupted work, along with concomitant rewards of accomplishment, etched into that marmoreal complexion, stretched tautly over those large, fine bones, poised on the light pink lips, thin almost to the point of non-existence, and embedded in the sleek, severely parted silver hair. And it was to him an entirely beautiful vision. Anyone, he realised, might have thought to call Christopher Noble-Nolan distinguished-looking – an epithet that, he reasoned, might be applied to a mere lawyer or diplomat – but, to John, the figure whom he beheld belonged to an infinitely superior cast. Looking at Sir Christopher lain out serenely on his bed, he thought he resembled the effigy of some Renaissance humanist or prince of the Church, Leonardo Bruni or the Cardinal of Portugal. *Resplendent*, he said to himself and smiled. Yes, that was the word he had been looking for. He now stared openly.

'Is everything all right?' Sir Christopher asked, looking up quizzically.

'Um, yes, um, of course,' John quavered as he knelt down by the side of the bed and leant across Sir Christopher's chest – their heads now but inches apart – to point out a word . 'I couldn't make out if you had written "yet" or "yes".'

'It's "yes",' Sir Christopher said, reaching up to touch John's hand. That day they read no further in the manuscript.

☥

It was clear to John that he should make a savoury to conclude the dinner, but that was *all* that was clear to him. After having united with Sir Christopher in his bedroom on Monday afternoon

– an encounter which had not repeated itself – he imagined that everything would simply resolve itself into a clarified dew, but now, five days later, on this Saturday afternoon, as he stood in the kitchen and wondered what to prepare for Alice Varrow, who was coming, *again*, to dine that night – at his suggestion, he had to admit – his position seemed to him more ambiguous than ever.

He opened the book by Lady Sysonby, grasping for ideas, but was unable to concentrate. What, he thought, should he do? Had he, he wondered, made some terrible mistake? He was not disturbed, per se, to have given himself to someone so much older than himself, but he *was* bothered not to know what, if anything, the exchange signified to Sir Christopher. To John, it meant everything: '*Tu se' lo mio maestro e 'l mio autore,*' echoed back and forth in his mind throughout the last few days.

Until now, John's sexual experiences, which could easily be counted on one hand, had invariably left him feeling dirty and disappointed. Intellectually, he had known from an unbearably early age that he was entirely homosexual, but he had never seen how, emotionally, he could gratify his desires. His sexual fantasies, as persistent as they were unwelcome – invariably involving some muscled athlete of the type who had taunted him during his school days for being an intellectual faggot – confirmed John's fear that he would only ever be attracted to someone who despised him and whom he, in turn, would resent for having aroused him. But he now found that the overwhelming, indeed devouring, intellectual fascination he felt for Christopher Noble-Nolan engendered a very real erotic attraction.

It has, of course, been claimed ever since Agathon that it is in the nature of youth to hate old age, that *youth is full of pleasance and age is full of care*, but it was precisely *because* John was young that he was so captivated by this man nearly half a century older than himself. Had he been forty-four years old, instead of twenty-four, it is unlikely that John would have experienced the same surge of emotion. But as a young man, anxious to shake off a past that he found unbecoming and eager to capture a future that appeared elusive, he was incapable of being attracted to a mirror image of himself. Of what possible interest was another 24-year-old American to him?

Through love, he sought the image of everything he had never been, everything he would like to become. But though he longed to believe that he had finally beheld that image in the flesh, there were torturous moments of doubt, when he feared that he had only closed his lips upon that lie which has but the *face* of truth. He did not even, he reproached himself, know how to address his newfound intimate. He had tried once or twice to utter aloud that (to him, beautiful) Christian name unadorned, but he found it worse than impertinent of himself to pronounce it thus; he found it unnatural. In time, quite a long time, he would learn to juggle, with consummate skill, the intricacies of employing Sir Christopher Noble-Nolan's title – when, and in front of whom, he should say 'Sir Christopher' or 'Christopher' or, most often, nothing at all – but in the secret chamber of John's heart, he would never, till his dying day, think of him as other than *Sir* Christopher, nor did he want to think of him otherwise. Over and over, he repeated those two incantatory words to himself, till the owner of that name knocked on the kitchen door himself.

'Do you have everything you need?' Sir Christopher asked, standing on, but not choosing to cross, the threshold of the kitchen.

'Um, yes, I think so,' John said, 'though I must admit that I am not terribly organised.'

'I'm sure that you'll manage beautifully – whatever you do.'

'There's the salmon that I bought this morning. I am going to poach that and serve it cold with a cucumber salad and a *sauce verte*. But I don't know what to begin with. And then for the sweet, I thought that I would just make a sorbet with these,' he said, picking up a fishnet bag of lemons. He didn't say anything about the savoury, as he wanted that to be a surprise, though he was so put off by some of the recipes he had come across – cheese ice and biscuits Casanova – that he was not sure how to proceed.

'But that's sounds perfect. Much better than old Alice has any right to expect, considering the nasty food she normally gives one. Well, if there's nothing else, I think I had better get back to Botticelli – now that we've finally got that blasted review off.'

'It's just, I was, um, wondering...' John hesitated, clutching the bag of lemons to his chest. 'Do you think it would be all right if we just had a cold soup to start with?' he asked, losing heart.

'I'm sure that would be fine,' Sir Christopher said.

'What with this heat,' John said feebly. 'And then, um,' he faltered, 'well, you know, um, what today is?'

'No,' Sir Christopher said.

'It's the sixth of August, the *Transfiguration*,' John said with great emphasis.

'And?' Sir Christopher asked, remaining in the embrasure of the door.

'*And* that means,' John said, laying the lemons on the table, as he tried to rip open their fishnet sack, hoping all the while to avoid looking Sir Christopher in the eye, 'that I will have to think about moving on. I haven't, you know, even been to Rome yet. And as for Naples or Venice, well, I'm afraid that I won't have time for that now, not before I head back to New York.'

'I don't follow you,' Sir Christopher said, stepping, for the first time, fully into the kitchen.

'I'm here, in Europe I mean, because of my PhD, and I will have to be getting back to that.'

'But do you want a PhD? *I*, after all, don't have one,' the autodidact, Christopher Noble-Nolan, who had been born into a world where art history was not an officially recognised academic discipline, said smilingly.

'I *want*,' John said, as he wrenched open the sack of lemons, spilling them on to the floor, 'to be an art historian.'

Sir Christopher calmly watched John collect the lemons and place them in a bowl on the table. He then said, 'But that is exactly what I thought you were in the process of becoming – here, with me.'

'Does that *mean*,' John asked, wringing the empty fishnet sack in his hands, 'that you want me to stay on, stay in Florence, with you?'

'Of course. I just assumed that that was *obvious*. Now, do you happen to know where on earth one put the Brieger, Meiss, what's-his-name volumes. I should be immensely grateful if you could find them,' he said, staunchly turning round to go back to his study.

Thus called, John forsook the net that was entwined round his fingers and followed his master.

BOOK SECOND

CHAPTER I

St Martin's Summer

SPRING IS THE most celebrated season in Florence, for then is it that sweet-blossomed shrubs and fruit-bearing trees and long-trailing vines break into a sensual riot and transform this art-drenched urban centre into a vision of arcadia. But to the cognoscenti of our day, it is the autumn, when the worst of the tourists have disappeared and the strident light of summer has melted, changing the series of noble hills by which the city is surrounded from striking stage set into serene vista, that is the most cherished time of year. And yet, John Forde, as he passed through a massive stone gate, the last vestige of the mediæval walls by which the city was once surrounded, and began a now familiar climb on this mid-November afternoon toward his favoured place of reflexion, could not help thinking back on the sticky, smog-ridden, sealed-up month of August without a certain nostalgia, for then he had had Christopher Noble-Nolan all to himself.

He continued his ascent up the via del Monte alle Croci, past an allée of cypresses and groves of olives, all under a cerulean sky. At the top of the winding path, he did not look back but went on his way and crossed the busy *viale*, leading to the beckoning church of San Miniato al Monte. It was a day all benignant, with the sun-dappled sky luxuriantly caressing this jewel of a Romanesque church, dedicated to the first Florentine martyr. There she reigned, a marble shrine – ancient already when Dante was born – majestically poised at the top of a steep flight of steps, with her central mosaic of Christ, enthroned between the Virgin and St Minias, refulgently reflected in the severely geometric pattern of her green and white stone façade.

Not till he had positioned himself on the perron did John turn round to take in the sweeping view of the Arno Valley. He was pleased to think that he knew, as a matter of course, that he was standing not far from the very spot where Corot had chosen to set up his easel or that it was just such an autumn afternoon in Florence that had inspired Shelley to write his "Ode to the West Wind". And yet, at the same time, he was saddened to think that it was only in recalling the emotional responses of other, earlier (and infinitely more distinguished) visitors that he was moved by the sight he had come in search of, but then this autumn in Florence had not unfolded as he had expected. He had spent much of the past few months working up to today, 11 November, Christopher Noble-Nolan's seventieth birthday, and now he found himself here, in the city of his dreams, alone, on that very day.

From the time he moved into Sir Christopher's apartment on 6 August, John had assumed that he was there to stay: he wrote cryptic notes to his parents and dissertation adviser, saying that he was, unexpectedly, going to remain abroad for the foreseeable future; he arranged for a fellow student to take over the lease of his apartment in New York; and he had his books, clothes and few possessions shipped to him in Florence. These had, rather propitiously, arrived during what was now Sir Christopher's brief absence, thus leaving John the opportunity to slip everything into what was meant to seem its unobtrusive place and so grant him the illusion that all of his things had reached their natural resting place in Palazzo Vespucci.

When he had been unpacking his belongings this very morning, he came across but one disturbing anomaly: a small album of family photographs, an identical copy of which his mother had presented to each of her five sons last Christmas. As he slowly turned the pages, he was horrified to note that in every image there was, invariably, some, no matter how small, jarring note or incriminating bit of evidence – a hideous vase of fake flowers, a bolt of shag carpeting, a box of ice cream plunked down on the table, a swatch of polyester – to betray the vulgarity of his background. Not wanting anyone, *himself* above all, to connect him with such a world, now that he felt he had found his rightful place in Sir Christopher Noble-Nolan's meadow of fresh verdure – *in prato di fresca verdura*, where the inhabitants spoke with gentle voices and cast gazes of grave authority – John took the photograph album into the drawing room and, with great ceremony, placed it in the fireplace and set it alight. When, finally, he had nothing before him but a heap of cold ash, he took up a handful of dust and put it, just as he had imagined doing on his very first day alone in this apartment, in the metal libation vessel in the centre of the chimney-piece.

In order to ensure that he undeniably and incontrovertibly belonged by Sir Christopher's side, John had sought, in the past few months, to make himself an indispensable secretary: he dealt with correspondence, made appointments, classified papers, prepared notes and continued (or tried to continue) serious art historical research. Quickly, he became initiated in the mysteries of the Kunsthistorisches Institut, or the German Institute as Sir Christopher preferred to call it. Eventually, he would come to know this institute – a monumental library funded by the German state and housed in an architecturally undistinguished palace on the other side of the river, whose open stacks and idiosyncratic filing system made it a Mecca for serious art historians round the world – better than he would ever care to; for the present, he had less time to spend there than he would have liked.

Constrictions of time notwithstanding, it was John who first suggested that he himself should sift through all the new periodical literature, bringing only the most germane to Sir Christopher's attention. He even proposed that he should look out in advance whatever books Sir Christopher might possibly need, so that, when he arrived at the Institute, Sir Christopher would find everything awaiting him.

The first time he had gone to the German Institute, back in September, when Sir Christopher presented him as his secretary and asked for a reader's card on his behalf, John was acutely attuned to the deferential nods and diffident glances that greeted Sir Christopher's appearance in the library. Such attention more than compensated John for his trouble-taking efforts: it enraptured him, for the grander was the image of the man with whom he had allied himself, the more hallowed did he feel his own position to be. Like Faust's attendant, he thought that to promenade with his *Magnificus* was but an honour to bring profit.

On the domestic front, intellect and Eros were fully wed, as John donned the mantle of *sweete-chamber fellow* and took to running the house. Knowing that Sir Christopher desired, above all, to be left in peace with his work, and wanting to assume absolute control himself, John had easily arranged so that no one but he should have direct access to the master. He answered the telephone, dealt with tradesmen and, just generally, fielded all household affairs, from arranging the linen cupboard to paying the bills.

Though there had been two maids working for Sir Christopher – the frequently flustered Rita and the persistently dour Piera – when he first arrived, and though breakfast and lunch were prepared every day, it was, curiously enough, the question of meals that seemed to occupy most of John's time. Much to Sir Christopher's dissatisfaction, neither woman seemed to know anything – nor want to learn anything – about serving the meal she had prepared. Near the end of September, John had ventured to suggest that they might do away with Piera, whose truculent nature disarmed him increasingly, and find a new maid who would come in to help Rita during the week and whom he himself would train to serve luncheon. He realised that he would be forced, if his plan succeeded, to cope alone on Sundays, but he was convinced that, if he could simultaneously establish absolute control *and* pacify an increasingly disgruntled Sir Christopher, he would have made a most favourable exchange. He also realised that the proposal would require all the artfulness he could muster.

'Of course, it was just a suggestion. And I'm afraid, to judge by the look on your face,' John had said by way of justification, 'a rather *bad* suggestion. Just forget that I mentioned it.'

'It's only that I don't see why we can't send that hysterical Indian packing and keep the other one, that Piera. She's an infinitely better cook, and, more important, she's exactly the sort of stalwart Tuscan peasant whom one has been served by for years. She just seems so much more trustworthy,' Sir Christopher said, not for the first time.

'I've already looked into that,' John said truthfully, for, having foreseen Sir Christopher's objections, he wanted to be fully armed, 'but, alas, there's no possibility of that. You see, she, Piera, works for Contessa Vespucci during the week. Remember, that's how you found her in the first place. And you can't very well steal a maid from your landlord's wife, can you?'

'No, I suppose not,' Sir Christopher admitted reluctantly.

'And it was Piera who approached *me*, saying that she found the two jobs a bit much and that she would like to be relieved of her post here. I just thought this might be the perfect opportunity to rearrange things, so that you can have everything just as you like. Actually, I was talking to Contessa Vespucci the other day about this problem, when she told me of a young, very reliable girl whom she knows of. But obviously it's up to you. Perhaps you prefer to keep things as they are?'

'No, I think the situation most unsatisfactory. As it is, one can't invite an even remotely respectable person to luncheon, but it's just... just that I'm afraid of things getting even more muddled. And now that one has found such a nice rhythm – working every single day – well, we don't want to do anything to upset *that*.'

'No, nothing,' John said.

'Well,' Sir Christopher said unenthusiastically, 'if you really think it a viable proposition, I suppose that we should give it a try.'

And try John did, so that Sir Christopher was soon delighted by an altered *régime*, whereby Rita, kept well out of view, was given all the time she needed excitedly to cook her meals behind closed doors, as the new recruit – a pretty girl, hardly twenty years old, called Annunziata, who proved not only willing to learn, but capable of doing so – calmly and professionally served the meals.

Within a week, the much trusted, stout *contadina*, Piera, was utterly forgotten, whilst a steady stream of visitors – generally just two at a time, never more than four, as the number of guests that could be squeezed round the unwelcoming porphyry-topped table was exceedingly limited – began to make their way to lunch in Sir Christopher's apartment. The rare dinner, when a butler was imported to serve whatever complicated menu John had arranged in advance, was reserved for only the grandest of guests.

But every meal, no matter how small, was a tremendously tense undertaking for John, not only because of the labour involved – and there was no detail he did not attend to – but, more, because he looked on every guest as a sounding board by which to divine what an outsider thought of his relationship to Sir Christopher. The litmus test of how he was perceived – mere factotum? efficient secretary? *fidus Achates*? beloved disciple? – was to see whether, when the guest in question returned the invitation, as invariably happened in one form or another, John was asked as well.

From the first, John had grasped that Sir Christopher would never himself suggest that he should be included, though he appeared to be happy – or, at least, he made no objection – when John *was* invited. Thus his public presence at Sir Christopher's side depended wholly, he thought, on the good will, if not the caprice, of strangers and the impression he made on them.

In this sense, Alice Varrow was the easiest subject to conquer. Old, lame, impecunious and terrified of being alone, her greatest pleasure was to cram her pocket-sized house at Bellosguardo full with people whom she could neither manage to accommodate nor afford to feed, so that she viewed the recent arrival of John – a young man who could be pressed into service, whilst masked as a guest – as something of a godsend.

The first time he had been invited to dine at her house, at the end of August, he had had the temerity to ask if he could bring anything, to which question Alice unhesitatingly replied, 'You do that tarragon chicken *en gelée* so nicely. Why don't you bring that along? We'll be fourteen.' And though he quickly learnt to circumvent her far from subtle stratagems, he could not really begrudge Alice, for, not only did he realise that it was out of necessity that she acted so shamelessly – she *was* hard up, she *could* barely walk, she *did* need to live by her wits – but also because it was primarily thanks to her and her jumbled gatherings that he met the vast number of Florentines whom Sir Christopher had known for decades, Florentines whom he wanted to disabuse of the vision of an *un*attached Christopher Noble-Nolan. What is more, Alice was the only person who invited him alone. Now, almost every Sunday afternoon, he climbed up the scenic hill of Bellosguardo to her house – a cottage with its own entrance, nestled at the back of a grand villa – bringing with him some item from town that she had forgotten or, more likely could not afford, on her weekly shopping spree. Of course, he knew that she was desperate for anybody who would make the tea and provide conversation, but he also believed that the lonely old woman looked on him as a reason, not an excuse, for company.

Amongst aristocratic Florentines – the only Florentines whom Alice appeared to know – Contessa Vespucci was the sole person with whom John had direct contact, but this was, for now, of a mostly practical nature, regarding the apartment. In time, however, she became his greatest support against the predators of emotion lurking along the Arno, but then – as all old Florentines were quick to point out – Antonia Vespucci, who was born on the banks of the Tiber, had *nothing* (marriage not withstanding) to do with the City of Flowers: she was an *importée*.

Someone like Tommy Tornabuoni, on the other hand, who had twice been to lunch at Sir Christopher's, though perfectly polite (achingly polite, John had begun to think) seemed incapable of, or uninterested in, registering him. John had not expected to be included amongst the guests for the enormous dinner being given in December in Palazzo Vecchio to honour Barone Tornabuoni officially for bequeathing his palace and its magnificent contents to the city of Florence, but he would like to have been asked to accompany Sir Christopher to Palazzo Tornabuoni when *he* was invited to lunch there.

And yet his spirits, far from dampened at what he viewed as a deliberate slight, only rendered him all the more determined. He studied Tommy Tornabuoni's memoirs, with an eye to dropping casual references into the conversation the next time he saw the author at Alice's, and even applied himself to the decades-old poetry. And though it unnerved him terribly each time Sir Christopher left the apartment on his own – whether it be to a luncheon in the palace of a Florentine grandee or to dinner with a modest academic was of little importance – John did, at least, feel secure in the knowledge that Sir Christopher would himself invite no one without him. At least, that is, till two weeks ago, when he rushed back to lunch after a busy morning of shopping for an array of essential trifles and found Sir Christopher in the unusual attitude of talking on the telephone.

'Right you are,' John had heard Sir Christopher saying, as he himself entered the front hall and dropped his bags on the floor.

'Exactly. Well then, you make the final arrangements and get back to one straightaway to confirm that everything is settled,' Sir Christopher concluded, ringing off without saying goodbye.

'Where *have* you been?' He turned smilingly to a mute John.

'I, um I,' he faltered, 'was out, you know, trying to find someone to mend your velvet slippers. And then there were the books you wanted. They didn't have the biography of St Augustine at Seeber's, but I've ordered it. I did get all the McBain books you wanted. Unfortunately, they were out of the chocolate-covered gingers at Old England, though I found – but is anything wrong?' he asked, breaking off his nervous litany.

'No. I wasn't making a reproach,' Sir Christopher said, continuing to smile.

'Has something happened then?' John asked, disarmed by what he considered Sir Christopher's almost jeeringly good humour.

'No. Well, nothing bad. But yes. Rather a lot. When you didn't come into my study with the post, I came down to look for you. But as you weren't here and there was an enormous pile of letters on your writing-table, I decided to open them myself. Amongst which were these,' he said, waving several papers. 'First, there was Dodo,' he said, holding up a large sheet of thick cream-coloured wove paper, covered in confident block writing, 'to say that she is coming to Florence for two nights, expressly – if you can believe it – for that rather ridiculous party for Tommy Tornabuoni in Palazzo Vecchio in December. I've already written back to her to say that I am sure she would prefer to dine quietly on the night following such an enormous party and that I will simply take her out to a restaurant, though she was agitating about seeing the flat, so that she can report back to everyone in London. You know, she always likes to be on top of things, but I think I can keep her at bay for the time being.

'And then there was Peter,' he said, brandishing a typewritten piece of crinkly airmail paper. 'I just had him on the telephone. He suggested that we make a little trip for my birthday – for about a week – in Germany. It's funny how he can be so efficient about some things and perfectly hopeless about others. But in this case, he's got it all arranged. He has the schedule for the opera in Munich, which does sound frightfully good – a new *Meistersinger* and then *Der Prinz von Homburg*, which is to be done in that ravishing little Cuvilliés Theatre in the Residenz, where I've never actually seen a production. He's even worked out a way for us to go to Stuppach, which I only casually mentioned to him last year as something one really *ought* to do.'

'Stuppach?' John asked in a daze.

'But yes, of course, Stuppach, near Aschaffenburg. To see the Grünewald *Madonna*, by my calculation the only supreme masterpiece of Western painting that one has never seen in the original. I do think it was clever of him to have remembered. I told him that I would meet him in Munich on the tenth...'

John stopped listening. He was more than adept at decoding Sir Christopher's references to know that there was no hope. Whenever, in the past, Sir Christopher had said, 'I am out to dine with——' or 'One is expected to luncheon next——' it was meant to be perfectly clear to John, as indeed it was – sometimes painfully so – that he was *not* invited; similarly, when Sir Christopher said, 'We are asked to——' he was expected (there was no choice in the matter) to come along. Thus, he had immediately understood that he was not invited to dine with Dodo Delfington, but, with Peter Mason's proposal – *He suggested that* we *make a little trip* – there had been a glimmer of expectation, a glimmer that was soon extinguished. *Who are* we? he had wondered, only to find himself quickly, all *too* quickly, answered. And as he sat surveying the view of Florence on this Friday afternoon, he could not help replaying the whole scene over and over and over again in his mind.

Before Peter's letter had arrived, they had already discussed plans for Sir Christopher's seventieth birthday, settling on a small dinner at home to which Alice Varrow was the only person yet to have been invited. But once Munich came up, Sir Christopher had laughingly said that there was no difficulty about chucking *her.* As to John, Sir Christopher seemed slightly, but only *slightly,* embarrassed about leaving him, insisting that he would probably be happy to have the time to himself to concentrate on the followers of Botticelli – the first mention, he thought bitterly, that Sir Christopher had made in months of the idea that John might actually have any work of his own to dedicate himself to.

Though he was crushed by the news of what he interpreted as a stinging rejection, he did his best to mask his disappointment, not out of pride, but out of fear, fear of losing the precarious position he had striven so hard to attain, for he knew Christopher Noble-Nolan well enough to realise that it would be positively counterproductive to go moping about like some put-upon victim. Sir Christopher would not be made to feel guilty – he would simply refuse to respond – but he *could* be made to feel extremely cross with anyone who tried to entrap him in a maze of emotional entanglement.

To forestall such loss, John had gone about the smiling charade of presenting Sir Christopher, the day before he left, with a specially made birthday cake and an array of gifts, including an enormous box of marrons glacés, a small square of baroque cut velvet, woven in the factories at Tours, which, he feared, might not look nearly so expensive as it was, and a first edition of Browning, called *Pacchiarotto and How He Worked in Distemper*. He had bought the book, which he found listed in a catalogue, only because Sir Christopher owned a picture by Pacchiarotto; when, however, he discovered that there was a poem in the volume entitled 'St Martin's Summer', traditionally 11 November, Sir Christopher's birthday, he found it difficult to believe that there was anything adventitious about his choice of book. For a card, he settled upon one depicting the Simone Martini fresco at Assisi of *St Martin Dividing his Cloak to Clothe a Beggar*, on which he had written: 'As for St Martin's Summer 1983, with love <u>forever</u> from John'.

He thought that Sir Christopher had seemed genuinely touched by the attention, but he could not help remarking that, though the marrons glacés were quickly devoured, the velvet had been put away in a drawer and that it was McBain, not Browning, that had been put in the suitcase for Munich. John had the discarded volume of poetry with him this afternoon and, after once again admiring its simple brown cloth binding, opened it to read:

> *Don't we both know how it ends*
> *How the greenest leaf turns serest,*
> *Bluest outbreak – blankest heaven*
> *Lovers – friends?*

He began quietly to moan but then stopped himself, refusing to attach any vatic significance to these lines. *Don't we both know how it ends?* Ends? No, he would have nothing of that. From his point of view, his life with Christopher Noble-Nolan had hardly begun.

He took out the postcard with the Simone fresco of St Martin, which he himself had slipped back into the book, and reread his own words. *Yes*, he said to himself, <u>*forever*</u>.

It consoled him to think that, as of today, the difference of forty-six years between himself and Christopher Noble-Nolan was now rigorously mathematical. This divergence of age, which, he knew, many a person – heterosexual *or* homosexual – would look upon as an unbridgeable gap, actually reassured him, for he imagined that, once he established himself as the champion of Sir Christopher's Third Age that he could never be dislodged. He did not, on the other hand, consider himself some sort of obsessive gerontophile, as there was no *other* old man to whom he thought of attaching himself. He wanted only Christopher Noble-Nolan. And he hoped that, by his steadfastness, his refusal to be discouraged, he would prove the extent of his devotion and, thereby, eliminate any competition.

Since discovering a copy of Sir Christopher's will back in September, he had been slightly less anxious about his imagined rivalry with Peter Mason. He had been relieved to read that Peter Mason was left just one (not very important) picture and the sum of £75,000 in Sir Christopher's will, though he was severely distressed to find that Peter had been appointed to the much-coveted position of literary executor. All the rest, not just works of art, but his entire personalty, was bequeathed to the Ashmolean.

John tried repeatedly to overconvince himself that the fact that an institution should take precedence over an individual was proof positive of the relatively unimportant place that Peter Mason occupied in Sir Christopher's affections, but, ever since Peter had whisked Sir Christopher off to Germany for his birthday, he felt himself invaded by all the old (and even some new) doubts. When, earlier, he had questioned Sir Christopher about his relationship to Peter Mason, Sir Christopher had freely replied that they had, years ago, been briefly together, but that it had quickly grown into friendship. John hadn't dared to press for a precise definition of 'it', but he frequently wondered: *was it love?* And, if so, can love ever *grow* into friendship? Does it not wither into friendship? He didn't want, at any price, for his love to proceed thus, and he would do anything necessary to protect it from such caducity.

Logically, he told himself, there was no reason to feel threatened. Above all, he knew that he should be grateful that there were no cloying relatives to vie with, for it is a well-established fact, as Hawthorne had plainly taught him, that there is nothing a man so rarely does as to bequeath his estate away from his bloodlines in favour of an outsider; even if the relatives in question are deeply antipathetic to the testator, consanguinity will invariably take precedence over affection.

But from what John had gathered, there were no relations – not even quite distant ones – to stand in his way. Sir Christopher's eponymous grandfather, an Irish peasant who had somehow climbed his way into Parliament, colonial governorship and a knighthood – transforming, along the way, his banal Irish surname, 'Nolan', into the grander double-barrelled one, 'Noble-Nolan' – had had two sons: the elder, also Christopher, was killed at the age of twenty-one in the Boer War, *sans posterité*; the younger son, Sir Christopher's father, the Major-General, had had two sons, neither of whom, as John knew all too well, had ever married or produced an heir.

On his mother's side, there had been but one female cousin, the daughter of Dame Sophia's only brother; she died whilst giving birth prematurely, and her husband, whose surname Sir Christopher could not even *remember*, had inherited her estate and passed it on to the children of his second marriage. Sir Christopher was, therefore, incontestably, the end of his line, the last Noble-Nolan.

And yet, the liminal figure of Peter Mason unnerved John as much as, maybe even more than, the threat of some shadowy relation lurking in the distance. He feared that it was going to require a superhuman effort on his part to behave with anything approaching naturalness when, next week, they would finally meet. On Thursday, 17 November, Sir Christopher was to return from Germany, accompanied by Peter Mason, who would stay with them for the inside of a week.

✟

'I *do* think it a most marvellous invention, this towel dressing gown. I suppose it must be American, don't you?' Sir Christopher asked.

'Hmm,' John mumbled, looking at the garment – what he would normally have called a 'terry-cloth robe' – strewn across the bed, a, to him, perfectly hideous thing, not least because it had been given to Sir Christopher for his birthday by Peter Mason.

'It's certainly an improvement on that one I had been wearing for years.'

'I quite liked your old dressing gown – all in camel hair. I can't believe you just *threw* it out in Munich,' John said.

'Oh, but that was perfectly threadbare.'

'Now, you'll have to stand still, if you want me to get your links through the cuffs,' John said, dismissing the subject, as he helped Sir Christopher to get ready before they left to dine at Alice's.

'It *was* practical of Peter to have known one needed a new dressing gown,' Sir Christopher persisted.

'More practical than he was about the driving licence anyway,' John said, unable to restrain himself.

'Yes, that was rather extraordinary. But the *most* extraordinary part of it was that he should have had the wallet returned to him at all. That's typical of Peter – getting into the most appalling muddle and then extracting himself at the penultimate moment.'

'I still don't understand exactly what happened.'

'Obviously, one couldn't very well have explained the whole story to you right there, in front of Peter, when we came in last night. That would have been too embarrassing, but it really is quite simple. You see, there I was sitting in the hall of the Vier Jahreszeiten, waiting for him to come down, so that we could leave, as arranged, at half past seven. The taxi to take us to the station was already ordered, and we had our reservations for the quarter-past-eight train from Munich to Frankfort. When he hadn't yet appeared at twenty-five minutes past, one began, *quite* naturally, to get rather fussed. And then, just as I thought of calling up to his room, who should barge through the front door but Peter, looking, I must say, rather the worse for wear. Of course, I knew that he had gone off on his usual louche tryster, following the opera, as he didn't want to dine with one afterwards.'

'You mean, he left you to dine *alone!*'

'Actually, I had said that I was feeling rather tired after the opera and that I just wanted to have an omelette in my room, which didn't seem to tempt him. He did come back to the *hôtel* with me and, to judge by the look of him the following morning, change his clothes before going off to Lord-knows-where. Anyway, he was in a great state that morning, saying that he had lost his wallet.

More likely had it stolen, I thought, though I didn't imagine there could have been very much money in it, in view of his perennially precarious finances.

'By the time he changed, checked out of his room and told the reception all about the missing wallet, you can imagine that we had long since missed the train, though we did get one later in the morning. But the worst of it was that his licence was in the wallet, so that when we finally did get to Frankfort we couldn't rent the car to go to Stuppach. I can't say that I did much to hide my displeasure, though one did rather thaw when he managed to make friends with a Frankfort taxi driver – in that extraordinary way he has of winning over the most unlikely characters – who agreed to take us the following day to Aschaffenburg and to Stuppach for a really quite modest sum.

'And yet, the most remarkable part of the story is that, when we got back to Munich three days later, there his wallet was, with everything in it – money, cards *and* the licence – waiting for him. Some boy or other, having found it in his flat, returned it to the *hôtel*, as Peter had mentioned he was staying there.'

'It was a bit *late* by then, though, to make use of the licence,' John said tartly.

'Yes, but now that he has it back we'll be able to go to Volterra tomorrow to get some more beautiful plants for the loggia – and one could never do *that* by taxi. I think you really will be surprised at how magnificent this nursery garden is – run by two charming Australian boys – one has never seen anything quite like it. I want mainly to concentrate on old roses, but there's also a ceanothus, *Gloire de Versailles*, that I'm particularly keen to get, as well as the *Convolvulus cneorum*. One had better tie a knot in one's handkerchief to remind oneself of them.'

'What about some more of those green zinnias I liked – the ones called "Envy"?' John asked.

'I admit,' Sir Christopher said, as he mangled an immaculately starched handkerchief, 'that the name is rather amusing – one *does* like to be envied – but they are much too common to be bothered with. Our attention must, above all, be focused on the *Selenicereus grandiflorus*. Most of the plants travelling under this name are hybrids, but it appears, from their catalogue, that the boys at Volterra possess the true species, which is of the *utmost* rarity in cultivation. And as for the scent, well – you'll discover – it's perfectly divine.'

'Hmm,' John said, nodding. Having already heard Sir Christopher go on about this plant several times, commonly known as night-blooming cereus, John had looked it up, only to find, to his horror, that it was a sort of cactus, meant to flower but *once* a year, for a few hours, at night.

'You know,' John continued in the hope of discarding horticultural pursuits and returning to the subject of Peter Mason's ineptitude, 'Peter rather makes me think of your brother, all this story about losing the wallet and making friends with the taxi driver.'

'That's true, perfectly true – just the sort of muddle Crystal was always getting into. I'll never forget when he was so foolish as to hand over the portrait that Lucian Freud did of him – much the best thing he owned – to a taxi driver, also from Frankfort, who was meant to put his finances in order. You can be sure that was the last we ever heard of *that* picture. Goodness, one was cross with him!'

'I suppose,' John said, stepping up to straighten Sir Christopher's tie, 'that they were really rather alike, Peter and your brother, never being able to hold down a regular job and that sort of thing.'

'But my brother could *write!*' Sir Christopher bridled, just as John had hoped he would. 'Very important books, really, he wrote, and I don't mean just that old life of Edward VII that Alice is forever going on about, but the books on Chateaubriand and Disraeli – those sort of literary/political figures that he was so good at. They were quite original, based on a lot of new material. Whereas Peter, with those pathetic little books he churns out for Vyvyan Virtue – all that recycled information – it's just no use. He's got to get some kind of permanent job if he's ever to settle down to Sir Joshua.'

John was almost frightened to see how easy it was to lead Sir Christopher into playing one figure off against another. John knew that he was good at the game, but he also feared that someone else, some unforeseen competitor, might be better. And might not that someone else try the same thing but against him? And would Sir Christopher, in that case, rise to *his* defence? He did not, unfortunately, feel sure. 'I, um, ah, suppose, you're right,' he spluttered and then stopped. 'But listen!' he added.

'To what?' Sir Christopher asked.

'The music,' John said, referring to the exceedingly faint hum coming from Sir Christopher's study.

'I don't hear anything,' Sir Christopher said.

'But yes,' John insisted, for *the ear of jealousy heareth all things*. 'It's that bit of Debussy you play every morning. Peter must be in your study at the piano.'

'Oh, yes, I hear him now, and I dare say that he plays it much better than one.' Sir Christopher laughed. 'Rather embarrassingly better.'

John knew that the composer was Debussy, only because he had often noticed the same closed score sitting on Sir Christopher's piano, but he had never been able to name the exact piece and would never have dreamt of asking. It was a short work, lasting not much more than two minutes, which he was longing to identify.

'I thought you would want a little drink before we go off,' he said agitatedly.

'I do think we will need a nip of vodka to fortify ourselves if we are to endure another of Alice's dinners.'

'Yes, exactly. I'll put the tray in the drawing room, but first let me go and call Peter,' he said and hurried off.

'We thought,' John said, as he tapped on the open door of the study, 'we might have a drink before going off to Alice's.'

'Just what the doctor ordered,' Peter Mason said as he looked up smilingly from the keyboard.

'I hope that I didn't interrupt you,' John said, stepping behind Peter to look over his shoulder at the score.

'Oh no, I was just pounding away.'

On the right-hand page John read the heading *Prélude IX. La sérénade interrompue.* As Peter had just that moment finished, John assumed the ninth *Prélude* was the next piece. He took a deep breath and ventured, 'Was that the eighth *Prélude* you were playing?'

'Exactly. I'm sure that you play it much better than one.'

'No, no. I don't play at all. Only the violin, a bit, when I was younger,' John said, failing to specify that he had, when he was twelve years old, taken lessons for all of three weeks. 'It's just that Christopher,' he continued, trying desperately to pronounce that unadorned Christian name as naturally as possible, 'plays that *Prélude,* the eighth, almost every morning before he starts work.'

'*So* appropriate, as we all know how Christopher adores flax-en-haired girls,' Peter said, laughing raucously.

'Hmm.' John smiled, not understanding the allusion. 'Well, I'll just get the vodka.'

'Actually, I'd rather prefer a whisky. If that doesn't present a problem?'

'No, not at all,' John said, amazed that *any*one, especially a non-entity such as Peter Mason, would so forthrightly state his preference.

John quickly laid out ice, glasses and bottles on a silver salver, which he placed on the low table in the drawing room – he even lit a small fire – and then waited behind the closed door of the kitchen, whilst slipping a batch of cheese straws into the oven. When he was sure that Peter and Sir Christopher had both assembled, he dashed up to the study, turned back the pages of the Debussy score and read the title: *Prélude VIII: La fille aux cheveux de lin*. He groaned to himself, now understanding Peter's little joke. He also thought it most unlikely that Sir Christopher should be devoted to a work with such a title – he even thought Debussy a bit out of charac-ter; he would have imagined Sir Christopher being drawn more to Bach or Scarlatti – but he was deeply pleased to be able, finally, to put a name to the piece of music whose haunting melody he had come to identify so intimately with Christopher Noble-Nolan. And yet he deplored that such knowledge should come to him by way of Peter Mason.

He closed the score and rushed back to the kitchen to take the cheese straws out of the oven, half regretting that Peter Mason had proved so undeniably likable, for there was a part of John – a too-large part, he feared – that genuinely wanted to hate Peter. But how could he hate someone so good-natured, someone who was forever smiling, forever at ease? How could he hate someone so physically unprepossessing, someone who was shorter, squatter and nearly twenty years older than himself? And how, above all, could he hate someone so transparently *not* jealous, someone who had known Christopher Noble-Nolan for years but who accepted that John's newfound presence was as natural as it was foreordained?

And yet, hatred was exactly the emotion he felt this morning when Sir Christopher rang up Alice Varrow to ask if he could bring Peter along to dinner tonight, recalling, as he eavesdropped, every time Sir Christopher had *not* telephoned to have him invited to some Florentine gathering. And hatred was again what he felt when he walked into the drawing room with a plate of cheese straws, crisped to a golden perfection, and saw Peter and Sir Christopher huddled agonistically on the canapé over a game of cards.

Before leaving for Munich, Sir Christopher had mentioned that he much looked forward to playing cribbage with Peter, so that John, who, lacked *any* competitive spirit and despised all games – bridge, Scrabble, backgammon, tennis, not to mention the vulgar sports of his childhood – was horror-struck by the sight he beheld.

He paused in the embrasure of the door for a moment and stared despairingly. He liked to think that his longing to have Christopher Noble-Nolan wholly to himself – the two of them not against but outside the world – was proof of the depth of his love, but in that buried, tacit part of himself, where feeling reigned stronger than thought, he knew that the desire exclusively to possess another human being is a manifestation not of love but of a gnawing sense of unworthiness, making one doubt the value of that most precious of gifts one has to offer and that it is precisely this demeaning need for sole ownership which, after having utterly polluted the spirit, delivers one, defenceless, unto a vain battle with interchangeable enemies, all the while blinding one to the fact that the enemy, if he ever existed, was right there, within. Who was the opponent? Peter? Sir Christopher? Himself? No one? Quivering at a roiling stream of sentiment, whose clash he could not subdue, John entered the room and, trying to regain control of the trembling plate, asked brightly, 'Cheese straws anyone?'

'Fifteen two, fifteen four, fifteen six and a pair is eight,' Sir Christopher, displaying his cards, said triumphantly.

'Goodness, they do look good,' Peter said with a greedy smile, as John proffered the dish with one hand and a stack of linen cocktail napkins with the other.

'Oh, *how* delicious,' Sir Christopher exclaimed, taking two cheese straws and turning back immediately to move his pegs along the board.

'It's you to deal,' Peter said to Sir Christopher. 'I'm just going to have another of these lovely things, whilst they're still hot. I see now that Christopher was not exaggerating' – Peter turned to

John – 'when he said that you have a marvellous gift for making the routine of ordinary life infinitely less *ordinary*.'

John smiled and, blushing, turned to pour himself a glass of vodka. He realised that he should be grateful to Peter for not simply praising his culinary skills but for having divined the intention that lay behind his work, and yet, somehow, he could not make the simple leap of generosity. He took a sip of vodka, and then *another*, remembering that only a few months ago he had never drunk spirits neat. Now, he found the idea of diluting alcohol with tonic or water terribly limp. He took a final gulp and said, 'I think we'd better be going down in five or, at most, ten minutes. The taxi should be arriving shortly.'

'Oh, one more hand,' Sir Christopher, who had just lost, whined. 'And I better have another one of those lovely cheese straws,' he said, 'as one never knows *what* one will be given to eat at Alice's.'

'As you like, but you know how agitated Alice will be if we're late. She said we're going to be twenty-three tonight.'

'Twenty-three! And to think that Alice would dare to invite even *three* people in that little matchbox of a house,' Sir Christopher said distractedly, inspecting his newly dealt cards.

'Speaking of invitations, I am going to lunch tomorrow with the "Whores of Virtue", near Lucca, at Pescia, and was wondering if you might like to come with me, John?' Peter asked affably.

'No, he most certainly does *not* want to go with you!' Sir Christopher, tossing his cards aside, cut in with alarming vehemence.

'But whoever are the "Whores of Virtue"?' John asked, choking back his laughter.

'Oh, don't you know?' Peter asked. 'James Hoare and Vyvyan Virtue. Absolutely everyone calls them the "Whores of Virtue". It's just *too* irresistible a name, isn't it? They've been together for donkey's years. They came out here right after the war and decided to try their luck as freelance art historians.'

'They are *hardly*,' Sir Christopher snorted, 'what I would call art historians – more like slick, superficial journalists. Hoare wrote one half of a not bad book on William Kent thirty-five years ago but was too lazy to finish the second volume or, indeed, anything else. And as for that perfectly ridiculous simpering queen, Vyvyan Virtue – he's really an embarrassment, you know, covered in powder and scent, even liquid make-up – well, the only thing that creature has done is cobble together endless dictionaries about art, architecture and interior decoration, all the material lifted straight from other sources, as well as to dash off those pathetic little books on every subject going: Mannerism, Neo-Classicism, Realism, Surrealism and on and on. To cap it all off, the two of them, Hoare and Virtue, published together – together, mind you – just last year, a survey of the entire history of world art in a *single* volume. It is the very jewel in their crown of journalistic whoredom.'

'You can say what you like, Christopher, but the fact of the matter is that they had to *earn* their living,' Peter replied with a confidence that left John gaping. 'I admire them for settling out here, divorced from the system and making a go of it on their own. I admit that James had a bit of money. His father was a doctor, and he inherited enough, *just* enough, to buy that charming villa at Pescia. But as for Vyvyan, well, his father sold silver – not even silver, but electroplate – from an outdoor stall in Eastbourne, till, that is, his business went belly-up and he got thrown into prison for all sorts of shady dealings.'

'I dare say that explains the grotesquely affected manner of that little Pesciatina queen. And where did he come up with the orthography of that ridiculous name – Vyvyan? Does he think he's the son of Oscar Wilde?'

'Actually, his real name is Patrick. I think he just wanted to—'

'I should have guessed as much,' Sir Christopher cut in. 'And as for his accent,' he continued, 'it's like something on a music-hall stage – a very *cheap* music-hall stage! The way he pronounces "involved" as if it were "in vō ved". Is *that* what Vyvyan Virtue considers chic? I mean, it's just too, too—' Sir Christopher broke off, shuddering.

'I admit that Vyvyan's an *outrageous* camp,' Peter said, trying to stifle his laughter. 'And old James is always feuding with his friends, the closer the better – you know, James has even recently set them at daggers drawn with Will Beevor, who wrote and dedicated to both of them his wildly distinguished biography of Verdi. To make matters worse, really pathetic, the row was all stirred up by an article written by that flaming – and I mean *flaming* – American fag, Daniel Shrube, in that worst of tabloids, *The Fitz-Boodle Papers*. But, be that as it may, James and Vyvyan are really—'

'They're really "The Whores of Virtue", if you want to know, the epitome of the *second*-rate. Yes, thoroughly second-rate, they are,' Sir Christopher broke in, employing the ultimate term of derogation in the Noble-Nolan lexicon. 'John wants nothing to do with them. And I don't think you should be having anything to do with them either, Peter,' Sir Christopher finished off.

'I don't really have much choice,' Peter said. 'You see, they've commissioned a new book from me.'

'Not *another* one,' Sir Christopher said.

'Yes. It's on Cubism, for that series they edit, *Style and Culture.*'

'Can you imagine anything *more* vulgar' – Sir Christopher turned to address John – 'than a series called *Style and Culture*? I mean, I ask you! Do you know that they even had the effrontery to write to one, years ago I admit, asking one to contribute the volume on the Early Renaissance to their ghastly little stable of books? I fired back at once, saying that, as there was no "ism" in Renaissance, I did not think such a volume would sit comfortably amongst the others they had commissioned. What really galls one, though, is that one was foolish enough to have written a letter supporting that cheap queen, Vyvyan Virtue, for a grant from the British Academy to work on Canova. And believe me, without my letter he never would have got it! That was nearly thirty years ago. And he hasn't produced a thing to speak of, certainly not the promised monograph. And meanwhile, he has actively prevented anyone else, any serious student, from working on Canova. If he had so much as a *shred* of decency, he would have returned that money to the Academy long ago.'

'Well, it looks, John, as though you're not, after all, going to get to see the really charming house, the Villa Marchì, where the "Whores" live. Unless, of course, you declare open mutiny,' Peter said teasingly.

'Actually, I'm quite busy tomorrow,' John said, scandalised at the idea of such disloyalty.

'I do think, Peter, you rather exaggerate the *soi-disant* charm of their house,' Sir Christopher said. 'I mean, by Italian standards, it is hardly more than a *casa colonica.*'

'You must admit that it's in a beautiful position,' Peter said.

'It's rather hard,' Sir Christopher stubbornly insisted, '*not* to find a beautiful position in Tuscany. And as for that wildly unkempt garden, well, it's the only such one I've ever seen that manages to be both pretentious *and* pedestrian at the same time.'

'You've been there?' John asked, surprised.

'Yes, once, years ago,' Sir Christopher said brusquely. 'They were trying to butter one up about writing to the British Academy and invited one to luncheon, if luncheon you could call it. Had the food been just a *bit* less nasty, one might have resented having been given so little to eat. As it was, one was just jolly grateful to get up from their filthy table as quickly as possible. I remember thinking that the wine must have been supplied by Lucrezia Borgia herself. And the cold of that house, one will never forget it. One came down with terrible influenza.'

'It's perfectly true,' Peter said, 'that the house is hardly heated – a veritable deep freeze it is in winter – and filthy *comme ce n'est pas permis*. Even the plates are dirty, and so far as the loo is concerned – well, that doesn't *bear* mentioning. And I'm afraid to stay the night there anymore, as the spare room is an absolute fire trap, what with loose wires dangling from exposed electric points and the paint peeling off the walls onto your pillow. I'll also admit that the wine, which they produce themselves, is sick-making. James, you know, is wildly mean, and it is he who controls the purse-strings. Poor Vyvyan, as the wife, of course, has to do all the cooking, and James practically makes her *beg* for the few shekels she gets to do the weekly shopping. The last time I was there for lunch, I was presented for the main course – the main course, I promise you,' Peter continued, starting to cry with laughter, 'with a cracked serving plate, on which swam five pathetic ravioli for the three of us. Not knowing what to do, I took one and a half. "They are very *large* ravioli," Vyvyan said meekly, taking the other one and a half ravioli. James, of course, helped himself to the remaining two. And yet, you know, the strange thing about going to see the "Whores of Virtue" at the Villa Marchì is that, each time I come away from them, I always feel what a lovely, life-enhancing experience it has been.'

'Do, by all means, feel free to go there tomorrow,' Sir Christopher said, '*alone*. And now, can we drop this unpleasant subject and get back to one last hand of cribbage before we have to go off to Alice's fraught entertainment.'

As he watched Peter all too obviously let Sir Christopher win the next round of cards, John thought how, far from minding that Sir Christopher should have silenced him, should have usurped his very voice when Peter asked if he would like to accompany him to the Villa Marchì, he was actually flattered to have had his *cher maître* speak for him in, what seemed to him, a vigilant, almost possessive, mode. The 'Whores of Virtue' might have been the proprietors of Caprarola, for all he cared, but he would still not have wished to visit them if it could be a source of displeasure to Sir Christopher.

He was, on the other hand, distinctly discomposed by the eruption of homophobic vitriol that spewed forth from Sir Christopher onto the pathetic Vyvyan Virtue. He was aware that, just as there is no one so anti-Semitic as a self-loathing Jew – he thought of Alice – so too is there no one so homophobic as the guilt-ridden homosexual, but this in no wise, he was sure, applied to Sir Christopher. John had, from the first, assumed that Sir Christopher, who appeared to view homosexuality as but the appurtenance of genius – a gift from God, accorded to the *happy few* – was immune to such sentiment. He could only ascribe this recent display of acrimony to Sir Christopher's inherent dislike of flamboyant mannerisms and exhibitionistic posturing. In truth, he was secretly thrilled by Sir Christopher's severe dismissal of Vyvyan Virtue's superficial little books, for it added weight to the protective veil behind which he felt Sir Christopher had shrouded him.

'And now,' John said, 'I think we really must go down. The taxi metre will be clicking through the roof.'

'Yes, I suppose we must. Anyway, the sooner we get there, the sooner we can get away, because I don't want to be late tonight – not if we're going off to Volterra first thing in the morning. You do still have your licence, I hope, so that we can rent the car tomorrow?' Sir Christopher asked Peter.

'I can see that it's going to be a long time till I live *that* one down!' Peter said, laughing with his usual insouciance.

'Will it not,' Sir Christopher said smilingly, as he finally stood up. 'Oh, look,' he continued, leaning against the chimney-piece, 'there's ash in this libation bowl. Mercy, how slatternly that Indian is. She can't even dust properly. There, and off we are,' he said. Whereon, turning back to his right, Sir Christopher flung John's burnt offering, in a long arc, into the smouldering pit.

Surely, John quoted to himself, *something strange will come of that gesture which my master follows so intently with his gaze.*

✝

'What a peculiar evening that was,' Peter Mason said, as the taxi wended the three of them down the hill of Bellosguardo back to the via de' Bardi.

'Peculiar? Whatever do you mean by *peculiar*, dear Peter? It was the most quintessentially Florentine gathering one could ever imagine. There they all were – supping at Alice's festively decrepit board – the twenty or so people who own most of Florence. And believe me, voraciously do they hold on to their property. They are, the Florentines, you know, the polar opposite of the prodigal Venetians, who have gambled away most of their patrimony. Here, in the "City of Flowers", there is hardly a hayloft – let alone a palace – that has been sold in the past five hundred years. Bibino, Bibi, Bobo, Baba, even Bobozzi, as all these aristocratic Florentines seem to be called' – Sir Christopher laughed – 'they know how to look after *their* inheritance.'

'I must admit,' Peter said, 'that I was more than a little amused to meet all these ancient Florentines, who, though speaking the archest of English, rejoice in the most absurd of Italian nicknames.'

'Oh, those silly nursery names are just meant to be proof of ancient lineage. But then, one must not forget that there is that whole other contingent that goes in for the anglicised version: Margherita "Daisy" Cavalcanti, Amerigo "Merry" Vespucci, Patrizia "Patsy" de' Pazzi and, not least, Tommaso "Tommy" Tornabuoni,' Sir Christopher said, shattering, with the mention of the latter's name, John's imaginary safety in the dark of the taxi.

'Speaking of Tommy,' Peter said, 'I can tell you that he was perfectly impossible. I tried to speak to him before dinner, but I think he was already tight.'

'Wouldn't surprise one,' Sir Christopher said. 'He's even been known to *arrive* blotto. That's yet another reason why one would like to throw something – something quite hard – at old Alice. When she isn't going on about my mother's delicious food, she's holding forth on how brilliant old Tommy is. In truth, his so-called historical works are all derivative. And as for his knowing anything about works of art – I mean, really, he's always backed the wrong people. In the thirties, he and his friends were free to champion any Baroque painter they wanted – the field was wide open to them – the Carracci, Domenichino, Guercino, Guido Reni. And whom did they choose but Magnasco? I ask you, Magnasco! And then there is that old Society of Dilettanti that he is so proud of being a member of. Such a bore! Needless to say, he had never heard of Stuppach. And as for those two volumes of mythomaniacal memoirs – *Confessions of a Florentine Art-Eater* and *More Confessions of a Florentine Art-Eater* – well, the less said the better. And the poetry – we won't even touch *that*. No, it really is too tiresome of Alice always to be droning on about Tommy – so brilliant, so charming, so—'

'Charming!' Peter Mason scoffed. 'I can assure you that he was anything *but* charming tonight. When I tried to talk to him before dinner, he just looked into his glass of whisky, granting me the occasional blank stare, even as I made the requisite allusions to Gertrude Stein and Picasso and his years in Paris before the war. I quickly gave up, but that was nothing compared to what happened after dinner. I'm sorry about that, John. I certainly had no intention of bringing up the subject, let alone making you the object of his fury.'

John looked out the window, saying nothing.

'What do you mean?' Sir Christopher asked excitedly.

'Well, I had been talking to Miss Varrow's sister after dinner, talking with some difficulty, I must say, as she is so hard of hearing, and I happened to mention that I was reading a new edition of Steven Spanday's criticism. She immediately got the bright idea of talking to Tommy Tornabuoni about it. I tried to stop her, but there was no making her understand.'

Sir Christopher laughed. 'Oh, she didn't!'

'She did.'

'It's too marvellous, Trixie's gift for always saying the wrong thing. Perhaps her *only* gift.'

'I don't think,' Peter Mason continued, 'that Tommy Tornabuoni can possibly know that Spanday's infamous review is reprinted in the volume in question, but just the mention of a book by Steven Spanday set him off on the most terrific tirade, a perfectly irrational tirade, directed mainly against Americans, and I am afraid that John had to bear the brunt of it, even though he hadn't mentioned a word. I've never seen such a sudden outburst. And it looked' – he turned to John – 'when we first came up to you, as though you had quite won him over, in a way that I certainly hadn't before dinner.'

'What review is that?' John asked dryly.

'It's a long review that Spanday did of Tommy's first volume of memoirs, *Confessions of a Florentine Art-Eater*, when it came out in the fifties. And it is, I am afraid, very severe, hilariously so at times. I remember, most of all, that he wrote that the noble Barone Tornabuoni does not so much drop names as he *hurls* them.'

'Yes.' Sir Christopher laughed loudly. 'He did say that, didn't he? And then there was all that bit about the war. He quoted Tommy as saying that he needs the beauties of art to live the way a labourer needs his daily crust of bread, but that he, Spanday, imagined that, in the five years of the war Tommy passed at the Beau-Rivage with his mother, on account of his so-called weak heart, he managed, just occasionally, to sample the *tiniest* morsel of brioche.

'We all thought that Steven went rather overboard about the war. To be fair, Tommy's mother, silly goose though she was, had been rather courageously anti-fascist. She even had to spend an entire night in prison before the war in Florence, locked up with a lot of prostitutes, though she did have the presence of mind to draw a circle round herself with a tube of lipstick, vehemently defying any of the tarts to cross the line. And she was absolutely obliged to leave Italy the minute the war started, whilst Tommy's father and perfectly simple elder brother, Bibi – both dyed-in-the-wool, fanatic fascists – remained behind.

'And it was, of course, the dreadful father, Barone Alberico, he who was longing for a military hero in the family, who pushed his son into Egypt, where he was eventually killed. All that bit that Tommy is forever going on about – the wicked strumpet luring his brother to Africa – is utter nonsense. It was entirely the fault of the old Barone; and his wife never forgave him, in particular, or Italy, in general. When she came back to Florence after the war, she never spoke a word of Italian again, nor a word of *any* language to her husband. And Steven recounts all of that in his review, blatantly contradicting the account in Tommy's book.'

'And I guess' – Peter turned to John – 'as they had once been such great friends, he could never forgive Steven Spanday for having written that review.'

'It's much more complicated than that,' Sir Christopher interjected. 'You see, Tommy and Steven had been together throughout most of the late twenties and early thirties. They lived together in Paris – more than just *friends*, I can assure you. Steven Spanday, of course, hadn't a penny to his name – son of an East End rag-picker, he was. And though Tommy did support Steven, he never let him forget it. Too embarrassing it was meant to have been. When they visited people in the country, he would make Steven take a third-class railway carriage, whilst he travelled first. He's even said to have sent him to fetch things – books or cigarettes – in front of guests.

'Of course, I didn't know them at that time, as they were both ten years older than one, but Mamma knew them. She always liked Steven, thought him frightfully clever, but Tommy, well she found him a bit precious, really thoroughly second-rate. And I don't imagine she did much to hide her feelings.

'Shortly after the two of them made their great trip through the Near East in the mid-thirties – having lived in Damascus for over two years – Tommy came back to Florence. I've never been sure how much he was actually *forced* to return, as he always insists, but I do know for a fact, as I was already in Florence myself by that date – thirty-five or thirty-six, it was – working on Taddeo Gaddi, that Tommy never invited Steven for so much as a weekend, saying kindly that he wouldn't mix with the local grandees.

'But then, when the tables were turned – and turn they most decidedly *did*, just after the war – poor old Tommy could never accept that he should have been eclipsed by the impecunious, unknown Steven Spanday, he whom he had abandoned to a London bedsit. It was simply too much for Tommy's ego. Of course, it proved to be the making of Steven – that Tommy should have dropped him. He just went from strength to strength. And then, in the end, the late sixties and early seventies, when Steven had that tremendous success in America – the lectures at Harvard, all those honorary degrees and that big poetry prize, whatever it's called – Tommy would become simply apoplectic at the mention of Steven's name.'

'To judge from tonight's performance, age has done little to diminish his ire, though it does seem to have helped him to forget that he himself is half American,' Peter said.

'Three quarters, actually,' Sir Christopher corrected.

'Really?'

'Oh yes. Not only was his mother American, but his paternal grandmother as well, a van der Luyden – old Dutch New York – she was. I remember her quite well from before the war. Frightfully impressive, she was. No nonsense about her. It was his mother, from Chicago, who introduced a strain of silliness into the family *and* all that department-store gold. So that his father, you see, old Barone Alberico, was only half Florentine, though, to hear him talk, you would have thought he was descended straight from St Zenobius himself. No, three quarters of Tommy's blood – and *all* of his money, I dare say – is American.'

'That makes this evening's anti-American philippic all the more incredible. Anyway, if you like, I'll lend you the book, John, so that you can see what all the fuss is about,' Peter said, as they arrived in the via de' Bardi.

Before going to get Sir Christopher ready for the night, John went to the spare room to retrieve the essays of Steven Spanday from Peter. 'Thank you,' he said quietly as Peter handed the book to him.

'Oh, you're more than welcome,' Peter said, as he began unselfconsciously to fling his clothes on the floor. 'And I wouldn't let old Tommy Tornabuoni get to you.'

'I couldn't care less,' John said unconvincingly as he modestly looked away.

'I've seen him launch much fiercer attacks than the one you were subjected to,' Peter, now near naked, continued. 'And always out of the blue like that. I suppose it was the mention of Steven Spanday that set him off tonight. Funny, you would think that people like Tommy or Christopher would be above caring about negative reviews. But somehow it rankles.'

'What does Sir Christo—' John faltered, 'um, Christopher, have to do with it.'

'I just meant that it's transparently obvious that the violent dislike of Vyvyan Virtue he betrayed before dinner has nothing to do with Vyvyan's character, per se – his brother Crystal was much more effeminate than poor old Vyvyan – and everything to do with the fact that Vyvyan wrote a critical, and really only *quite* critical, review of Christopher's book on Piero della Francesca, for which he has never forgiven him.'

'What on earth does Vyvyan Virtue know about Piero?' John asked indignantly. 'Though I must say that I'm surprised that a *nobody* like old Virtue would be brave enough to come out in the open and criticise someone of Christopher's stature.'

'That's what made it so galling: he *didn't* come out in the open. It was published in the *TLS*, on the front page, not long after I first met Christopher, back in the days when all the reviews there were still anonymous. Christopher literally bribed Albert Ryce-Smith, the editor – I think he paid him a hundred quid – in order to get him to divulge who had written it. I thought it would all blow over – Vyvyan even wrote a grovelling letter of apology – but, as you saw before dinner, Christopher is not to be dissuaded.'

'No wonder,' John said. 'I mean, I do call that pretty slimy, writing a hostile anonymous review, and all of that presumably after Christopher had secured the grant from the British Academy for him to work, or rather *not* work, on Canova.'

'Goodness, I can see whose side you're on,' Peter said, smiling.

'Well, goodnight, and thank you for the book,' John said, hurrying off to Sir Christopher's room, where he immediately began to turn down the bed, lay out pyjamas, pour water and line up pills.

Last night, when Sir Christopher had returned with Peter Mason, John had taken enormous pleasure in going through this ritual, as if to prove to himself that, though Peter Mason might travel with Sir Christopher, it was he, John, who oversaw intimacy. Tonight, however, he had not the heart to indulge in such inventions. He was deeply embarrassed to have pandered so brazenly to Tommy Tornabuoni near the end of Alice's dinner – comparing his pathetic poetry to Wyatt's, his supercilious memoirs to De Quincey's. *Have you* no *shame?* he interrogated himself.

But he was, above all, positively conscience-stricken to have sat quietly by whilst the noble Baron regaled him with tales of Dame Sophia's blatant preference for her younger son and told him – told him *twice* – which he had already read in Jo Leigh-Fiennes's diary, that at Oxford Christian Noble-Nolan was known as 'Botticelli', the incarnation of Pateresque ethereal beauty, whilst the elder, hard-working brother, Christopher, was dismissively labelled 'Botticini', the plodding, uninspired follower. John even wondered if the crushing rebuke he had endured at the end of the evening – *All of you idiotic Americans absolutely* worship *Steven Spanday!* – was not some sort of divine retribution for the mute voice he had maintained in the face of Tommy Tornabuoni's not so subtle jabs at Sir Christopher. He tried to reason that he had had no time to reply, but he was unconvinced by his own argument, for he knew that silence can be tantamount to denial. Had he heard the cock crow?

He looked down at the now recumbent figure of Christopher Noble-Nolan, who, already drowsy with sleep, had, to John, the air of a child, so untrammelled did he seem by worry, by desire, by jealousy, by envy. So utterly whole in himself did he appear, shielded by his vast erudition and his unassailable sense of self, that John feared he would never be able to penetrate his autarky. John did not see that Sir Christopher was forever at rest because he was his own repose. If someone could have taught John to understand this truth, he might have walked easier himself. But *what angel can teach it to an angel? What angel can teach it to a man?* And so, not knowing where to seek such fulfilment, where to knock, John would never receive what he asked, nor find what he sought. The door would be forever closed to him.

Bending over to kiss Sir Christopher on the forehead, he said, as if to reassure himself, 'I love you.'

'Yes, one sees that.'

You see nothing, nothing at all. Thank God, he said chokingly to himself as he turned off the lights and stumbled back to his own room.

Once in bed, he opened Steven Spanday's book to the table of contents and immediately spotted an essay called *Conceits of a Florentine Art-OWNER*. John smiled to himself but felt too depleted to take any real pleasure, vindictive or otherwise, in such an attack. He turned off the light and fell straight asleep.

CHAPTER II

Tender Buttonholes

'BUT YOUR BUTTONHOLES, they, ah, they... *open!*'

'What?' Sir Christopher asked.

'Your buttonholes, here on your suit, they actually open,' John said in amazement, dropping his notes about photographs to be ordered for Sir Christopher's forthcoming book.

'Don't they open on all suits?' Sir Christopher asked, looking up incuriously from his writing-table. 'I don't, after all, see that there would be much point in a buttonhole that *didn't* open. And as for the Berlin photos—'

'Well, of course, they all open in the front,' John interrupted. 'But I mean here,' he continued, 'along the outside sleeve or cuff – or whatever you want to call it – of your suit coat. There, your buttonholes open. I guess that it's just because you've lost a button – the first one on your left sleeve, you see—'

'So one has.'

'—that the buttonhole has popped open and I'm noticing it for the first time,' John said, taking Sir Christopher's coated arm in his hand and stroking it gently.

In the eight months since he had been installed in the via de' Bardi, John had become intimately familiar with every article of Sir Christopher's clothing, as well as with each item of his toilette. He knew the exact number of shirts Sir Christopher possessed: how many striped and how many white – no checked. He had quickly caught on to the precise rôle of each pair of shoes: during the day, it was brown tie when in the house, but black tie when out of the house; in the evening – inside *or* outside – it was black slip-on, with no tassels or buckles of any description. He had memorised the exact placement of each instrument of grooming: the silver-backed hairbrushes stood on the dressing table in the bedroom, with the ivory shoehorn to the left, the nail scissors to the right, and the comb in the centre; the eau de Portugal, decanted, remained on the glass shelf in the bathroom.

He also appreciated that Sir Christopher owned twelve scarves but no sweater; fourteen pairs of braces but no belt. It was, however, to Sir Christopher's fifty-six suits that John had devoted the most minute attention, so that he was distinctly disconcerted never to have registered this matter of the buttonholes. He had personally arranged the congeries of suits so as to form a coherent body: the few Prince of Wales plaids were hung together at the beginning of the clothes press, followed by the numerous pin-stripes, after which came the even greater number of staid solid colours.

When he first inspected these suits back in the summer, he had been struck immediately that there was nothing so vulgar as a vendor's label to disfigure the lining of any of them but that, *inside* each right-hand breast pocket, a small tailor's tag was sewn in, upside down, on which was printed: H. HUNTSMAN & SONS L^{td} 11. SAVILE ROW LONDON W1X 2PS, with Sir Christopher's full name and the date of fabrication typed below, followed by the initials of the cutter and a, to John, mysterious string of numbers; MADE IN ENGLAND was written at the bottom. Eventually, John became familiar with the weave, the weft, the weight and, above all, the cut of each suit. There were some three-button suits, many two-button ones and no double-breasted. The trousers were pleated, cuffed and trimmed at the waist with two adjustable tabs; there were no belt loops, but there were numerous interior buttons to which braces could be attached. All of this, he knew by heart. *So how, how on earth*, he asked himself, as he stood behind Sir Christopher's chair distractedly collecting his notes, *could I ever have overlooked those* real *buttonholes?* Aloud, he absent-mindedly said, 'But we already have photographs of all the Berlin drawings.'

'I was speaking about the *comparative* photographs,' Sir Christopher said sharply.

'Um, yes, of course,' John said, snapping back to attention. 'I've also ordered a completely new set of photographs of the Yates Thompson codex.'

'I know *that*. But we still don't have any photos of the manuscript in the Bibliothèque de l'Arsenal. I want a clear photo of the scene showing Dante and Beatrice before St Peter in the *Paradiso* from, ah, well from whatever Canto it is.'

'Twenty-four,' John said swiftly.

'Yes, twenty-four,' Sir Christopher said. 'We'll compare that with the Botticelli drawing in Berlin. Now, the *Purgatorio* is all taken care of, but as to the *Inferno*, well, I think we'll want all of the Master of the Vitæ Imperatorum illuminations in Imola. We already have enough of those from the Bibliothèque Nationale.'

'I should probably write direct to the Biblioteca Comunale in Imola for that.'

'Right you are. And finally, for the last Canto of the *Inferno*, um – what is it?'

'Thirty-four.'

'Yes, thirty-four. Good of you. We'll need to show Lucifer clawing the back of the writhing Judas. But I would like, at the same time, to see the other two traitors, Brutus and Cassius, depicted.'

Three Judases, each one thrice worse than Judas! John quoted to himself. Aloud, he said, 'I think it would be easiest if I were to go straight to Alinari this afternoon to see what they have in stock.'

'That would be splendid.'

'Is that all?' John asked, closing the cap of his Mont Blanc.

'It seems more than enough, doesn't it?' Sir Christopher smiled. 'But wait, there is just one more, quite important, thing. Could you find an early illustration, very early, in which Brunetto Latini is depicted actually grasping Dante's cloak? It would be useful to compare that with Botticelli's illumination of Canto XV of the *Inferno*.'

'Maybe Guido da Pisa?' John said.

'Yes, that would be perfect, if it corresponds.'

'I'll look that out at once. I couldn't agree more that the meeting of Dante and Ser Brunetto needs to be emphasised. In fact, I've been thinking for quite some time,' John said in a sincerely reflective voice, as he brushed all thoughts of buttonholes aside and sat down, 'that it would be interesting – more than interesting – really wonderfully felicitous, if you could expand or enlarge, just a *bit*, your commentary on Canto XV.'

'How so?' Sir Christopher asked, suspicious.

'Well,' John said, trying desperately to avoid any trace of fulsomeness, 'I wouldn't say this if I didn't honestly think that your manuscript on Botticelli's illustrations for the *Divine Comedy* is one of the best things you've ever written – and I don't mean that as idle flattery. I do believe that the marriage between great painter and great poet that you conjure up is unlike anything that anyone else has ever written on the subject. No one before has come *close* to conjoining the gravity of the text with the sublimity of the images. And if you're right, which I am sure you are, that Botticelli kept the manuscript in his own possession, working on it right up until his death—'

'It seems to one self-evident,' Sir Christopher broke in. 'There's just that mad German, who's proposed – without so much as a shred of evidence – that Lorenzo di Pierfrancesco de' Medici gave the manuscript as a present to Louis XII in 1501. Imagine giving a not even half-finished manuscript to a king – a *French* king at that! It might, just might, have been commissioned by Lorenzo di Pierfrancesco, but there's no proof that it was ever delivered to him. I am sure that it had intense personal significance for Botticelli and that he worked on it sporadically, for years, up until he died.'

'I quite agree, now that you've written about it so lucidly. And that's exactly why I think you should expand, ever so slightly, your commentary about the personal nature of the illustration to Canto XV. I really see it as a reflexion of Botticelli's anguished state of mind at the time. It would be the perfect place to bring up Botticelli's own homosexuality and the fact that he was denounced to the Night Officers in 1502 for keeping a boy.'

'I don't see how that's relevant,' Sir Christopher said stiffly.

'But if you look,' John said, opening a book to a pre-marked page, 'at his depiction of the so-called "Violent against Nature" in the third ring of the seventh circle, one sees that it is the *only* one of the ninety-two illustrations in the manuscript in which Botticelli heightens the pale pink of the flesh with cooler shades of mauve, thereby emphasising the cruelty, indeed the inhumanity, of the punishment meted out to these sinners, condemned to perpetual motion on a field of burning sand. And the image, from a strictly formal point of view – flattened and peculiarly close-up, with an abrupt, almost brutal, cropping at the sides – is unparalleled in the cycle, almost as if its composition were emblematic of the very nature of homosexuality.'

'I *have* looked at the illumination, and I've said all that I want to say about that Canto.'

'Right you are,' John said, knowing when to drop a subject. He assumed, wrongly, that Sir Christopher's refusal to address the subject of Botticelli's homosexuality was a manifestation of generational pudicity, whereas, in fact, it was Christopher Noble-Nolan's sure sense of self that preserved him from the fanciful self-identification to which an insecure being, such as John himself, was prone. Christopher Noble-Nolan had, from an early age, made a conscious choice to write in a frigid style, with accuracy and clarity as his guide and unimpeachable historical scholarship as his goal, thereby obliterating his personality from his work. Any suggestion that his own emotional experience might be grafted on to Botticelli's artistic vision was, to him, utter anathema.

In time, an inexpressibly protracted efflux of time – so long a time that its duration could hardly be appreciated – John came to understand, even to admire, Sir Christopher's intellectual detachment; for now, he merely felt frustrated, wondering, but not daring to ask, why Dante had consigned his revered teacher, Ser Brunetto Latini, to writhe in sodomitical hell. Did this, he wondered, make Dante himself treacherous to his master? Or was it, as Boccaccio had commented, simply a question of *pedagogus ergo sodomiticus*? John could only say for sure that he thought it frightfully unjust of Dante – *he*, who was so judgmental of everyone else – to have condemned the sodomites to a lower rung of hell than he did the heretics, the tyrants or the murderers.

'Now,' he continued, 'I've got to look something up. It will only take a minute. Do you want to go to the drawing room before luncheon? I've already put the sherry out. I'll be with you in a moment.'

'Well, one is feeling rather hungry after all that work this morning.'

'I should probably warn you that lunch is going to be just a little bit late.'

'And what muddle has that Indian created *now*?' Sir Christopher asked good-naturedly.

'Actually, I tried to teach Rita how to make a soufflé. So we'll see the result today. And she said that lunch will only be about ten minutes late, which, I admit, probably means twenty minutes. But still, it's nothing to fuss about.'

'It *is* good of you to try, though I fear you are only wasting your time on that woman. I'll just take these along,' Sir Christopher said, collecting the magazines and reviews that had arrived that morning, 'to keep me company.'

As soon as Sir Christopher was safely out of the way, John stole into the latter's bedroom and unlocked the doors to the tabernacle of a clothes press. And there they all were, a sacrosanct display of *real* buttonholes, staring out at him. *How,* he asked himself again, *could I have failed to notice them? Fifty-six bespoke suits, four buttonholes per sleeve, one hundred twelve sleeves, equals four hundred forty-eight buttonholes! How?*

He thought of his one 'good' suit, from Brooks Brothers, or his perennial blue blazer, and cringed. There was no need to examine those sleeves, for he knew that they contained no buttonholes of any description.

He closed the doors despondently and, overcome by a sense of non-admission, made to return to Sir Christopher. On his way, he stopped in the kitchen to inspect the soufflé, which, he was happy to see, appeared to be rising nicely.

☦

Directly luncheon was finished, John went out in the direction of Alinari, the celebrated photographic archive, on the other side of the river. As he made his way there, he did not fail to recall that most of Florence's more expensive clothing shops were located in the same neighbourhood. Though he had already passed many an hour pressing his nose to the glass of these temples of luxury, fixating on cashmere sweaters, silk dressing gowns and sundry other items which he imagined it necessary to possess in order to be accepted by, or at least to pass amongst, the privileged few, he had never devoted much attention to that most basic staple, the suit.

Today, he looked at nothing else. But before entering any shop, he dutifully headed for the offices of Alinari, housed in Palazzo Rucellai – the most perfect example, to John, of humanist architecture in Florence. He quickly searched for (and found) every photograph Sir Christopher had asked for, so that he might all the sooner resume his own quest.

In order fully to unravel the mystery of the buttonholes, he slunk into one shop after another. It did not take him long to grasp that, whereas off-the-peg American suits had two, occasionally three, buttons nonsensically sewn on to the cuff of the sleeve, with no trace of a buttonhole, their European counterpart was generally furnished with ersatz buttonholes, of which there were normally four. It was only on the most expensive suits, generally sold in small shops with their own label, that one found buttonholes that actually opened along the sleeve. But as all of these suits were of a cut – cinched waist, flaring lapel and belt loops on the trousers – at variance with Sir Christopher's sober taste, John did not feel tempted, as he usually did, by things beyond his means.

Wandering home, in a rather aimless fashion, he stopped first in a music store in via de' Ginori, where he bought a CD of the orchestral version of Haydn's *Seven Last Words of Christ*, in the hope – vain though he feared it be – that he might convince Sir Christopher to convert from long-playing records to compact discs. He then turned round, went into via de' Tornabuoni to buy a cake for tea and then ambled down the via de' Fossi, where he transferred his attention to the many antique shops lining this street. He was already thinking, months in advance, that he might come upon a small but precious object suitable for Sir Christopher's next birthday. He dreamt of discovering some unidentified or, more likely misidentified, work of art, not only because he might then be able actually to afford it, but, even more, because he wanted to impress Sir Christopher with the excellence of his own eye.

Crossing the street in pursuit of a late Baroque bronze which, at least from a distance, looked promising, he was suddenly arrested by a small window farther along. He ran forward, finding himself confronted by a tailor's dummy, dressed in what appeared to be an exact replica – not least the buttonholes – of one of Sir Christopher's pinstriped suits. There was no name on the shopfront, but there was a small, handwritten placard, discreetly placed at the foot of the model, which read, '*Su misura*'. 'Made to measure. Exactly,' John tremulously whispered to himself.

He cautiously pushed the door open and walked into a long, narrow room, furnished only with a refectory table, on which sat pile upon pile of leather-bound rectangular books containing fabric samples. A smiling middle-aged man, with a tape measure hanging round his neck, appeared from behind a curtain and asked if he could be of service. John explained, trying to convince himself more than the tailor, that he wanted to have a suit made and that he was very taken with the model in the window.

'*Lo stile inglese*,' the man said proudly.

'*Si, molto, um,* molto *inglese*,' John stammered.

The tailor seemed only too happy to display swatch after swatch, minutely detailing the quality of each one. John soon fixated on a specimen of wondrously light worsted wool in charcoal grey that could, he thought, be worn all year long and which, though it closely resembled many of Sir Christopher's suits, did not exactly copy any of them. Screwing up his courage, he looked off to the side and asked the price. Horrified though he was by the answer, he calmly said that he would come back soon and thanked the tailor.

He hurried home to prepare a late tea for Sir Christopher, fantasising all the while about a beautiful grey suit with *real* buttonholes, even though he knew that there was no possibility of acquiring such a thing. *At least not for the moment*, he said to himself. Important though it was to John to have *everything handsome about him*, he did not want, by asking outright for the money for a bespoke suit, to put any strain on his financial relationship with Sir Christopher. Since September, Sir Christopher had been more than generous about money: he had shown complete trust, a trust that John wanted passionately to maintain.

They generally went together to the bank at the beginning of the month, when Sir Christopher withdrew a substantial sum of money, which he handed over to John directly, telling him 'to take care of things'. Sir Christopher liked at all times to have 500,000 lire in his wallet – in case, he said, he should ever fall down in the street when alone – but, like royalty, he did not like to be bothered by the squalid tedium of handling cash. He owned no credit cards, and only when obliged, in a restaurant or *hôtel* for example, did he write a cheque. Otherwise, John typed out cheques, which Sir Christopher blindly signed, and dealt with all incidental expenses.

He had also come to learn that Sir Christopher was not nearly so rich as he had at first imagined, a fact that actually pleased John. For, though he was not so self-deluding as to pretend that Sir Christopher's money played no part in the attraction he felt for him – how, after all, could their civilised coexistence go on without the requisite funds? – he did not want to be accused, least of all by himself, of being some sort of vulgar fortune hunter. He knew that Sir Christopher had never owned the freehold on his house in London and that he now rented, for a not inconsiderable sum, his apartment in Florence, whilst his pension was pathetically paltry and his books produced a risible income that no one – not even the *most* devoted votary of Sparta – could ever live off.

Sir Christopher's wealth, such as it was, was almost entirely based on the Italian Baroque pictures he had astutely bought just before and after the war, when they were completely out of fashion and to be had for very little money by the discerning connoisseur. From what John could gather, Sir Christopher occasionally sold a picture to support his more than comfortable *train de vie,* one which was utterly incompatible with an academic's salary. He knew that, ten years ago, Sir Christopher had auctioned off an Annibale Carracci altarpiece, which he had bought in 1946 for £32, for several hundred thousand dollars, but that precious little of that money remained. And just the other day, Sir Christopher had said, with a nonchalance which surprised John, that he thought it might be a good time to sell his Domenichino of *St John the Evangelist,* certainly the most important picture he owned.

It was not, definitely not, the moment to bring up the subject of money, he said to himself, putting the latchkey in the door.

✝

'Tea will be ready in a minute,' John said, rushing into the drawing room, where he was sure Sir Christopher would be waiting for him.

'Right you are,' Sir Christopher said, without looking up from his magazine, one which John instantly recognised as a dense monthly on opera with a few black-and-white illustrations and much – rather too much, John thought – text.

After he poured the tea and served the beautiful glazed orange confection – dubbed 'the marmalade cake' by Sir Christopher – which he had bought earlier at Giacosa, John cautiously ventured,

'I got this compact disc for you, just so you can see what one looks like. It's a recording of *The Seven Last Words*.'

'Why don't you put it on the machine then? That way, we can hear if the sound really *is* better, as you are always insisting it is.'

'But you can't,' John said, laughing, 'just put it on the "machine". You need a special CD player to make it work.'

'That sounds infinitely *too* complicated,' Sir Christopher said dismissively. 'I think that we will just stick to the regular gramophone records. Now *that*,' Sir Christopher said in a suddenly agitated voice, as he glanced back at his magazine, 'is exactly the opera that Peter was talking about!'

'Which?' John asked warily.

'*Il viaggio a Reims*. It's being done at Pesaro this summer as part of the Rossini festival.'

'Oh yes, I saw that in New York a while back,' John said, trying desperately to sound *au fait*.

'But you *can't* have!' Sir Christopher said with distracted indignation. 'It was specially written as part of the festivities surrounding the coronation of Charles X at Rheims in 1825 and only performed in Paris four times that year. It has never since been done. The production at Pesaro will be the first modern revival.'

'Oh, I meant, actually, I meant, just that I had seen an opera by Rossini at the Met last year. It was, um, *Le comte Ory*,' John said, almost choking on his lie, though wildly relieved that he could think of the title of even *one* work by Rossini.

'According to this article here, Rossini actually recycled about half of the music of *Il viaggio a Reims* for *Le comte Ory*.'

'I guess that's what got me confused,' John said lamely, cringing at his own Trimalchio-like pretensions.

'Yes,' Sir Christopher said inattentively. 'Now I wonder what one should do about tickets?'

John sensed that he had escaped, if only just, from his lie, not so much by any special cleverness on his part as by Sir Christopher's indifference. Though he had in the past months come to a much greater appreciation of music, he was still intimidated by the subject, and, like the dream-merchant of Vienna, a part of him rebelled against being moved by a work he could not analyse. It perplexed him that, whereas a word can be demonstrably proven to mean one thing and not another, there was no way to define, for example, the emotional modulation from C-major to F-sharp minor. *The White Devil* is a tragedy – there is no arguing otherwise – but the Brahms clarinet quintet has, plausibly, been called both melancholic and rapturous. Such ambiguity disarmed John, leaving him afraid to reply to Sir Christopher.

'I do only hope,' Sir Christopher continued, 'that Salzburg doesn't conflict with Pesaro. That would be too maddening. If forced to choose, I can only say that it would be infinitely more enjoyable to see a Rossini opera which is completely new to one than the hundredth, or more likely five-hundredth, production *of Il barbiere.'*

'Does it say anything about ordering tickets?' John asked tentatively.

'I haven't got to that yet. In any event, I suppose we'll have to wait to see what Dodo Delfington has planned. I did absolutely promise her, when she was here before Christmas, that I would really go with her to Salzburg this year. She has invited one so often in the past, and one has always made excuses. Of course, it also means wearing a dinner jacket in the middle of August, which I find a frightful bore.'

'I've never seen you in a dinner jacket,' John said, thinking wistfully of Sir Christopher's evening clothes, sealed up, along with his academic gowns, in plastic bags that hung in the hall cupboard outside his bedroom.

'No, one doesn't have much need of a dinner jacket in Florence. Not even for Tommy's party at Palazzo Vecchio, but there were, then, all those dreary little professor types present. London, of course, is quite a different matter. There, it is not uncommon for one to be obliged to wear white tie and decoration.'

'Actually,' John said, 'I'm invited to a party next week to which I have to wear a dinner jacket.'

'Really?' Sir Christopher asked, curious.

'Yes. An old friend of mine from Newport,' he said, inventing as he went along, 'a childhood friend, has invited me to a party her parents are giving at the Excelsior, where they're staying. And it says black tie on the invitation. I wouldn't normally have accepted, but, as it is the same night when you are out to dine with Baba Braccio, I didn't think that you would mind.'

'No, not in the least,' Sir Christopher said.

As if I still had any childhood friends, not to mention one who would invite me to a black-tie dinner, a black-tie dinner in Florence! John cried to himself.

'I'm sure it will be amusing for you,' Sir Christopher, who did not believe that he in any way curtailed John's social life, continued.

'I haven't worn my dinner jacket either for quite some time,' John said, thinking of the garment he used to call a tuxedo, which he had bought at a thrift shop, when he was seventeen, for a dreaded high-school prom. He had always imagined that it might come in useful one day, and he was grateful that he had had the foresight to have it shipped from New York to Florence with his books and few other possessions. Now, he hoped that this ruse of being invited to a black-tie dinner by some childhood friend would colour Sir Christopher's image of him, render him worthy to be invited with the likes of Lady Charles Delfington.

John wanted to believe that his interest in this old woman had been aroused because Sir Christopher always spoke so respectfully of her – he seemed, in fact, to fret over her opinion in a way that he did about no one else's – but in another, jumbled part of John's psyche, he knew, even if he couldn't quite admit it, that his longing to construe a supernal link between himself and Dodo Delfington was based on the idea (however convoluted it might be) that they had *both*, when young, fled Rhode Island in pursuit of grander designs.

Frustrated by the disjointed fragments he could gather about her from Sir Christopher, John turned to Alice Varrow, who regaled him with endless (though not always reliable, he realised) anecdotes, all of which revolved round a ball Dodo's father supposedly gave in Alice's honour in Newport in the summer of 1939, and always ended with the, to John disquieting, refrain: 'She is remarkable, Dodo, but then there's *nothing* like a cultivated Jewess.'

Desperate for hard facts, he decided finally to ferret out information on his own. He tracked down a biography of her father, entitled *Leopold the Magnificent: The Many Lives of Leopold Kline*, from which he learnt that the object of his fascination was born Dorothy Kline, in Newport on 4 July 1901, the only and much beloved child of Leopold Kline, who had started life in Mannheim, worked as an office boy in Karlsruhe and finished in New York as a colossus of Wall Street, President of the Metropolitan Opera and trustee of the Metropolitan Museum. In 1921, Dorothy Kline married Lord Charles Delfington, the younger son of a Scotch duke, in a terrific ceremony at St James's Piccadilly. Metamorphosis complete: Dodo Kline, who had been refused the honour of coming out in Newport when she was seventeen – due to her father's 'immigrant' background, as the local grandees explained – became Lady Charles Delfington and never looked back; John Forde planned, similarly, to don his dinner jacket and move only forward.

'Speaking of dinner jackets, we really must find the gold repeater that Dodo gave to one. One can't very well meet her in Salzburg without it. She'll expect to see that fob chain dangling across one's waistcoat. You know how she never misses a thing,' Sir Christopher said.

'Find what?' John asked.

'The gold repeater watch and chain that belonged to her father, which she gave to one as a going-away present when one left London.'

'You mean a pocket watch?'

'Yes, of course. You know exactly what one means,' Sir Christopher insisted. 'I remember quite clearly that we came across it when we were unpacking everything, right at the beginning. You must surely recall that.'

'I wasn't here,' John said defensively, '*right* at the beginning, when you moved in. You must be thinking of Peter Mason.'

'That's quite true,' Sir Christopher said. 'Yes, it was Peter who was here at the time. I remember now that it was he who said that it should be wrapped in tissue paper to protect it – but that we couldn't find any – everything being in such a muddle before you turned up. Anyway, I think that I eventually hid it away myself, after Peter left, though I can't for the life of me think where.'

'I'm sure that I'll find it,' John said and smiled, basking in the reference to the muddle *before* his arrival. 'What does it look like?'

'Well, you *know*,' Sir Christopher huffed, 'like a normal, gold repeater watch. Only very grand, of course, with the initials of Dodo's father inscribed on the reverse.'

'I imagine that it must be at the back of some drawer or other in your bedroom. I'll go and have a look for it,' John said, clearing away the tea things.

'I should think that the most likely place,' Sir Christopher said, returning to his opera magazine.

✝

'Don't you look smart,' Sir Christopher said when, one evening the following week, John entered the former's bedroom at half past seven.

'I don't know,' John said, looking at his black-and-white image in the mirror.

'No, really,' Sir Christopher said admiringly, 'you *do* look smart.'

'I suppose that it will do,' John said, tugging at himself. He didn't like that his dinner jacket had a cummerbund, rather than a waist-coat, like Sir Christopher's, but he did not actually think that he had much right to complain, considering that he had only paid forty-five dollars for it back in 1977. *Frightfully good investment. Providence to the rescue*, he said to himself with a smile, straightening his bow tie.

'Only, seeing you like that reminds me that we still haven't found Dodo's watch,' Sir Christopher said.

'I'm sure that it will turn up as soon as we stop looking for it. Now, turn round. Your braces aren't properly done in the back.'

'I only hope that it wasn't pinched by that dreadful Indian.'

'The repeater? Pinched by Rita? Don't be absurd,' John said, laughing. 'She may not be wildly intelligent, Rita, but I've no doubt that she's completely honest.'

'I wish I could be so sure. It really would be too unlucky to lose another watch,' Sir Christopher said.

'What do you mean by *another* watch?' John asked.

'Mamma's watch,' Sir Christopher said.

'I don't know anything about that,' John said.

'But of course!' Sir Christopher chafed, as though John should know everything about his master's past life. 'It was a beautiful gold watch, with the same inscription on the dial-plate that Dr Johnson had engraved on his: Νυξ γαρ ερχεται. It was inherited – and lost – by Crystal, who did not believe that the night would ever come. But *come* it most certainly did.'

John assumed that the Greek quotation must be from the *New Testament*, though, rather than ask, he thought it best to wait to look it up himself in Boswell. For now, he simply said, 'You had better put on your jacket, so that I can brush you off before I go out.'

'Yes, my coat. Where is that?'

John would have liked to slap himself for tripping up. He knew perfectly well that Sir Christopher always said 'coat', never 'jacket', and he rarely failed to mimic him on this point.

'There,' he said, brushing imaginary lint off Sir Christopher. 'Now, I've ordered the car to take you to Baba Braccio's at five minutes to eight. You just have to go downstairs and it will be waiting for you. It's charged to the new account I opened with the taxi company, so that there's nothing to pay.'

'That *is* a blessing,' Sir Christopher said.

'I shouldn't be late, though I imagine that you'll be home before I am. If your light is still on, I'll look in,' John said, pecking Sir Christopher on the cheek.

He went back to his own room, wrapped a thin scarf round his neck, put on his rather worn overcoat, buttoned it to the top, turned up the collar and slipped out. He was thankful that it was already dark and still just cold enough to wear an overcoat, or his plan would never otherwise have worked: he had decided to hide himself, during the hours when he was meant to be at his imaginary smart dinner party, in the protective dark of the cinema. But he had to get there first – get there undetected. He figured that if he kept his coat closed that no one in the street – even if he crossed someone he knew – would notice that he was in black tie and that, once inside, he would be safe for the rest of the evening.

As Sir Christopher had complete contempt for the cinema, John had had no opportunity in Florence to indulge a passion he had nurtured from earliest childhood.

'I do not, you see, like pictures that *move*,' Sir Christopher was fond of saying. And he would have laughed in anyone's face who referred to film as an 'art'. The only movies Sir Christopher could abide were gruesome police stories or convoluted action fantasies.

At least, John thought, as he stole along the streets, obsessively adjusting his coat collar, *this charade will allow me to see something that actually interests* me. He would never, of course, have considered leaving Sir Christopher to fend for himself one night, whilst he went out, alone, to the cinema.

He had noticed in the newspaper that there was a film set in India, adapted from a novel he had read not long ago, playing (in English) in a theatre in via Romana. Everything – India, sensitive women, oriental costumes – that Sir Christopher would have hated. He also knew that the novelist on whose book the movie was based had written the screenplay herself, so that he was curious to see what, if any, changes had been made to the narrative. And yet, he now felt himself unable to concentrate on the images that flashed in front of him.

He found that the time sequence, constantly shifting between the present and the 1920s, left him feeling slightly queasy. He feared that he was creating the distance between himself and the screen and forced himself to concentrate on the beautiful face of the young blonde Englishwoman tramping through the dust and dirt of modern India, but the moment the scene switched back to the 1920s, and he was confronted by a Maharaja entertaining a party of foreigners in evening clothes, John knew that he had completely lost the thread.

Why, he began to interrogate himself, looking away from the screen, *should I be here in the first place? Here, at the movies, in a dinner jacket! And why on earth should I have been embarrassed to have said 'jacket', back in Sir Christopher's bedroom, instead of 'coat', when it's perfectly acceptable, even correct, to say dinner jacket? Why should I care about these trifles?*

But care he did, for he spent most of the rest of the film lost in a search for simple everyday words whose usage differed in British and American idiom.

Granted, he thought, *'dressing gown' is nicer than 'bathrobe'; 'biscuit' preferable to 'cookie'; and 'mackintosh' superior to 'raincoat'. But is 'stick' really more pleasing than 'cane'? Or 'stuff' better than 'material'? And is 'pudding' any chicer than 'dessert'? No!* he began to scream to himself. *'Pudding' is really a very nasty word, no matter* what *Miss Mitford might say. And as for 'thriller'! Surely, 'mystery' is infinitely less vulgar. If only the tables were turned and it was the British who called a detective story a 'mystery', they would not hesitate to label 'thriller' a dreadful* Americanism.

He remembered that he had read that the most fanatically anglicised of twentieth-century American expatriates had once asked the most fatuously anti-American of English writers how he would describe a particular garment: 'A great coat'? 'An overcoat'? 'A topcoat'? 'That way,' concluded the Englishman, 'lay madness.' And mad John thought he was going, as he hovered in the dark, watching the film begin for a second, excruciating time. He knew that he had to bear with it, but he could not wait to get home and throw off the trappings of his self-imposed costume.

✝

As he stood on the platform waiting for Sir Christopher's train to arrive from Pesaro, John was acutely aware that his first full year in Florence was drawing to a close. Taking, or attempting to take, stock of his position, he had to admit that all of his sorry schemes for advancement – the feigned knowledge of opera, the dinner jacket – had done little to reconfigure his horizon. Sir Christopher had, as John feared, gone off to Salzburg alone to meet Dodo Delfington at the beginning of August and he had, even more humiliating to John, left at the end of the month to hear his recherché Rossini opera with Peter Mason in Pesaro, and yet, as John wandered round the station, absurdly in advance of the train, he felt a certain sense of, if not tranquillity, at least stability. On a purely material level, he was more than happy to have left behind the anxiety of his New York life. The memory of what it is like to fret over the electric bill or to long passionately (but futilely) for an expensive new art book was not so distant as he would have liked, but the impression of menace *had* receded.

As he looked up at the arrivals board – still another fifty-five minutes to go – he recalled a recent scene in Sir Christopher's bedroom, a scene that allayed any fears he might still harbour.

One evening, a few weeks back, Sir Christopher had not, most uncharacteristically, appeared at the regular hour in the drawing room before dinner. Hesitating for some time, John finally went to Sir Christopher's bedroom, where he found him fast asleep.

'One must have nodded off,' Sir Christopher said, on hearing John enter the room.

'I didn't want to bother you. It's just that I was getting a bit worried, as it is now half past eight,' John said, sitting down on the edge of the bed.

'Goodness, that is rather shocking. But mightn't we,' Sir Christopher asked in a drowsy, childlike voice, 'just lie here a few moments?'

'If you like,' John said, tentatively arranging himself on the bed next to Sir Christopher. There they both lay, fully clothed, in pregnant silence, John resting his head on Sir Christopher's shoulder, whilst thinking that, much to his own regret, they had never, not even *once*, passed the night together, for Sir Christopher insisted that he was unable to sleep in the same room, let alone the same bed, with a breathing body next to him. And how often had John lamented that he could not suppress his own breathing! Though gladly would he spend and be spent for Sir Christopher, he secretly feared, as St Paul had warned him, that the more abundantly he loved the less would he *be* loved.

'I suppose,' Sir Christopher finally said, 'that it is because one has been working so hard lately that one is this tired. You know, I don't think that I've written quite so intensively or so concentratedly in years, not since the period back before one was director of the museum. Of course, it's all really thanks to you,' he said, running his fingers through John's hair, 'that one has been able to resume working in this way.'

The remembered sensation of that touch more than sustained John in the time that remained for the train to arrive. He stood on the platform and, smiling to himself, longed for the reappearance of the man to whom those fingers belonged.

'Thank God you're here!' Sir Christopher exclaimed, hurtling himself from the train almost an hour later.

'Of course, I'm here,' John said, his inner smile transforming itself outwards.

'Because I don't have a penny on me!'

'What?'

'That's right, not one *red* cent. I seem to have lost all my money.'

'Did you lose your wallet?'

'No, thank goodness. Nor my chequebook. But when I had the *hôtel* call me a taxi this morning – by which time Peter had already left – the only thing I could find was one 10,000 lire note. Barely enough to pay the taxi. And you know, I had an enormous wad of money with me. Well, it can't be helped. I must say that I am delighted to see you. Otherwise, I don't know what one would have done.'

'I can't think,' John said, his smile evaporating.

'We shouldn't let the porter take this. You'd better look after it.

But be careful. It's frightfully fragile,' Sir Christopher said, handing a bulky package, wrapped in brown paper, to John.

'What is it?' John asked, signalling to the porter, whom he had engaged before Sir Christopher's arrival, to collect the other bags.

'You will *never* guess!' Sir Christopher said, smiling. 'It's something that I came across at an *antiquario* in Pesaro. But I don't want to spoil the surprise, and we'll have to wait till we get home to open it.'

'Whatever you say,' John replied, wondering if the curious package might not be a belated birthday present for himself.

Sitting in the taxi, pretending to listen to a discourse about the marvels *of Il viaggio a Reims* – Ramey's singing, Abbado's conducting, Roncone's staging, it all ran together – John remembered that Sir Christopher had never had the curiosity to ask him, nor he the confidence to offer, the date of his own birthday. Sir Christopher had once told him that Andrew Bruntisfield used to mark his own birthday in Sir Christopher's diary, so as to prod his memory, but John felt that he would have preferred no recognition whatsoever to one that was manufactured. When, at the end of May, however, the subject of his birthday had still not been broached, and the actual day was fast approaching, John, in spite of his own misgivings, left prominently positioned on his writing-table a card he had received from his mother, on which was printed in large, distinctly tacky, lettering, 'Happy Birthday, To Our Son'.

When Sir Christopher noticed the card, as John had intended he should, he merely said, 'Of course, you also must have a birthday. But it's funny, I never think of you as being *anyone's* son.'

Hath the rain a father? John had asked himself at the time, wondering if the seeming parthenogenesis Sir Christopher attributed to him were not meant to be a compliment. *Did he want to say that I belong completely to him? Or less flattering,* he feared, *simply that I have no life outside of him? As if I came into being on that fateful day when I first heard him lecture at Villa Belcanto, on the Vigil of the Baptist, and would, by implication, cease to exist if I were ever to be separated from him.* John was unsure. In any event, the displayed birthday card inspired no gift. Today, as he clutched the crinkly brown paper, John asked himself, *Is this some sort of reparation, three months late?*

As soon as they entered the apartment, John dropped the bags in the hall and walked into the dining room with the tantalising package, which he ceremoniously placed on the porphyry-topped table.

'Now,' Sir Christopher said, 'I'm longing to see your reaction. But do be careful.'

John began gingerly to undo the paper, underneath which were several more protective layers. Having the strange sensation of not knowing if the thing he was unwrapping was actually intended for himself, he proceeded with great caution.

'There,' Sir Christopher said triumphantly, as the object came into view, 'you see, we have a perfectly preserved set of Renaissance bellows! I've never seen anything quite like them before. All the carving on the front side is really magnificent. They must be Ferrarese. Don't you think?'

'I suppose so,' John said weakly.

'They remind me of the Sala degli Stucchi in Palazzo Schifanoia.'

'Domenico di Paris, you mean?'

'Exactly. Frightfully good of you. I don't say that they were actually carved by Domenico di Paris himself, but certainly by someone very close to him, someone who was trained in his shop. Those rollicking putti really couldn't be anything *but* Ferrarese.'

'No, of course not. Where do you intend to put them?' John asked, awaiting confirmation of his *non*-gift.

'I thought we'd put them in the drawing room,' Sir Christopher said. 'Of course, we can never actually *use* them – they're much too fragile for that – but still, I'd like to leave them lying on the floor, next to the fender, if only you can prevent that idiotic Indian from banging into them with her broom.'

'I think I can arrange that,' John said, placing the bellows as Sir Christopher had indicated, wondering all the while how much they could have cost. *A fortune, no doubt*, he said to himself. *And there they are, lolling about on the floor!*

'Oh, don't they look smart there,' Sir Christopher said, sitting down contentedly in his usual armchair. 'Of course, it *was* rather extravagant of one, but, now that we've sold the Domenichino, I think one can indulge oneself a bit.'

'Yes, they do make quite an effect,' John said, stifling his disappointment. He tried to convince himself – and he *almost* succeeded – that, more important, infinitely more important, than any gift was Sir Christopher's recent adoption of the first-person plural: 'I thought *we*'d put them...'; 'Now that *we*'ve sold the Domenichino...' Was this not proof positive of the acceptance he had so desperately been seeking?

'Would you like something to drink?' John asked with a forced smile.

'For the moment, just a glass of water. And maybe we can have tea later on.'

'Yes, of course. I've even got the marmalade cake from Giacosa.'

'How delicious,' Sir Christopher said as John went in search of the water.

'Oh, there's something I quite forgot to tell you, what with all the excitement about the bellows,' Sir Christopher said, when John returned.

'Yes?'

'You'll never guess who appeared in Pesaro?'

'Who?'

'Dodo! I made the mistake of telling her about the Rossini festival when we were in Salzburg, and she just decided, without saying a word to one, to turn up. Once we met there, she confessed that she just couldn't have borne the thought of missing something so rare. She really is amazing, coming all the way by herself at that age.'

'It's not as though it's so very far from Venice,' John said.

'But that's just it. She wasn't even in Venice. She doesn't go there till the middle of September. She came from London, perfectly unaccompanied. It really is proof of a rather remarkable intelligence.'

'We shouldn't forget,' John said, unable to restrain himself, 'that she came here from London in December, perfectly unaccompanied as you say, for that party of Tommy Tornabuoni's, which you called mind-numbingly dull. I don't exactly call *that* proof of remarkable intelligence.'

'True. But then, one cannot expect the very rich to have the same standards that we do. And believe me, she's got more standards than most people, rich *or* poor. She had even been reading Stendhal, just to prepare herself for Rossini. No, it really was a great pleasure to see her in Pesaro, and then there wasn't all the incessant *mondanité* that there was in Salzburg. She also got on with Peter.'

'*Did* she now?' John asked more hostilely than he would have liked.

'Yes, frightfully well,' Sir Christopher replied, oblivious. 'I do hope she takes him up in London. It would do Peter no end of good to start seeing people who actually accomplish things in this world. In any event, Dodo gave Peter a lift back to London in her æroplane, so it looks as if things are off to a good start.'

'I had better go and see to your bags. If you want, you can look through the post and papers that arrived while you were away. I've put them all here, on the low table, for you,' John said calmly, turning away.

✞

John had been rather proud of the self-possession with which, after the initially aching disappointment, he had accepted the news of Peter Mason's accompanying Sir Christopher to Pesaro. It was, after all, Peter, he admitted to himself, who had discovered the opera. Moreover, he had so often told himself that he had nothing to fear from Peter Mason that he had almost begun to believe his own words: *Peter is simply a friend, a friend whom Sir Christopher sees out of habit, a habit that can be broken.*

Now, however, as he set about opening Sir Christopher's suit-cases, he could not dismiss the matter so readily. *Why,* he shouted to himself, as he began irascibly to fling Sir Christopher's travelling clothes across the bed, *should Peter Mason still be able to upset one so? Why should the mere mention of his name be capable of spoiling everything?* And yet, he knew perfectly well the answer to his own questions: Christopher Noble-Nolan's will.

Though John had thought obsessively about this question of the will over the past few months, it was Sir Christopher himself who first referred to the subject, on a warm June afternoon, when they stood together in Seeber's Bookshop looking for suitably distracting reading material. After Sir Christopher had brushed aside any number of suggestions, John designedly pointed to a book called *The Penultimate Will and Testament of Lord Rostellan* by U.C. Birch.

'No,' Sir Christopher said dismissively, 'I've already read that. And jolly good it is. Though it reminds me – I want to change my will. Don't let me forget.'

John was, simultaneously, too discreet and too self-interested overtly to mention the matter, though he did try indirectly to allude to it several times. When, after ten days, the subject had still not been broached, he decided to adopt a more offensive attack. That morning, he noticed a printed card from Sir Christopher's solicitor in London, announcing the appointment of a new partner to the firm. He put aside all the other letters and papers that had arrived and went with the single card to Sir Christopher's study at a quarter to one.

'There was nothing but this in the post,' John lied as he entered the room.

'Is it important?' Sir Christopher asked, looking up from his type-writer.

'No. Not at all,' John said, handing the notice to Sir Christopher.

'But that reminds me,' Sir Christopher said, dropping the card in the wastepaper basket, 'about my will. I might as well do it now, as we're thinking about it,' he said, inserting a fresh sheet in his typewriter, on which he pounded away for a few frantic moments. 'Now,' he continued, 'if you could copy that out on a proper sheet of writing-paper, we can send it off and the matter will be settled.'

As he went on unpacking, John vividly recalled the heartbreak he had felt on reading that one single sentence:

I, Christopher Anthony Edward Charles Henry George et omnes sancti Noble-Nolan, on this day of 14 June 1984, hereby make a codicil to my Last Will and Testament of 25 March 1975, in which I bequeath to John Forde of Providence, Rhode Island, the sum of £10,000 and my red chalk drawing of the Stigmatisation of St Catherine of Siena *by Francesco Vanni.*

A codicil! John cried to himself, hanging up one of Sir Christopher's suits. *More like an afterthought!*

When Sir Christopher said that he wanted to *change* his will, John had assumed that he meant to draft an entirely new document, not merely to add to a pre-existing one. Though he was undoubtedly stung to learn that he should have been left less money and a less valuable work of art than Peter Mason, he was truly wounded to discover that Peter Mason should remain Sir Christopher's literary executor, the guardian of his Word. So completely convinced had John been that Sir Christopher intended to appoint him to this coveted *rôle* that, on learning this was not to be, his heart was permanently invaded by a shade of rancorous disappointment. He readily acknowledged that he had known Christopher Noble-Nolan for a much shorter period of time than Peter Mason had, but he could not admit that intensity of love should be measured chronologically.

Maybe I was wrong? Maybe Peter does mean more to him than I thought? Or maybe, I just don't mean as much to him as I would like to? he said to himself, hanging up the last suit coat. He rubbed his face against the seductively rich wool and, looking down at the buttonholes, felt himself consumed by hatred – hatred of Peter Mason, whose pre-eminence he envied; hatred of Christopher Noble-Nolan, whose emotional self-sufficiency he resented; hatred of, above all, himself, whose devouring need to be loved he despised.

Burying his face in the shroud of Christopher Noble-Nolan's suit coat, he wanted to scream but only managed to whimper. He rubbed his head back and forth and, hearing something rustle, reached into the lower inside pocket, where he found the money that Sir Christopher thought he had lost.

In the first week of September, John returned to the via de' Fossi and, with this purloined trove, ordered for himself a bespoke suit in grey worsted wool with *real* buttonholes.

CHAPTER III

The Wives of Geniuses

JOHN'S SECOND AUTUMN in Florence was colder and wetter than his first one had been, but never was it so cold nor so wet that his new grey suit of light worsted wool, for which he had endured five fittings, could not be pressed into service. He was convinced that this suit had already eased him through several anxious occasions, not least Sir Christopher's recent birthday which, to John's great satisfaction, had, this year, been celebrated in Florence, whilst Peter Mason remained in London, brushed off with the vague promise of a Christmas meeting. Now, on this rainy Friday night, the last day of November, as he stood in the dining room and inspected the table once again, he touched the sleeve of his coat and congratulated himself on his foresight. Tonight, more than ever, he felt reassured to be vested in this shield of woollen armour.

Waiting for Sir Christopher to appear so that they could review the *placement* together, John fussed obsessively with his already carefully executed work, straightening a straight candle, smoothing a smooth mound of salt in a gleaming cellar, biding bided time. As was usual on such occasions, the effect for which he had striven – a Paduan bronze as centrepiece, the decoration of fresh herbs in place of flowers (which *might* be considered vulgar), the best eighteenth-century Doccia service – was intended primarily to impress (and hence to please) the host, though he did have to admit that, this evening, he was also anxious about the guests, none of whom he had met before.

The date of the dinner had been fixed long in advance to coincide with the brief Florentine visit of Jefferson Birstein. Though he had vaguely heard of Jefferson Birstein back in New York, John had since made himself thoroughly familiar with the man's work – at least his published work. He read, with mixed pleasure, the one youthful novel, the two collections of poetry, the five volumes of memoirs and the numerous critical studies, all of which concentrated on Birstein's abiding passion: dance, not a subject of great interest to John. From the autobiographical writings, which John thought veered perilously close to auto-hagiography, he learnt that Birstein had made several forays before the war, in Paris and in Monte Carlo, as choreographer and director, but that it was in his native America, after the war, that he transformed himself into a ballet impresario of renown. That John should have heard this man described by Sir Christopher – described more than once – as 'perhaps the only *true* genius one knows' both intrigued and alarmed him.

Thus it was with a certain anxiousness that, a few weeks ago, John had posed the question: 'Whom do you think we should ask to dine with Jefferson Birstein, when he turns up here at the end of November?'

'With Jefferson? Well, well, um,' Sir Christopher said with an uncharacteristic waver to his voice. 'One certainly wouldn't dream of asking old Alice. Jefferson wouldn't have any time for her, as she's perfectly tone-deaf and wouldn't know a work of art if she tripped over one. And I think that any of those old Florentines, Tommy Tornabuoni or Daisy Cavalcanti, would appear hopelessly provincial to him. He has, after all, known absolutely everyone, everyone of any intellectual stature. One can't invite him with just anybody. He is, perhaps, the only *true* genius one knows.'

'Do you want to be alone with him, then?' John asked circumspectly.

'No, you should certainly meet him, and then I'm sure that he will be accompanied by Young Winston.'

'Young Winston?'

Sir Christopher laughed. 'Yes, rather ridiculous, isn't it? Particularly as, I suppose, Young Winston is not so *young* anymore. But that's what he's always been called. Winston Young, you see, is his actual name, and then he did look so very young, really *indecently* young, when Jefferson first plucked him out of the corps de ballet in the fifties and tried to groom him for stardom. He was meant to be a vehicle for reviving Jefferson's pre-war ballet, *Flesh is Heir* – indeed, Jefferson sent him round the world for several years, at vast expense to himself – but I am afraid that Young Winston was no more destined to be an *étoile de ballet* than Jefferson was to be a great choreographer. And, of course, by the time Young Winston finally returned from his abortive world tour, it was rather too late for him to go back into the chorus. Rather a pity, really, as one finally realised that what Young Winston was born to be was an absolutely first-class dancer of the *second* rank. But by then, Jefferson had gone on to find his vocation as ballet impresario – one might say that he is Diaghilev's real heir – coupled with his work as critic and poet. Yet, all was not lost; one might almost say that all was found, as Young Winston came back to New York and discovered *his* vocation: looking after Jefferson.'

'It's funny,' John said, thinking it anything *but* funny, 'I don't remember Jefferson Birstein ever mentioning the name Winston Young in all those endless volumes of memoirs he's published.'

'Oh, but Young Winston pertains to Jefferson's private life. Dante, after all, never mentioned his wife in any of his published writings. It is quite a normal practice – or so it seems to one – to keep one's private life *private*. A person like Young Winston was always meant to be a background figure, and very well he has done it. I cannot begin to tell you how much I depended on him during that frightful year – which was it – when I was at the Institute for Advanced Study.'

'Nineteen fifty-five,' John said, finding it perfectly normal that he should have this fact at his fingertips.

'Yes, exactly – '55. Really, he saved one's life, Young Winston did,' Sir Christopher continued. 'One came up to New York every weekend – anything to escape the intellectual smugness of that old Institute – and Young Winston arranged positively everything: finding tickets for the opera, getting one into exhibitions and always organising a marvellous Sunday lunch party in Jefferson's house off Gramercy Park, with delicious food *and* the most amusing people.'

Exactly, John had thought, *why we ought to have some wildly distinguished person to meet Jefferson Birstein.*

And so it seemed to him nothing short of providential that Sir Christopher should, a fortnight ago, have received a simple white postcard, across which was scratched: 'We shall be staying at the Pensione Beacci from 27 November through 3 December. Lettice Brompton-Corlett.'

'Look!' John had said, walking into Sir Christopher's study. 'You've received this from Dame Lettice Brompton-Corlett.'

'Old Lettice, mercy! What can she want?'

'She's coming to Florence,' John said, proffering the postcard.

'So she is. Well, I suppose that we will have to do something for her. She certainly seems to expect it – to judge by this terse little note.'

'But don't you see?' John asked. 'She's going to overlap exactly with Jefferson Birstein. And wouldn't she be the perfect person to ask to dinner with him? I mean, you were complaining that there was no one grand enough to invite with him, and now here she is, one of the greatest living novelists in the world, right on your doorstep.'

'Now, that *is* a clever idea.' Sir Christopher smiled. 'It would be rather a pleasure, I must confess, to be able to introduce Jefferson to someone he doesn't know. And I should think it highly unlikely that they've ever met – Lettice being so entirely English. I'd bet that she's never even been to America. It is rather hard for one to believe that little old Lettice could be quite so celebrated now.'

'Well, I can assure you that, even if she's never been to America, she's *very* well known there,' John gushed, unable to distinguish between his admiration for this writer, which was genuine, and his curiosity, which was overwhelming, to meet someone who had known the entire Noble-Nolan family.

'The one drawback, however, to inviting Lettice is that you cannot have her without Miss Hudson.'

'Maud Hudson, you mean?' John asked.

'Yes, of course,' Sir Christopher said. 'Hence the "we" of the postcard. I cannot tell you how absolutely impossible Maud can be – always pushing herself forward. But one would hope that, now that Lettice has been made a Dame and her books are taken so seriously, Maud has finally mastered the art of playing second fiddle.'

'But isn't Maud Hudson a sort of art historian? A textile expert or something?' John asked. 'I seem to remember that Jo Leigh-Fiennes recounts in one of his diaries that he had gone with you and your mother to a lecture she gave during the war and that your mother found it very scholarly.'

'You can always count on Jo Leigh-Fiennes to get a fact wrong. Art historian, indeed!' Sir Christopher huffed. 'Maud Hudson is really nothing but a covert vendor of moth-eaten old linen. I remember all too well that interminable lecture she gave at the Royal Society during the war about the history of damask table settings, or some such nonsense. When it finally ended, Mamma turned to Jo and said, "And thus *The Napkin Scholar* concludes her oration." Thereafter, Maud Hudson was always known, in our house, as *The Napkin Scholar.* I suppose that is what silly old Jo must have been thinking of, in so far as he was thinking at all.'

'*The Napkin Scholar,*' John repeated to himself, as he refolded the napkins once again and wondered what to expect of the evening.

'Doesn't that look nice,' Sir Christopher said, admiring the table as he walked into the room.

'I assume that you'll go here, in your usual place,' John said, indicating the chair placed at the centre of the circular porphyry-topped table. 'And then, do you want to take Miss Hudson or Dame Lettice on your right?'

'Oh, Lettice, surely,' Sir Christopher said. 'Even if Maud be the senior of the two, Lettice is the infinitely more distinguished.'

'I suppose that it doesn't much matter,' John said, 'so long as you go between the two of them.'

'I was just thinking, whilst having my bath, that it might be more amusing to split the ladies up. I could take Lettice on my right and Jefferson on my left. And you can go between Young Winston and Maud. That way, we'll have two nice, distinct groups for conversation, you see.'

'Yes, I do see,' John said, trying to convey no emotion. *The geniuses came and talked to Gertrude Stein and the wives sat with me*, he quoted to himself, thinking of the book that he had, with horrified fascination, read last week.

'That's all settled then. Now, we just have to wait. What time is it?'

'A quarter to eight,' John answered.

'We might as well sit in the drawing room and have a nip of vodka before they come. I do hope they won't be late.'

'I shouldn't think so. I gave them very precise instructions on the telephone,' John said, handing a drink to Sir Christopher.

'Thank you,' Sir Christopher said, taking the proffered glass whilst simultaneously reaching over to pick up the latest instalment of the 87th Precinct by his beloved McBain.

'You're welcome,' John said, sitting down with a calf-bound volume.

'Goodness!' Sir Christopher said disapprovingly, as he glanced over at the book in John's hand. 'You do seem rather besotted by all these lady writers. Last week, it was Edith Sitwell and Gertrude Stein, and now, this week, it's been nothing but the endless correspondence of that old Madame du Deffand.'

'I can only tell you that I find the blind old marquise the most fascinating of the three.'

'I would have thought you could get by quite nicely without *any* of those ladies.'

'Your brother, Crystal, certainly seems to have been interested in Madame du Deffand. He had quite a collection of books about her,' John, by way of defence, said.

'Crystal was absolutely determined to write about her at one point, though I told him over and over again that it was quite useless to do so, as there was that American with the rich wife who had devoted his entire life to her and Horace Walpole. There really wasn't room for another book on so slender a subject. He finally admitted that one was right, but not until after he had wasted a lot of time on her.'

'Anyway,' John said, 'it's all rather new to one, the eighteenth century in Paris, and I find the world she describes – the intrigue, the etiquette, the romance – rather fascinating.'

'Fascinating!' Sir Christopher roared. 'I find it a *repulsive* world – all those menacing women controlling everything, what with their *salons* and their incessant fornication. In fact, I think the eighteenth century altogether a terribly sterile period, except for the music, and none of the *decent* eighteenth-century music – Handel, Mozart or Gluck – is French. And as for the art! Well, how anyone can take eighteenth-century French art seriously is beyond one. Watteau, Boucher, Fragonard – it's all the sort of underbred trumpery one detests.'

Mercifully, the ringing of the doorbell absolved John from the burden of even attempting to reply to Sir Christopher's outburst of Francophobia. He was, however, disturbed to witness that, on hearing that it was the two American men who arrived first, Sir Christopher had, quite exceptionally, come into the entrance hall himself to welcome the guests. *Does he think Jefferson Birstein that important?* John asked himself, whilst taking note of the complete absence of introductions.

Jefferson Birstein was just as tall and imposing as John had pictured him. Wide-shouldered, sure of step and firm of grip, he was dressed in a double-breasted black suit, black tie and white shirt with single button cuffs. No overcoat. His enormous, completely bald head, from which emitted a booming, aggressively American, voice, dwarfed his already large frame. John found it hard to believe that Jefferson Birstein had not consciously tried to cultivate the image of an intimidating clerical inquisitor, though he thought he actually looked more like a belligerent labour lawyer.

Winston Young, on the other hand, bore not the slightest resemblance to the thin, lithe figure John had conjured up. Though still possessed of the graceful posture and walk of a professional dancer, his small body had run to fat, and his sallow skin appeared to have been pickled in alcohol. The few tufts of grizzled hair that remained on his skull had been left to run in any number of conflicting directions. Despite the fact that there was a difference of twenty-five years separating the two men, John was unnerved to find that it was difficult to say, on first glance, who was the older. *Young* Winston, indeed!

Once drinks had been served by a white-gloved butler, the four men sat down, awaiting the arrival of the two ladies. Sir Christopher and Jefferson Birstein instinctively placed themselves in facing armchairs, whilst John and Winston Young were paired together on the canapé. John attempted to block out the spirited rally, in which Sir Christopher and Jefferson Birstein volleyed names and reputations and titles back and forth, and concentrate on his own charge. But try as he might, he found it impossible to engage Winston Young on any but the most trite of subjects: travel schedules; food; even the unseasonably cold weather in Florence. When John asked him about his career as a dancer, Winston Young dreamily said that it was all so long ago that he could hardly remember, and when he spoke to him about a young choreographer who was often in the news, Winston Young replied that he didn't much like contemporary dance, though he would *like* to know the recipe for the deliciously puffed *gougères* that the butler was just now passing round.

John could see that this studied effort at indifference was not directed at him personally. He felt that Winston Young's refusal to be interested *or* interesting, coupled with his wan smile, might even be intended as a covert form of solidarity between them, but John had no desire to be pinned with the medal of dejection which, he thought, Winston Young wore with such perverse pride. Had he, however, lived in the shadow of a 'great man' for nearly thirty-five years, as Winston Young undeniably had, John might have been less quick to judge. As it was, he turned away to listen to the more animated conversation.

'Perfectly absurd,' he heard Sir Christopher concur.

'Yes, they want to turn her into a saint or, even worse, some sort of *victim*,' Jefferson Birstein thundered. 'Why shouldn't she be offered up, I ask you? What does her measly little life mean in comparison to *The Waste Land*?'

'You make one quite glad to have missed the play.'

'Complete trash, I assure you!' Jefferson Birstein persisted. 'I saw it in London, not long ago. There she was, this little chit of a girl, stalking poor Eliot at performances of that pageant play, *The Rock* – she stood outside the theatre, wearing a placard round her neck on which was scrawled "I am the wife he deserted" – and barging into his office at Faber's at any hour of the day or night. And they want you to pity *her*. Well, I think that life's entirely too short to feel sorry for the wives of geniuses! Quite right he was, Eliot, to have that first wife locked up in a loony bin.'

'But when one arrives at that level of intellectual authority, I don't think it matters *what* one does in one's private life,' Sir Christopher said serenely. 'It's the work that counts.'

John blenched but refrained from commenting on the play he would very much liked to have seen himself and thought, instead, about all those 'wives' sacrificed on the altar of art: from the reviled Xanthippe, through the passed-over Signora Alighieri, right up to the effaced Mrs Henry Adams, the scratched-out Watts-Dunton, the purloined Alice B. Toklas, the maligned Kenneth Halliwell and, of course, the incarcerated first Mrs Eliot.

'*Alas*,' Jefferson Birstein said with a sententious sigh, 'that is not the opinion of the masses. All those pathetic non-entities are out there, just waiting to pounce on the decaying carcass of genius. How dare they think they have the right to judge! And the men are as bad as the women. It was written by a *man*, you know, that pathetic play about Eliot and his first wife, whatever she was called.'

You don't even know her name, *you fool. She was called Vivienne, Vivienne Haigh-Wood*, John moaned to himself, whilst turning away from Jefferson Birstein's enflamed visage.

'But you can't imagine what trouble these feminists are now causing in art history. Once they get their claws into a subject there is no fighting them off,' Sir Christopher said laughingly.

'Oh, but I *can* imagine. They're everywhere now,' Jefferson Birstein answered. 'Though I must admit,' he continued, 'that I just read a highly intelligent review about Auden in the *London Review of Books* by a woman I've never before heard of called Victoria de Vere Greene.'

'No, that doesn't mean anything to one, de Vere Greene,' Sir Christopher said.

'Actually,' John, daring to join in the conversation, said, 'I just read a book by Victoria de Vere Greene last week – a frightfully good book, in fact, a biography of Edith Sitwell that she wro—'

'*Not*,' Jefferson Birstein interrupted snappishly, 'a writer I care about, Edith Sitwell. That lady was nothing but an affected, pushing, publicity-mad fraud.'

Blushing, John turned in the direction of Winston Young, who smiled and gave him an *I-told-you-so* sort of look.

'Speaking of ladies,' Sir Christopher intervened, 'I wonder where on earth Lettice and Maud can be. It's now twenty past eight.'

'That's odd,' Winston Young said with deliberate provocation, 'because lesbians are usually very punctual.'

'Now that, my dear Young Winston,' Sir Christopher said, suppressing a laugh, 'is the *one* subject you mustn't mention in front of them. It would make them both frightfully uneasy.'

'Why?' he asked. 'I just assumed, from what you told us about them, when we first arrived, that they were a couple of old dykes.'

'It's much more complicated than that.'

'How so?' Winston Young asked.

'Mamma, who was so frightfully clever,' Sir Christopher said, 'had the theory that Maud, who doesn't look like a lesbian, is, *au fond*, one, though she doesn't know it; whereas Lettice, who does rather look like a lesbian, is not in the least one, but has always been astute enough to play on Maud's weakness. I suppose that is really the secret of how they've managed to stay together all these—'

'Weakness?' Winston Young interrupted.

'Well, you know what I mean.'

'No. No, I *don't*.'

'Now don't be tedious, Young Winston,' Jefferson Birstein said, effectively silencing his companion. 'In any event, there's nothing about lesbianism in her novels, nothing that I remember.'

'Nothing at all,' Sir Christopher said. 'But, you see, I don't think Lettice is very interested in women, per se. The two subjects that *do* interest her are incest and money. You know, her most celebrated novel, *Twin Brothers Entwined* is virtually a literal transcription of the incestuous relationship between her brothers, Castor and Pollux. Just as in the novel, so in real life did her twin brothers convert to Catholicism, in rebellion against their strongly Scotch Presbyterian background, and they did, the two boys, *actually* stab each other to death on the high altar of the Oratory. If one did not know the facts, one would have thought the story *peu credible*. But there it is, the truth: twin brothers *entwined*. It might, however, be thought rather indelicate to bring up that subject during dinner, though if you were to talk about Dorothy Wordsworth's incestuous passion for her brother, Lettice would be delighted. And if that doesn't take, you only have to compare notes with her about the varying prices of apples in Kensington and Chelsea.

'Finally, if you get *really* stuck for conversation, you just have to run down one of her rival lady novelists, and she will be your friend for life.' Sir Christopher laughed wickedly. 'But the truly extraordinary thing about little old Lettice, I can tell you, is that when I first met her, oh well over forty years ago that is, she was entirely in Maud Hudson's shadow, simply pouring the tea and not daring to say a word. Back then, no one took much notice of her, except for Mamma – but then *she* had a special flair for spotting talent. Of course, it was Maud who was a bit older and she who had the money – a little, that is – but, still, it's hard to imagine how Lettice put up with all those years of being tyrannised by *The Napkin Scholar*. It is really through sheer force of character that Lettice has managed to come out on top. Now, here they are—' Sir Christopher interrupted himself at the sound of the bell.

'Shall I go?' John asked, standing up.

'Yes, do,' Sir Christopher said, remaining seated.

Greeting the women at the door, as the butler took their coats, John was immediately struck that neither one of them looked like what would, stereotypically, be thought a lesbian – nothing 'butch' about them. Gertrude Stein and Alice B. Toklas they were not.

Maud Hudson, the taller and handsomer of the two, dressed in a navy blue skirt, matching cardigan and well-starched floral blouse, resembled, to John's eye, a prim suburban librarian; Lettice Brompton-Corlett, shorter and plumper than John would have guessed from her photographs, but coiffed with her signature meringue-like mass of beige hair and wearing an acid-green silk*ish* dress, to which was pinned an enormous diamond and turquoise brooch, he would have described as a concierge decked out in her Sunday best. Having introduced himself, he escorted the two women to the drawing room, whilst making polite enquiries about their journey.

'Lettice! How nice,' Sir Christopher cried. 'And Maud also,' he added with noticeably less enthusiasm. 'Now, I think that we will have to go straight to table, as you are so frightfully late. We'd almost given up on you.'

'I am afraid that it's my fault that we're late,' Maud Hudson said with no trace of fear. 'I insisted that we must go to Lucca for the day, which Lettice didn't know. I did most particularly want her to see the textile collection in the museum, where there are some very interesting examples of early damask. And what with the buses and the peculiar opening times in Italy – well, it all took rather longer than one would have thoug—'

'You've never been to Lucca, Lettice? Never been to *Lucca*!' Sir Christopher said, twisting and strangling the name of that city in his throat. 'I do call that highly eccentric, never having been to *Lucca*.'

'Nor Florence either,' Dame Lettice said proudly.

'How perfectly extraordinary!'

'You know, Christopher, I never did much care for abroad. I once accompanied Maud to Lyons, so that we could see the Musée des Tissus. Very interesting it was, I am sure, but the *food*. Onions over everything! One was sick for a month afterwards. It's only because the Italians are bringing out an edition of my complete works, all in new translations, that one has consented to come here. They are, of course, paying all our expenses. Perfectly frightful what travel costs today, isn't it?'

'Now, we really must go to table,' Sir Christopher said, raising an eyebrow at Jefferson Birstein.

'We brought these for you, Christopher,' Maud Hudson said, extending a bedraggled bunch of pansies, held together by a snippet of string. 'We collected them ourselves, whilst walking round the walls of Lucca. Rather like Ruskin circling the same walls, don't you know. Just the sort of thing we thought you would appreciate.'

'How nice,' Sir Christopher said, as he immediately pressed the flowers into John's hands.

'I'll put them in some water,' John said, awkwardly clutching the spurned offering.

Passing from the drawing room through the dining room, John felt himself followed by Winston Young, who whispered to him, 'Christopher's coarsening.'

'What?' John asked suspiciously.

'Coarsening, I said – the way he just shoved those flowers at you. Yep, Christopher's coarsening,' Winston Young smilingly repeated himself. 'Of course, they all do in the end.'

John replied with a blank stare and hurried off to the kitchen. Plunking the flowers in the ugliest vase he could find, he was assailed by the memory of a photograph that had, as a child, fascinated him: it showed the most famous of America's First Ladies, standing in a receiving line at the White House, extending her right hand in greeting, whilst, without turning round, she pushed the evening bag in her left hand into the grasp of an attendant servant. He could clearly remember being entranced, when he was nine or ten years old, by this image of the woman's *total* assurance that there was someone behind her, just waiting to attend to her. But back then he had imagined himself as one of the distinguished visitors shaking the hand of the celebrated lady; now, he saw himself as the retainer collecting the cast-off effects. Whether it be an evening bag or a bunch of wilting flowers did not much matter; the result was the same: humiliating. Curiously, it was Winston Young's blundering attempt at complicity that brought him round. He had no intention of being consoled by, let alone identified with, an embittered aging has-been such as Winston Young.

Taking a deep breath, he went back to the dining room, where the guests were already seated, placed the flowers on the console, so as not to disturb his table arrangement, and sat down.

Avoiding Winston Young's glance, John turned to his right, seeking to attract the attention of Maud Hudson. Though she politely answered his questions, she posed none in return. It was clear to him that she intended, by her aloofness, to make it known to all assembled how deeply offended she was by her *place à table*.

'Lettice, Jefferson has come from New York with his ballet company to perform in Milan,' Sir Christopher said in an attempt to unite his half of the table according to his preconceived notions.

'Did you hear that, Maud?' Dame Lettice crowed across the table, as if intentionally to thwart Sir Christopher's too transparent intentions. 'Mr BEERstein has come all the way from New York with his ballet.'

'Humph,' Maud Hudson snarled.

Almost mockingly, Winston Young suddenly jumped into the conversation, 'I must say, Dame Lettice, that is a simply *stunning* brooch you are wearing.'

'Oh, yes, it is *Twin Brothers Entwined*,' Dame Lettice said, stroking the unspeakably tawdry – even if real, or *especially* if real – trinket on her breast.

'But it doesn't look like an image of twin brothers to me. May I?' Winston Young asked, practically rubbing his face in Dame Lettice's capacious bosom.

She giggled. 'Oh, not literally. You see, over the years, I have offered myself a jewel on the publication of each book, and this lovely one was to commemorate *Twin Brothers Entwined* in 1947. That was my first really big success and hence my first really *big* jewel.'

'I remember, Dame Lettice,' John hesitantly spoke up, 'that Jo Leigh-Fiennes recounts in one of his diaries your coming to tea with Dame Sophia in the spring of 1947, just as *Twin Brothers Entwined* was published, and how much she admired the book.'

'She was very intelligent, your mother,' Dame Lettice said, ignoring John, as she turned to Sir Christopher.

'Was she not!' Sir Christopher proudly agreed.

'Dear old Jo, of course, presents a rather severe portrait of your mother, "The Dame", as he always referred to her. But then, I think he was quite terrified of your mother,' she said.

'As well he *should* have been!' Sir Christopher exclaimed.

'Of course, nowadays, everything has changed, and Jo himself is taken so terribly seriously. His diaries are even going to be adapted into a play for the BBC,' Dame Lettice said.

'How extraordinary,' Sir Christopher – he, who could not abide the unstinting praise and critical attention now lavished on the diarist whom the entire Noble-Nolan family had long ago dismissed as thoroughly 'second-rate' – said.

'Yes, it *is* extraordinary. Dear Jo just goes from strength to strength. You know, there was a long, and frightfully amusing, interview with him in *The Telegraph* the other day,' Dame Lettice said, addressing Jefferson Birstein with a challenging stare, 'in which Jo said that the great regret of his life was not to have gone to fight in the Spanish Civil War in the 1930s – on the side of Franco, naturally.'

'*Naturally*,' Jefferson Birstein repeated the word with a sneer.

'I'd feel sorry for *any* army that had Jo Leigh-Fiennes fighting on its side,' Sir Christopher said, laughing almost uncontrollably at his own joke.

'And how,' Jefferson Birstein said.

'Now, Lettice,' Sir Christopher said, trying to stifle his laughter, 'you really ought to go to Milan yourself and see Jefferson's ballet. It's not so very far from Florence, you know.'

'And will you be dancing yourself, Mr BEERstein?' Dame Lettice asked in a tone that seemed simultaneously naïf and insolent.

'No.' Jefferson Birstein laughed. 'No, no. I am bit old for that, don't you think?'

'I suppose that one of the great advantages to being a writer is that one just gets better with age. How old were you when you had to stop dancing?'

'But I've never been a *dancer*!' Jefferson Birstein said indignantly. 'I was in the past something of a choreographer, but for years now I've run the company in New York. I am what is known as an impresario. And like you, Dame Lettice, I write and continue to do so. But an actual dancer? No. Never! Dancers are acrobats, not artists. It's purely physical what they do, and the truth of the matter is that I was always too big, too rich and too intellectual to be a dancer.'

John felt a pang of sympathy for Winston Young, who appeared in no wise offended. *Is he simply all too accustomed,* John asked himself, *to being dismissed as a small, poor, moronic dancer? A mere* acrobat.

It also disturbed him to recognise that the contempt with which Jefferson Birstein appeared to regard the practitioners of his preferred art was not unlike that with which Sir Christopher looked on contemporary artists. He remained silent.

'Which ballet is it, Jefferson, that you are bringing to Italy?' Sir Christopher, in a desperate bid to salvage the conversation, asked.

'*Orpheus* – Balanchine's *Orpheus*,' Jefferson Birstein answered. 'I wanted to bring something that had been created in New York, specifically for the company. We've even got Noguchi's original sets and costumes. Historically, I thought it would be much more interesting that way. They wanted us to bring Petipa's *Don Quixote*, but I insisted on *Orpheus*.'

'I am sure that you were right,' Sir Christopher said. 'To tell you the truth, I find everything to do with Cervantes a colossal bore. Is there any celebrated writer whom you don't like, Lettice?'

'I've never been able to get on with that German, what's his name, uh, Goethe,' Dame Lettice said distractedly, as she wincingly scraped the white truffles off her *risotto alla Milanese*.

'I have to admit,' Sir Christopher said, 'that I do find Goethe's scientific works, even the colour theory, all but impenetrable. But there is the *Italienische Reise*, which one greatly admires, and I've always had a particular weakness for the *Conversations with Eckermann*.'

'And one shouldn't forget the drama,' Jefferson Birstein added.

'I tried *Maria Stuart*, but I'm afraid that I found it unreadable,' Dame Lettice said.

'But that's Schiller!' the two older men exclaimed in unison.

'I suppose,' Dame Lettice, not in the *least* flustered, said, 'that I was thinking of the opera by Verdi. But then, I've never understood why all these foreigners should be mucking about with *our* history.'

Sir Christopher ran an anxious finger across each of his severely raised eyebrows, as though to dispel the string of mistakes, but said nothing.

'Speaking of opera,' Maud Hudson suddenly bawled, 'I took

Lettice to see that new film about Mozart last week. Most extraordinary it was to hear all the characters chattering away in American.'

'I thought it a masterpiece,' Jefferson Birstein said aggressively.

'*Really?*' John could not restrain himself from asking. 'It's so completely unhistor—'

'But it's not a documentary. It's a work of art. An absolute masterpiece. I saw it seven times. In fact, I'm meeting the director next month and hoping to interest him in a film about Diaghilev. He's the only person I can think of who's capable of making a film about a genius. The only one who would approach the subject on the same level of...'

John looked straight at Sir Christopher, who did not return his gaze. Several weeks ago, when they had gone to see this film together, Sir Christopher had insisted on leaving the cinema after three quarters of an hour. 'Insupportable rubbish,' he had said. And yet now, he offered no opinion. While it disappointed John to think that Christopher Noble-Nolan, whom he revered as the personification of intellectual integrity, should be, if not intimidated by, at least unduly impressed by a bombastic, self-promoting, cultural dictator like Jefferson Birstein, it positively grieved him that Sir Christopher had made no effort to come to his defence, that he left him there, dangling in the grasp of the enemy.

With a mixture of determination and resignation, John turned to Winston Young and spoke to him for the rest of the evening about the restaurants and *hôtels* he was likely to come across during his stay in Italy.

✞

'Did you catch Lettice's *double* howler?' Sir Christopher asked as soon as the guests had departed.

'Did I not!' John said with false confidence.

'I didn't think that one could very well correct little old Lettice twice in a row – after that mishap about Goethe and Schiller – but it was *deeply* embarrassing, her muddle over Verdi and Donizetti. Can you imagine anyone *not* knowing that *Maria Stuarda* was composed by Donizetti? Too extraordinary! Thank God Jefferson managed to control himself. He's not always so restrained, you know.'

'So I gather,' John said.

'That's why I immediately steered the conversation away from music and ballet, indeed away from anything European. I forgot how pathetically provincial old Lettice actually is. Once I got on to English subjects – books and history – she was really quite intelligent, in her, admittedly, idiosyncratic way. But it wasn't till Jefferson said that he couldn't abide Iris Murdoch *or* Muriel Spark that old Lettice positively lit up. In the end, I think Jefferson was really quite amused by her.'

'Thank goodness,' John said.

'Though I must say that I *do* find it rather hard to take little old Lettice quite so seriously as she now takes herself.'

'I suppose,' John said, 'that she will be getting the OM next.'

'I wouldn't go *that* far,' Sir Christopher bristled. 'Andrew Bruntisfield is, after all, the only person one knew – the only person one knew well – to have received that distinction. Though Lettice did say – did you hear that? – that there is even someone now writing a biography of her. I do call that quite extraordinary.'

'No, no, I didn't hear most of your conversation. You know, I was busy trying to keep up my own end of the table.'

'Yes, I saw that. I thought you did beautifully, in particular, with Maud.'

'It wasn't easy, as she hardly spoke.'

'Yes, I noticed that she was unusually silent tonight, except when she occasionally shouted across the table to Lettice in that shrill voice of hers. I did tell you, in advance, how difficult she can be. Not at all like Young Winston. You see how charming he is, in his unassuming way.'

'Um,' John said.

'I like the way he holds back – so unlike Maud's pushing manner.'

'I had better go and pay the butler, and then we can go to bed,' John said, hoping to close the subject.

'Anyway, thanks to you, the dinner was a great success,' Sir Christopher said.

After he had put Sir Christopher to bed and arranged the silver in its proper place, John settled down in front of the still blazing fire and resumed his reading of the correspondence of Madame du Deffand. He was determined to block out the, to him, disastrous evening and to lose himself in the eighteenth century. That he read slowly in French, and with great concentration, helped his cause. He took up at the exact place where he had left off before dinner, thinking, as he continued, *Even if Sir Christopher despises the eighteenth century, he resembles Madame du Deffand more, much more, than he knows.*

He read over again the same letter, addressed to the old woman's future companion/traitress, Julie de Lespinasse, and translated to himself:

> *I will at no time give the impression of wanting to introduce you. I intend to make you sought after, and, if you know me well, you will not worry about my treatment of your* amour-propre. *You must trust to my knowledge of the world.*

As he moved on to the next letter of the Marquise to Mademoiselle de Lespinasse, John gasped. Again, he translated to himself:

> *A favour I want to ask of you, which is the most important thing of all, is not even to think of coming to one unless you have completely forgotten who you are and unless you have firmly resolved never to change your situation.*

'*Si vous n'avez pas parfaitement oublié qui vous êtes,*' he said aloud. He wondered if that was what Sir Christopher expected of him – completely to forget who he himself was, to sit there, silently, with the 'wives', whilst the 'geniuses' held forth?

So downcast was he by the realisation that the eighteenth century, far from providing a bulwark against anxiety, simply led him right back to himself, his wretched self, that he closed the book, went in search of the excellent (and still plentiful) claret left over from dinner and proceeded to get blindingly drunk.

CHAPTER IV

Old Roses and New Rancour

IN THE WEEKS leading up to Christmas, the cold weather abated. Short days of clear, intense sunshine lit up the surrounding hills, drawing ever more people out into the already crowded streets. Pairs of Sardinian shepherds played their pipes, chestnut vendors hovered round their braziers and country gardeners hawked their plants and shrubs, jostling the throngs of holiday revellers, whilst even the smallest of shops remained open on December Sundays. The palpable air of festivity, so different to the commercialised shopping-mall holidays of John's youth, inspired him to suggest, which he had not quite dared to do last year, that they give a Christmas Eve *réveillon* at home. Though Sir Christopher was originally opposed to the idea, claiming that it would cause entirely too much interruption to his work, it was he who appeared to have most enjoyed the evening. That night, after the guests had departed and Peter Mason had retired to the spare room, Sir Christopher pecked John on the forehead and told him that he thought it was the nicest Christmas he had ever known. 'And without you,' he had said, 'there would have been *nothing*.'

Now, two days after Christmas, as he sat staring out the window of the rented car in which Peter Mason was driving them back to Florence from the nursery garden at Volterra, John thought how right he had been to insist on the dinner and, even more, how right he had been to make such an enormous effort. The tree (decorated with dried fruit, real candles and old ornaments), the *chapon demi-deuil* (stuffed with foie gras) and the elaborately wrapped presents (laid at the places of Alice Varrow, Daisy Cavalcanti, Tommy Tornabuoni, Peter Mason and, of course, Sir Christopher) were all remarked upon, all appreciated.

Turning to look at the back of Peter's squarish head, John was happy to realise that he didn't even mind *his* presence. Though he found Peter as disarmingly friendly and easy-going as he had been on his other visits to Florence, John could not help thinking that his imagined rival now seemed preoccupied, somehow less prepared to play the game of entering into Sir Christopher's inflexible universe. He was also sure that Peter had lost weight. And he thought that his thinned-out cheeks had a better, brighter colour, making him look a few years younger. He wondered if Peter Mason didn't have a new boyfriend. He very much hoped so.

When Peter stopped the car before the large double doors of Palazzo Vespucci, John jumped out and began to unload the numerous plants they had purchased in Volterra. He placed them inside the entrance before the grille and then, in stages, transferred them in the lift to the second floor. Once he had them all in the apartment, he carted them up the narrow staircase to the loggia. Ever since his arrival in Florence, John had been disconcerted to learn what an important part gardening played in the lives of most rich people – not least Sir Christopher. Having grown up in the midst of suburban tract housing, John associated 'gardening' with weeding, watering and, worst of all, mowing the lawn, just as he connected 'nature' with hiking, fishing and, worst of all, camping – everything he hated. He knew that he was only comfortable with the beauties of the outside world once they had been filtered through the alembic of artistic vision and transferred to the sanguine surface of canvas, but he had, at first, made a real effort to cultivate an interest in gardening, as he was loath to leave any avenue of Sir Christopher's sympathies unexplored, but he increasingly came to resent the time and energy that this required. He was willing to cook, to type, to edit, to answer the telephone, to make appointments and to spend endless hours at the German Institute checking the most obscure of references, but that he should also be expected to tend to the plants seemed, to him, to be asking too much. Like Alice B. Toklas before him, he resented that his monomaniacal master should see fit to add yet another task to his already bulging roster of duties.

There was no morning John dreaded more than Thursday, when he was obliged to accompany Sir Christopher to the weekly plant fair, *Sotto i portici,* in Piazza della Repubblica; there, he would

torpidly trail after Sir Christopher, dragging home whatever eso-
teric thing had struck his guide's fancy. And though it was true that
Sir Christopher liked watering and puttering about with the plants
himself, all of the unpleasant work – lugging the earth up to the
loggia, transplanting from one pot to another, clearing away the
debris – fell to John. And it was not as if he had any say in which
plants were chosen or how they were arranged.

He soon learnt that, as a basic (but unspoken) tenet of 'good
taste', scent was to take precedence over abundance, single flowers
were to be favoured rather than double, small narcissus rather than
large, blue flowers rather than red, flat petals rather than ruffled
– and that there was not the slightest excuse for chrysanthemums.
As for poinsettias, the very name could not even be *mentioned*. But
important though all these delicate distinctions were, the over-
riding criterion according to which a plant was granted admit-
tance to Sir Christopher's utopia was rarity. Any concern for what
would actually *grow* – grow in a pot, under a covered loggia facing
north – was disdainfully brushed aside. The result, John thought,
was distinctly draggle-tailed and unsatisfactory. *Even Alice's garden,*
suburban *though Sir Christopher might find it, with its oleanders and*
red salvia, John said to himself whilst arranging the new purchases
from Volterra on the loggia, *does at least have the merit of possessing*
plants which actually flower. Not like that thing, nothing but a hideous
cactus, requiring full sun. No wonder it never produced one *trace of a*
bloom, at night or any other time, he went on grousing to himself as
he glanced over at the all but dead *Selenicereus grandiflorus.*

'Now how many of these old Florentines, who *think* they know
about plants, do you imagine have *Tradescantia* in their gardens?' Sir
Christopher asked, proudly holding up one of the scraggier arrivals
from Volterra.

John smiled. 'Not many, I'm sure.'

'And I should think even fewer of them know who Tradescant was.'

'Hmm,' John said noncommittally, making a mental note to look
up the, to him, unfamiliar name.

'And do be careful with the *Fremontodendron californicum,*' Sir
Christopher ordered, pointing to the plant in John's hands. 'It's not
nearly so tough as it looks.'

'Shall I put it here, in the corner?' John asked.

'No, no, no. I want it over there, next to the *Hamamelis*,' Sir Christopher continued in a tone of ever-mounting authority.

'I must say that it certainly does not look as if the *Hamamelis* is going to flower next week for Epiphany, as you have so often claimed it is meant to do,' John replied tauntingly, feeling rebellion reflexively rise in his breast when faced with what he considered his horticultural enslavement. 'Not a *single* bud on that poor, pathetic little thing.' He ventured to laugh aloud, whilst bending down to push aside the plant, which, he remembered, Sir Christopher had told him, the very first time he sat under this loggia a year and a half ago, was a great rarity that came from the Himalayas. What a sense of vindication he had experienced when, later, he had discovered that *Hamamelis* is nothing but common witch hazel, which grows wild all over Virginia!

'It must be its propinquity to that, uh, that *thing*,' Sir Christopher said, pointing to the impertinently robust poinsettia that Alice had given to him as a Christmas present, 'that is sapping the life out of the *Hamamelis*. I do think that old Alice has positively outdone herself in bad taste this year. You had better get that enormity away from our lovely specimens. Just throw it *out*,' Sir Christopher said, kicking the poinsettia.

'Right you are,' John answered. *Poor Alice*, he said to himself as he lifted up the maligned plant and removed it to the adjacent room.

'I'm afraid that it took longer than I thought to find a parking space,' Peter said, poking his head round the door.

'We're just getting things arranged before planting,' Sir Christopher said, bending over a pot.

'Yes, I see. It looks as though you've got everything under control. I'll just leave you both to it then, as I've got something I want to do downstairs,' Peter said and smiled, before disappearing.

'I do think Peter's behaving very strangely, slipping away all the time,' Sir Christopher said disapprovingly.

'Maybe, he's just not very interested in gardening,' John offered, as he trod gingerly round the piles of rose bushes spread across the brick flooring.

'Nonsense. He used to be passionately interested in my garden in London. Rather knowledgeable, even. *Quite* inexplicable, his attitude is.'

'I've got a notion,' John said, 'that he's in love.'

'Well, he's always had something up his sleeve, ever since I've known him. There's no reason why it should suddenly change him.'

'But I don't mean just another of his usual flirtations. I mean really *in love*.'

'I don't see how he can have time for *that*, not if he's meant to be getting on with Sir Joshua.'

'Perhaps it will settle him down. Make him really concentrate on his work.'

'Hmm,' Sir Christopher said, uninterested. 'Now, what *we* must concentrate on are all these magnificent old roses. Whatever you do, don't take the tags off. We don't want to get them muddled up.'

'These two bushes are labelled Madame de Staël,' John said. 'They're the ones that I thought you would like to have in honour of your mother.'

'Yes, that was rather a nice idea you had,' Sir Christopher said, 'even if it is not a particularly celebrated rose.'

'And these three all say Joséphine de Beauharnais,' John said, making a new pile.

'We'll start with those,' Sir Christopher said. 'I'm particularly glad that we found them, as Joséphine was one of the greatest of all patronesses of the rose. Do you have that bit of paper on which that nice Australian boy at Volterra wrote down the names of the breeders of the roses?'

'No,' John answered absently, as he knelt down to line a pot with fertilizer.

'You lost it? *Lost* the paper with the notes about the roses?' Sir Christopher demanded.

'No.'

'What do you mean "no"?'

'I *mean*,' John said, standing up in an unusually assertive fashion, 'no, I did not lose the paper. I never actually had it. I saw the boy give it to you.'

'But you were supposed to look after it.'

'I noticed,' John said in a tone of mock boredom, 'that you put it in the left inside pocket of your suit coat. I imagine it's still there.'

Sir Christopher withdrew a crumpled sheet from the pocket that John had indicated and, unrepentantly, said, 'That's okay, then.'

Okay? Is it really okay? John asked himself. Okay *by whom?* So offended was he by Sir Christopher's brusque manner that he suddenly pictured himself sneaking up to the loggia in the middle of the night to poison all of these wretched roses. The image both titillated and shocked him.

'Vibert,' Sir Christopher said.

'What?' John asked, confused.

'Vibert, I said. Jean-Pierre Vibert is the name of the breeder of the Joséphine rose, according to what the boy wrote on this slip of paper. He introduced it in 1823 and named it in honour of the late Empress.'

'I see,' John said.

'That leaves us with the Banksia roses. Funny that he hasn't given one any notes about them. Hand those to me, would you?' Sir Christopher asked, pointing to the shrubs at John's feet.

'But this says Alba Plena,' John said, bending down to read the attached label.

'Well, that must be wrong. I'm sure it's a Banksia, because it's thornless, as you can see. It was brought to England from China at, I think, the beginning of the nineteenth century. I had an enormous one growing up the back of my house in Bedford Gardens. I think it would look frightfully smart to have it climbing up this column here. I must admit' – Sir Christopher smiled – 'that I do like the idea of a thornless rose, as it makes it a great rarity amongst even the most recherché of old roses.'

'What actually makes a rose *old*?' John asked.

'What?' Sir Christopher asked back.

'I was just wondering who decides if a rose is "old" or not. Is there some sort of cut-off date? Or are they a particular species?'

'They're not a *species*,' Sir Christopher said scornfully.

'Yes, but, uh, I mean,' John persisted, 'I was curious to know how old roses came into being.'

'They're hybridized from the seed of other roses by breeders.'

'Not from the wood?' John asked.

'You only have to go downstairs and get your beautiful book,' Sir Christopher said impatiently, 'to have all your questions answered.'

'Yes,' John said, turning toward the door. *Phoney*, he said to himself, descending the stairs. *And he's meant to be such a great authority on horticulture. That's why he doesn't like being questioned.* Stunned by his own accusations, John stopped at the bottom of the stairs and tried to collect himself. He reminded himself that, as he hated gardening, there was no need to take offence. To remain aloof from Sir Christopher's snappishness would, he thought, grant him power over the older man, render him the dominant, all-seeing lover. But his reasoning failed to persuade: the bitterness oozed out of him. He turned round and looked back at the flight of narrow steps, admitting that he had come to know, as his master had taught him, *how hard the path to descend and mount by another man's stairs, how salt is the taste of another man's bread.*

Regretfully, he went in search of the 'beautiful book', a large illustrated manual that he had given to Sir Christopher for Christmas, called *Almanack of Old Roses*. Finding it in the drawing room, he could but note that, as on other occasions, the least expensive of the presents he had offered to Sir Christopher seemed to be the most appreciated. He turned to the section on *Rosa banksiae* and read:

> *Species: banksiae; variety: Alba Plena. It is of the utmost difficulty to obtain hybrids of the Banksia type from seed, as the flowers, being early, have finished by the time other species bloom. It cannot be stressed too strongly that one should avoid, at all costs, growing the Banksia type in a pot...*

italic font

One should avoid, one should avoid... avoid *getting mixed up in this* mess, John stammered to himself. He was not interested in the difference between a genus or a species or a variety – Linnæan systems of classification being utterly alien to his own, unsystematic trains of thought. Nor did he care whether an old rose was hybridized from seed, or from wood, or from both, or from neither. He did not want to be proven right or wrong. He only wanted to be free from conflict, in pursuit of which he thought that he must remain patient. And patience was, he believed – in spite of what Queen Christina of Sweden may have said – his greatest strength, *a strength made perfect in weakness.*

'You were quite right about the Banksia being introduced to England from China at the beginning of the nineteenth century. It was exactly in 1807,' John said in an affectedly cheerful tone, trying to spit the salt taste from his mouth, as he reappeared on the loggia with the book.

'Do let one see that,' Sir Christopher said, holding out his hands.

'Here you are. Now, why don't you sit down?' John said, pulling up a wicker chair. 'You must be exhausted. We've been at this all afternoon, without even a break for tea.'

'Well, yes, one *is* rather tired.'

'Just sit and read – if there's enough light – while I pot these last remaining bushes. You're not too cold, are you?' John asked, having regained his natural voice.

'Not a bit,' Sir Christopher said, wrapping his mackintosh about him as he settled in to read.

John knelt down and, making no effort to keep clean, as he normally did, dug deep into the mounds of earth.

'Now, *that* I had no idea of,' Sir Christopher said.

'What about?' John asked, looking up.

'That the Banksia was named in honour of Sir Joseph Banks's wife. He was, you know, the great naturalist who travelled with Captain Cook and who, on his death, left his magnificent collection of books and botanical specimens to the British Museum.'

'No, I didn't know that,' John said, as he plunged deeper and deeper into the soil, intentionally letting the grime lodge beneath his nails and burrow up the sleeves of his jumper. He then swiped his sweat-stained brow with his filthy hands and, as a final gesture of expiation for lack of faith in his master, surreptitiously shovelled a small mound of dirt down his throat.

'I must say that this is a simply beautiful book. But then, one does love all manner of systematised knowledge. I suppose that is why one likes to read railway timetables,' Sir Christopher, oblivious to John's wretchedness, said cheerfully.

Making no reply, John continued with his work. When he had finished planting the roses and had carefully aligned the pots, he stood up and, turning to Sir Christopher, said chokingly, 'Well?'

'Doesn't that look smart,' Sir Christopher said. 'Now, according to this book, we must be quite particular about the Banksia. I'll read you what it says: "They are not, like other roses, to be pruned at set seasons. In summer, when their shoots have grown to about a foot long, one should pinch off the tops. In consequence, they will form laterals that will, with certainty, flower."'

With certainty? John asked himself. He realised that, if Sir Christopher had read thus far, he must also have come across the phrase warning that 'One should avoid, at all costs, growing the Banksia type in a pot.' He could only surmise that Sir Christopher thought himself above any such prosaic admonition. As in religion, so in gardening, John divined that there were certain rules that do not apply to *one*.

Surveying his work, John said to himself, *At least I won't have to bother poisoning these wretched roses myself. They will,* with certainty, *have the goodness to die of their own accord.*

As he closed the door of the loggia behind himself, John realised that he still had no idea of what made an old rose 'old'.

✞

Peter Mason left the following afternoon. Though John made a show of sharing Sir Christopher's consternation at Peter's early and (most offensive of all) unapologetic departure, he was happy that they should now be alone, free to pass a quiet New Year's Eve together. Walking back from the station, where he had gone to accompany Peter, John dawdled deliberately. He looked in shop windows, lit a candle in Orsanmichele without any specific intention and sat down to drink a coffee in Piazza della Signoria, where he was prompted to think more of Lucy Honeychurch's awakening than of Savonarola's demise. And he was content to note that the lowering sky, which he normally found oppressive at this hour of the afternoon, seemed to press down on the art-filled square not with the intention of effacing her monuments but with the desire of caressing them in a cloud of welcome. Even the Palazzo Vecchio, whose hulking mass and severe stonework were deeply at odds with John's æsthetic vision, seemed to take on a new elegance and nobility of form in this shrouded light.

He looked round at the familiar sculptures – the lumbering *Neptune,* the anodyne copy of the *David,* the surprisingly small *Judith and Holofernes*, the graceless *Hercules* and the lithe *Perseus,* preening triumphantly under his loggia – all of which he could identify, even date, with precision and felt an elated sense of belonging. How remote the past seemed to him; how palpable the present.

Having paid for his coffee, he got up, wandered next door and entered the familiar premises of his favourite stationer. Not wanting to attract the attention of the staff, he glided stealthily round the busy shop. He fondled some of the paperweights on display, tested

165

a few pens and inspected the vast array of writing-paper, imagining which he would, one day, choose for himself.

Just as he was preparing to leave, however, his wandering gaze was arrested by the sight of a large shagreen-skin volume. He had never liked the binder, filled with loose-leaf sheets, on which Sir Christopher had his address book typed – thought it, in fact, entirely unworthy of him – and immediately decided that the one before him would make the perfect *étrennes*, even though he had had, until that moment, no idea of making such a gift. Having already spent most of the money Sir Christopher had given him for Christmas on two Loden coats – unable to choose between navy blue and the traditional hunter green, John had, without reflecting, bought both – he knew that he ought now to make some serious effort at economy; it had been quite unnecessary to buy *two* coats, but his desires were not to be reasoned with. Like poor King Reignier, John's large style did not agree with *the leanness of his purse*. And so it was that he crept up to the front desk and bought the luxurious book.

He spent the entire weekend, staying up late Saturday and Sunday nights, transcribing Sir Christopher's old address book into the new shagreen one. He did this in his closest approximation to copperplate, in Prussian blue ink he had bought in Basle on a recent trip with Sir Christopher.

On Monday morning, the last day of the year, he reread his efforts with immense pleasure and decided that he would present it as a gift to Sir Christopher whilst they sat before the fire, sipping an ancient Château Peyraguey – a favourite wine of Sir Christopher's and one which, he insisted, was not to be served chilled – on New Year's Eve.

Though John had anticipated, and was ashamed to have anticipated, the snobbish satisfaction that it gave him to write out the names of the many grandees with whom Sir Christopher was associated – the lords and ladies, even the occasional duchess – he had not counted on the wonderful feeling of release that the finished product gave him. As if to underscore this sensation, he got up, went into his bedroom and ferreted out his own address book, stashed away at the back of his clothes press. Returning to his writing-table, he flipped through the little red book, the size of a pocket diary, which he had had since he was sixteen, and almost began to laugh. Far from finding its contents reproachful, as he often had in the past, he now saw the list of names – Professor Isner, fellow graduate students, even the odd acquaintance from school, as well as the myriad relations scattered in and around Providence – as merely superannuated. What had any of these people to do with him? They were incapable of touching him now.

Convinced that he would never need this pitiful little book again, he thought he might as well throw it out but then decided that destruction would provide a more fitting symbol. And yet, as he began joyfully to rip out the first random pages, his eyes fell upon a forgotten annotation that quashed the momentary exaltation he had just experienced. There, under the letter *P*, was written, in a transparently American, parochial-school handwriting – a script that John had long since transformed – the name and address of a Benedictine boarding school, just north of Newport, that he had longed to attend when he was a boy. At the age of thirteen, when he was in the eighth grade, he had written off in secret for a pro-spectus from this school. He knew that his parents would never allow him – on trumped up religious grounds – to attend one of the grand New England boarding schools, but he thought they would acquiesce when it came to a Benedictine Priory *if*, needless to say, he won a scholarship. Here in Florence, all these years later, John could still see – see with repulsive clarity – his father seated at the kitchen table, callously brushing aside the application form that he had solemnly placed before him, as he said, 'You'd better learn to accept your place in life, John. Believe me, you can put on all the airs you like, but you're still going to the same high school as everyone else in this family. The Christian Brothers will be good for you. They'll keep you from getting above yourself.'

Crushed though he had been by his father's rebuke, John dared not to defend himself. Instead, he answered, in his most emotion-ally turbid fashion, that he understood his father's position perfectly well, whilst he sheepishly collected the spurned papers and silently absented himself from the room.

Like many homosexuals, John had learnt, when *very* young, to lie *very* skilfully. Never would he acknowledge what he was attracted to but, rather, feign interest in that which bored him; never would he speak of the longing that choked his heart but, rather, muffle up in his mantle the cries that besieged him. As a child, he harboured the formless fear that his secret – and he knew he had a secret, even before he could name it – would be found out and that he would be severely punished for it, shunned, maybe even killed. In adolescence, his fear was less dramatic but more preponderant. From the age of fourteen on, he thought that, were he ever so foolish as to tell the truth – something that, ironically, he was always being exhorted to do – his parents would, at best, deliver him unto the filthy hands of some incompetent Catholic counsellor who would try to 'cure' him; at worst – and he considered this far from impossible – he imagined that they would have him locked him up in a godforsaken asylum, where he would be plied with drugs and subjected to electroshock therapy.

Most galling of all was that he was sure that his parents would have claimed, and indeed honestly believed, that they had acted out of love. He knew that they would, in fact, be deeply indignant, if he had ever suggested that they did not love him. And yet, John realised quite early on that his parents' so-called 'love' was nothing but a sublimated form of egotism attempting to impose its Manichæan notions of right and wrong on an alien spirit. You cannot love someone whom you refuse to know; and John's parents chose – chose quite consciously – not to know their middle son.

In time, John came to accept, as André Gide had taught him, that it is better to be hated for who you *are* than to be loved for who you are *not*, so that he would eventually cherish the distance he felt from these people with whom he had so little in common. His abjectly conformist father was hostile to all deviation from the norm: he never questioned authority, rigorously subscribed to all social conventions and unblinkingly accepted the religion, education and class assigned to him at birth, expecting his children to do likewise. So unimaginative was his father that he had even taken to running – running right into the ground, John could not fail gloatingly to note – *his* own father's once thriving real-estate business. Though his mother was less overtly opposed to her son's temperament, she was infinitely more judgmental, for, unlike his father, she minded – minded terribly – about the good opinion of others. It was of paramount importance to her that people – even, or perhaps most particularly, people she hardly knew or actively disliked – should think well of her or, ideally, envy her. And in her maniacal pursuit of extramural approbation, she felt compelled to condemn any action that her provincial relations, friends and acquaintances might stigmatise. And so it was that she did not flinch from sacrificing her son's every inclination, every ambition, every longing on the altar of middle-class respectability.

From as far back as he could remember – when he was four, even three, years old – John had been discontented with his surroundings. He longed to be elsewhere, far from his antagonistic brothers – two older, two younger – and his censorious parents. At times, he seriously believed that his destiny had been tampered with by some evil spirit. At about the age of seven or eight, he became mesmerised with tales of changelings and foundlings, wondering if a similar fate might not have befallen him, thus leading him to fantasise that he, appearances to the contrary – for John could not deny that he, of all his brothers, bore the closest physical resemblance to his father – might actually be the proud possessor of beautifully aristocratic blood.

By the time he was twelve or thirteen, this interest had segued into impostors, and the more he delved into the subject, the more was he inclined to sympathise with the interloper, for he really did want to believe that Anna Anderson *was* the Grand Duchess Anastasia and that Perkin Warbeck actually *was* Richard of Shrewsbury, Duke of York. It was not, however, till the summer of 1973, by which time he had just turned fourteen, that the long festering revolt of his spirit colluded with a new (and most unwelcome) mutiny of his body.

In July of 1973, his parents had taken him and his four reluctant brothers on a tour of the grand houses at Newport open to the public. As they drove away, he had let slip that it must be magnificent actually to *live* in such a world. His mother had cut him off abruptly, addressing all those packed into the car, 'John's problem is that he's very easily impressed. He's going to have to get over that or he'll wind up being disappointed by life. People who are easily impressed are followers. You want to be a leader, not a follower. Do you *hear* me,' his mother said in her all too typical tone of hectoring termagant, as she turned round to stare at her son in the back seat, 'when I say you shouldn't be so easily impressed?'

John heard her then, and he still heard her, but he thought then, and he still thought, that he himself was, on the contrary, difficult to impress. Now, he could, of course, see through the sort of vulgar ostentation by which he had been dazzled at the age of fourteen, but he reasoned, and not without justification, that his mother had been annoyed not because her son was awed by the splendour of Newport but because the wonder he voiced clearly implied the dream of a life beyond the limited confines of the family he had been born into. His misery was crowned that afternoon, when, on leaving that fabled summer resort, his father drove north on Aquidneck Island, heedlessly passing right before a set of elaborately worked gates that opened on to five hundred immaculately maintained acres, perched on the edge of Narragansett Bay. There in the distance, John caught his one and only glimpse of the Benedictine Priory he had longed to attend. But sad though the sight of his withheld dream rendered him, it also strengthened his resolve.

That evening, when they got back to Providence, he took the *H* volume of *The World Book Encyclopedia* from the one bookcase in the house and tremulously began to turn its pages. Here, he found seventeen pages on 'Hawaii' (yes, seventeen); seven pages on 'Hobby' (not one of which interested him); four pages on 'Hockey' (which repulsed him); five pages on 'Homemaking' (all the pictures showing women); and ten pages on 'House' (every example being American); but not one single word about the subject on which he sought illumination. The following day, he went to the public library and consulted the *Encyclopædia Britannica*, where he found a long, fear-inducing article on the *H* word that possessed him. Thenceforth, he became a grand master at the art of lying.

As his seemingly interminable youth stretched on and on, the need for secrecy expanded exponentially, but rather than be oppressed by the weight of this accumulation, he felt emboldened by the knowledge of his separateness. A child's vision of his own self-worth is generally assumed to be predicated on his parents' perception of him, but the esteem a child holds for his parents equally determines the extent to which he himself accepts their opinion, and, as the years inched along, John's estimation of his parents diminished, dwindled and finally evaporated altogether, leaving him immune to their incessant reproofs. For a long time, he had simply been embarrassed by them. The vulgarity, the coarseness, the utter lack of chic in his parents appalled him. He had only to recall that day in Newport for him to wince: his skinny father in baggy shorts and white socks; his overweight (soon to be obese) mother in a clinging polyester trouser suit; and his youngest brother – by far the most sympathetic of the four – tearing round The Breakers in a football jersey, emblazoned with the words 'Our Lady of Perpetual Sorrows, '73 Catholic League Champs'. At The Breakers, of all places!

And the more he saw of the world, the more did his distaste for his entire family metamorphose into revulsion. First, it was the *way* they ate that appalled him – pushing their food with their fingers and chewing with their mouths open; then, it was *what* they ate – a profusion of pork products, frozen vegetables reduced to a state of indescribable mushiness and viscid sweets; finally, it was *when* they ate – wineless suppers at six o'clock, occasionally even at half past five, accompanied by the flimsiest of paper napkins, the remains of which (scrunched up!) were left carelessly strewn about the table. By the age of sixteen, he could hardly bear to be seated at table with any member of his family.

But more important, and therefore more liberating, was his realisation of just how pharisæan and delusional his parents were. Surely, it was his father, not himself, who was the 'follower', he who never once dared to stray from the path ordained for him; just as it was his mother, rather than himself, who was 'easily impressed', she who set such store by the opinions of her wide (but pathetically constricted) circle of lady friends. He was convinced that it was precisely because he *did* know his place – knew that his place was elsewhere – that his parents made such desperate attempts to reign in his imagination. 'John likes the *finer* things in life,' his father had often tauntingly said of his adolescent son before a roomful of strangers, not realising that his mockery only further persuaded John of the unbridgeable gap that separated him from the rest of his family.

And yet, when he finally did get away from Providence at the age of eighteen, he did not have the courage to sever all ties. Though he had won a generous scholarship to the University of Chicago – his education cost his parents much less than that of his brothers at local second- (if not third-) rate Catholic colleges – there always seemed to be some small fee to pay or financial-aid form to file, thus keeping him loosely tethered to his parents. Then, when in graduate school in New York, it hardly seemed worth the effort definitively to break off relations, as he only saw his parents two or three times a year. He would sit by silently as his father intoned that AIDS had been sent by God to rid the world of faggots, whilst his mother, pretending to look shocked, would reply that that was not a very 'Christian' thing to say but never fail to add, 'Of course, *they* did bring it on themselves.'

Today, however, as all the old indignities assailed him – just the name of that Benedictine boarding school, which he had been barred from even *applying* to, was enough to set him aquiver – he felt inspired to action, irreversible action. On the verge of hysteria, he began to shred the pages of his old address book, whilst he attacked the red leather cover with a large pair of scissors. He shoved the remains into a manila envelope and then looked out a postcard. On the reverse side of an image of the *Doni Tondo*, he frenziedly wrote to his parents that he would be travelling round Europe for the next several months and that he would be in touch later, once he had established himself somewhere. It was his last direct communication, *ever*, with his family.

☦

Not wanting any trace of his old, cast-off life to remain in his presence, John gathered up the envelope and postcard and slipped out of the apartment. He crossed the Ponte Vecchio, making his way to Piazza della Repubblica, where, with a tremendous sense of liberation, he dropped the card in a postbox and the manila envelope in a soot-stained rubbish bin. As a sort of congratulatory confirmation, he went on to buy a large plate of white truffle sandwiches – small, oval-shaped treasures of *pain brioché*, which could only be had at Procacci in via de' Tornabuoni – to serve this evening with the bottle of old Sauternes. On re-entering Palazzo Vespucci, he ran into the portress, who handed him the morning post, which, directly he was again seated at his writing-table, he began to sort through. The Christmas season had brought with it an influx of cards and letters, in addition to the usual bills, statements and photographs, all of which he began to separate and prepare for answering. He put to one side the only envelope addressed to himself. He read the return address – SAFS, P.O. Box 1329, Lombardy, Illinois

– and shrugged. To him, Lombardy was a region, not a city, and he found the four-letter acronym meaningless. He assumed that it must be something to do with the importunate alumni association at the University of Chicago; he did not stop to think how they could have got his address, as he had completely cut himself off from his undergraduate past since moving to Florence.

When he finished organising Sir Christopher's papers, he turned to the curious missive and thoughtlessly opened the envelope. He extracted a sheet of coarse white paper and read:

Society of Academic Financial Services
P.O. Box 1329
Lombardy, IL 60698-1913

December 21, 1984
A51429-J FORDE
RE: Student Loan from University of Chicago
Account Number: 51429-791-54-9871-A
Loan Type: National Direct Student Loan

Your National Direct Student Loan is past due in the amount of $1,032.76.

As we have been notified that you have not been officially registered in an American Graduate Study Program since the spring term of 1983, the deferment you claimed regarding the repayment of your undergrad-uate Student Loan is declared null and void. Furthermore, you have violated the terms of the contract you signed by not personally notifying us of your change in status.

You are hereby given notice that your Student Loan will be reported to a credit bureau, assigned for collection, or litigated in accordance with the provisions of your promissory note, unless appropriate action is taken within 30 days of the date of this letter.

Additionally, the entire principal balance of $3,6037.90, plus accrued interest, will be accelerated as outlined in the promissory note you signed.

These actions can be avoided by immediately paying the $1,032.76 due on your account. Send your check TODAY.

John's first reaction to this most unwelcome news was indignation at having been sent a letter that contained neither salutation nor valediction. *How dare they write to one in so peremptory a fashion!* he said to himself, trying to imitate Sir Christopher's authority. But no sooner had the disdainful words formed on his lips than he was utterly cowed by the flimsy piece of paper.

After a moment of stunned silence, he scanned the letter again. He assumed that it must have been the head of the Academic Office in New York, who, knowing his address in Florence, had notified the student loan authorities that he was no longer enrolled in graduate school. He could not imagine *how* he ever could have forgotten about such an important – oppressively important – aspect of his past, but he did understand that, whatever the origin of his oversight, he had no time to waste. He would have immediately to ask Sir Christopher for the money. He didn't like – indeed dreaded – doing so, but he could see no alternative. He knew that Sir Christopher could be generous, at times very generous, but such acts of largesse as he was capable of had always to originate with him. And yet, considering how much time and energy he devoted to the older man, John thought that he more than deserved this paltry sum, for, though it was true that he was housed and fed in a luxury such as he had often read of but never actually known, it was equally true that the sporadic remuneration he received was in no way commensurate with his ceaseless efforts.

He decided to ask Sir Christopher that very evening, simply to state his position, after they had sipped a bit of wine, but before he presented his gift of the new address book. And yet, when faced with the task, John balked: the words refused to form on his lips. He rationalised that he had not wanted to spoil their New Year's Eve dinner and that he would broach the subject on the morrow. But when the following day came, and the one after, and the one after that, he still had not found his voice.

Each day of silence made the threats from Lombardy, Illinois seem ever more menacing to John. Visions of collection agencies and litigation officers haunted his nights, whilst awkward pauses and missed opportunities disfigured his days. Finally, on the Sunday, Epiphany, he decided that he could postpone the matter no longer. When they returned from Mass, an unusually long Mass, in Piazza Santissima Annunziata, John installed Sir Christopher in the drawing room with a large stack of the English Sunday papers and went to put the finishing touches on his elaborate luncheon. After he had served the first two courses, but before he brought out the final one, John explained his need for the money in as poised a fashion as he could muster.

'But I just gave you several thousand dollars for Christmas,' Sir Christopher said flintily, interrupting John in mid-sentence.

'Yes, I, uh, know that,' he stammered, 'but this could not have been foreseen. And anyway, I'm not asking you to *give* me the money, just to lend it to me.'

Sir Christopher raised a quizzical eyebrow, forcing John, or at least making him *feel* forced, to justify himself.

'You, uh, you see, I've been promised,' John started to invent, 'an inheritance from my grandmother. You remember, don't you, that I told you, just a month or two ago, that she had died and that I was particularly close to her? It's quite a small inheritance, but it will be more than enough to pay you back when it does come. I should have it within a month or—'

'Why don't you go and get my American chequebook right now?' Sir Christopher said, cutting John off again. 'And then we can get this over with at once.'

John rose from table and did as bidden. Gravely, he laid the chequebook in front of Sir Christopher and withdrew in search of the sweet. Returning with a dish of Virginia Woolf's Burgundy pears, a jug of Devonshire cream and a plate of home-made ginger biscuits, he immediately noticed the cheque at his place. Without examining it, he folded it, slipped it into his pocket and mumbled a few words of thanks.

'Is there *no* sugar?' Sir Christopher asked by way of reply.

'How stupid of one!' John said, tapping his forehead and jumping up.

'Very delicious this looks,' Sir Christopher said when John reappeared with a silver castor. 'And as for the proofs of the book on Botticelli's illustrations for the *Commedia*,' he continued, while liberally sprinkling sugar on the glistening pear, 'I think we should be finished with them as soon as possible. Wednesday, I should say, at the absolute latest. Don't you think that should be...'

†

When John had received his first cheque from Sir Christopher a year and a half ago, he thought it an auspicious omen that it should be drawn on a bank in New York, for the existence of an American account seemed both to promise transition and to forestall complication. What, he had often asked himself, would he have done with an English or Italian cheque? But today, as he stood in the kitchen after lunch and withdrew the new cheque for inspection, he felt sickened by its distinctly American aspect. It was, effectively, made out for one thousand dollars to the order of John Forde, but in the bottom-left corner, where American cheques provide a space marked 'memo', Sir Christopher had printed in large, wobbly letters: *Loan*.

Loan, Loan, LOAN! John shouted to himself in disbelief, as he lurched round the kitchen. *What*, he asked himself, *does a thousand dollars, a mere* one *thousand dollars, represent to Sir Christopher Noble-Nolan? Nothing*, he answered, *nothing at all*. Certainly, it did not equal the price of a pair of Renaissance bellows, and it did not come even close to approaching the value of any number of works of art he owned, and yet it was not the niggardly sum of money, per se, that rankled, but the demeaning position to which he had been reduced. Such pathetic servility utterly eviscerated the love he desperately tried both to show *and* to win.

John had no illusion about the one-sided nature of his obsession, but he did hope that by proving himself useful he would, eventually, become indispensable, and that this indispensability would, in turn, ignite a passion – even a muted passion – in Sir Christopher's heart. Traditionally, it is, of course, the older man, conscious of his spent youth and missed opportunities, who courts the younger one, who inclines himself before him in the hope of provoking but a glimmer of genuine desire in spite of his advanced age; and yet, John knew, such was not their case, leaving him to feel both rebuffed and ashamed that it should be he – he, who was forty-six years younger – who was in relentless pursuit. *Does my youth count for nothing? Or am I to be accused of wanting to exchange bronze for gold?* he asked himself with increasing frequency as he watched the little intimacy that he did still enjoy with Sir Christopher grow ever more limited.

The first time they had passed the afternoon together in Sir Christopher's bedroom, almost a year and a half ago, it was John, at the age of twenty-four, who had said to the then 69-year-old man, with a spontaneous sincerity of which he had not thought himself capable, 'I love you.' But when, thereafter, John had repeated himself, as he often did, so far from eliciting the reciprocal declaration for which he longed, he only rendered Sir Christopher weary, almost exasperated he feared.

Eventually, Sir Christopher took to cloaking whatever emotion he felt in silence; sometimes, he responded by rubbing John's cheek, while other times he simply turned away, depending on his mood – a mood which John could, almost invariably, predict – till one night a few months ago, Sir Christopher had surprised him. After placing a perfectly starched handkerchief in the pocket of Sir Christopher's pyjama jacket, John leant over and, without forethought, kissed the supine figure on the forehead and said, 'Goodnight. I love you.' To which the beloved, with closed eyes and expressionless mouth, replied, 'Yes, of course. But there is no need to *say* it all the time.'

John recoiled but, wounded though he was, could not restrain himself – he felt physically incapable – from all such utterances in future, though he did manage greatly to curtail them. Nor did he want absolutely to dumb his sentiments, for, like the sickly poetess more than a century before him, he felt that to give voice to his deepest emotion, yet once over again, was no mere hollow melody but the *silver iterance* that granted credence to the love in the labyrinth of his soul, a labyrinth which now echoed with the word 'loan', as he scraped the remains of Cumberland sauce from eighteenth-century Tournai plates.

Having protracted the washing-up as long as possible, John sat down at the kitchen table and rapidly polished off the bottle of wine that had remained untouched at luncheon. Though he had hoped the alcohol would drown out the voice of his own demons, as well as the insistently bellicose sound of Christopher's clacking typewriter, he found, when he finally placed himself at his own writing-table, pretending to correct the captions for the forthcoming book on Botticelli's illustrations for the *Divine Comedy*, that he had only managed to implant the warring factions – *clack, clack, clack* versus *loan, loan, loan* – all the more deeply in his throbbing head. Inutilely shifting through a sheaf of photocopied illustrations, he replayed over and over again in his mind each word, each gesture, each silence of his exchange with Sir Christopher. It incensed him most particularly that he should have been reduced to introducing his grandmother into the conversation, less than a week after he had destroyed his address book and, he thought, definitively expunged his family from his life. It was true, as he had claimed at luncheon this afternoon, that he *had* spoken of the death of his maternal grandmother to Sir Christopher some two months ago, but it was perfectly laughable to think that she, the child of Irish immigrant peasants, had anything to bequeath to anyone, let alone to John, her least favourite grandchild.

John could distinctly remember that he had brought up the subject of his grandmother's death, not out of any sense of familial piety, but as a conscious experiment by which to gauge Sir Christopher's reaction. Though he himself knew almost everything possible about the Noble-Nolan family – Sir Christopher sometimes joked, not unpleasantly, that John knew more about his family than he did himself – he was acutely conscious that the Forde family was a complete blank to Sir Christopher. He was sure that, though Sir Christopher knew John was born and raised in Providence, Rhode Island, in a Catholic family, he would have been incapable of situating, in any concrete way, the milieu from which he sprang; he was equally sure that, though Sir Christopher was aware that John had several brothers, he had no idea of exactly how many and was ignorant of all of their Christian names; and he was convinced that, though Sir Christopher did realise that John's parents, both young enough to be his children, were alive, he could not have specified the occupation of either one, having been content to accept John's evasive description of his father as working in 'business' and his mother in 'charity'. And yet, John had from the start, indeed from the very first night he dined with Sir Christopher, been delighted *not* to be obliged to speak about his background. And so it was that he had mentioned, with the most premeditated calculation, but in what he trusted seemed an utterly natural fashion, as the two of them sat reading peacefully in front of the fire one night after dinner at the beginning of November, that his grandmother had died.

'I didn't know you had a grandmother,' Sir Christopher had said, barely looking up from *The Art Bulletin*.

'Yes, my mother's mother. As a child, I was particularly close to her,' John lied. In fact, he had long harboured a distinct aversion to his maternal grandmother, finding her coarse and bigoted, in a stereotypically Irish Catholic fashion, and he was sure that she returned the compliment, never ceasing to make fun of what she called her grandson's 'highfalutin' ways.

'Were you now?' Sir Christopher asked with even less interest.

'She was called Dorothy Knowles Donaldson,' John said, transforming his real grandmother, Dolores Norah O'Donnell, into someone who, he hoped, might impress Sir Christopher. 'She was from an old Providence family, but she was converted when she was a young woman, like your mother, which is why my mother was raised a Catholic.'

'I thought your family was of Irish Catholic origin?' Sir Christopher said in a tone that compounded bewilderment with irritation.

'My father's side of the family, like yours,' John said.

'Right you are,' Sir Christopher maundered, as he looked back at his magazine. 'Now, just when one thought one had seen everything, here is *this*,' Sir Christopher, holding up *The Art Bulletin,* said a few minutes later in a completely altered, forceful tone of voice.

'What's that?' John asked.

'Do look! This perfectly lunatic lady scholar, who has had the effrontery to write on Luca della Robbia, describes the reliefs of the *cantoria* as depicting *male* youths. I mean really, *male* youths! One might just as well speak of *female* lasses.'

'I quite agree,' John said, standing up to peer over Sir Christopher's shoulder, 'that it is quite preposterous – *male* youths – but I can't say that I am totally surprised. It's typical of the perverted jargon that has infected art history in America.'

'*Too* extraordinary, is all one can say,' Sir Christopher exclaimed. 'And tell me,' he continued animatedly, 'can Barbara be a *man's* name in America?'

'Not that I've ever heard. But I suppose *anything* is possible. Why?'

'At the beginning of this number of *The Art Bulletin*, there is a long letter from someone described as the legal counsel to the College Art Association of America, signed by one Barbara Cooke, Esquire.'

179

'Oh that,' John said, glancing at the published letter, 'just means that she is a lawyer. In America, lawyers have long called themselves "Esquire". Why, I have no idea. And now all these ferocious feminists insist on doing the same – totally oblivious are they to the real meaning of the word. And what's worse, these women see nothing in the least ironic about it.'

'*Male* youths indeed.' Sir Christopher laughed heartily. 'Next thing you know, they will be referring to a *male* esquire.'

John smiled and went back to his armchair, realising that, in introducing the subject of *The Art Bulletin*, Sir Christopher had consciously cemented the closure of the conversation about ancestry. Though he had hoped that Sir Christopher might draw some parallel between his own convert mother, Dame Sophia, and John's imagined New England matriarch of a grandmother, he knew in his heart that Sir Christopher never did think of him as having a life prior to his appearance in Palazzo Vespucci. And so, ductile that he be, John let the subject drop.

After he had seen Sir Christopher to bed, he went in search of a plastic rosary that his mother had sent him, along with a short note in which she said she was sure that he would want to have something that had belonged to his grandmother. That November night, he had dumped both the rosary and the letter into the wastepaper basket, just as he had, a few days ago, done with his old address book. But today, Epiphany, the discarded contents of all these wastepaper baskets seemed to be forever flying back in his face and unsettling him.

The next day, he did, however, have the presence of mind to post the cheque, with its humiliating 'Memo', to his account in New York, so that it would clear as soon as possible. And the following week he sent off a cheque to Lombardy, Illinois for $1,032.76, along with a photocopy of the threatening missive but with no letter of his own. The intervening days had not, however, helped to heal the wound to his pride, a wound that seemed, if anything, to fester and suppurate over time. So obsessed did John become with the idea that he must pay back this 'loan' of one thousand dollars, so as to right himself in Sir Christopher's eyes, that he decided to resort to a drastic but, he reasoned, foolproof measure.

From the beginning, he had been struck by the disorder that reigned in Sir Christopher's financial affairs. Before he had taken to typing out Sir Christopher's cheques for him and filing his bank statements, John was surprised to observe that Sir Christopher kept several chequebooks in circulation at once, pouncing on whichever one was at hand, and never bothering to note the amount of the cheque on the counterfoil. And he certainly never attempted anything so banal as balancing his own chequebook: such, John had often bewailed, was the privilege of the rich. But more to the point for his present scheme was the fact that, except for very large sums, such as something that would result from the sale of a work of art, Sir Christopher paid not the slightest attention to what was deposited in any of his accounts. His pension, royalties, lecture fees were, to Christopher Noble-Nolan, just so many meaningless digits printed on never perused monthly statements. *What*, John wondered, *if I were to pay him back, or pretend to pay him back, to give him a cheque for one thousand dollars, claiming that I had finally received the inheritance from my pathetic grandmother – Dorothy Knowles Donaldson indeed! – but then never deposit the actual cheque for him? Would he ever notice?* He figured that, if he could but screw his *courage to the sticking place*, he could not fail.

He devised a plot whereby he would, in the most seemingly innocent manner, present Sir Christopher with the cheque for one thousand dollars, just at the moment when they were going through the morning ritual of the post. He would then produce a stamped, addressed envelope in which to stash his worthless cheque. Meanwhile, he would have prepared another, identical envelope filled with a blank piece of paper, which he would post in front of Sir Christopher's very eyes later that day. He did not see how his scheme could go awry.

He did not like being forced into such a duplicitous rôle, but forced he felt, for the position of grovelling employee would choke him to death. And so, in the hope of restoring himself to what he considered his rightful place of beloved disciple, he decided to go ahead with his contrived plan. Now, he had only to choose – choose most carefully – the date of execution.

✝

On 21 January, a Monday, they were meant to go to Naples – a trip that John had anticipated eagerly. In the year and a half that he had been in Florence, he had not seen nearly so much of Italy as he imagined he would have. Though he realised that he should be grateful to have accompanied Sir Christopher to Bergamo and Milan (again) and Piacenza, not to mention numerous day trips to Prato and Pistoia and Pisa — adventures of which he could have but dreamt a short time ago — he was, nonetheless, conscious that all such travels were rigorously orchestrated round Sir Christopher's work, with never a thought given to what might interest him. The one time they went together to Rome, he had even been told, in all seriousness, that he should concentrate his entire thought on the Sistine Chapel *before* Michelangelo. Naples, which John had long imagined as the last great tourist-free capital of Europe, would now be a first, and as Sir Christopher was to be ensconced in two days of meetings about the restoration of the Triumphal Arch by Francesco Laurana — the ostensible reason for their visit — John assumed that he would have time on his own to explore the eighteenth-century Bourbon extravagances of the city, sites of which Sir Christopher would surely disapprove.

They were scheduled to leave at noon, lunch on the train and arrive in Naples in the late afternoon, spending three nights. John was certain that the morning of their departure would find Sir Christopher seated at his writing-table, reviewing his notes on Botticelli's *Madonna* in the Museo Nazionale di Capodimonte. Having meticulously rehearsed his plan, John tapped on the door of Sir Christopher's study at a quarter past ten that morning, his heart pounding wildly, and walked in.

'Do you have everything you need?' John asked, desperately trying to control his wobbly voice as he approached Sir Christopher.

'It's *too* marvellous what you've done about the Farnese provenance of the Botticelli. Thank you for leaving it out for one. It's so well done, in fact, that I think it can go straight into the catalogue raisonné as it is.'

'I'm glad you approve,' John said, breathing more easily. He had worked with especial diligence on the project, intentionally keeping it aside for this morning, so as to soften up Sir Christopher.

'It's frightfully interesting what you've written about the dispersal of the Farnese collection at the time of the Austrian takeover, when Charles de Bourbon was permitted to remove all the family holdings from Piacenza and Parma — even that marble staircase!

– to Naples. I suppose that old Tommy Tornabuoni's book on the Farnese must have come in rather useful for once.'

'Actually, I found that riddled with errors,' John said, hoping to appeal to Sir Christopher's competitive streak.

'Not surprising, considering that he is incapable of *serious* research.'

'The most useful source was a French book, by someone called Peyre. Though it did take one more than a moment to work out that, when he was writing about "Plaisance", he meant Piacenza.'

Sir Christopher laughed loudly. 'They *are* incorrigible, the French.'

'Hmm.' John smiled, relieved to have succeeded in creating the desired climate. 'Now, the post has arrived miraculously early this morning, and I thought you might just want to go through one or two things before we set off.' Fearing that the caprices of the Italian postal system might jeopardise his scheme, John had put aside several letters from Friday's and Saturday's delivery so as to ensure its execution.

'Anything interesting?' Sir Christopher asked.

'There's a letter from the Bayerische Akademie der Wissenschaften asking you to lecture.'

'I don't suppose that one can very well refuse – not to the Akademie – but I don't know *when* we will find the time,' Sir Christopher said.

'And a letter from your college at Oxford, asking you to dine.'

'That we can decline.'

'Yes, I've already drafted the reply. You just have to sign it. And then, there are a few practical things. First, your yearly membership to the London Library. You said you want to keep that up?'

'Yes, certainly.'

'And then, there's the subscription to *The Burlington* – and jolly expensive it is,' John said.

'And so it is, but there's nothing to be done about that. One would rather die than live without *The Burlington Magazine!*' Sir Christopher Noble-Nolan exclaimed.

'I've typed out those cheques,' John said, breathing deeply. 'You just have to sign them.'

'My, how wonderfully organised you are. Is that all?' Sir Christopher asked.

'There's also some reading material that's arrived – a copy of the *Proceedings of the American Philosophical Society.*'

'How nice,' Sir Christopher said. 'You know, the American

Philosophical Society really is the learned body that one is most proud to be a member of, so distinguished is its history – *much* older than the British Academy, it is.'

'Yes.' John replied nervously, 'We've also received copies of the *New York Review* and the *Gazette des Beaux-Arts,* as well as the *Mitteilungen.* I thought you might want those for the train. And then, last of all,' John said, trying not to tremble, 'there's this, um, you know, this matter of the—' He stopped himself, having lost courage in his plan of deception and, turning round, changed tack and pointed to the picture that hung above the piano. Not forgetting that he had been unable to identify this work on his first visit to Palazzo Vespucci, he said, with false confidence, 'I really do think that that panel of the *Lamentation* is an absolutely autograph Giovanni Agostino da Lodi.'

'Obviously,' Sir Christopher said, 'no one but a blind person, of which there are all too many amongst the art historical clerisy, could doubt its attribution.'

'Obviously,' John repeated the adverb. He was now aware, as he had not been a year and a half ago, that many scholars – not least his former dissertation adviser, Milton Isner – labelled this picture 'school' of Giovanni Agostino da Lodi, but John was prepared to accept the work simply because it hung on the wall of Sir Christopher Noble-Nolan's study. Its *ownership* was, for him, proof of authenticity. 'Yes,' he continued, 'it must be Giovanni Agostino da Lodi, or the Pseudo-Boccaccino, as they used to call him. And now,' having regained a shred of confidence, John said, 'there is just this last matter of the cheque to settle.'

'What cheque is that?' Sir Christopher asked vaguely.

'The one thousand dollars you lent to me. I told you that I would pay you back as soon as I received the money from my grandmother's estate, which I now have,' he said weakly, suddenly overcome with guilt, as he imagined that Sir Christopher was about to refuse the repayment.

'Right you are,' Sir Christopher said, proposing no such refusal.

'You just have to endorse the back,' John said in an eerily calm tone of voice.

'Now where,' Sir Christopher said, 'is an American chequebook, with one of those wretched deposit slips at the back?'

'I've already done it for you. It's in here,' John said, brandishing a stamped, addressed envelope.

'Good,' Sir Christopher said expectantly, extending his right hand.

Confusedly, John handed over the envelope with the deposit slip inside.

'That's all right then,' Sir Christopher said, putting the endorsed cheque inside the envelope. 'I can post it when we arrive at the station.'

Tugging frantically at what was meant to have been the 'replacement' envelope, stashed inside his blazer, John looked on, dumbstruck, as Sir Christopher sealed the other envelope and folded it into the breast pocket of his own coat. In the one and half years he had been with Sir Christopher, John had never known him, not once, to post a letter by himself. And when, an hour later, he watched him drop that white envelope into the metal box at the station of Santa Maria Novella, he found that he had also never known such a visceral, coruscating sensation of hatred to swell up in his own heart.

To his surprise, this raging hatred granted him, at least initially, an unexpected deliverance. Generally, whenever he had been upset, or even just slightly nonplussed, by Sir Christopher's behaviour, John found it almost impossible to concentrate – he did not like to think of the number of times he had pretended to read whilst seated in front of him, wondering all the while what was going on behind that inscrutable façade – but today, with his body literally shaking and his blood rushing furiously, he was astounded to find that he was able to focus all his attention on the copy of *Macbeth* that he had brought along with him.

As he sat there, reading raptly in the fast-moving train, there was a part of him that was aware that he should be fretting about the thousand-dollar cheque that was – unless he came up with some radical solution – most certainly going to bounce, but so outraged did he feel that he willingly let himself be swept up by the story of vaulting ambition and merciless plotting, which he only *thought* he knew well. He even managed to sail his way faultlessly through the good lunch they were served on the train, regaling Sir Christopher with alternate tales of Alice Varrow's indiscretions and of art historical ineptitude, whilst never for a moment losing sight of the betrayal to which he felt he had been subjected, *false face hiding what false heart did know.*

Well before the train approached Naples, Sir Christopher got up, as John knew he would, and planted himself near the door; and John obediently followed suit, piling up the luggage in the passage, so as to block anyone passing before them. Watching Sir Christopher frenziedly twirl and trundle the handle, as they bumped into the station, and open the door before the train came to a full stop, John's hatred redoubled. The overweening impatience, the complete self-absorption, the ruthless determination that John now imputed to Christopher Noble-Nolan all seemed to be completely embodied in this agitated desire to alight from the train, a desire John had seen manifest on every train ride they had ever taken together but which had never before affected him in the same way. Today, he suddenly thought how easy it would be to give Sir Christopher a little shove and send him tumbling out of the still moving train to his death. With just a flick of the hand, he surmised, he could kill him and so put an end to his own poisoned obsession. He was suddenly terrified to admit the depths to which his own hatred could descend, and, in admitting this terror to himself, the strange sense of self-control he had known during the train ride instantly evaporated.

That evening, after they had dined at the *hôtel*, Sir Christopher asked, in a declarative fashion, if, it being such a fine evening, it would not be nice to take a walk after dinner. As they strolled along the via Parthenope, rounding the corner by the port of Santa Lucia, John looked back at the view of Posillipo across to Capri and then over to Vesuvius. He knew that this small strip of coast, which had inspired countless painters and not a few poets, was one of the glories of the civilised world, but, try as he might to let himself be seduced by the incomparable splendour, he could feel nothing. All of his emotions dwelt in Christopher Noble-Nolan, who moved out in front of him, leaning perilously close to the edge of the Lungomare. He was appalled to find himself assailed by the same murderous thoughts that had invaded his mind on the train. *Just the merest tap and I could push him over the edge*, he said to himself. He looked up at the glittering sky and, quoting from his reading of this afternoon, whispered aloud: *Stars, hide your fires! Let not light see my black and deep desires.*

✞

Voltaire, who was rich, wrote that poverty saps courage, but John's financial worries rendered him neither cowardly nor courageous; they simply emboldened him into action, a state which was, otherwise, antithetical to his nature. Whilst wandering inattentively round the museum of Capodimonte, John had resolutely decided that he would steal a small piece of jewellery, something that had belonged either to Sir Christopher's mother, Dame Sophia, or to his brother, Christian – the hiding places of which he knew better than their rightful owner – and that would never, he trusted, be missed. He would then hock said jewel to raise the money necessary to pay off his debt. And roused as he was, he did not hesitate to ferret through Sir Christopher's possessions as soon as they returned to Florence, even before he went about unpacking the bags.

The affairs of Sir Christopher's younger brother – silver hair-brushes, several pairs of cufflinks, studs and a platinum wristwatch – were stored, pell-mell, in the top drawer of the highboy in Sir Christopher's bedroom. John thought that a pair of silver links, set with square-cut diamonds might do nicely for his purposes, though he feared the risk of taking something from Sir Christopher's bedroom, as he imagined that there was the possibility, albeit remote, that their absence might one day be noticed.

The personal effects of Sir Christopher's mother, on the other hand, had the advantage of being scattered in various cupboards and cabinets throughout the apartment. He knew well the contents of a handsome magenta-coloured leather box, embossed with the initials S. N-N., which stood on a shelf in the hall cupboard, but had already decided in advance that anything to be found therein – a sixteenth-century silver and pearl rosary that was *said* to have accompanied Robert Southwell to the scaffold, various decorations and an old (if not actually, as Sir Christopher claimed, Elizabethan) diamond cross, inscribed with the words *Hagia Sophia* on the reverse – were too personal and might be traced back to their source.

As soon as he heard the clack of Sir Christopher's typewriter – for once a reassuring sound – John swept down upon a Flemish ivory-inlaid cabinet in the front hall, removed its central drawer and ran off with it to his own bedroom. Behind the security of a locked door, he extracted a mound of yellowing tissue paper from the drawer, in which was encased a pearl necklace, a sapphire ring and three brooches, all of which he laid out on his bed. He feared that the necklace and ring might be *too* valuable and settled finally on an amethyst and diamond pin as the perfect solution to his problem.

Determinedly, he shoved the object in the pocket of his trousers, but, as he picked up the empty drawer of the ivory cabinet, in which he had intended artfully to redistribute the remaining jewels, he was surprised to hear that it rattled as he handled it. Bewildered, he turned the drawer upside down, only to discover that there was a secret compartment. He slid its trap-like door open and out tumbled a gold pocket watch and chain. Instantly, he assumed – with what luck he could not imagine – that he must have stumbled on the missing gold repeater given to Sir Christopher by Lady Charles Delfington. He clicked open the back panel of the watch and, seeing the initials *LK*, encircled in diamonds – *Leopold Kline*, he said to himself – had his assumption confirmed. Without the slightest hesitation, John replaced the brooch in his pocket with the gold repeater. He then wrapped up the jewels and put the drawer back in place.

That night at dinner he told Sir Christopher that he would have to go to Rome tomorrow for the day to renew his visa – even though he did not have a visa – at the American Embassy.

'Can't that be done at the consulate in Florence?' Sir Christopher asked, vexed.

'I'm afraid not. And it must be done right away. The letter was waiting for me when we got back this afternoon.'

'Well, that's a bore.'

'Yes, it is, but it cannot be helped,' John said firmly.

Having decided that it would be more prudent to sell the watch in Rome than in Florence, John was not to be dissuaded. The following morning he took the six-o'clock train; by half past one, he was lunching in the shadow of the Pantheon, having already sold the watch to a dealer in via del Babuino and wired the money to his account in New York from the American Express office in Piazza di Spagna. Poverty had not sapped *his* courage.

CHAPTER V

The Cost of Discipleship

THROUGHOUT THE WINTER of 1985, John Forde constantly thought of leaving Christopher Noble-Nolan. Though he feared that he had no one and nowhere to leave him *for* – graduate school in New York having been precipitately abandoned and his parents in Rhode Island remorselessly forsaken – he felt incapable of remaining in the suffocating miasma that was his present position. In his bitterness and disappointment, John had convinced himself that Sir Christopher saw him not as his beloved disciple but as an Eckermann, an Eckermann as Sainte-Beuve described him:

> *Of a subservient nature, one of those men who is a born acolyte, and who, supported by a reserve of intelligence and devotion, by a youthful inclination to pious admiration, is destined to become the secretary of a superior being. Such was Nicole for Arnauld, and the Abbé de Langeron for Fénelon...*

But *such* did John Forde not want to be for Christopher Noble-Nolan. He would not, could not, stay if he believed that his gift of discipleship were to be perverted into a mere conduit of utility. And yet he knew, knew well from his reading of the Lutheran pastor martyred on the altar of Nazi baseness – he whom John had discovered (and revered) as a schoolboy, but whose exigent standards left him feeling forever inadequate – that *true* discipleship must be sought again and again, must be asked for: such is the kingly rule, the call at which the disciple leaves his nets. He reproached himself (and Sir Christopher) for having succumbed to cheap grace, that is grace without discipleship, over the costly grace whose treasure lay hidden in the field and for the sake of which one needs forsake all that one has, one's own self above all. And yet, John could not imagine what *more* of himself remained to be sacrificed.

Hiding under the upstairs loggia on one particularly anguished afternoon in early February, whilst Sir Christopher pounded away ferociously at his typewriter in the study below, John stared into the heart of a moiling storm and gave way to desperate brooding. As a haunting view of the blackened Arno valley dangled before him, he recalled the exiled Florentine asking the despised simoniac: *What treasure did our Lord require of St Peter before he delivered the keys unto his keeping? Surely, he asked nothing save, 'Follow me'.* For the very first time, John began to fear that, follow his guide and master though he might, even until the ends of the earth, Sir Christopher would never confide unto him the keys to *his* kingdom.

In the weeks since he had stolen the gold repeater watch, weeks during which he had detected not the slightest flicker of suspicion, John had to acknowledge that Sir Christopher seemed actually to have softened. Not only was he less ready to snap, but he was more prone to thank, showing unsuspected depths of consideration as he did so. One bright winter afternoon, Sir Christopher went so far as to say, 'We really should visit the Protestant Cemetery some day. I don't think you can ever have been there, as it's been closed for so long, and it's just the sort of place that you would like, as you seem to be so taken by all those nineteenth-century literary connexions to Florence.'

'I'd love to see it,' John said, touched, even astonished, that his own interests should be accorded such importance by Sir Christopher. 'I've tried to get in there several times, but always to no avail. I read in the *Nazione* this morning that it has just reopened after a long restoration.'

'So did I. Why,' Sir Christopher asked even more unexpectedly, 'don't we just drop everything and go now? It's such a beautiful, crisp winter day, and tea can surely wait.'

Only too happy to comply, John rang up for a taxi, and off they sped to Piazzale Donatello on the other side of the river in search of the verdant oval-shaped island of a cemetery, marooned in a sea of swirling traffic.

By long, strictly observed tradition, all non-Catholics – Protestants, Orthodox and Jews alike – who died in Florence were obliged to be buried in Livorno, over one hundred kilometres distant – their bodies often decomposing on the way, before the earth could receive them. In 1827, however, the Swiss Evangelical Reformed Church purchased a plot of land outside the gate of the now destroyed porta a Pinti from Leopold II, Grand Duke of Tuscany, in order to consecrate a burial site welcoming those of all confessions; the cemetery created there remained the preferred resting place of almost all foreigners born outside of the Church until 1877, when new law forbade the burial of any *body* within the city limits. As the various inscriptions – in Greek, Russian, Danish, Swedish, Italian, French, German, Romansh and, above all, English – attest, a true spirit of ecumenism reigned for half a century on this grassy knoll, but it was the English and American Protestants who largely predominated. Hence, its Italian appellation, '*Cimitero degli Inglesi*' or '*Cimitero degli Protestanti*'. Sir Christopher greatly preferred the latter toponym, as, so he liked to point out, English Catholics *had* been buried within the sacred precincts of Florence. Thus it was, as he tugged on an old-fashioned metal bell pull, that John said smilingly, 'You can't imagine how I've wanted to visit the Protestant Cemetery.'

They passed through a rusted iron gate, paid the modest entrance fee to the oscitant caretaker and stepped inside the marble wilderness. Side by side, they walked up a steep allée, framed by waist-high boxwood, toward the central mound, without seeing another soul. The presiding spirit of desolation – for there was precious little evidence of the '*restauro*' touted up in the newspaper – was, if anything, enhanced by the cacophonous din of the persistent motor traffic churning round this abandoned plot, a forsaken oasis of loftier aspirations in the midst of a prosaically flattened world. Like most visitors, they were instinctively drawn to the grave of this cemetery's most famous occupant, so famous, indeed, that only her initials, EBB, were inscribed on her tomb.

'It was designed by Lord Leighton,' John said.

'It looks it too,' Sir Christopher said disdainfully.

'I admit,' John said, surveying the ungainly grey-white sarcophagus, incongruously plunked down on six squat, pseudo-Romanesque columns, 'that it *is* rather ill-proportioned, but still she was so important to Italy in general, and Florence in particular, in the nineteenth century that one really cannot begrudge her its fastuousness.'

'Yes, it is true that she was important, or, to be more exact, *represented* something important to the Italian politics of unification, but all that nonsense about table-turning spiritualism, I mean really, and as a poetess, well, Mamma,' Sir Christopher said with the confidence of a lawyer brandishing an incontrovertible piece of evidence, 'never thought much of her.'

'I once read,' John persisted, as he would not have dared to do even a few months ago, 'that Emily Dickinson kept a photo of this tomb in her bedroom at Amherst, Massachusetts. On it, she had inscribed a line from *Aurora Leigh*: "The soul selects his own society",' John said, intentionally inverting the pronoun.

'That *is* rather nice, I must admit, but still, given a choice between the two poetesses, I would pick Emily Dickinson any day of the week. And are not the wild cyclamen lovely?' Sir Christopher asked, pointing to a mauve carpet of flowers that was meant to lead them on their way, far from the sickly spiritualist.

'As you're so keen on Emily Dickinson,' John said, 'I assume that you won't mind if we look out some of my compatriots, those happy few who interest one.'

'No, not at all,' Sir Christopher said good-naturedly, extending his arm for John to guide him down a slope. 'Whom were you thinking of?'

'I'd particularly like to find the tomb of Henry Adams's sister, Louisa, who's meant to be buried here someplace. There's an incredibly moving chapter in *The Education*, called "Chaos", in which he describes the disquieting effect of her death on him.'

'That doesn't sound very healthy.'

'It can't,' John insisted, 'be any less "healthy" than Adams never having mentioned, not even once, the name of his dead wife in his autobiography.'

'Did Adams's wife do anything *worth* mentioning?' Sir Christopher asked.

'She was an amateur photographer of distinction, whom the feminists now puff up. She committed suicide by swallowing the potassium cyanide that she used to develop her photos.'

'Jolly well *right*, Adams sounds, never to have mentioned her,' Sir Christopher said firmly.

'Why don't we move on to the sculptor Hiram Powers,' John

asked, as a way of changing the subject. 'I believe that he's right over here. Luckily I did mug up on this place a few weeks ago at the Gabinetto Vieusseux.'

'Oh look,' Sir Christopher said, stopping abruptly, 'here's Mrs Trollope. Mamma was quite keen on her.'

'She must have been rather terrifying, Mrs Trollope,' John said.

'Quite,' Sir Christopher said with a sly smile.

'And that's her daughter-in-law, Theodosia, next to her. I only know of her,' John explained, 'because she is meant to have been the model for Miriam in *The Marble Faun*. And there, just to the right, that's Hiram Powers.'

After they surveyed this grave, they turned round, traversed the central allée and sought out the tombstones of the sculptor's three children – who had died at, respectively, ages five, eight and seventeen – all of which he had carved himself. *How, in the face of such tragedy*, John asked himself *did Powers find the fortitude to carry out this work?* But then, even if the circumstances had been propitious, perhaps especially if they had been so, John would have posed the same question.

Happily, they wandered round a decaying maze of obelisks, sarcophagi, columns, cinerary urns, busts, cenotaphs, globes and crosses, stopping to inspect whatever monument caught their attention. Sir Christopher seemed content to follow John's lead and joined him in deciphering any number of nearly effaced inscriptions. Though there were several memorials to people from Philadelphia, and a few to those from Baltimore or New York, the vast majority of the Americans interred here were from New England, inspiration to not a little appropriation, and to a great deal of pride, in John's breast. Most of his own ancestors had not even arrived in America by the time these venerable (if now mostly forgotten) New Englanders had gone to their reward, but John still sought to construe a bond of spirit and sensibility between himself and these departed souls – a kinship that overrode mere consanguinity. Above all, he hoped that Sir Christopher viewed him as squarely belonging amidst this distinguished company.

'Oh, do look!' John exclaimed delightedly. 'Here's someone from Providence.' Gravely, he read aloud:

Roger Williams Rivington Pyne
Born at Williams House
Providence, Rhode Island
29 May 1859
Died at Villa Grifoni
Florence
23 June 1872
Beloved only child of
Roger Williams Pyne and Charlotte Rivington Pyne

'For what thou art is mine;
Our state cannot be sever'd, we are one,
One flesh; to lose thee were to lose myself.'

He started to repeat the quotation but then stopped, swallowing the lump in his throat. Obviously, John could not *but* notice that this boy had been born exactly one hundred years before himself, nor that he had died on the Vigil of the Baptist. And though John was not above devising some convoluted connexion between himself and the dead child whom he had never before heard of, such sorrow as surged up in him – and it was very real sorrow – was not a manifestation of retrospective grief for the death of an unknown thirteen-year-old boy, but, rather, the product of his own prevailing sense of discordance. Directly he read the epitaph, he conjured up a vivid picture of a frail, languidly handsome boy, with alabaster skin and auburn-coloured hair. To be such a boy – scion of wealth, status, beauty, intelligence – to be the offspring of civilised parents, parents who would install one in a Renaissance villa on the slopes of Arcetri and surround one (as John was sure they had) with the finest tutors, parents who would think to inscribe one's tomb with sonorously mournful Miltonic blank verse, was for John the very stuff of dreams. Choking back tears, he said, 'Shall we move on to the next section?'

'Does that mean,' Sir Christopher, not budging and staring searchingly at John, asked, 'that the poor boy is a descendant of Roger Williams, the Roger Williams you mentioned not long ago as having taken Hebrew lessons from Milton at Cambridge?'

'I should think he must be. A direct descendant, I would say.

But why do you say *poor* boy?' John could not help himself from asking, for he was overwhelmed by the knowledge that he would honestly have preferred to have been that privileged boy (dead at thirteen) than himself (he, the pilferer of gold repeater watches; he the eschewer of his own past), alive and well at twenty-five.

'Well, he did die at, what age was it?' Sir Christopher asked.

'Thirteen, um, I make it,' John said softly. Attempting to pull himself together, he turned to Sir Christopher and continued, 'I suppose that we had better be about it, as you know how suddenly the night can fall at this time of year. I rather despair of ever finding Henry Adams's sister. I wish I could remember her married name. I think it forms part of the "Philadelphia Rosary" – Rittenhouse or Hollingsworth or Logan or Biddle, something like that – but even so, one would have thought that the name Adams would feature prominently on the headstone. Anyway, there's just one other American whom I'm particularly keen to find, and I know that he is in quite a different section, in the upper right, near the Russians. I guess they couldn't fit him in here.'

'Who's that?' Sir Christopher asked.

'Well, I don't want you to think,' John said, as he resolutely led Sir Christopher away from the shrine to his now beloved Roger Williams Rivington Pyne, 'that all of these Prō-TEST-ənts have driven one round the bend, but there is one minister – Unitarian, if you please! – who is of particular interest to me. I doubt you would ever have heard of him: he's called Theodore Parker. Emerson described him – very unfairly described him, I dare say – as the Savonarola of the Transcendentalist movement. I once wrote a paper on him for an undergraduate English class I took called "The Heart of New England".'

Normally, John would have found someone like Theodore Parker – he is recorded to have said that he would rather be 'such a great man as Benjamin Franklin than a Michelangelo' – deeply antipathetic, a philistine with a social conscience, who preferred the coarse basics of shelter and nourishment to the fine arts of transformation and redemption. But he knew that he had stumbled on his *âme soeur* when he read that this same figure asserted:

Every man has at times in his mind the ideal of what he should be, but is not. The ideal may be high and complete or it may be low and insufficient; yet in all men, that really seek to improve, it is better than the actual character. Perhaps no one is satisfied with himself...

And the fusion he felt with Theodore Parker was all the more strong on account of the dissimilarity in their natures.

'But I *do* know who Theodore Parker was,' Sir Christopher said. 'Wasn't he born at Lexington, Massachusetts?'

'You never cease to surprise one,' John said.

'You mustn't forget that one spent several summers as a boy at Manchester-by-the-Sea, soaking up the local atmosphere. Back in those days, when my father was military attaché to the embassy, all of Washington used to decamp to the North Shore in summer.'

'No, I don't forget,' John said. 'Anyway, let's go over here,' he continued, as they threaded their way through a throng of opulent Russians and a smattering of impoverished Greeks till they found the lone testimonial to puritan conscience amidst a field of alien Orthodox corn.

'There he is. Just as I remembered,' Sir Christopher said proudly, 'he *was* born at Lexington, Massachusetts. In – what year was it?'

'1810 it says. He died here, in Florence, in 1860. Not quite ~~forty~~ fifty years old,' John said.

'Rather moving, that inscription is: *His name is engraved in marble / His virtues in the hearts of those he / Helped to free from slavery / And superstition*,' Sir Christopher read aloud.

'Yes, it is,' John agreed. 'You know that when Frederick Douglass first arrived in Florence he came direct from the train station to the cemetery to pay homage at this tomb.'

'Frederick *who*?'

'Douglass,' John repeated the name. 'He was an escaped slave who sought sanctuary in New England and wrote a celebrated autobiography.'

'Now that is *not* the sort of atmosphere one soaked up at Manchester-by-the-Sea,' Sir Christopher said, proud of his ignorance.

'The headstone, you can see, is rather fine,' John replied, refusing to acknowledge the quip. 'It was carved by William Wetmore Story, the sculptor about whom Henry James wrote that two-volume study.'

'You don't have to tell me about *that* book,' Sir Christopher broke in. 'My brother wrote an endless review of a reprint of it.'

'*Really*? Where did he publish that?' John asked, undone by his own curiosity.

'In the *TLS*, back in the days when the reviews, there, were still anonymous.'

'I am going to have to make a proper inventory of all those anonymous reviews,' John said, forgetting his own plot of departure. 'But still,' he said, resuming character, 'you must admit that it is a rather begrudging memoir on the part of Henry James.'

'I don't exactly know what you mean by *begrudging*, though I can tell you that I had to wade through both those volumes, explaining to Crystal all about Palazzo Barberini, Lago di Vallombrosa, the villas of Siena and the frescoes of Signorelli. You see, Crystal knew little, in general, about Italy and nothing, in particular, about works of art.'

'What I mean by *begrudging*,' John said, overlooking the reference to Sir Christopher's brother, upon which, in other circumstances, he would have pounced, 'is that, after nearly six hundred pages and two volumes of padded digression, old Henry dismisses poor Story's entire career, his slavish devotion to his art, as but "a beautiful sacrifice to a noble mistake". Now *that* is what I call begrudging, even *méchant*.'

'I must say that I wouldn't much like to have *my* career reduced to such a summation,' Sir Christopher said with a smile.

'Hmm,' John said noncommittally, thinking all the while that, much as he himself professed to revere 'The Master', he felt greater kinship to the obscure Unitarian preacher upon whose worm-devoured remains he now trod. 'I suppose,' he continued, 'we should wend our way through the English section, back toward the gate. I believe,' he said, pointing in the distance, 'that the sculpture of that hulking woman on her knees is Mrs Landor, lamenting the death of her son, not of her husband, whom she couldn't abide. Of course, he was known to be quite a difficult old thing, Landor.'

'But then, *some* people merit being difficult,' Sir Christopher said slyly.

John didn't ask *which* people, as he thought was expected of him, but said, 'Here's someone called Sir Grenville Winthrop, 9th Bart, 1768–1829.'

'Doesn't mean anything to one,' Sir Christopher said.

'There was an important American collector,' John said, 'before the war, called Grenville Winthrop, a direct descendant of *the* John Winthrop.'

'But how extraordinary! I met him, Grenville Winthrop. Papa arranged for one to be taken round his collection in New York when I was about twelve or thirteen. His house, right near the Metropolitan Museum – East 80th Street or 81st Street – was absolutely chock-a-block, with everything from ancient Chinese bronzes and pre-Columbian gold to post-Impressionists. Not many Italian pictures, but still the congeries of Ingres and Blake were quite impressive. Obviously, there was no comparison between his collection and Mr Mellon's in Washington. But then, it was a few years later that one saw that, right after he had purchased the pictures from the Hermitage, so that the effect was positively colossal. I remember that, with Mr Mellon, one had to excuse oneself and run off to the loo. One was made quite sick, literally sick, by such a dense conglomeration of masterpieces in a private collection. One had never seen anything like it – never *has* again, in fact. I believe that the Mellons tried to convince Grenville Winthrop to bequeath his collection to the nascent Gallery in Washington, but that he would have nothing to do with it. He left everything, every last object, to the Fogg, disinheriting his two daughters.'

'True enough,' John said briskly, regretting that the conversation should have turned to the benefaction of university museums, 'but it mustn't be forgotten that *both* the poor old man's daughters had eloped the same night, one marrying his chauffeur and the other marrying his electrician. It apparently was on the front page of the *New York Times*. It was really more than Mr Winthrop – a Lambert Strether figure, if ever there be one – could take. That's why he didn't leave either of his daughters a thing from his precious collection – not to mention,' he added pointedly, 'the fact that he knew that they were both heiresses in their own right from a trust fund on their mother's side.'

'Well, I suppose that Harvard, at least, was glad that the two little hoydens had run off,' Sir Christopher said with a laugh. 'All this talk of bequests reminds me that I want to add another codicil to my will. Don't let one forget.'

Unmoved by the promise of another mere *codicil*, John mechanically nodded assent. Looking at the nearest tomb, he said with unnatural authority, 'Here's Vieusseux himself. It's extraordinary to think of the number of great writers who passed through the doors of the Gabinetto Vieusseux in Florence to borrow books and read the foreign newspapers – Heine, Stendhal, Fenimore Cooper and, above all, Dostoevsky.'

He then turned his attention to an imposing sarcophagus and began to read aloud: '*Charlotte Maria (Keppel) Bowes-Lyon, Countess of Strathmore and Kinghorne, Baroness Glamis, 1826–1854.* I imagine she must be an ancestress of the Queen Mother's.'

'Certainly. But it's pronounced *Glams*,' Sir Christopher said.

'What?' John asked warily.

'*Glams*, just one syllable. It really has to be pronounced that way because of Shakespeare: *Glamis thou art, and Cawdor; and shalt be / What thou art promis'd.*'

And what exactly am I promised? John asked himself bitterly. Aloud, he said, 'Yes, of course. And now, I really do think we should be getting back, as the sun is starting to go down.'

'I suppose,' Sir Christopher said reluctantly, as they continued slowly to roam toward the gate. 'But it really has been a most enjoyable afternoon. And I don't know anyone else with whom I'd have rather seen all this.

'Now *that*,' he stopped in his tracks before a sombre stele and said, 'is a poet worth reading.'

'I am afraid that I never have,' John said.

'Never read Clough? Never read *Clough*? Oh, but you must put that right!'

John felt a pang of relief that he had refrained from pronouncing, or rather mispronouncing, the poet's name, for he had no idea that one said, as Sir Christopher had just done twice in a row, 'Cluff'. He had always assumed that the poet's name was pronounced to rhyme with 'plough'.

He knew that he shouldn't mind so terribly about being corrected, but mind he desperately did, for he lived in mortal dread of appearing a fool to the one whose good opinion mattered to him above all others. The irony of the situation was brought forcibly home to him, just a few days ago, when, waiting for Sir Christopher to go through the post, John idly took off the shelf a small olive-coloured volume, *Early Florentine Architecture and Decoration*. Though he had filed this book himself, he had never before looked inside it. That day, he opened it and read on the flyleaf: 'To Christopher Noble-Nolan, the youngest and most promising scholar of Florentine art I know. With warm wishes from the author, Edgar W. Anthony. Manchester-by-the-Sea, August 1927'.

Turning round to Sir Christopher at his writing-table, he had said, as if visited by a miraculous apparition, 'I didn't know this book on early Florentine architecture was inscribed to you by the author. Goodness, you hadn't yet turned fourteen that summer when he gave it you. Still thirteen, you were.'

'I quite forgot about that. Do give it one.' Sir Christopher extended his hand.

'Who exactly was Edgar W. Anthony?' John asked, intentionally suppressing the *h* in imitation of Sir Christopher's usual pronunciation of the Christian name – one of his own many middle names.

'It's pronounced "Ant<u>h</u>-ə-ny". I quite clearly remember him correcting one as a boy.'

'Oh,' John whispered apologetically, as he fell into a brown study. He felt suddenly besieged by the gaping disparity between the thirteen-year-old Christopher Noble-Nolan – he, the dweller of North Shore summers; he, the recipient of art-historical books inscribed by the author; he, the visitor to celebrated private collections – and the thirteen-year-old John Forde – he, the mower of lawns in Providence, Rhode Island; he, the unwilling participant in Little League baseball games; he, the petrified guardian of his own unvoiced secrets. And yet, even more troubling to think of was the contrast between the 25-year-old Christopher Noble-Nolan, who had already published two highly respected monographs, and the 25-year-old John Forde, who had published nothing, not even a book review, for John could blame this adult divergence on no one but himself.

'He was a sort of gentleman-scholar of the old school, Mr Anthony,' Sir Christopher went on explaining, utterly insensitive to John's chagrin. 'And very charming he was. He lived with his mother in a beautiful eighteenth-century house at Manchester-by-the-Sea. Frightfully nice, his inscription is. One had forgotten all about it.'

John, on the other hand, was sure never to forget about it. Certainly not today, as he stood in the Protestant Cemetery and stared at the memorial to the poet whom he had already decided to dislike. *Snuff Clough!* he said to himself, vowing that he would definitively and irrevocably leave Florence, set off on his own, before Easter.

'I suppose the *Amours de Voyage* is the most celebrated of Clough's poems,' Sir Christopher said, returning to the unwanted subject once they had settled into the back of a taxi, 'but the one I really remember being struck by is called "Easter Day, Naples, 1849". Of course, one doesn't believe a word of it – it's all a lot of heretical poppycock – but it is, poetically speaking, superb.'

'I'll have a look at it, though I don't recall any volume of Clough in the house,' John said, staring out the window and trying not to give undue emphasis to the pronunciation of the poet's name.

'And speaking of Naples,' Sir Christopher went on, 'what would you say if we went back there? That last visit was so unsatisfactory.'

'Unsatisfactory?' John asked flatly, thinking all the while that 'devastating' might be a more fitting adjective to describe those days of turmoil, starting with their departure from the station in Florence, when he had watched, horror-struck, as Sir Christopher posted the cheque himself. Just the *thought* of Naples unsettled him. It was, to him, pitiable that, in spite of the fevered anticipation in which he had cloaked that visit, he could remember but one single picture from the gallery at Capodimonte. He might just as well never have seen all those sublimely important works of art – the Simone Martini, the Masolino, the Botticelli, the Bellini, the Titians – that he had come in search of. They constituted nothing but a tremendous blur to him. The only work that John could recall with *any* vividness was a, to him, erotically charged double portrait by an obscure counter-Mannerist artist, depicting a white-bearded man at a drafting table, tenderly guiding the hand of a handsome youth. In many ways, the picture represented, to John, the polar opposite of his own relation to Sir Christopher, for it was painfully obvious, in the portrait, that the elegantly dressed young man was of aristocratic status, whilst the older one – presumably a professional architect – was employed to give instruction. With Sir Christopher locked away in meetings, John had stared for hours at this picture, vainly hoping to appropriate for himself the confidence and allure that the young nobleman embodied. The mere mention of Naples brought the picture, and his own failed efforts, menacingly back to life.

'Well, yes, *unsatisfactory*,' Sir Christopher explained, 'in that all one's time was taken up with meetings about the Triumphal Arch, so that one was hardly able to study the Botticelli. And now that one is reviewing that dreadfully vulgar book on Titian by Neville Pounder, one would really like to go over all those Farnese pictures again.'

'When did you want to go?' John asked.

'Ash Wednesday is next week, isn't it?'

'Yes,' John said.

'Well, as we've agreed that all of Lent would be devoted to the page proofs of the Botticelli monograph, I don't see how we can go before Easter. But we really must plan on it sometime.'

'Hmm,' John said vaguely, as the car pulled up in front of Palazzo Vespucci.

Once he had prepared tea for Sir Christopher, he went to his own study, sat down at his writing-table and flipped furiously through his pocket diary, wondering what day *before* Easter, which fell in the first week of April this year, would provide the fateful moment for his departure. Sir Christopher might, John thought, make as many allusions as he liked to further changes in his will, he might show him any depths of unsuspected affection, as he had this afternoon in the cemetery, but no second codicil, no unfurrowed brow could alter the fact that the 'loan' had been made, the watch stolen, the trust shattered. His rôle had been irrecoverably compromised, his desire indelibly stamped in humiliation. *After such knowledge, what forgiveness?* he quoted to himself. He must act.

In the coming weeks, he had occasionally gone through the motions of preparing his departure, stacking piles of clothes and books and papers on his bed, sometimes even stowing them away in suitcases, only to unpack everything the next day. At such moments, usually in the early hours of the morning, he would stand in the centre of his bedroom, much the largest room he had ever occupied in his life, and gaze longingly at its decoration – the Empire *lit à traversin*, whose ends tapered off into elegant swans; the red chalk Sienese drawings; the eighteenth-century Roman landscape; the

Flemish ivory crucifix; the oak dresser; the fine large Turkoman carpet – and admit honestly how achingly difficult it would be to separate himself from these surroundings, to go out into the world with nothing but the clothes on his back.

And yet, the greatest wrench would not be material, for the mere idea of willingly separating himself from Sir Christopher rendered him physically ill. He quivered. His insides twisted round. His heart pounded with an insistence he had not thought possible. But still, he did *think* of leaving, invoking the Bishop of Hippo to ask where his heart could find refuge from itself, where he might go, yet leave himself behind. Was there any place where he should not be prey to himself? No, he knew all too well, there was, for him, no Carthage to which he might decamp.

Thus it was that he stood forlornly by and, with a sense of desperate helplessness, watched Lent mercilessly exfoliate: Passion Sunday rolled into Palm Sunday, and Easter Day itself drifted by under an evanescent cloud of but fruitless intention, so that he was now, near the end of April, no closer to action than he had been, when, in the middle of February, he stood in the gloaming of the Protestant cemetery and swore an oath of imminent departure.

☩

Unfortunately for John, Sir Christopher kept his promise about planning a return visit to Naples; fortunately for John, he was spared – through no effort of his own – such a harrowing reprise. On the second Sunday after Easter, one week after the Botticelli proofs had been despatched to London, John found Sir Christopher unconscious in his bed. As on all servantless Sundays, John prepared their breakfast of grapefruit juice, Lapsang, *frutta fresca*, grilled Tuscan bread, marmalade and butter – a great deal of the latter, as Sir Christopher generously slathered *both* sides of his toast, except during Lent, when, as a special sacrifice, he buttered but one side.

This morning, as it seemed a particularly glorious spring day, John had taken the unusual (and time-consuming) decision to bring the breakfast things up to the loggia, so that he was relieved when Sir Christopher failed to appear, with his usual Kantian precision, at a quarter past eight. At half past, he listened at the door but could make out nothing. At quarter to nine, he knocked on the door and went in. He found Sir Christopher sprawled out in a strange position, with the bedclothes twisted uncomfortably tight round him. He could hear Sir Christopher breathing loudly, but, when he bent forward and tried to rouse him, he got no response. He then walked cautiously round and, from every angle, inspected this body that he knew so well. Standing at the foot of the bed and looking at the hunched-up figure, he was compellingly reminded of Mantegna's foreshortened *Christ* in the Brera, the thought of which made him smile, as he was sure that Sir Christopher would be pleased by the allusion.

He was struck that, for the first time in the nearly two years they had known each other, the reins of power were reversed. Sir Christopher, who had been to him the see of all knowledge, the vortex of all emotion, was now utterly in his thrall. John could, if he wanted, do nothing. It was a Sunday. No one would know. He could even, if he so chose, smother him – the most difficult method of murder to detect, or so Sir Christopher had not long ago told him, as he looked up from a particularly gory thriller – or he could save his life, render Sir Christopher forever indebted to him.

The realisation of his own power so terrified John that he immediately ran to the front hall and telephoned Dr Werner, a Swiss physician who seemed to look after all the foreign residents of Florence – at least all the well-off ones. When he got no reply, he then rang up the *pronto soccorso* and arranged to have Sir Christopher taken by ambulance to the public hospital of Sant'Egidio. Once he finally got on to Dr Werner in person, later in the afternoon, he arranged to have Sir Christopher transferred to a private clinic in via Cherubini, where he woke from the coma. The following morning Dr Werner explained to both of them that the situation, though serious, could be controlled.

'There is a problem with the liver,' Dr Werner said in his flawless English. 'It's not cirrhosis, and it's certainly not cancer. Just a minor form of sclerosis of the liver which, with medicine and diet, can be controlled. It's called hypoalbuminemia, but we needn't worry too much about the technical terminology. You should just realise that it was a chemical imbalance of the liver that pushed you into the coma. For now, you will need a daily drip of albumin, though that should soon be reduced to once a week. But the most important thing is really rest and diet – no salt or alcohol, above all. And luckily for you, you have your devoted secretary, John, to look after you. He helped to save your life, you know.'

'I do indeed,' Sir Christopher said in a disorientated voice.

John spent the rest of that week in a flurry of activity, trying to smooth over Sir Christopher's stay in the clinic. From home, he brought dressing gowns and monogrammed handkerchiefs and silver hairbrushes, whilst, from London, he ordered a luxurious assortment of nightshirts, to which Sir Christopher thenceforth swore complete allegiance. He covered a hospital table with a piece of eighteenth-century Lucchese velvet, on which he displayed Renaissance plaquettes, gold snuffboxes and jade amulets. He traversed Florence in search of books and scent and forbidden delicacies. And he imported every meal, serving it on the best china and silver from Palazzo Vespucci. In the hours when he was not running errands, he simply sat with Sir Christopher, fending off visitors, whilst self-consciously reading Jean-Jacques's *Confessions*. Once he had conferred with the doctors and established the exact dosage of the medicines, his main concern was to find a sympathetic confessor.

Though Sir Christopher was strictly observant in matters liturgical, he *never*, not even at Easter, communicated. Naturally, John imitated Sir Christopher in this matter. As a child, John had, like the rest of the congregation in Providence, unthinkingly glided up to the altar-rail every Sunday; *not* to have done so would have called attention to himself, and this he would never have risked. Though the adolescent John Forde dreaded eternal damnation for receiving the Holy Sacrament in a state of mortal sin – and he had no doubt that he was so condemned, not by any specific action of his own but by his very nature – he feared, even more, to have his shameful secret revealed, and so, for years, did he choke down that, to him, far from insipid little wafer, at *least* once a week.

By the time he had gone away to university, his corrosive fear had largely metamorphosed into disdainful ambition, but he still continued to communicate regularly, only now it was sacrament as symbol rather than reproof. He might never have given the transubstantial doctrines much more thought, had he not been made to feel so intensely Sir Christopher's disapprobation for anyone who failed to sense the gravity of the matter. And so, when he saw that unconscious body lying on the bed, he was overcome by a paroxysm of responsibility. He did not want to be held accountable for the state of Sir Christopher's immortal soul: he must pave the way for him to repent and communicate before dying, even if this meant, as he was sure it would, a formal end to their intimacy – their now exceedingly rare intimacy. He was, therefore, reassured to have made contact, through the good agency of Antonia Vespucci, with a kindly old Irish Jesuit called Father Hennessy. And his conscience was set even more at ease to learn that Sir Christopher appeared positively delighted by the idea that the priest should come to hear his confession in the clinic. Thereafter, Sir Christopher was to communicate every Sunday. In this *one* instance, the disciple did not follow his master.

John did not, however, find it difficult to define the religious attachment he felt to the Roman Catholic Church. To him, the acceptance or rejection of a greater being (and its attendant doctrine) was not simply the result of man's reasoning but the logical outcome of the whole impression the world had made upon him. He found it more poetic and, therefore, more aristocratic to be *croyant*, and so he allied himself to the theists. Princes of the Church, Brahmins, High Priests, the Chosen People were all, to him, reassuring indices of grandeur in a banal world. He infinitely preferred the ornate mystery of a Gerard Manley Hopkins to the plebeian starkness of an Arthur Hugh Clough, the *Sonnets of Desolation* to *The Bothie of Tober-na-Vuolich*.

His *spiritual* belief in the Church was, on the other hand, more resistant to codification. The only convincing explanation he had ever come across was to be found in the tortured meditations of the *janséniste* of Port-Royal des Champs, who wrote of Catholicism:

No other religion has ever proposed that her adherents should hate themselves. No other religion can, therefore, please those who both hate themselves and desire to love another unreservedly. Thus would such as those, even if they had never heard of the religion of a humiliated God, embrace it forthwith.

And so did John believe that Pascal alone had understood the devotion he felt both to Christ and to Sir Christopher. In these words he understood the truth of the Fall and the Redemption, embodied in the contradictions of human nature – the turpitude of man's actions contrasted with the loftiness of his aspirations; the temptation to let someone die coexisting with the desire to lead him to grace.

John could not, of course, ask Sir Christopher, ask him outright, about his encounter with absolution at the hands of Father Hennessy, but he did want to allude to it.

'That volume of Clough,' he began carefully, as he sat in Sir Christopher's room at the clinic the day after the priest's visit, 'the one I ordered ages ago from Heywood Hill, finally turned up. For once, I must say that I simply cannot imagine *what* you were thinking of.'

'Oh really?' Sir Christopher, still subdued, asked.

'Yes. Naturally, I didn't bother with that long poem with the unpronounceable Scotch title, not when I read in the introduction that it was meant to be about a Highland socialist reading party, during which the protagonist falls hopelessly in love with a local proletarian girl – symbol of the earth, or some such nonsense. I did, however, dip into the exordia of *Amours de Voyage*, but was immediately put off by his dismissing Rome as "rubbishy". Can you imagine? *Rubbishy?* Rome! I mean, the utter insolence of Clough.'

'How extraordinary,' Sir Christopher said weakly.

'And it only gets worse, really heretical,' John said, testing the waters of absolution. 'Listen: *No, the Christian faith, as I, at least understood it, / Is not here, O Rome, in any of these thy churches.* And as for the poem you particularly recommended, "Easter Day, Naples, 1849", well, that's out and out blasphemy.

'There is *one* verse I quite liked in the poem: *We are most hopeless, who had once most hope, / And most beliefless, that had most believed.* But as for the rest of it, that clanking refrain, above all – *Christ is not risen!* It's too awful,' John quivered.

'Here, let me see,' Sir Christopher said, without extending his hand.

'To tell you the truth, I am not sure that, in your newly immaculate state, you should even *touch* this book,' John said, pressing the volume on Sir Christopher.

After quickly glancing through the poem, Sir Christopher gently closed both the book and his eyes, saying, 'No, I don't suppose Father Hennessy would approve of this promenade through *the great sinful streets of Naples*, now that one has been cleansed and made whiter than snow – *super nivem dealbabor.*'

John sat silently next to the bed, rejoicing that his essay at absolution should have succeeded, when, after a fairly long interval, he was surprised to hear Sir Christopher say in a much more animated voice, 'And as for Naples, we'll have to put off that trip. When was it to be?'

'Actually, we were meant to have left today. But don't worry. I've cancelled all that.'

'Good. Because now,' Sir Christopher said, feebly trying to hoist himself up, everything – what with this recent setback – will have to be focused on work.'

Whose work? John sneered to himself, trying to think of the last time that any reference had been made to independent research of his own. Aloud, he said, 'Well, at least we can be thankful the Botticelli proofs got off before *this* happened.'

'Yes, thank God. But we really have no time to lose. I'll have to start preparing my Slade lectures on Botticelli and the Medici, but the first thing I want,' Sir Christopher said, banging on the side rail of the bed, 'is to get that review of Neville Pounder's bloody little book done. It's been languishing for ages, and I really do want to give it to him. Imagine writing that Titian didn't know Latin. Not know Latin? *Titian!*' he very nearly screeched.

'Now, don't get worked up. That's the last thing Dr Werner would want,' John said, smoothing out the bedclothes.

'The only thing that wretched dedication of Dolce's proves,' Sir Christopher said more calmly, 'is that Titian couldn't read the sixth *Satire* of Juvenal. Even the monks at Downside had trouble with Juvenal; he's notoriously difficult, and the sixth the most difficult of all the *Satires*. By the same token, one could say that anyone who has ever poked his nose into the Loeb Classical Library doesn't know Latin or Greek. No, it's all rubbish. How could an educated artist in sixteenth-century Venice *not* know Latin? His elder son, Pomponio, was even a priest! You can tell old Pounder didn't have a proper Christian upbringing. Only the son of an atheistic barrister could come up with such an idea.'

'I quite agree,' John said.

'And as for the vulgarity of the rest of that book, you can't imagine it.'

"I *have* actually read the book,' John reminded Sir Christopher.

'Then you know that he calls the Farnese picture *Paul III and His Grandsons*. Everybody is aware that they were his grandsons, but the picture is always, out of simple respect for the office, labelled *Pope Paul III with His Nephews*. And he doesn't even know what a mozzetta is! He calls it a stole, if you please. But the coup de grâce is that frontispiece: nothing but the right breast of Danaë. It's enough to make one's blood boil.'

'That's just what it *shouldn't* do. Now please don't think about it,' John said.

'But one does. I suppose it's the idea of him as keeper, there at the Ashmolean – where one has bequeathed all one's own pictures – that really irks one.'

'We all know that it is the institution that endures, while the staff come and go,' John said, hoping to fan the flames of Sir Christopher's indignation with pacific logic.

'One likes to think so. Now,' Sir Christopher said in a (once again) weak voice, 'would you hand me that little book, *Ancient Devotions for Holy Communion*? It's a very nice compilation, you know, of Eastern and Western early sources. I'm sure Father Hennessy would approve of *that*.'

✝

When he brought Sir Christopher home from the clinic in the first week of May, John found that the alternating bouts of kindness and sharpness – of spiritual surrender and worldly determination – to which his master seemed ever more prone, only intensified. As Dr Werner had promised, the medical condition could be treated by a weekly treatment – a costly drip of albumin that could only be obtained at the distant hospital of Careggi – and diet; Sir Christopher, however, was having no part of the latter, which he dismissed as 'frightfully American'. John thought that if Sir Christopher were to follow a stricter *régime* – no salt and no alcohol, above all, and maybe not so much butter – his moods might fluctuate a bit less, though he knew better than to suggest such a thing.

The first jolting swing of the pendulum came just one day after their return home, when Sir Christopher, of his own accord, spoke himself on the telephone to the bank in Florence, informing them that he was sending his secretary with a letter authorising his signature on the account. Thereafter, Sir Christopher never again, not *once*, set foot in the bank, and John took complete control of the household expenses: he signed the cheques; he even got a credit card.

The following day, in the same spirit of rupture and again of his own volition, Sir Christopher drafted an entirely new will. As Peter Mason had shown no sign of life during Sir Christopher's stay in hospital – he had, indeed, been conspicuously distant all the last year, a lapse that John had not failed to point out several times – Sir Christopher cut him entirely out of his will, naming John to the much-coveted position of literary executor, as well as heir to several small works of art and a not insubstantial sum of money. The Ashmolean, however, remained his principal beneficiary.

John was, of course, pleased with his transformation in status, feeling that he now only had to persevere, with his preternatural patience, in order to obtain the full recognition he craved. At the same time, he was honest enough to admit that, if he had had any money of his own – even a *little* – he would never, ever have remained at Sir Christopher's side. But then, if he had been financially independent, he would not have got entangled in this position in the first place; it was, he knew, inconceivable that the 25-year-old Christopher Noble-Nolan would ever have condescended to be anyone's secretary. Only the poor accepted – let alone ran after – such posts. John was not, however, honest enough to recognise that it was his lack of belief in himself that led him to hide behind someone else, to seek sanctuary in the work of another, rather than to risk failure on his own. For now, he merely acknowledged that he was here, in Florence, to stay. There was no point in wasting any more time with futile schemes of departure.

As if to cement his position in Palazzo Vespucci, John had, whilst Sir Christopher was safely ensconced in the clinic, taken the high-handed step of exchanging his study with the spare room, the latter being much the nicer of the two chambers. He also established an archive, as he liked to call it, in the abandoned room upstairs, next to the loggia, where he slowly began to sort and file the voluminous correspondence, manuscripts and photographs of Sir Christopher's mother and brother, as well as all of Sir Christopher's personal papers.

As he set about ordering these documents, his greatest attention was reserved for the correspondence between the two Noble-Nolan brothers, both sides of which he held in his watchful grasp. John had initially assumed that Sir Christopher's reticence about his younger brother was born of the grief he must have felt over his brutal murder: in January of 1974, Christian Noble-Nolan had been tied to a chair by an Australian gigolo, beaten and left to fall backward, choking to death on his own blood. And though John never doubted the genuine sense of loss Sir Christopher had experienced, he came to believe that it was, nonetheless, clouded by long-simmering jealousy. John couldn't pin it down to a particular phrase or anecdote, but he felt intuitively that Christopher Noble-Nolan, like the duteous elder brother he was, resented the attention and the indulgence that had long been lavished (by both family *and* society) on the younger, prodigal son.

This evening, in the hope of unveiling the secret surrounding the fraternal alliance, John had the intention of asking Sir Christopher about a few carefully selected letters and photos that he had been sorting through in the new archive. After dinner, exactly the sort of rich meal of which Dr Werner would have disapproved – *velouté périgordine, filet de bar-en-smoking* (which is, to say, sea bass smothered in caviar) followed by a sweet puffed omelette *aux abricots*, accompanied by a bottle of Sir Christopher's favourite Pouilly-Fumé, *Baron de L* – John said, 'Would you like to begin with the photos?'

'Right you are,' Sir Christopher said.

'Here's one of your father, decked out in full uniform – at what, I assume, must have been the height of the war. Doesn't he look terribly intimidating?' John said admiringly.

'But intimidating is exactly what he was *not*. Mamma, you know, would have made a much better solider that poor old Papa,' Sir Christopher said.

'Hmm,' John muttered, for he had long felt sorry for the brushed aside Major-General. It was not for nothing, he thought, that the old man's favourite book was *The Ordeal of Richard Feverel*. *One might well*, he said to himself, *write a novel entitled* The Ordeal of Major-General S.P.H. Noble-Nolan, CB, DSO.

Aloud, he said, 'I've long been meaning to ask you, why was your father known as "Benjamin", when his initials were S.P.H.?'

'Oh, that's quite simple,' Sir Christopher said. 'Mamma didn't like *any* of Papa's Christian names: she found Stanislaus too foreign, Patrick too Irish and Bertie, short for Herbert, as he had been known before his marriage, simply impossible. She rechristened him, therefore, "Benjamin", in honour of Benjamin Constant, the *cavaliere servente* of Madame de Staël. Mamma, you know, worshipped the Baroness.'

'Of course,' John, with defeated blankness, said. 'And don't you look smart here in *your* uniform?' he continued falsely, proffering a new image, as he reflected on the fact that, though the young Christopher Noble-Nolan was a commissioned officer in the RAFO, in the Intelligence Department of the Air Ministry, he lived throughout the entire war with his parents in Avenue Road and never once saw the inside of a barracks, nor stepped into an æroplane. His war 'effort' consisted almost entirely of cataloguing the drawings of Domenichino in the Royal Library at Windsor. *Who* pulled *what strings?* John said to himself but did not dare to ask.

'And this photo – a rather typically theatrical Beaton shot,' he went on further, 'is one of the few that shows all three of you together – your mother, your brother and you.' *The Holy Trinity*, he thought.

'So it does,' Sir Christopher said, staring intently at his own image.

'What year do you think that was?'

'Oh, I suppose near the end of the war, '44 or '45.'

'I should think,' John said, 'that it must be post June 1944, when your father died. Otherwise, he would surely have been in the picture.'

'I wouldn't count on that,' Sir Christopher said.

John grieved for the poor old Major-General but ploughed on. 'You look quite natural, but your brother's stance is rather contrived. I suppose that was the Beaton effect.'

'Oh no. That was just Crystal. He was always like that, even as a child, always demanding attention. I remember that, if he didn't get *exactly* what he wanted, he would throw his shoes at one across the nursery. Looking at this photo, some people might think he had more character than one, but it simply wasn't true. He was just always acting, always trying to steal centre stage.'

'Your mother seems to be looking at him apprehensively,' John said, pleased with the direction the conversation was taking.

'She *was* always worried about him. Rightly so, it turned out. Some stupid people, those like Jo Leigh-Fiennes and Tommy Tornabuoni, thought she preferred Crystal to me, but it was much more complicated than that. She simply knew that he needed more attention, due to his deeply flawed character.'

John was discomfited by Sir Christopher's frequent habit of flippantly referring to someone's 'flawed' character – in the same way that one might speak of a flaw in a celadon vase or a golden bowl – but said nothing. Instead, he went on showing Sir Christopher a few anodyne photos, so as not to set off any alarm bells. Finally, he produced the last snapshot and asked, though he full well knew the answer to his question, 'And where was this one taken?'

'That's Crystal's flat in Ladbroke Grove.'

'And is that Andrew Bruntisfield with you and your brother?' he said, going on with another question to which he knew the answer.

'Yes, it is, rather unusually,' Sir Christopher said.

'Why unusually?' John asked.

'Well, they didn't really get on. They didn't detest each other. They just didn't have much in common. Crystal was not in the least interested in architecture, and certainly not in Andrew's stark modernism. And then, you can see in that photo the way Crystal is posing.'

'He does look rather affected there,' John said, treading cautiously.

'Well, he *was* wildly affected. And that wasn't Andrew's sort of thing at all. Crystal always said that Andrew had no sense of humour. But that wasn't the case. It just wasn't Crystal's sense of humour.'

John was quite prepared to believe that the severe Andrew Bruntisfield was completely lacking in humour – New Brutalist, indeed – but that was incidental to his purposes at the moment. 'I think you look very protective of them *both* in this photo,' he said, pursuing his prepared line of enquiry.

'One was. They both required looking after, albeit in different ways. But then I have always been the one to do the looking after. Till you came along, that is. For the first time in my life, I have someone to look after me. You really are a sort of extraordinary combination of Nicky Mariano and Watts-Dunton,' Sir Christopher said with a mellow warmth.

'Um, ah, yes,' John said, stunned by Sir Christopher's avowal – not at all the revelation he had been in pursuit of. Following a few speechless (and more than guilt-ridden) moments, he finally managed to ask, 'Shall we move on to the letters?'

'Right you are,' Sir Christopher said tranquilly.

'Oh, but first there's this rather curious thing that I came across,' John said, producing a long, typewritten horoscope of Christopher Noble-Nolan, across the top of which was scrawled, in a large, untidy hand: *Darling Christopher, Don't blame me if you are frightened by its uncanny accuracy. With Christmas love from Crystal. Washington, DC, 1944.*

'What's that?'

'It appears to be some bizarre sort of horoscope, cast for you at the behest of your brother, when he was posted in Washington during the war,' John said, feigning ignorance. In truth, he knew all about this horoscope, which Jo Leigh-Fiennes had referred to at length in his diaries and which he had urged Christian Noble-Nolan *never* to present to his brother, so distinctly unflattering did he find it as a portrait: *His planets absolutely prevent his having emotions about people or even liking them.* John felt almost sure that the selfish, profligate younger brother had taken a perverse pleasure in baiting his responsible, efficient elder brother, and he was more than prepared to take umbrage on behalf of his master: Botticini-Botticelli, indeed!

'Oh, *that* rather silly thing,' Sir Christopher said, brushing aside the horoscope. 'Just the sort of game that Crystal loved, though I must admit that it did rather put one off driving a motorcar for life.'

'Did you *ever* drive?' John asked, shocked.

'A little bit, in the North of England in the late thirties, when my father was posted near Durham. But Crystal's Washington astrologer, Miss Bartleman, put paid to that, insisting that the stars absolutely *proved* that, were one so foolish as to go on driving, one would die in an accident,' Sir Christopher said.

'And did your brother ever drive?' John asked, still, after all this time, avid for every niggling detail concerning the Noble-Nolan family.

'Good heavens, no!' Sir Christopher cried. 'Crystal could never have managed a motor – nor, indeed, anything practical.'

'Now, to move on to the letters,' John said, disconcerted to note that Sir Christopher was not nearly so offended by the horoscope as he himself was. 'This batch here was written to your brother in the mid-thirties through the late forties, at which point the correspondence abruptly breaks off. They are all signed merely *C*. I assume that they,' John continued, holding up a large stack of gauzy (now yellowed) paper, covered in spidery handwriting, 'come from Clementine Arden, or Chamberlain as she was then. They are all quite short, but nonetheless rather passionate, letters.'

'Yes, that certainly must be Clementine. She and Crystal were frightfully close for a time. You know that he dedicated his first two books to her. Mamma thought that *rather* an exaggeration. One dedication looks admiring, she said; two dedications, she declared, seem cloying. And right, as always, Mamma was, for, as soon as Clementine married, she dropped Crystal and sold out to the conventions of political life.'

'Yes, I was sure that they were from her. Now these' – he moved on to a clutch of thick grey-green writing-paper – 'though less numerous, cover a much longer period, from the late forties, right up till Crystal's death in '74. Having read them quite carefully, I would say that they are less passionate than Clementine's but, somehow, more tender, more thoughtful. All of these are just signed *J*. Would that be Jane, Marchioness of Dorset?'

'I should think so,' Sir Christopher said, extending his hand.

'Here,' John said, giving over the letters.

'Yes, they're certainly from Jane Mooreshead, the pianist,' Sir Christopher said, after cursorily examining a few pages. 'She was wildly clever, as well as frightfully kind. Canadian, of course. And supremely talented. She could have had a proper career as a pianist, a really successful one. Her Liszt was extraordinary – you cannot imagine, not even *begin* to imagine, her rendition of the *Années de pèlerinage*, above all the "Raphael *Sposalizio*" – but she gave it all up when her husband, Garrison, unexpectedly succeeded to the marquessate. Rather a pity, really. She ought to have put herself first. It's actually quite amazing that she should have been such good friends with Crystal, who was entirely unmusical.'

John was quite used to hearing Sir Christopher list the subjects – works of art, architecture, music, abstract ideas, domestic practicality – about which his brother knew nothing, but did not think it a propitious moment for exploring this avenue. Even *less* did he want to test Sir Christopher on the merits of putting oneself first, and so he moved on to a new bundle of letters. 'These,' he said, pointing to a group of divers papers – ranging from sheets engraved with a royal coat of arms to tattered scraps of loose leaf – all covered in the same wobbly script, 'were the hardest to make out, and the tone is strangely variable – sometimes businesslike, sometimes broodingly romantic. I wondered if they might not come from the Royal Archivist, the Hon Sir St John Vascelles, though the signature, which is almost indecipherable, appears to be "Teddy".'

'But he was always called "Teddy", *Sin-jin Vas-əls* was,' Sir Christopher said, correcting John's pronunciation of both Christian *and* family names. 'And perfectly charming he was, old Teddy. Do let one see those. He had a terrible crush on Crystal, though I never knew how far things actually went between them.'

'Right you are,' John said, blushing deeply at his phonetic mistake, whilst upbraiding himself for not having remembered from Jo Leigh-Fiennes's diaries that the Hon Sir St John Vascelles was known as 'Teddy'.

'We can keep these aside, if you like, to look over later on, but finally I wanted to show you these three letters,' John changed course, hoping to jettison his pronunciation blunder. 'Though they are all, obviously, from your brother to you, none of them, most unusually, is dated. I was hoping that you might be able to tell me, roughly, when they were written, so that I can file them properly. I'll go and get the Armagnac, whilst you're reading them. I also have to fetch something in my study. I'll be back in a minute.'

Having planned his exit in advance, John sat in the dark of the kitchen for ten minutes, quietly sipping a snifter of brandy, after which time he returned to the drawing room, finding, as he imagined he would, Sir Christopher in a state of some agitation. 'Would you like a drop of that?' he asked, pointing to the bottle on the silver salver he had just placed on the low table.

'More than a *drop*,' Sir Christopher said excitedly.

'Is something wrong?' John asked.

'Have you actually read these letters?'

'No,' John lied.

'The first two,' Sir Christopher said, 'obviously come from some time in the early fifties, when Crystal was at work on that biography of Edward VII, interviewing and staying with one deposed German royal after another. They're quite amusing, even perceptive, letters, in their way, filled with gossip about the idiosyncrasies of superannuated despots, burdened by a misplaced sense of self-importance, but, amusing or not, it was really exposure to this world that set in motion all the snobbishness that eventually got Crystal into such a financial muddle. And as for this, this, *uh*,' Sir Christopher changed his tone, holding up a single, typewritten sheet of chartreuse-coloured paper, 'I think he must have been going off his head. It certainly was sent from Ireland, where he went in '71 or '72 to escape taxes. Imagine, someone on the brink of ruin, going abroad – to Ireland, of all places – in order to avoid taxes! It was only because I stepped in to put his affairs in order that he was able to avoid having to file for bankruptcy. And here he is accusing one of engineering his demise, so that I could swoop down and cart away his remaining possessions. I can't think why one ever saved this really quite disagreeable thing in the first place,' Sir Christopher concluded, tearing the letter to shreds.

'I'll just throw this out,' John said, bending down to collect the scattered pieces, pieces that, he knew, he would tape back together later that night. Though he was sorry to have snipped the thread of intimacy that the photos had inspired – above all, Sir Christopher's explicit gratitude for John's looking after him – he thought the sacrifice worthwhile, if it had helped him to penetrate the smokescreen that Sir Christopher had constructed round his relationship with his younger brother. In the nearly two years that John had known Sir Christopher, this was the first time that he had ever heard him speak – speak with anything approaching openness – on the subject.

Tentatively, John continued, 'And I wouldn't worry about that stupid letter. Obviously, as you said, your brother was going off his head in the end – what with drink and financial worries and the rough company he kept – so that that letter doesn't really signify. What *is* clear is that he always depended on you, could never have got on without you. But now, as you so rightly said, it's time for you to depend on me. Come, to bed it is.' John smiled, extending his hand pacifically.

'Yes, bed, as there is a great deal to do tomorrow,' Sir Christopher said in a markedly altered voice. 'I must get back to that blasted Pounder review. And have you been to the German Institute yet? To look up the transcription of Dolce?'

'One couldn't very well have gone today, what with all the practical things there were to do,' John defended himself.

'Well, tomorrow then. I also need information about *all* the translations of Ovid available in Venice in the 1530s, so that I can give Pounder a proper thwacking over the *Danaë*, which I simply know he's got wrong. You might also look out some Juvenal, whilst you're at it. And the *C* in my typewriter is sticking. Could you see if you can somehow put it right? At least, till I get the review out of the way. It might, then, need to be properly mended. And please, do tell that Indian not to touch *anything* on my writing-table this week, whilst I am at work on the review. I don't want her muddling things up.'

'I'll tell Rita,' John said.

'And I think it would be nice if we could have the marmalade cake for tea tomorrow.'

'Fine,' John suspired. 'Now, let's go to bed.'

For the next ten days, Sir Christopher worked steadily – the mornings on Botticelli and the afternoons on his review of Neville Pounder – going out only to Mass on Sunday, and then by taxi. On Monday, 13 May, however, when John presented him with a freshly typed copy of his finished review, Sir Christopher proposed that he accompany him to the post office. 'It's a perfectly lovely afternoon. And then, having written such an *un*favourable review has quite restored one's spirits. I am sure one is up to a walk now,' Sir Christopher said with a smile.

After Sir Christopher approvingly watched John post the manuscript of his review to London, he suggested that they stop at Seeber's in via de' Tornabuoni. 'One has earned a rather good dose of McBain, after working so hard on that review. And we might stock up on some Simenon. It would do one no end of good to be reading French trash – very helpful it is for one's vocabulary – particularly as we are meant to be going to the festival at Aix-en-Provence this summer.'

'Yes, do let's go to Seeber's,' John agreed heartily. 'And if it's French you want to be reading, perhaps I could get you a copy of

Mémoires d'Hadrien. You remember that we spoke about it the other day, after that long, laudatory article about Madame Yourcenar in the *New York Review*.'

'Yes, one would like to read her. It's rather a lacuna not to have done so. She's not too *sensitive*, is she?' Sir Christopher asked worriedly.

'Not in the least. She's a tough old dyke, if ever there were one. I'd also like to get a paperback of *Richard II* whilst we're about it.'

'Whatever for?' Sir Christopher asked. 'We have that beautiful edition of Malone in the house.'

'I'm afraid,' John said apologetically, 'that I just prefer to read a version with modern annotations, though not, of course, modern spelling.'

'That seems highly eccentric to one,' Sir Christopher said. 'And anyway, I thought you were still busy with Rousseau?'

'I abandoned that some time ago. You know, I couldn't get past the end of even "Book Two", in which Jean-Jacques recounts how, as a young man, he stole a pink and silver ribbon from the lady of the house, where he was employed as a sort of secretary-cum-valet. To protect himself, he then blamed the theft on a perfectly innocent serving girl – saying she had given the ribbon to him. The poor thing – called Marion, I believe – was, thanks to his calumny, thrown into the streets, destitute and alone, presumably ruined forever. Writing about the incident forty years later, Jean-Jacques was still preoccupied by his own villainy, but only in so far as it compromised *his* spotted soul. No, I found him unbearably antipathetic, that querulous Swiss Calvinist.'

'Now,' John said, stopping in the street, 'why don't I pop into the chemist by myself – you need some more talcum powder – whilst you wait for me at Procacci? You can sit down and have a white truffle sandwich and a *succo di pomodoro*. Then, we'll go on to Seeber's together.'

After they finished in the bookshop, they headed home, proceeding at a stately pace. When they got to the swarm of tourists round Ponte Vecchio, Sir Christopher slowed down noticeably, looking in various shop windows, more to grant himself a pause than to satisfy curiosity. Not quite halfway across the bridge, he stopped and let out a tremendous squeal. '*Look* – there it is!'

'There's what?' John asked as he peered in the vitrine and gasped.

'It's Dodo's watch, the gold repeater.'

'I don't think it can be. I mean, uh, I don't, uh, know,' John stammered. 'I never, um, actually *saw* the watch. Remember, you were with Peter when you first unpacked it. But still, I don't see how it could be for sale, here, on the Ponte Vecchio.'

'Well, there's one way to find out,' Sir Christopher said, tugging determinedly on the door of the shop.

John followed recklessly behind, convinced that his end was near. He listened passively as he heard Sir Christopher imperiously ask to inspect the repeater. Standing in the tiny shop, he watched, from what seemed to him a great distance, Sir Christopher fiddle with the globular mechanism at the top of the gold object. Eventually, through no intervention on John's part, Sir Christopher managed to pop open the cover on the reverse of the dial-plate, the underside of which, they both saw, was engraved with the intertwined letters *LK*, surrounded by a wreath of diamonds.

'Well, there you have it, the proof,' Sir Christopher said. 'Dodo's father, Leopold Kline. I am sure that it was that Indian who pinched it.'

'Rita?' John asked, horrified.

'Yes. Who else could have taken it? *Allora*,' Sir Christopher said, turning to the shopkeeper to ask if he knew anything of the watch's provenance. When this elicited nothing but the vaguest of replies about a colleague in Rome, Sir Christopher closed the cover and, without having asked the price, said, '*Va bene. Lo comprerò.*' He then turned to John and said, 'You can come back tomorrow afternoon to pick it up and leave the cheque at the same time. And then, we'll get to the bottom of this with that old Indian.'

The trance-like state that had overcome John in the shop boiled up into one of near hysteria by the time he was ready for bed. For most of the night he prayed, if praying it could be called – it was closer to something like supplication, if not actual begging – for some sort of divine intervention. He sought God's mercy, tried to appease His anger, to avert His chastisement. Thus far, it appeared that John had no material loss to fear for himself (Sir Christopher suspected nothing) but that he should be the agent of poor besieged Rita's demise – she, the nervous, twittering abandoned wife with two children; she, who had been so trusting of John, looking on him as her protector against the potential wrath of Sir Christopher – shamed him endlessly.

After a few hours of fitful sleep, he got up at about five and went in search of the volume he had discarded in disgust more than a week ago. Obsessively, he read and reread Rousseau's twisted tale of blaming his own theft of *un petit ruban couleur de rose et argent* on the unsuspecting Marion. John tried to convince himself that he, unlike the Geneva apprentice, had never falsely accused an innocent girl, but he knew in advance that, whatever cruel fate might await *his* poor servant woman, he also would never confess. Exactly like his despised Rousseau, John feared, above all else – more than death itself – disgrace. And there was no lie that he would not tell in order to avoid ruining himself in front of Sir Christopher.

How, John asked himself, *can I not lie to him, if he confronts her with my crime?* Overcome with remorse, he burst into convulsive sobs, ripped the accusatory book apart and, bending forward, spat on the mutilated pages of the *Confessions.* Had he been a little less quick to judge, he would have learnt from Jean-Jacques that, whilst remorse may lie dormant in times of prosperity, it invariably rears its pathetic head in adversity.

At breakfast, he announced that he needed to spend the entire day at the German Institute – anything to avoid Rita's unsuspecting, smiling visage – to which Sir Christopher raised no objection, though he did remind him to collect the gold repeater on his way home. John did not, in fact, go anywhere near the library. Instead, he headed straight for Santa Croce, the church that, to him, seemed the most perfect incarnation of the cross itself – the cross not as triumph but as testament to the wounds of the Master, the true Franciscan inheritance. He never forgot the sensation he experienced when, in that summer of 1983, he had advanced, awestruck, up the massive nave of this church for the first time. He felt then, and still felt today, as if he were scaling the wood of Golgotha itself. And for him, this manifestation of the cross as trial reached its apogee in the refectory of Santa Croce, where Taddeo Gaddi, Giotto's most faithful disciple and the subject of Sir Christopher's first book, produced a colossal fresco of Bonaventure's vision of the crucified Christ as *Lignum vitae*, the Tree of Life. Now, gazing up at this imposing depiction of the crucifixion, surrounded by prophets and saints, from which all humanity seemed to descend, he thought he understood perfectly the Early Christian motto, *amor meus crucifixus est.*

Yes, he said to himself, *my love has been crucified.* His gaze then trailed down to the *Last Supper* – the prototype of refectory decoration for generations to come – that Taddeo Gaddi had frescoed beneath the crucifixion scene. He knew this work well, had studied it on any number of occasions, but today he saw it quite differently.

All of his attention was focused on his namesake, *the disciple whom Jesus loved*, collapsed on the breast of his impassive Master, whose hand he clutched desperately, as if to reassure himself that it is not *he* who will commit the great betrayal, a crime of which he obviously thought himself capable.

How alike we are, my brother, John said to himself, staring fixedly at his namesake. He admitted to himself that Sir Christopher had been right, in *part*, not to trust him – he had intended to deceive him over the cheque back in January – but John also felt that Sir Christopher accepted the advantages of discipleship without fully assuming his own obligations of master. John was even ready to acknowledge that he, unlike the Galilean disciples, had not been called and chosen by his master, but had, in the orthodox manner, sought out his own master. Like Alyosha, he had consciously chosen his 'Elder', but, unlike the saintly Karamazov brother, John had refused (or was unable) to renounce his own will. And so it was that he would never find himself in himself, would never attain freedom from himself, could see only what he might have been, what he would like to become, not who he was. Thus blinded, he sat before this image of the perfect marriage of loyalty and betrayal for hours, wondering if he too, like the bewildered disciples spread out before him in the fresco, was not capable of the gravest of all sins – treachery to his master.

He then let his gaze wander to the reviled figure of Judas Iscariot, *sans* halo, cast out alone on the other side of table, dipping his hand in the sop. John was aware that there had been numerous attempts to rehabilitate the great betrayer – from Goethe through the young Dr Goebbels, with diversions by way of Browning and Borges – claiming that, through his 'kiss', Judas had hoped to force Christ to reveal His power and glory to the whole world, thereby freeing His people and convincing all mankind of His divinity. And though John remained unconvinced by any such apologia, he had always pitied Judas, who, both Sts Luke and John assert, was pushed to his treachery by the devil who had entered into him. He had had no choice.

How much more wounding, more human, John thought, would it not be if the *Disciple whom Christ loved* had betrayed his Master? Zarathustra, of course, went so far as to encourage his disciples to denounce him: 'Only when you have denied me will I return to you,' he enigmatically pronounces. *Is not betrayal, therefore, the* truest *most perfect manifestation of loyalty?* John asked himself over and over again as he stared up at this harrowing image? Unable to persuade himself of such Jesuitical casuistry, he pushed himself out of the church and spent the next few hours aimlessly wandering round Florence.

Shortly after four o'clock, he entered the shop on the Ponte Vecchio and, with trembling hand, wrote a cheque for exactly double the amount he had received for the watch in Rome back in January. For the first and only time ever, he left Sir Christopher on his own for dinner that night; he pled ill health, for he did not trust himself to cloak sufficiently his secret. Fuelled by alcohol, he spent the night locked in his bedroom in a torrent of obsecration: he asked, but he did not receive; he sought, but he did not find; he knocked, but the door was not opened to him. In the morning, he found Sir Christopher already seated at table, buttering both sides of his toast.

'Are you feeling better?' Sir Christopher asked.

'Yes, much. Thank you.'

'I was rather worried about you. You almost looked a bit squiffy last night.'

'Hardly,' John said feebly. 'I just wasn't feeling well, but I'm fine now. Anyway, I'm sorry, terribly sorry, that I left you to dine with Duke Humphrey last night.'

'Actually, I rang up Alice yesterday evening, *all* by myself, and took her to dine at Campidoglio. She was delighted to be invited, of course. And she was actually able to produce the telephone number of a maid who, she said, is perfectly reliable. A straightforward Tuscan peasant – no more of this Indian nonsense. Now, shall we get this over with? Rita!' Sir Christopher screeched, producing the gold repeater from his pocket and laying it on the table.

John would not remember the particulars of the confrontation, though he could, till the end of his life, hear Rita's plaintive voice ringing in his ears, imploring him to come to her defence, extolling his virtues, his past kindness to her and his trust in her, beseeching him to deny Sir Christopher's accusations of thievery. *Unqualitied with very shame*, John stood up in the midst of the agon, left the room and ran to the loo, where he was as sick as the young Christopher Noble-Nolan had been after viewing Mr Mellon's pictures. A great storm broke within him, and, unable to bear that *deceit should dwell / In such a gorgeous palace*, he randomly grabbed a book and ran out of the apartment. He left Palazzo Vespucci along the side of the Arno, slipped through a narrow door in the exterior wall of the gravel park surrounding the palace and entered into the public garden in Lungarno Torrigiani, where he cast himself on a bench under a fig tree and gave full vent to his tears. He thought not of his victim, but of himself, wondering how long, just *how* long, his uncleanness would endure.

After what seemed but a few moments, he became aware of a vague chant or incantation – *Tolle, legge* – coming from he knew not where. Attempting to check the torrent of his own tears, he picked up his book and, opening it at random, fell upon these lines: *I'll read enough / When I do see the very book indeed / Where all my sins are writ, and that's myself.* An influx of anxiety infused his heart, and all the darkness of doubt descended. He had stumbled upon his own epitaph.

BOOK THIRD

CHAPTER I

The Veiling of Images

ON SUNDAY MORNING, 12 March 1989, John Forde awoke to find himself fat. He had, of course, been aware for some time that he had gained weight – a good deal of weight – but, so long as he could squeeze into his clothes, he had been able to discount the gravity of the situation. He had, however, taken up smoking a little over a year ago – on the sly, of course, as Sir Christopher hated cigarettes – in the vain hope that this would help him to reduce, which, needless to say, it did not; he only managed to add one more arm to his arsenal of vices. Intentionally, he did not own a scale and shunned all attempts at dieting – in imitation of Sir Christopher – in the deluded hope that, if he succeeded in not acknowledging the problem, it would have no grip on him.

This morning, however, as he struggled desperately to button the trousers of his best suit, the bespoke grey worsted, he split the seam along his bulging left thigh, ripping the material in what, he feared, was an irreparable fashion. He had long since abandoned trying to get into his off-the-peg suits, but he had twice returned this one to the tailor in via de' Fossi for professional alterations. Today, he despondently threw the tattered suit on the floor and yanked a pair of incidental trousers (bought recently) and a navy-blue blazer – of which he possessed a profusion, in various sizes – from his clothes press, saying to himself, *This will just have to do.*

He was particularly distressed that the disturbance should have occurred this morning, the very day they were invited to lunch by Tommy Tornabuoni in honour of Lady Charles Delfington and her daughter, Mrs L. Biddle Hollingsworth, the latter of whom he had never met, but he knew that he did not have time to dither. It being a Sunday, he was obliged to prepare the breakfast himself, and he was already running late. In addition, he agreed yesterday – or, rather, Sir Christopher informed him that he *had* agreed – that, in the hour they would have between Mass and Tommy Tornabuoni's lunch party, they would review several old book contracts as well as a new one concerning the Botticelli workshop, so that he would not have a minute to spare this morning in which to address his vestimentary emergency.

When, later in the morning, he was sitting next to Sir Christopher at Mass on this, the fifth Sunday in Lent, Passion Sunday, he glanced round the chapel from one shrouded image to another, thinking that he would have liked to conceal his corpulent self behind just such a veil of dark, collusive purple velvet. Succumbing to the naïf mythology that to be thin is an inherent proof of refinement, he was now bound in with shame at the thought of his own coarseness: *Approaching down a ruined corridor, / Strode someone with his own distorted features / Who wept, and grew enormous, and cried Woe,* he quoted to himself several times, whilst mouthing the words of the Confiteor. Whereas, hitherto, he had consistently refused to address the question of his unwanted girth, from this day forward it would be the constant focus of his attention, so much so that when, an hour later, he was going over the contracts with Sir Christopher in his study, he had immense difficulty concentrating.

'*This letter advises,*' John read in a mechanical voice, '*that under clause sixteen of the Memorandum of Agreement, dated 29 January 1965, concerning* Piero della Francesca, the Complete Works *by Christopher Noble-Nolan, all the Publishers' rights in this book have reverted to the Author, without prejudice to the Publishers or any third party, in respect of any agreement properly entered into by the Publishers hereunder with such party.*'

'I think that's frightfully well done. You've got the tone just right,' Sir Christopher said.

'Um, ah, good,' John said, happy that he had prepared the necessary paperwork the night before.

'I am sure that, now, we'll get the rights back to all my books,' Sir Christopher said, flipping through a stack of similar letters written by John. 'I must say that I do think it jolly clever of you to have gone through those old contracts and to have discovered that we could reclaim the rights to the out-of-print books. I never imagined that would be possible. How did you know that? And where did you learn all those legalistic ambages?'

'Oh, when we were in London last month, I just looked up a few things in a law book on contracts at the London Library. It was all clearly spelt out.'

'Still,' Sir Christopher said approvingly, 'you could have been a good lawyer yourself.'

I could have been a lot of things – quite *a lot of things,* John, overdone with bitterness, said to himself. *Instead, I keep here, wasting precious time, but,* Being your slave, what should I do but tend / Upon the hours and times of your desire?

The knowledge, or rather half knowledge, that he was himself the architect of his own enslavement only further stimulated John's resentment. Aloud, he simply said, 'Hmm.'

'And as for the new book contract about the Botticelli workshop, your points are, of course, all perfectly valid, and yet I don't think I'm going to sign it,' Sir Christopher said provocatively.

'Why ever not?' John, suddenly more attentive, asked. 'You seemed so pleased with the new publisher.'

'Oh yes, one is. It's just, I've been thinking—' Sir Christopher hung fire.

'Thinking what?'

'Well it seems to one, what with this beautiful new book on Botticelli and the Medici just out,' Sir Christopher said, looking admiringly at the stack of freshly delivered books on the chair next to him '—oh, and do remind me to take a copy of this to Dodo, and I suppose I'll have to give one to old Tommy, as he's giving the lunch party and he's always foisting copies of his own awful books upon one – but, as I was saying, what with the publication of the new book, I think one really has cornered the market on Botticelli. I mean, if you count the early book on the drawings, this makes it my fourth book on the subject. So, this morning, as I lay in bed, I decided it might be better if one moved on to something quite new.'

'What did you have in mind?' John asked warily.

'What would you say if I told you that I was going to work on Leonardo?'

'Leonardo!' John exclaimed.

'You sound surprised,' Sir Christopher said leadingly.

'Yes, I *am* surprised,' he replied. In truth, John was shocked by Sir Christopher's change of direction. A well-known poet has claimed that the 'intellectual dandy' can be recognised by the unpredictable nature of his work: none of his previous books provides any clue as to what the subject of his next one might be. By this definition, Sir Christopher Noble-Nolan was the very antithesis of the 'intellectual dandy', for each of his books had been built steadily, some might say stodgily, on its predecessor, mounting, like capital well and cautiously invested, toward an enviable principal.

Christopher Noble-Nolan began writing about the trecento, marched logically into the quattrocento – with but one wartime deviation into the seicento – but he had never before ventured into the High Renaissance. And yet, the reticent resistance with which John greeted Sir Christopher's announcement had roots deeper than mere surprise: he was not simply taken aback; he felt taken from. Leonardo had been John's earliest boyhood love, the first artist whose work had inspired in him an æsthetic as well as an intellectual response, that *hard gemlike flame of ecstasy*. But though John had abandoned this budding passion, transferring his allegiance to Botticelli – not least as a means of wedding himself to Sir Christopher Noble-Nolan – he had never entirely forsaken the enigmatic master from Vinci, who lingered in the recesses of his soul as his preferred artistic personality.

The only other artist whom John would have admitted to this pantheon was the architect Leon Battista Alberti – also illegitimate, also intellectual, also elusive, also unmarried. Much as John actively disliked the personality of Michelangelo – the titanic ego and the furious temper, the self-promoting arrogance and the material stinginess – he worshipped the aura of Leonardo: aloof and secretive; calm and reserved; elegant and extravagant; lover of personal luxury and of beautiful young men; utterly detached from the competitive brutality of mankind. He seemed, to John, the very quintessence of an artist *and* a gentleman; he thus felt cheated to learn that *his* Leonardo was to be snatched from under him. Nor did he like the idea that Sir Christopher should write on another homosexual artist and never mention, as he was sure he would not, his *true* nature, cloaking his personality in a mantle of unspoken assumptions. John was also more than a little fascinated by Leonardo's seemingly neurotic compulsion *not* to finish things, though this he could not yet admit to himself.

'So, you don't think it a good idea for one to write on Leonardo?' Sir Christopher asked.

'Goodness, I don't know what I think. Except, I mean, that it would involve a whole new arena of research, including Milan, not to mention the court of François Ier,' John said.

'Don't think one doesn't realise that.'

'I mean, uh, I mean,' John floundered, 'it just seems to me that you are creating the most unnecessary struggle for yourself.'

'Struggle? Struggle!' Sir Christopher said indignantly. 'But one has never had to *struggle* oneself. Everything has just always come naturally to one.'

Never had to struggle! John wailed to himself, thinking that his own life was but a continual struggle, a struggle to be what he is not and to spurn what he is, to aspire to what is beyond him and to repudiate that which he was capable of. Contrary to the English poet, writing about the Florentine painter, John thought that a man's reach should *not* exceed his grasp. Or what's a hell for?

'A challenge it will be, but certainly not a *struggle*,' Sir Christopher said firmly.

'And then it's such a specialised field – Leonardo is,' John persisted. 'Most Leonardo scholars have dedicated their entire lives to him and no one but him.'

'But don't you see,' Sir Christopher said with a smile, 'that's exactly the point. They're all so limited. Whereas I, an interloper of sorts, will be able to bring a much wider range of knowledge and criteria to the subject. And provided one lives long enough to produce a really splendid monograph, the definitive monograph in fact, well, it would lend such beautiful symmetry to the arc of one's scholarly writing, establishing one as the undisputed authority in the field, from Giotto right through the High Renaissance.'

'And are you planning just to chuck all the research about the Botticelli workshop?' John asked.

'Not in the least,' Sir Christopher said. 'You see, I think you should take it over. After all, most of it *is* your doing. And this way, you wouldn't be studying just a few miscellaneous followers but a whole, coherent entity.'

'I don't quite know what to say,' John answered, stunned.

'Why not just say "yes"?'

'Okay, *yes*. I mean, uh, of course, I agree, and, um, thank you,' John, who had no intention of devoting any further effort to the followers of Botticelli, said nervously. It was not, not *exactly*, that John had become bored with the history of art but, rather, that he had grown weary of the series of endless epigones to whom he had chosen to commit himself: the Master of the Castello Nativity; the Master of the Gothic Buildings; the Master of the Lathrop Tondo; the Master of this; the Master of that – none of whom had *mastered* anything. For some time now, it had struck John as more than odd, really quite mysterious, that, whereas great thinkers spawn great disciples – and the greater the thinker the greater the disciple he will bring forth: Socrates begat his Plato, Christ his John, Marx his Engels, Husserl his Heidegger – great artists rarely (if ever) produce but the most mediocre of pupils. Consider those who hovered round Giotto or Leonardo or Rembrandt: a blurry band of brothers, of nothing more than academic interest – if *that* – as John knew all too well from the legion of second-rate followers who had overrun the Botticelli workshop. No, he thought, he himself merited allegiance to an order higher than Botticini & Co.

'Good, that's settled then,' Sir Christopher pronounced. 'Now where's that letter from the man who's writing the biography of little old Lettice? What's his name?'

'Norman Port. Here it is,' John said, retrieving a sheet of coarse beige paper from the bottom of a bulging stack of correspondence.

'Funny name, isn't it? Porter would be one thing. But Mr Port? Why not Mr Sherry? He sounds just like the sort of odd character who *would* have latched on to Lettice. To judge from his curious letter, it would appear that it was old Lettice who first came up with the idea of a biography – in the end, she *did* have a very good opinion of herself – but that she then did an about-face and tried desperately to block the book's publication. I imagine that Mr Port dug up a few too many skeletons in the Brompton-Corlett cupboard. He has, you know, established beyond the shadow of a doubt not just the reciprocal stabbing of the incestuous twin brothers, Castor and Pollux, on the high altar of the Oratory – that we all knew about – but also that, of the nine Brompton-Corlett children born to Lettice's benign Presbyterian pastor of a father and her Scotch shrew of a mother, Muriel Spartachey, not *one* of them ever married or produced an heir and that five, possibly even six, of them committed suicide. And now that Lettice has died, Miss Hudson has apparently readmitted Mr Port back into the fold. I wonder if old Maud is not being intentionally mischievous, trying to exact some sort of retrospective revenge on Lettice for having dared to upstage her. Do you remember exactly when it was that old Lettice came to dine here with Jefferson Birstein?'

'Yes, it was in November of 1984, nearly five years ago,' John said.

'Five years!' Sir Christopher said. 'Goodness, it seems like yesterday.'

'Yes,' John said, thinking that it seemed as if the dinner had taken place in another lifetime.

'I'll just mark that down,' Sir Christopher said, turning to his typewriter. 'I think that I've answered most of Port's other questions, but he also wants some sort of general impression. What do you think of this? I dashed it off this morning, whilst waiting for breakfast.'

John took up the proffered sheet of paper and read:

My mother was not much interested in Maud Hudson – thought her, indeed, thoroughly tiresome, what with all that talk about napkins and white linen damask – but she greatly admired Lettice's books, most particularly Twin Brothers Entwined, *and she was fascinated by her whole identity. For me, Lettice was an acquired taste, and the better one got to know her the fonder one became of her. Her inscrutable visage and indirect manner of speaking were all of a piece. One was conscious of a great depth of feeling that was never, or scarcely ever, articulated. The books were the only true repository of the profound emotions stirring within her. I sometimes think the most important thing in life is how one tends one's talent, and Lettice tended hers with marvellous disinterest and conviction and consistency.*

'I think you've quite captured her. I particularly like the bit about *tending one's talent*,' John said, uttering both a lie that was a truth and a truth that was a lie.

'Yes, obviously. I mean, just think of poor Peter and the way he squandered his talent. Such a waste!'

'I suppose that we shouldn't speak ill of the dead, particularly as he was struck down by the plague,' John said, finding it easy to stand up for Peter Mason, of whom he had once been so ravenously jealous, now that he was safely dead and buried. 'Anyway, I am sure Mr Port will be happy to have your words.'

'If you could just type up a proper copy of that, we could send it off to him tomorrow. And when we come back from luncheon, we ought to make a definitive list of the articles to appear in the new volume of my collected essays, as the publisher seems keen to bring out the book as soon as possible. And then tomorrow, we should really go to the German Institute together and survey the Leonardo landscape.'

'But I'm meant to be taking Dodo and her daughter round some of the more obscure Florentine churches this afternoon, and then tomorrow I've gone to all that trouble about arranging a private visit for them through the *Corridoio Vasariano*, to see the collection of self-portraits,' John said, as though expressing a great burden. He thought back to his first year in Florence, remembering how he had *longed* to make the acquaintance of Lady Charles Delfington, convinced that, if he could but infiltrate her world, he would automatically be accepted by Sir Christopher. Now, here he was, almost six years later, lamenting the successful realisation of his schemes.

'Oh blast,' Sir Christopher said. 'I'd quite forgotten about that. Thank God she's leaving tomorrow afternoon, as all this social whirl does cut terribly into one's work. I must say that I do think it good of you to look after Dodo each time she turns up. One couldn't, of course, very well leave her on her own, but, still, I know how time consuming it is. And then, you know exactly how to handle her. The only problem, now, is that you will have to put up with the younger daughter, Mrs Hollingsworth. I don't know what *she*'s doing here.'

'Dodo told me on the telephone,' John said, 'that they were coming here together in order to meet up with Princess Bonamici at the Villa Reale di Montalto, near Lucca, which Mrs Hollingsworth is hoping to rent for her daughter's coming out ball in August.'

'How frightful!' Sir Christopher quailed. 'We shall have to make sure to steer well clear of anything to do with a ball. Don't let them ensnare you in *any* way, though I do warn you that Permelia

Hollingsworth can be very tenacious when she wants something. The elder daughter, Lady Gaylord, is quite another matter – frightfully clever she is – but Mrs Hollingsworth, well, I'm afraid that you'll find she's completely lacking her sister's, not to mention her mother's, astringency. Very literal minded, she is – and *appallingly* earnest. After all these years as the wife of Ambassador Biddle Hollingsworth, she's become more American than an American.'

John knew that, though Lady Charles Delfington was one of the few society ladies whom Sir Christopher both genuinely liked and admired – he had heard her praised, praised more times than he could count, as 'wonderfully astringent' – Sir Christopher soon tired even of her: three or four dinners in a row, punctuated by a few interrupted workdays, sent him flying back to the isolation of his study. John could not, on the other hand, be sure if he should regard his hard-won rôle of escort to the rich and entitled as a sign of acceptance or if, as with the discarded Botticelli material, he should suspect the motivation behind the gift. He merely said, 'I suppose we should be leaving now. We wouldn't want to be late for old Tommy. You know how fussed he gets.'

'Yes,' Sir Christopher said, 'I suppose we must. We'll have to let the German Institute wait till Tuesday, but when you're out tomorrow, after you've finished with Dodo, you might want to have a look for some new black velvet slippers; mine seem to be getting terribly shabby. It would also be rather nice to have some of the delicious marmalade cake for tea tomorrow. It's simply ages since we've had that. And whatever you do, do not forget about the Brendel tickets. It would be perfectly *catastrophic* if we missed that concert.'

☦

Throughout the Lucullan banquet of a luncheon in Palazzo Tornabuoni – consisting of truffled lasagne served as a *first* course, poached turbot *au beurre blanc*, wild boar, a mountain of white asparagus, bathed in butter and melted parmesan and culminating in an unctuously rich chocolate meringue concoction – John's thoughts alternated between the problem of his weight and Sir Christopher's disturbing proposition about the Botticelli workshop. John rarely ate much in public, and never with the slightest trace of avidity, so that he found it possible to keep the former state of distress in check, though he was seriously embarrassed to be lunching amongst such grand company in a blazer rather than a proper suit.

The confusion he felt over Sir Christopher's offer could not, on the other hand, be so easily tamed. He imagined that Sir Christopher intended to be generous, maybe even magnanimous, in suggesting that he should take over the project of the Botticelli workshop, but he could also not *but* believe that his proposition was motivated mainly by concern for the contours of his own glittering career, as well as disbelief in the possibility that John ever could establish intellectual independence. John wondered if, in passing the Botticelli material on to him, Sir Christopher might not, in some perverse and underhand way, actually be trying to thwart him, to hold him back, to keep him in place?

Could he fear, John asked himself, *that the disciple might overtake his master? Might spread his wings and fly away?* He knew that Sir Christopher wanted, indeed insisted, that John himself should lead a serious, scholarly life – he would never have countenanced a frivolous creature like Tommy Tornabuoni's Woodstoke by his side – but he did not, on the other hand, leave him any reasonable opportunity to realise his potential gifts.

And yet, the most unsettling aspect of the morning's exchange, to John, had been Sir Christopher's letter about Dame Lettice Brompton-Corlett: *I sometimes think the most important thing in life is how one tends one's talent…* John repeated that phrase to himself over and over, asking himself how he was meant to tend *his* 'talent', if indeed he possessed one.

Several months ago, when he read for the first, but far from last, time the novella *The Lesson of the Master*, John had felt visited by an epiphany. *Why not,* he asked himself, *produce a modern pendant to Henry James's story?* He would call it *The Tuition of the Disciple*. The mere idea of such a book had thrilled him inordinately, for he envisaged, therein, his liberation from the bonds of intellectual servitude – something that would grant him his own terrain, away from Sir Christopher's clearly delimited plot. But aside from buying an expensive notebook in which he jotted down a few disjointed ideas, he made no concrete progress with the plan and eventually abandoned the project for the ignis fatuus it was. The ambition to create something of his own remained, however, immured within his breast, inchoate, but all the more convulsive for not having been localised.

Today, as he pondered the advice about tending one's talent, he dared to think that he was capable of something larger and bolder, something brutally honest and shamelessly autobiographical: simply and grandly and beautifully, *The Disciple*, his own story. He need no longer bother himself with Sir Christopher's cast-off subjects; he would dedicate himself to a higher cause. Like Paul Overt, he would be supremely strong. He would, following the master's exhortation, make his work 'divine'. Intoxicated by his own hubris, he tried to picture the day when Sir Christopher Noble-Nolan would be mainly remembered to posterity for having known one John Forde.

Who, today, has heard of Anna Jameson? he asked himself, summoning up the name of the author, famous and fêted in the nineteenth century for her six-volume history, *Sacred and Legendary Art*, though now all but forgotten, even by most specialists. *But the outcast, reviled Melville*, he continued his orgulous associations, *he reigns forever.*

He vowed to tend ferociously to his new plan. (Tellingly, in all his fantastical delusions, he never once dwelt on the components that Sir Christopher had enshrined as the handmaiden of Dame Lettice's talent – 'disinterest and conviction and consistency' – qualities in which he himself was notably deficient.) Buoyed up by visions of literary glory, he turned, with consummate grace and vast self-deception, to chat away animatedly to his neighbours on left and right.

✝

As coffee was served by liveried footmen in the library of Palazzo Tornabuoni, John walked over to the window and gazed out on the enormous private garden. Here was his preferred vision of nature – seen through a glass darkly and tended to by someone *else*. After a suitable interval, he turned round and surveyed the room: Alice, now the centre of attention, was purring between Barone Tornabuoni and Sir Christopher; Mrs Hollingsworth, off to one side, was desperately trying to converse with Alice Varrow's sister, Trixie

Giraldi; Montgomery Woodstoke, Tommy Tornabuoni's *once* good-looking kept boy, was brushing back his tinted mane with one hand, whilst fondling a cigarette with the other; the haughty Duchessa de' Portinari and her even more disobliging mousta-chioed niece, Mrs Bentley-Gordon, were conniving together in a corner; and Lady Charles – or Dodo, as John had been instructed to call her several years ago – stood alone, intently inspecting the three Botticelli panels that, unlike Alice or Lulu, she admired, as only a seriously rich person can, not for their commercial value, but for their intrinsic beauty.

Looking at her from a distance, one might, John thought, be forgiven for assuming that Dodo Delfington was a devastatingly chic, unremittingly exigent, magisterial old dyke. She stood not quite five feet tall and, though thin, was not achingly so; her short, crimped white hair, coiffed in a distinctly masculine manner, with side part, was pomaded down and ritualistically kept in place by a single bobby pin. Her jewellery, though impressive, was invariable: a triple strand of large globular pearls, fastened by an emerald and diamond clasp that exactly matched her earrings. There was no watch, no bracelet and certainly no brooch to to blemish her severe silhouette. Like Gertrude Stein before her, Lady Charles Delfington preferred to spend her money on pictures rather than on clothes; John could not, however, help surmising that *her* wardrobe, though simple, must have cost a tad more than old Gertrude's. To John, Lady Charles Delfington presented a stark, elegant, exceedingly refined and wholly original profile.

'It *is* extraordinary to think, Dodo,' John said, as he inched up alongside the old woman, 'that these pictures were given as a wed-ding present by Lorenzo the Magnificent to Alberico Tornabuoni in 1483 and that they have never since left this Palace.'

'Yes, extraordinary,' she said, staring intently at the pictures. 'And to have all three of the series is even more extraordinary.'

'Actually,' John said, 'there's a fourth panel, but that's—'

'Oh *please*, I implore you,' Tommy Tornabuoni cried, struggling to rise from his bergère, 'don't rub the salt in the wounds. The fourth panel – the only one to bear the coats of arms of both the Tornabuoni *and* the Medici – was virtually stolen from us. That,' he said, pointing to the one empty wall in Palazzo Tornabuoni, 'is why I leave that space blank over there, as *testimonianza* to the duplicity, nay the crime, to which we were subjected. You see, my poor trusting grandfather – a gentleman to the very tips of his fingers – was taken in by that Hebrew chap who lived up the hill at Settignano.'

'Do you mean—'

'Don't *mention* that name in this house,' Tommy bleated, cutting Dodo off. 'Woe betide him for the chicanery he wreaked on poor Grandpapa, for destroying the perfect symmetry of the Tornabuoni legacy. Do you know he had the audacity – so typical of his race – to push his way into the Palace and then to pronounce that the fourth panel in the *Nastagio degli Onesti* series was workshop – by one Jacopo del Sellajo. Workshop? *Workshop* amidst the Tornabuoni collection! Impossible, you might well think. But he insisted, and poor gullible Grandpapa fell right into the trap. And is it *par hasard* that the fourth one is generally considered the most magnificent of the group? That scoundrel from Settignano – *scoundrel*, I tell you – he walked out of the Palace with the picture right under his arm. He practically made Grandpapa pay *him* to take it away. And do you know, the very next year he sold it as a perfectly authentic Botticelli – sold it for a colossal sum, I dare say – to the Prado, where it hangs in ignominy to this day. Mummy and I even went together to Madrid in the early thirties to try to get the picture back. But by then, the Bolshevists were already vying for power, and they wouldn't even discuss the matter with us. They honestly seemed to believe that they possessed rightful ownership of *our* picture.'

'Museums can be like that,' Dodo said proscriptively. 'When Papa died, just after the war, the Metropolitan simply swarmed round, like a kettle of vultures, thinking they had the right to his entire collection. They assumed that, because I was in England, they could make off with what they liked. One trustee even threatened to sue me over the Carpaccio, saying that it had been promised to the museum. Well, one wasn't going to put up with *that*. I just had all the pictures packed off to London and put up for sale at once.'

'I would never like to speak against museums,' Sir Christopher joined the conversation, 'but I do think they, or at least some of their more benighted staff, can sometimes step out of bounds. You know, I had made it clear, years ago, that I was planning to leave my entire – albeit quite modest – collection to the Ashmolean, until, that is, a junior curator there had the extraordinary impertinence to attack one's Botticelli work, attack it in print. His arguments were, of course, utterly suppositious, but attack one he nonetheless did.'

'No, I don't believe it. That doesn't seem possible. Attack this beautiful new book?' Dodo said, sitting down to pat the gift Sir Christopher had offered her this morning.

'No, not the new book,' Sir Christopher said, placing himself next to Dodo on the canapé, 'but my two-volume monograph that came out a few years ago.'

'But I thought everyone,' she said, 'considered that *the* definitive work on Botticelli.'

'So most people – most *intelligent* people – do,' Sir Christopher immodestly agreed, 'but that didn't stop one person, a fool named Neville Pounder, from wielding his sledgehammer into my book. Of course, I knew that his damp squib was nothing but a puerile payback for a review one had written of a little book that he turned out on Titian a few years back, a work which, for vulgarity of statement and dearth of historicity, could hardly be surpassed. One was really *very* restrained in reviewing it; he should actually have been grateful to one. Instead, he turned round and produced the most vitriolic ad hominem attack you can imagine on my Botticelli monograph – for which he ought rightly to have been sacked. I didn't see why, after that sort of treatment, one should leave one's things to the Ashmolean. Talk about biting the hand that feeds one! I can assure you that, thanks to him, I've made an entirely new will, with nary a bequest to the Ashmolean. Old Neville Pounder has only himself to blame for doing Oxford out of my pictures. So aptly named is he: penny wise and *Pounder* foolish!' Sir Christopher said with a flourish, failing to acknowledge, as he did so, that Pounder, so far from having been fired from his position as curator at the Ashmolean, in the wake of the damning review, had actually been promoted to the directorship of the museum.

John stood to one side, sipped his coffee and pretended to inspect the much disputed Leonardo *Portrait of a Youth*, displayed on an easel in the corner, whilst half listening to Sir Christopher expound on a subject he knew by heart. Two years ago, a few months after the publication of Sir Christopher's monumental monograph, *Alessandro*

Filipepi, Commonly Known as Sandro Botticelli of Florence, Two Volumes, Including a Catalogue Raisonné, Neville Pounder published an excoriating article in *The London Review of Books*, entitled 'Christopher Noble-Nolan, Commonly Known as the Savage Noble of Florence, One Review, Including a Catalogue of Errors'. Rather than lash out with a reply, Sir Christopher had, most uncharacteristically, brooded for some time before taking action.

Several months after Pounder's review had appeared, Sir Christopher called John into his study one afternoon and said, 'Here, read this. That should put paid to old Neville Pounder.'

John was presented with several sheets of paper that named him as the sole legatee of Sir Christopher's estate. After he made a sufficient show of gratitude – for 'show' it was – John was instructed to type up a fresh copy and post it to Sir Christopher's London solicitor, who was to draft a new will that would eventually be signed and witnessed at the British consulate in Florence. John did as bidden, but with none of the elation he might once have imagined such news would fill him. Though he admitted to himself that the passage from complete preterition to unencumbered heirdom in less than six years was a fairly remarkable transformation, he would still have preferred to have been chosen not in reaction against Neville Pounder but for himself alone, in acknowledgement of his indefeasible right to inherit; he did not want to be employed as the instrument of revenge but recognised as the object of love.

Glancing round the room today, John unquestioningly thought Sir Christopher the most distinguished, the most handsome, the most intelligent, the most fulfilled of the present company, and he could not deny that he still, after all the deception – deception in which he himself had indulged and to which, he thought, he had been subjected – longed to be loved by Sir Christopher, to be loved as passionately as he loved him. *Will I never be satisfied?* John asked himself.

No, not till you tend your own talent, another self whispered to him, whispered so softly that John did not hear – or chose not to hear. And yet, the truth was that, even if all his dreams were to be realised, John Forde would remain forever unsatisfied, for he could not cease to yearn, to imagine, to regret, as there was within him a devouring impulse toward self-detestation that he could neither appease nor exorcise.

'But Mr Forde here would know that; he knows all about Florence,' Mrs Hollingsworth called out, desperately seeking guidance in her topsy-turvy conversation with Trixie Giraldi.

'I'm sorry, what was that?' John asked politely, trying to shake off his inner colloquy.

'Oh, John, I was just telling Signora Giraldi that you had arranged to take us, Mummy and me that is, to see this enchanting secret corridor.'

'A secret garden? *Giardino segreto*? Nothing special about that. They're two a penny in Florence,' Trixie Giraldi said in her typically dismissive fashion.

'No, not a garden. What *is* it called, John, this corridor? The Fazari corridor?'

'It's the Vasari Corridor, connecting the Pitti Palace to the Palazzo Vecchio, with its splendid collection of self-portraits. That' – he turned to Signora Giraldi – 'is what Lady Charles and Mrs Hollingsworth and I are going to see tomorrow. And it is true that very few people, even very few Florentines, get to visit it.'

'Oh, but I have. Pifi and I were part of *the* most marvellous private tour in May of 1938, the historic tour that is,' Trixie Giraldi said proudly.

'What tour was that?' Mrs Hollingsworth asked.

John rolled his eyes.

'You don't know, my dear? Honestly don't know? The ninth of May, 1938, a Monday. A day too, *too* beautiful. I shall never forget it. All of Florence had been preparing for weeks. And Pifi, my husband, being the *vicesindaco* of Florence was right in the thick of things. In fact, he and a charming engineer, called Giuntoli, organised all the decorations. You've never seen the town looking so lovely and gay. Banners and flags of the *giglio* were draped from every window and balcony.'

'What's the *giglio*?' Mrs Hollingsworth continued her litany of artless questions.

'It's the fleur-de-lis, or a sort of stylised iris that is the symbol of Florence. Unlike the French version, it always shows a stamen posed above each folded petal. It appeared thus, on the reverse of the first gold florin ever struck, in 1252 in Florence,' John explained.

'That's right. The fleur-de-lis, or the *giglio* as we prefer to call it,

belonged to Florence *long* before the French had the cheek to pinch
it from us. Some people date its association with Florence – *Flor-entia*, as she was originally known – back to the first century BC,'
Trixie Giraldi, who always believed what she wanted to, said. 'And
so there it was, the *giglio*, hanging from every window, on the ninth
of May 1938. And for this special occasion, when *tutti quanti* would
be here, our Leader had the brilliant idea of installing three large
windows smack in the middle of the Vasari Corridor, right over the
Ponte Vecchio, so that, as we ambled from Palazzo Pitti toward the
Uffizi, all the dignitaries could stop and behold a marvellous view,
west, toward Santa Trìnita.'

'Windows? Three windows?' John asked sceptically. 'I can hardly
believe that even *he* could just have three windows hacked into the
Vasari Corridor.'

'Oh yes, three large *lovely* windows. All on the Duce's express
orders. You'll see the windows tomorrow. You can't miss them;
they do introduce some much needed light into that dank old
Corridoio. But then, everyone knows that the Duce was a man of
exquisite taste, not to mention an unwavering perfectionist, and he
did want everything to be just *so* for that special day. Of course, Pifi
and I were very well placed in the cortège. We were even amongst
those invited to meet our German friends at the train station. I'll
never forget the thrill of it: the ninth of May 1938, two o'clock in
the afternoon at Santa Maria Novella train station, platform sixteen
he was to arrive—'

'Well, I think we really must be off, if we are to see any of those
churches later this afternoon,' John said firmly, cutting off Trixie
Giraldi, before she floated away on the flood-tides of fascist nostalgia. He then stood up and made a motion to leave, a motion with
which Sir Christopher was more than happy to comply.

✝

Everyone departed together – Alice and her sister sponging a lift
in the taxi of the Portinari ladies; Dodo and her daughter escorted
to their *hôtel* by their driver; and Sir Christopher and John returning home on foot – leaving Tommy Tornabuoni and Montgomery
Woodstoke to commune in silence, or so John imagined, for he was

convinced that, when alone, the noble baron and his aging catamite had nothing, but absolutely *nothing*, to say to each other.

Once out in the damp, grey air of this March day, Sir Christopher said to John, 'Well, you certainly do seem to have made a conquest of Permelia Hollingsworth.'

'That wasn't difficult. She is, as you warned one, appallingly earnest. But, you know, in the end, I really rather liked her,' John said, failing to specify that it was Mrs Hollingsworth's labile nature – she being the daughter of a German American Jewess and a Scotch aristocrat, who, through marriage, had reinvented herself as a Philadelphia Quaker grandee – that particularly appealed to him.

'And then,' he added, 'next to Mrs Bentley-Gordon, on my right – well, *anyone* would be preferable to her. She really is thoroughly disagreeable. And her moustache is thicker than ever! She now looks like an adipose version of Alice B. Toklas.'

'Yes, I rather pitied you that,' Sir Christopher said, 'but you seemed to put a brave face on it.'

'I did, as a matter of fact, manage to extract one interesting bit of information from her. She told me that her husband, her notably absent husband – I gather that he is off cavorting in Amsterdam – is not, as we thought, working on Masaccio, but, if you can believe it, on Leonardo.'

'Well,' Sir Christopher said, 'we've nothing to fear from that quarter – if his Masolino work is anything to go by.'

'No,' John agreed. 'Though I was led to understand, even if Mrs Bentley-Gordon didn't actually come right out with it, that her husband is prepared to say that Tommy Tornabuoni's portrait is an authentic Leonardo.'

'Do, by all means, let him. It will only make one's case for Verrocchio that much the stronger,' Sir Christopher said.

'I noticed,' John changed course, 'that you, on the other hand, did not make much effort with the neighbour on *your* right, Trixie.'

'I don't see why one should be bothered. She really is *too* moronic, that woman. And as for old Alice, do you think she's finally going off her head? Screaming up and down the table as she was about her *placement*. I mean really. She'll have to be locked *up*, if that continues.'

'That was just her sister,' John explained, 'driving her mad. You know that whenever Alice has Trixie to stay for more than a day or two – and now it's over a fortnight – they invariably lapse into their Betty Davis and Joan Crawford routine.'

'I've no idea what *that* means,' Sir Christopher said, 'but I did find her behaviour highly eccentric throughout all of luncheon.'

'At least she didn't mention your mother's food,' John said.

Sir Christopher laughed. 'Quite true. But did you notice the way she devoured those asparagus? One spear after another, she took in her hand – she obviously thought that was more "ladylike" – with mounds of butter and cheese drooling down her cheeks. *Too* disgusting, it was.'

'Well, as Dr Freud asserted,' John said, 'sometimes a cigar *is* just a cigar. But much worse than any of Alice's little attention-grabbing antics was the vomition of fascist fanaticism over coffee. First, there was Tommy's slur about "that Hebrew chap up the hill at Settignano" – and that in front of Dodo.'

'Yes, I heard that. Tactless, I admit. But then, Dodo wouldn't mind. She's so infinitely superior to that sort of thing. It never ceases to amaze one that they were able to reconstruct this bridge so convincingly. One would have no idea that it had been blown up by the Germans,' Sir Christopher said, stopping in the middle of Ponte Santa Trìnita.

'Speaking of Germans,' John rejoined, refusing to be quashed by Sir Christopher's abrupt turn in the conversation, 'Tommy's sniping was far from the worst of it. After that, we had Trixie regaling Mrs Hollingsworth with the beauties of the Führer's visit to Florence in 1938. I managed to put a halt to the conversation before she could quite get out the name Hit—

'But look!' John interrupted himself excitedly. 'There are the three windows. I thought she was simply demented when she was going on about them. But there, there indeed, they are – three large, hideous windows.'

'What on earth do you mean? Three windows?' Sir Christopher asked, turning round.

'Right there,' John said, pointing toward the Ponte Vecchio. 'Those three ghastly picture windows – if that's what you would call them – let into the Vasari Corridor. She, uh, Trixie, said that Mussolini had had them specially installed, so that Hitler could stop, when he was walking from Palazzo Pitti to the Uffizi, and enjoy an unobstructed view of Santa Trìnita and all the north-west of Florence. I just assumed that she had got things muddled up, as usual. But, my God, there they are, those three monstrous windows. They look like something in Florida!'

'They are perfectly awful, I admit,' Sir Christopher agreed, 'though I don't remember ever having noticed them before.'

'Now, one will never be able *not* to notice them – thanks to Trixie. You should have heard the way she went on, waxing nostalgically about the good old days, with flags of the *giglio* waving from every window in honour of the Führer's visit in May of 1938.'

'I can assure you that it wasn't just the *giglio* that was flying proudly in Florence that day. I well remember that street leading up to Santa Croce – via de' Benci – being absolutely swathed in flags of swastikas, not a *giglio* in sight, as Hitler was stopping at the church to pay his respects at the shrine to the so-called martyrs to the fascist cause.'

'What? You mean that you were in Florence for Hitler's visit?'

'One wasn't here *for* Hitler's visit. I was here to put the finishing touches on my book about the Master of Saint Cecilia,' Sir Christopher said. 'I remember being absolutely livid that not only the German Institute was closed – not surprising, I suppose – but even the Archivio di Stato. It was a Monday, and one couldn't get a jot of work done. The city was simply awash with Italians frantically flinging their arms about in mangled *Heil Hitler* salutes. One old woman even knocked me in the head, just back there in via de' Tornabuoni, right by Tommy's Palace. Tommy's father and elder brother were, of course, part of the inner circle of guests. And believe me, you wouldn't have dreamt of going anywhere near Piazza della Signoria, so jam-packed was it with zealous Italian fascists, panting to salute the Führer, as he stepped onto the balcony of Palazzo Vecchio.'

'You never told me,' John said, disappointed.

'It never seemed important. It is, of course, perfectly farcical when one hears Italians, today, going on about the "Liberation" of Italy. Italy wasn't *liberated* from German occupation. The Italians were the allies of the Germans – thick as thieves they were. Everyone knows that it was only because the Nazis started losing the war that the Italians switched sides. The most opportunistic people one has ever met, the Italians are! But I suppose that is what makes them so charming – like something straight off the operatic stage – *Così fan tutte* come to life. Now, why don't we pop into Cammillo on the way home?' Sir Christopher asked, speaking of the trattoria that was the preferred eatery of them both, which also possessed the incalculable advantage of being open on Sundays. 'That way, we can double-check that they have a suitable table for Dodo tonight. It's not every multimillionaire that you can bring to such a simple place.'

'Okay, but do let's hurry, as Dodo is meant to be picking me up at a quarter to five, and I want to look up something first,' John said, casting a last, aggrieved glance at the odious three windows.

⚜

'Wasn't that a curious lunch party?' Dodo Delfington said as John settled himself in the front seat of the car.

'I'm afraid it's rather standard fare for Florence,' John said, turning round to address the two ladies in the back.

'Well, I've never seen Alice quite like that – all of that shouting and making such a fuss about her *placement*.'

'Christopher thinks she's going off her head, but it is, I promise you, just her sister, her deaf old fascist sister, who drives her round the bend, when she overstays her welcome in Florence.'

'It wasn't her sister who got her going on about Papa giving a ball in her honour,' Dodo said. 'I've never heard such nonsense. Papa might, just *might*, have invited her to a party in Newport right before the war – I had long been in London by that point, of course, married to Charles, so I wouldn't know – but the idea that he gave an enormous ball in her honour, in honour of Alice Varrow! I mean, I ask you – it's just too preposterous, too preposterous even to contemplate.'

'Oh, Mummy, I'm sure that she didn't mean any harm,' Permelia Hollingsworth intervened. 'You know how people misremember things.'

'Speaking of *mis*remembering things,' John said, 'I just had time, when we got back, to verify Tommy Tornabuoni's story about the "scoundrel from Settignano", as he called him, intentionally misattributing the Botticelli and then selling it for great profit, directly he got his hands on it. Well, I can tell you now that it's a fact, *fact*, that the picture was bought by the Prado in 1868, and a fact, *fact*, that the "scoundrel" was born in 1865. Now, many people have praised him for being a precociously gifted connoisseur, but I don't think anyone – not even his greatest admirer *or* detractor – has ever claimed that he was pronouncing on Botticelli at the age of three.'

'No.' Dodo laughed. 'Not even Papa, who depended on him for countless attributions. He would never have bought the Carpaccio but for him. But then, I didn't believe a word of what Tommy had to say. Like many disappointed people, he believes his own lies, which is why, I suppose, he goes on repeating them.'

'As Dr Goebbels,' John chimed in, 'is meant to have said, "A lie told once remains a lie, but a lie told a thousand times becomes the truth." '

'Hardly the truth, in Tommy's case,' Dodo said, 'as we've all seen through him. Now, to speak of more life-enhancing matters,' she went on, 'do tell us about the churches that you are taking us to this afternoon?'

John realised that he had been, if not rebuffed, at least rerouted. Anti-Semitism, he was left to understand, was not a subject capable of penetrating Lady Charles Delfington's veil of protection: it did not define her; she defined herself. Though she spoke openly and proudly of her accomplished father, Leopold Kline – German Jewish banker, turned New World Mæcenas – she also insisted on referring to the Anglican communion, in which both her daughters had been baptised and married, as 'our' church, and though she would never, like Alice Varrow, be so crass as to spew forth anti-Semitic vitriol in the hope of deflecting suspicion about her own past, she did make it known that she felt no connexion to the modern state of Israel, which she made a point of never having visited, saying on more than one occasion in John's hearing that one must never confound anti-Zionism with anti-Semitism.

John himself could not, however, cast off the subject of anti-Semitism so easily. During his childhood, he had been repulsed by the mentality that fuelled his parents' bigotry – indeed their hatred. The revulsion they felt for 'kikes', as they called them, was second only to that they harboured for faggots, the latter being a tribe so reviled that his parents could only rarely bear to call them by name – 'they', generally, were just dismissed as degenerates like *that*. No Jew, let alone black, had ever crossed the threshold of his parents' split-level aluminium-sided sanctuary (and they would never admit that they sheltered a fag under their very roof), and so were they, in their deeply ingrained ignorance, free to indulge in the crudest of stereotypes.

But the very real aversion John felt toward his parents' obloquies was motivated as much, if not more, by embarrassment of their unenlightened, lower-middle-class values. Anti-Semitism, like all forms of racism, he felt, was not just wrong; worse, it was *vulgar*. He was, therefore, shocked, when he came to Florence, to find noble barons and counts spewing forth similar prejudice.

At least, John had often consoled himself, Sir Christopher took no part in such villainy. On the other hand, he had to admit that, though Sir Christopher would actively denigrate no one for racial reasons, he was totally *un*interested in the 'Jewish Problem'; and he could certainly never be made to read a book on the Holocaust, let alone to visit a concentration camp, whereas John himself was deeply preoccupied by the matter. As a young boy, he had felt very much deprived not to have so much as a *drop* of Jewish blood, though he could not deny that such Hebrew association as he longed for was always of a Rothschild/Sassoon hue rather than of a Bronx/Brooklyn tincture; as an adolescent, terrified of the opprobrium that knowledge of his own homosexuality might elicit, he developed a profound sense of kinship with this most despised and rejected of people and vowed – a vow he did not always manage to keep – never to give way to the obscenity of anti-Semitism.

With great affection, he looked straight at Dorothy Kline Delfington and said, 'I thought we would start with the church of Santa Maria Maddalena de' Pazzi.'

'Whatever you think,' Dodo said affably. 'We're entirely in your capable hands, John.'

'Afterwards, we might try Sant'Ambrogio and San Simone, and anywhere else you like, if we have time, but I am particularly eager to start with Santa Maria Maddalena de' Pazzi whilst we still have good light, as there is the most beautiful late quattrocento open courtyard designed by Giuliano da Sangallo that repays careful study. And then there is a great hidden gem in the church, which I don't want to spoil for you.

'Oh, look, here we are,' John said, as the car slowed down in Borgo Pinti. 'You see how beautifully concealed it all is. From the street, one can hardly tell that there is a church lurking behind this high wall.'

On the qui vive not to inundate his charges with more information than they could easily digest – a fatal flaw of the overzealous cicerone, as he had long ago grasped – he gave but the briefest sketch of Giuliano da Sangallo, the architect whose work most perfectly embodied Lorenzo the Magnificent's intellectual and artistic credo. Briefly, he pointed out the graceful silhouette of the unfluted Ionic columns and the archæologically correct entablature, but he left the two women to soak up the elegant sobriety of the unadorned courtyard in silence.

After listening to her daughter splutter forth a few trite remarks of admiration, Dodo Delfington said, 'The architecture is so perfect, this extraordinary union of austerity and grandeur – like the ingeniously simple solution to some very complicated mathematical problem – that one's almost afraid to spoil it with words.'

Deeply pleased by Dodo's response, John added nothing, leaving her to feast her eyes on the noble spectacle before them. This was, indeed, one of his favourite places in Florence and not one that he was prone to share. He often stopped here when walking home from the German Institute, no matter the weather, to sit alone under the sentient shade of the archways, the ideal niche for him in which to immure his thoughts, to bemoan his fate, to plot his future or simply to sigh his soul away.

Leaving Dodo alone in the atrium, he led her daughter toward the church, stopping outside the main entrance to indicate a chapel on the right. 'That,' he said, turning toward Mrs Hollingsworth, 'is the chapel of Santa Maria del Giglio. And I don't have to tell *you* what the *giglio* is. I was sorry about the way she went on, Alice's sister, Trixie. I did my best to break it up.'

'Don't be silly. It was nothing to do with you. Poor old thing, she's so deaf that I don't think she can even know what she was talking about,' Permelia Hollingsworth said, brushing aside the matter of Trixie Giraldi's fascist encomia.

'Yes, of course,' John said, realising that Mrs Hollingsworth, just like her mother, was not going to implicate herself by any show of Hebrew indignation.

'This, in any event,' John continued, as they entered the chapel, 'is the real *giglio*, the true Florence. The frescoes, as you can see, are rather second-rate – Bernardino Poccetti, the artist is called – but it's the image of Philip Neri that I like, done just two or three years after his death, well before he was canonised. Many people think of him, mistakenly, as Roman – because of the Chiesa Nuova and so on – but I can assure you that St Philip Neri is as Florentine as the *giglio* itself, for he was born and raised here and even educated at the convent of San Marco by the Dominicans.'

'How fascinating,' Mrs Hollingsworth said. 'Oh look, here's Mummy.'

John led them inside the church, where he explained to them that the choir is the fullest and most coherent expression of high Baroque taste in Florence, enlightening them with a few (but not too many) dates and names. He also informed them – sure that it would warm the cockles of their secular hearts – that the titular saint of the church, Mary Magdalene de' Pazzi, whose supposedly incorrupt remains the high altar still houses, was born of one of the most noble of all Florentine families, a family that, needless to say, strenuously objected to their daughter submitting herself to the debasement of Carmelite seclusion. John desisted, on the other hand, from recounting either the spiritual or mystical excesses of this saint, the very incarnation of masochistic *anorexia mirabilis* – she who sheathed herself in a nail-studded corset; she who trod barefoot through the snow to lick the wounds of lepers; she who begged her sisters in arms to tie her up and hurl hot wax at her scarred body – or the fact that his own birthday fell on her feast – *fell*, that is, until Vatican II wreaked her calendrical havoc, thus depriving him, in his mind, of a supernal link to this most aristocratic of Florentine saints.

After covertly dipping his hand in a holy water font to the left of the high altar, he turned to Dodo and said, '*Now*, the real treasure waits in store for you. We have to go down to the crypt, which leads into a grandly austere, late fifteenth-century chapter room, where you will be confronted by one of the great secrets of Florence. It's a work of art,' he continued, turning to Mrs Hollingsworth, 'that

I have never looked at in the presence of another person – except for Christopher, of course. Just let me go in search of the sacristan. He'll let us in.'

As John stepped back into the nave, he made out a lone figure advancing toward him. This man was, unmistakably, his one-time dissertation adviser, Milton Isner. Fearful that his former professor should convince him of sin, that his truth should not be believed and accusations flung at him, John hid himself and went out of the temple.

CHAPTER II

Mental Reservation

'GOODNESS, YOU DO look soaked right through,' Sir Christopher said, standing at the door of his study, as he watched John wriggle out of his dripping coat in the front hall.

'It's positively torrential out there,' John said, shaking his umbrella.

'I wouldn't open that thing in here – frightfully unlucky that would be.'

'No, I wasn't planning to,' John said, knowing all too well of Sir Christopher's, to him unfathomable, adherence to superstition. 'I'll open the umbrella on the loggia.'

'It's after five, you know,' Sir Christopher said, descending the steps to meet John.

'Yes, I'm perfectly aware of the time,' John said snappishly. 'Don't worry, I'll make tea as soon as I dry off.'

'I wasn't worried about tea,' Sir Christopher said in a wounded tone of voice. 'I was *worried* that something might have happened to you in this god-awful weather. Weren't you meant to be coming home directly you finished lunching with Dodo and her daughter?'

'Yes, I was, but lunch went on forever,' John said not untruthfully, though nonetheless misleadingly. In fact, when he met Dodo Delfington and Permelia Hollingsworth this morning at their *hôtel*, they had both apologised profusely for not being able to lunch with him, as planned, after the tour of the Vasari Corridor, for they had just been asked, not an hour before, to arrive in Lucca earlier than expected and did not want to jeopardise their chances of renting the Villa Reale di Montalto. John had said that, much as he regretted not lunching with them, he perfectly understood, whilst secretly rejoicing in the idea of having a long, leisurely, drunken meal – alone. Yes, lunch had gone on *forever*.

253

'And then,' he continued, 'I had so many errands to run, as you can see from all these packages. Once I disburden myself of them, I'll prepare the tea. But I can light the fire first, if you like, as it's such filthy weather,' he offered as a piacular gesture, for he felt both touched and guilty that Sir Christopher should have been worried about him, whilst he had fribbled the afternoon away, lending a thought to no one but himself.

'That *would* be welcome,' Sir Christopher said. 'But what beautiful things do you have in all those parcels? That tube there looks the sort of thing in which they roll up honorary degrees.'

'No, nothing to do with doctorates of honoris causa. And it's not even a tube. It's, uh, it's, well, it's a – a mat that's rolled up.'

'What sort of mat?'

'Just a mat. Something I need,' John said brusquely, opening the door to a hall cupboard, where he shoved the offending item out of view. 'But I did get the marmalade cake and the new slippers and, most important, the Brendel tickets. I also went all the way to Careggi to get some more of your albumin drip.'

'Oh yes. I suppose that is wanted. And what's in that big box there?'

'That,' John hesitated and then blurted out, 'is a scale.'

'A scale? You mean something for the kitchen?' Sir Christopher asked.

'No,' John said emphatically, preparing himself to be completely forthcoming, 'it's for the bathroom, my bathroom.'

'Whatever for?'

'What do you think it's *for*? So that I can weigh myself. I'm planning to go on the strictest of *régimes*.'

'Why would you want to do that?'

'Because I've become so appallingly fat.'

'You don't look any fatter than usual,' Sir Christopher said placidly.

'Thanks. Thanks a lot.'

'I think you look fine the way you are.'

'Well, I don't *feel* fine!' John nearly yelled. 'I feel absolutely dreadful, dreadfully embarrassed about the way I look,' he continued, his voice now sinking to the merest whisper. He turned away, fearful of breaking into tears, and then said, 'Let's go light the fire in the drawing room. Then you can sit there, as I'm preparing the tea.'

'Yes, that sounds a good idea,' Sir Christopher, who was unsettled by John's outburst of emotion, said in a subdued tone of voice.

'I also got a copy of *The New Yorker* for you in Piazza della Repubblica,' John said, as they walked into the drawing room together.

'That was very thoughtful of you,' Sir Christopher said.

You've no idea how *thoughtful,* John said to himself, regretting that it increasingly seemed to him that every gesture he made toward Sir Christopher – especially the benevolent ones – every word he spoke to him – especially the kind ones – should be mired in obfuscation. People speak reprovingly of thoughtlessness, but it was, he feared, his own thought*fulness* that corrupted his every good deed.

'Here,' he said aloud, handing over the copy of *The New Yorker*, to which they did not subscribe – entirely too much about left-wing politics, jazz, photography and other such non-subjects for both Sir Christopher's *and* John's taste – 'you're in luck. There's not only a wildly long critique of several recent productions of *Parsifal* by Andrew Porter, but what appears to be a never-ending "true crime" article – something about Orthodox Jews murdering one another in Forest Hills – that should appeal to you.'

'How delightful,' Sir Christopher said.

'Good,' John said, bending over to stoke the fire. 'I'll be back in a moment.'

After he dried himself and slowly put away his purchases, he set to making the tea. He opened the canister of Russian tea he had bought this afternoon in via de' Tornabuoni, the very same oblation he had made to Sir Christopher back in the summer of 1983, and thought ruefully of the person he had been six years ago, of the aspirations he had harboured and the future he had envisaged for himself. Whereas it had, six years ago, been a time for making plans, it was now, he realised with trepidation, a season for taking stock, but the courage for such an undertaking escaped him, and so it was that he walked into the drawing room with the tea tray and, with manufactured cheerfulness, said, 'Here is the marmalade cake from Giacosa.'

'How delicious! But do tell one,' Sir Christopher said, looking up from his magazine, 'what is a bag-əl?'

'What?' John asked.

'A bag-əl,' Sir Christopher repeated himself. 'It says here, in this perfectly fascinating article in *The New Yorker*, that there are these extraordinary people in Queens – creatures such as one has never imagined, much less *met* – who are forever hatching the most vicious murder plots over a cup of coffee and a bag-əl.'

'Oh.' John laughed. 'I think you mean a bā-gəl.'

'What on earth is that?' Sir Christopher asked.

'It's a sort of Jewish bun, with a big hole drilled into the middle of it.' John smiled, delighted by Sir Christopher's blissful benightedness. Ignorance can be as carefully and self-consciously cultivated as knowledge – many an intellectual is as proud of what he does *not* know as of what he does know – which goes far toward explaining why John took such pride in living with someone who refused categorically to temporise, for he viewed such bewilderment not as betokening discontinuity but as providing a bulwark against the vulgarity of the modern world, a means to keep them both not simply from but above the herd.

'And jolly nasty that sounds,' Sir Christopher said, 'a Jewish bun, with a great big hole drilled in the middle.'

'Yes, it is,' John said, 'thoroughly nasty, really quite disgusting, I assure you. But the extraordinary thing is that you find them all over New York – not least in Queens, I imagine, where, I am happy to say, I have never been. But I can tell you that even in Manhattan there are entire shops dedicated to selling them.'

'How EXTRAORDINARY!' Sir Christopher said.

'But you needn't worry,' John said. 'I couldn't, for love or money, find you a *bag-əl* in Florence. You'll have to make do with marmalade cake and white truffle sandwiches. And as a matter of fact, I found the Russian tea this afternoon. They've finally got it back in stock at Procacci.'

'The Prince Vladimir?'

'Yes.'

'Oh, then the tea today will be especially lovely,' Sir Christopher said. 'And what with this horrid weather, it couldn't be more welcome.'

'And here are the Brendel tickets. You can see that they are beautiful seats in the centre stalls,' John said, standing behind Sir Christopher's chair as he handed over both a plate of cake and the concert tickets. 'The program is to be all Schumann, starting with the *Kinderszenen*,' John continued, laying a hand on Sir Christopher's right shoulder.

'We'll have to listen to it after dinner,' Sir Christopher said, reaching back to touch John's hand. 'But aren't you having any of this delicious cake?'

'No, I'm beginning my *régime* immediately,' John lied, having already rationalised that he could not possibly start to transform himself until the day *after* Dodo had left, when he would wake up fresh, free from all constraints.

'What strength of character you have,' Sir Christopher said, taking his cake in his hands and biting into it. 'But you haven't yet mentioned your visit to the *Corridoio*.'

'It was quite a success, I think. Of course, it was a bit rush—' John stopped short, realising that he had almost unmasked himself by alluding to the fact that the two women had had to leave early in order to get to the Villa Reale di Montalto.

'Well, I didn't mean rushed, not exactly,' he corrected himself. 'It's just that there was so much to see, don't you know, and rather a lot of walking involved. Mrs Hollingsworth was perfectly all right; she didn't ask too many tiresome questions. Above all, she was delighted – the way rich people always are – about gaining entry to a place closed to the general public. Dodo, on the other hand, was absolutely splendid. She looked at everything, every single thing, with the utmost scrutiny, and, you know, when one made but a passing reference to that haunting self-portrait by Annibale in the Hermitage, she knew exactly what one was talking about.'

'That doesn't surprise one, not in the least,' Sir Christopher said.

'For one mad moment, I thought of asking Permelia which of the Carracci she preferred, but I rather feared that she wouldn't have known that there were three of them.'

'My dear, I rather doubt that she would know that there is even *one* of them.'

'I do see what you mean. She *is* rather uncivilised, especially for someone who had the great fortune to be raised in such extraordinary circumstances. She doesn't know the first thing about works of art. She did, rather tellingly, notice the three windows.'

'Three windows?' Sir Christopher asked.

'Yes,' John said frowningly, 'those three disfiguring windows that Mussolini had specially installed for the Führer's visit to Florence, the ones that stopped us in our tracks, yesterday, on Ponte Santa Trinita.'

'I wouldn't pay much attention to them,' Sir Christopher said.

'I don't very well see how one can ever again ignore those windows. But,' John hesitated, deciding to change tack, 'the rest of the visit seemed to go off frightfully well.'

'I'm glad of that, especially after the problem you had yesterday in Santa Maria Maddalena de' Pazzi.'

'Oh, *that*,' John said, trying to dispel the memory of Professor Isner's apparition. 'It's just that I couldn't find the sacristan to let us in to see the beautiful Perugino fresco. I'm quite sure he wasn't there, that lazy old lout. I looked all over for him, even went out of the church, which is why Dodo and her daughter had to wait so long for one.'

'Where did you lunch today?'

'Funny, you know, Dodo so much liked Cammillo last night that she wanted to go back there today, but I told her that it was closed on Mondays.'

'You see, I told you that she's not like other rich people. Quite exceptional she is.'

'I couldn't agree more. Anyway, we wound up going to Harry's Bar.'

'Did you see anyone you know?' Sir Christopher asked.

'No,' John said aloud; to himself, he added, *Thank God*.

'Well, I ran into someone at the German Institute. You'll never guess who,' Sir Christopher said.

'I thought you weren't going out today?' John asked worriedly.

'One wasn't planning to, but, as it was so nice this morning – unlike now; just look at it coming down – I thought one might as well pop into the Institute, for an hour or two, to begin poking about Leonardo. I had Annunziata ring up for a taxi. The *mere* idea of working on Leonardo excites one so. Imagine writing—'

'You haven't yet told me whom you met at the Institute,' John, assailed by frightful premonition, interrupted.

'Old Milton Isner, if you can believe it.'

'Good God in heaven!' John cried.

'Of course, one *should* have recognised him, as he is the only person I've ever known to wear such ill-fitting suits – they would appear to have been made for someone twice his size, with the trousers coming halfway up his chest – but I'm afraid that one didn't. Nowadays, he looks so entirely Cincinnati that it's hard to believe he was actually born in Europe. I suppose that it was somewhere *very* far to the east – Poland? Maybe even Lithuania or Latvia?'

'No,' John said nervously, 'Milton Isner was born in Hamburg – a nice, fitting art historical town – in '34 or '35. His family got out just in time.'

'I must say that he was perfectly affable, in his dour little way, when he came up to one in the periodical room and introduced himself. He asked after you quite warmly.'

'I'm sure he did,' John said, biting his lip.

'He was with his research assistant, who also sent you messages. A nice enough seeming young man – though I can't remember his name – who said that he is working on Francesco Vanni and would like to come to see the drawings.'

'Oh, God, you mean Vincent Casey. He's a colossal bore,' John said.

'Anyway, Milton Isner said that he's nearly finished his book on Gentile da Fabriano.'

'He's been saying *that* for years, ever since I first started graduate school in the autumn of 1981. I don't believe it in the least.'

'Well, you can ask him yourself on Wednesday,' Sir Christopher said.

'Whatever do you mean?'

'I invited both him and his assistant to lunch on Wednesday. You can ask him about Gentile then.'

'You did *what?*' John asked, springing up from his chair.

'I invited them to lunch.'

'But you can't have,' John said, supporting himself on the chimney-piece.

'Well, one did. I thought you'd be happy to see him,' Sir Christopher said airily.

'But we've already got the recently widowed Virginia Stewart Lambert and her young son coming to lunch on Wednesday. And she – a Maryland huntswoman and great heiress – certainly wouldn't go with Milton Isner and his pathetic little research assistant,' John said, desperately trying to stall.

'Oh, Virginia is so well-bred that she can mix with anyone!' Sir Christopher said with a laugh.

'Hmm,' John said.

Walking over to the window to stare out at the storm, he trembled to recall the proud disdain with which he had, six years ago, written to Professor Isner, announcing his intention to abandon the pedantry of graduate school for the Elysian Fields of Sir Christopher Noble-Nolan's universe, and was wildly intimidated by the prospect of being obliged, now, to justify those puffed-up assertions. Had he been less intelligent, the thought of intimidation would not even have occurred to John, for he then would have been able to deceive himself of his own exceptional nature; had he been more intelligent, he would have had enough confidence in himself to assume the mantle of his decisions, not to pander to the opinions of others. As it was, he was trapped in a crippling twilight of inaction: on the one hand, he was consumed by a burning desire to prove his own originality, the longing to display his superior artist's soul to a profoundly peccant world; on the other hand, he was unarmed by a worm of self-doubt, the gnawing sense of his own inherent mediocrity. Dismayed by the apocalyptic scene playing out before him – on both sides of the window – he reluctantly turned back to Sir Christopher and said, 'Here's another slice of cake and some more tea.'

'It *is* delicious, this marmalade cake.'

'If that's all for now, I'll leave you here by the fire. I have something I want to do in my study.'

'Oh, there is that old lecture on Alberti, the one I delivered to the Royal Society just after the war. Do you know where it is? I thought it might be a good way to open the new volume of collected essays, particularly as it has never before been published, in *any* form. I know I had it a couple of months ago, but I can't lay my hands on it now.'

'I'm quite sure,' John said calmly, 'that I put it back in place with the other lectures, in the *archivio* upstairs, back round Christmas. I'll look it out later. Okay?'

'There's no rush,' Sir Christopher said, returning to his copy of *The New Yorker*, with its thrilling account of murder on demand in Queens.

As soon as John deposited the tea tray in the kitchen, he hacked off an enormous wedge of cake and poured a large tumbler of white wine. *How, how*, he shouted to himself, whilst jamming his face with food and drink, *can I face Professor Milton Isner? And how, even worse, could Sir Christopher ever put me in this position? Can he misunderstand me so much? Or does he simply care so little?*

Though John heartily agreed with the tentmaker from Tarsus that no one can truly *know* another man's thoughts – *save the spirit of man which is in him?* – he believed that this instance of Sir Christopher's miscomprehension seemed, in its perversity, positively wilful.

Feeling suddenly sick from the cake he had gobbled and the wine he had swilled, he pressed his head against the cold tile just above the sink and, bending forward, stuck a finger down his throat and retched violently. He reeled backward, bumping into the kitchen table, whereupon his gaze fell on the new canister of Russian tea; he picked this up and, with great force, hurled it into the vomit-stained sink.

☦

That evening John did not even pretend to follow his *régime*. He ate with abandon, savouring the cheese soufflé, sprouting upright penne – a dish that Sir Christopher had affectionately christened the 'Threatened Porcupine' – the roasted squab *sur canapé* and the lemon tart, all accompanied by an ample quantity of red Burgundy. Sir Christopher noticed no contradiction in such behaviour.

'Now, to prepare for the Brendel concert: how many versions of the *Kinderszenen* do we have?' Sir Christopher asked near the end of dinner.

'I don't know exactly,' John answered. 'Shall I just bring them all to you in the drawing room, once I've stacked the dishes in kitchen?'

'That would be splendid,' Sir Christopher said.

'We seem to have rather an *embarras de richesse*,' John said on re-entering the room. 'There's the celebrated Horowitz recording, of course. But we also have Schnabel and Kempff and Buchbinder and Martha Argerich – even Horszowski.'

'And to think,' Sir Christopher said, as John handed him one disc after another, 'that, not so many years ago, one was adamantly opposed to switching over to CDs.'

'To *think*?' John replied caustically, for he remembered all too well the years of peaceful pleading on his part.

'Would it be nice to start with Schnabel, move on to Buchbinder and conclude with Horowitz? We can save the others for later in the week,' Sir Christopher said, leaving John to understand that there was nothing optative in the mood expressed.

As they sat listening to the final recording, John sipped a snifter of Armagnac and tried to think of nothing but the music. This was exactly the sort of seductively lush Romantic music that he had first felt instinctively drawn to as a boy, so different to the harsh sonority of a Wagner or the vulgar histrionics of much nineteenth-century Italian opera that, for the sake of Sir Christopher's approval, John now pretended to admire.

He closed his eyes and, trying to keep his head from drooping, gave himself over entirely to the music, feeling that he heard all the sorrow of the world – and all the joy too, he had reluctantly to admit – encapsulated in these thirteen little impressionistic cameos. When the, to him, slightly too rousing Fantasie in C major followed, intruding on his reverie, John took up a thick biography of Schumann that, in his perennial struggle to redress his musical inadequacies, he was wading through. He looked up the Fantasie in the index, which, he learnt, was composed as a 'profound lament' over the fifteen-year-old Clara Wieck.

As he read on, he was more than intrigued to discover that, less than a year before composing this work, Schumann had been engaged to the adopted daughter of a rich Bohemian noble, Ernestine von Fricken, but, on learning that the girl had been born illegitimate and would, therefore, receive no dowry, he brutally severed all relations with her, for fear that he would be obliged to earn his living like a mere 'day-labourer'. Pondering the transparently self-interested motives of this high priest of Romanticism, he whom John had always imagined to be the very avatar of artistic purity – utterly immune to petty materialistic concerns – he could but be reminded of his own, oft-times duplicitous, dealings with Sir Christopher.

Attempting to chase such unwelcome thoughts away, John stood up as soon as the disc was finished and said, 'It was too marvellous, the way Horowitz played the *Träumerei*, wasn't it?'

'Yes, it was,' Sir Christopher agreed. 'All of it, really, was spectacular. One finally begins to understand why the French prefer Schumann to Schubert.'

'I didn't know they did,' John said.

'Oh, yes, it's a well-known fact, that *all* French people prefer Schumann to Schubert,' Sir Christopher, without any trace of irony, said.

John smiled. 'If you say so. I think we should probably go to bed now. I'm sorry dinner was so late, but then I was running terribly behind schedule all afternoon.'

'Right you are,' Sir Christopher said, standing up. 'Oh, but that,' he continued, pointing at the manila envelope that John had earlier left on the low table, 'is quite the wrong lecture.'

'I thought you said that you wanted the Alberti lecture?'

'I do.'

'Well, that's what it is. The one you delivered to the Royal Society back in '48. I've got it typed right on the front label,' John said, whilst poking the fire.

'It might *say* that on the label, but inside, I can assure you, is the lecture on Baldovinetti that I delivered, but a year or two ago, to the Accademia del Disegno.'

'I suppose the lectures must have got inadvertently exchanged, one for the other. In any event, I think we should be wary of any future lectures.'

'Why ever so?' Sir Christopher asked. 'One has lectured all one's life.'

'It was, if you remember clearly, on the occasion of your lecture to the Accademia del Disegno that your tremor became so pronounced,' John said cautiously, as he referred to the now alarmingly shaky condition of Sir Christopher's hands *and* voice – though not his mind – a state that all doctors insisted was not Parkinson's disease but which, nonetheless, defied diagnosis.

'Yes, I *do* remember,' Sir Christopher said glibly, as John accompanied him to his bedroom and started to lay out his nightshirt.

'There you were,' John continued more assertively, 'getting all worked up over that lecture to the Accademia del Disegno, pumping yourself full of Dexedrine, whilst all the other speakers at the conference appeared to have brought themselves *down* with Valium.'

'Do you honestly mean to say,' Sir Christopher asked, incredulous, 'that people take a depressant *before* speaking in public?'

'Yes, I do.'

'No wonder that most art historical lectures are so boring!'

'Now,' John said, kissing Sir Christopher on the forehead and tucking him into bed, 'I'll look out the Alberti lecture for you first thing in the morning.'

'Goodness, what would one do without you?' Sir Christopher said, closing his eyes.

The following morning, however, John had little time to think about misfiled lectures. His entire attention was occupied with unpacking his new scale – though he did not yet dare to step on this instrument – and, even more, with jotting down detailed conversions of kilos to pounds in a snakeskin pocket diary he had specifically bought to serve as a *carnet de poids*. Finally, shortly before noon, he absent-mindedly went upstairs to the meticulously organised archive in search of the missing lecture. Without the slightest difficulty, he laid his hand on an envelope labelled: '*Alessio Baldovinetti and the Development of Landscape Painting in Fifteenth-Century Tuscany*'. *Delivered to the Accademia del Disegno, Friday, 29 May 1987*. But rather than find the missing Alberti lecture therein, as he had expected, John came across thirty sheets of blank paper. Overwhelmingly bored, he went down to Sir Christopher's study and, on entering, said, 'It's not there.'

'What's not where?' Sir Christopher asked, looking up from his typewriter.

'The lecture. The lecture on Alberti. I can't find it.'

'Well, what did you do with it?'

'What did *I* do with it?' John shot back, barely able to mask his anger.

'Yes. You must have done something with it,' Sir Christopher said in an exasperated tone of voice. 'I gave you the envelope with the lecture inside, round Christmas, and you were meant to have filed it.'

'It's perfectly true,' John said, trying to steady himself, 'that you handed me these two things to put away in the week between Christmas and New Year – when I was trying to clear up all the debris you had left strewn about your study – but you muddled them up,' John said, slamming two manila envelopes down on Sir Christopher's writing-table. 'You put the landscape lecture in the Alberti envelope and thirty sheets of blank paper in the Baldovinetti one. I never thought that I had actually to check that you were capable of stuffing the right lecture in the *right* envelope.'

'Well, you should have thought of that,' Sir Christopher said fractiously.

What I should *have thought of is leaving you to die a few years ago, all shrivelled up in your bed, alone,* John said to himself; aloud, he said, 'Hmm.'

'Good,' Sir Christopher said. 'Now, please just go find the lecture and leave one be. I am frightfully busy, blocking out a chapter on the young Leonardo.'

John turned away without replying and, closing the doors of the study even more gently than usual, gasped for breath. At luncheon

— before which he had already quaffed a bumper of sherry — John pretended as if nothing had happened to offend his sense of self; he talked easily and intelligently of the recent state of Leonardo scholarship, leavening the conversation with the occasional tale of Florentine squabbles. He even mentioned — only because it represented the polar opposite of what he felt — that he thought they were terribly lucky to have engaged the new cook for the daytime, the third in as many years. 'So much better than poor old Rita,' he said.

'Rita?' Sir Christopher asked.

'The Indian, as you used to call her. Remember?'

'No, I don't remember any Rita,' Sir Christopher said.

'Of course you remember her, the one who *denied*,' John said emphatically, 'having stolen the gold repeater.'

'Oh, her. One's forgotten that creature ever existed.'

'That's natural, I suppose,' John, who was plagued by the memory of Rita, said, whilst looking at his watch and wondering just how many undetected lies he could tell in the span of five minutes. 'Yes,' he continued, 'one has quite forgotten her, poor old Rita.'

'Well, whatever *you* do, please don't forget about the Alberti lecture. It really is essential for the new book of collected essays. And I believe that it was the only copy. Mamma, you know, thought very highly of one's Alberti work. That was the last lecture she ever heard one deliver.'

'Oh, in *that* case,' John said, cutting himself off, as he could think of no further lies — only a surfeit of accusations — to recount.

Having dawdled in his study after luncheon, John reluctantly returned to the archive at about three o'clock, where, to no avail, he continued his search. He clearly remembered that this lecture, '*Leon Battista Alberti: The Theory and Practice of Early Renaissance Painting*', had been typed on exceedingly thin, indeed flimsy, pale blue sheets — a relic of wartime rationing, John thought — more like tissue paper than airmail stationery, and did not doubt that its thirty or so pages could have been folded in half, even in quarto, and thus easily misplaced. Nonetheless, he was now absolutely sure that this lecture was not lurking anywhere in *his* beautifully arranged archive.

Much as he realised that Sir Christopher's study was the most logical place to continue his search for the missing manuscript, for it might have been unwittingly shoved into any book or thrust behind any shelf, he was loath to suffer the slings and arrows of his master's contumely – the censorious gaze, the rasping impatience, the derisive exasperation – that such an intrusion would inevitably call forth. John had not known Sir Christopher to be so captiously restive for years and decided, therefore, to focus his attention on the hall cupboard, leading to his own study and bedroom, where he had recently transferred all the offprints and photocopies that had been clogging up the shelves of Sir Christopher's study. It was possible, he thought, *just*, that the lecture might have slipped between the cracks of this less than perfectly arranged ensemble.

When he opened the door of the cupboard, the mat he had stowed there yesterday afternoon immediately tumbled out. Groaning, he bent down to pick this up and carried it off to his bedroom. Unfurling it, he looked despondently at the exercise guides drawn across the mat's surface – sit-ups, press-ups and Lord-knows-what-ups – that he had implausibly imagined himself performing. *Will this blasted régime ever begin?* he asked himself. Glumly, he kicked the reproachful object and went to prepare Sir Christopher's tea.

'I thought,' John said, walking into Sir Christopher's study, 'that you might prefer just to have your tea in here today.'

'Yes, that's a good idea. But aren't you going to have any?' Sir Christopher asked, looking at the single teacup.

'No, I'm still quite busy. But look, there's some cake left,' John said, producing a scrappy slice of what remained from yesterday's, once quite large, confection.

'How delicious. And is this still the Prince Vladimir?' Sir Christopher asked.

'Yes,' John lied, thinking of the vomit-soaked tea he had had to throw out last evening.

'Now, I really must be getting back. I've just begun to go through all the offprint envelopes in the hall cupboard, in the hope of finding the Alberti lecture muddled up there.'

'What about the archive? It's much more likely to be there,' Sir Christopher said.

'I've already been through that with a fine-tooth comb. And I promise you, indeed I am willing to stake my soul on it, that it is not there.'

'Well, I'm sure you *will* find it,' Sir Christopher said in a not altogether pleasant manner.

John went back to his own study, a retreat he had slowly and lovingly created. For years, long before he had known Sir Christopher, John had dreamt of a room of his own, an adytum where he might consort with master spirits of time past. And so it was that, when Sir Christopher had been taken ill four years ago, and John claimed this room for himself, he devoted such perfervid attention to its decoration. He employed the services of an old-fashioned artisan – someone who might have stepped out of the pages of *Romola* – to create a precise shade of green paint: enamelled green, *verde smalto* of the fourth Canto; he had had the large, glass-fronted bookcase from Sir Christopher's London study reassembled here and filled it with works of literature, all of his own choosing; and he hung the remaining walls with photos and drawings of the Noble-Nolan family, as if to arrogate them for his own ancestry.

Yes, the perfect sanctuary – perhaps too perfect, he whispered to himself as he looked round and thought of all the work that had *not* been accomplished within this setting.

As if to repudiate the useless idyll he had created, he grabbed pile after pile of the bulging, battered manila envelopes from the hall cupboard and scattered them wildly, indeed recklessly, round the room, hoping to cover his *Earth in forgetful snow*. But still, he found no trace of any Alberti lecture. At a quarter to eight, he gave up and, having no idea of what he was going to give Sir Christopher for dinner, wandered into the kitchen. He opened a cabinet, reached for a bottle of Tío Pepe and took a long swig. Just as he removed the bottle from his lips, the door of the kitchen glided open and Sir Christopher stepped halfway in.

'Oh, there you are,' Sir Christopher said good-naturedly.

'Um, yes,' John said, hiding the bottle behind his back. 'Listen, um,' he continued nervously, unsure if he had been caught in the act, 'I am afraid that I am going to have to give you an ad hoc sort of dinner tonight because, you see, I'm still busy looking for that old lecture. Would it be all right if we just had an omelette *aux fines herbes* and then, for the sweet, some of the *macedonia* left over from luncheon?'

'Right you are. I am sure that one can make do, this *once*, without a first course, though it might be nice to have some fried potatoes with the omelette.'

'Yes, of course. Would you like a nip of vodka before dinner?'

'That would be most welcome.'

'Fine, uh, fine. I'll bring it in to you. Now, why don't you just go and sit in the drawing room? I'll be there in a minute,' John said, nudging Sir Christopher out of the kitchen.

John drew a long breath and then took another gulp from the bottle of sherry that he was still clutching in his right hand, whilst extracting the vodka from the deepfreeze with his left. He then dug out a lone, rarely used, eighteenth-century Venetian glass and poured Sir Christopher more, much more, than a 'nip' of the iced nectar.

As he took a final sip of sherry before putting the bottle away, he could not help but recall that, when he first met Sir Christopher, it had seemed to him that the older man drank rather a lot, but then, at that time, the 24-year-old John Forde had only partaken of alcohol when offered, which was not very often. Now, he had to concede that, though Sir Christopher had steadfastly refused to heed Dr Werner's advice to foreswear all alcohol, John had never once seen him abuse drink, not even remotely so. Moreover, and even more tellingly, Sir Christopher's intake of alcohol never varied: save one thimbleful of vermouth or sherry before luncheon, he remained abstemious during the day, so as to be completely alert to work; in the evening, he had only one (sometimes very large) glass of vodka or whisky – he disliked gin and thought champagne an abomination, expecting John to feel likewise; at dinner, he generally took two glasses (never more than three) of full-bodied wine and was quite prepared, when in restaurants, to leave half the bottle behind – he abhorred 'house' wine but could not, at the same time, abide too much œnological fussing; after dinner, he was prepared, occasionally, to take a brandy -- he distinctly preferred Armagnac to Cognac.

John's consumption of alcohol was, on the other hand, wildly inconstant: sometimes, he could go for days, even weeks, without touching a drop, which irritated Sir Christopher to no end; at other times, such as today, when anxiety or disappointment descended on him, he could tipple on and off for hours and then, after Sir Christopher had gone to bed, down an entire bottle of wine by himself. He was not, however, concerned by his own erratic indulgence, as he did not believe that one *could* become an alcoholic before the age of thirty. He was only twenty-nine – at least for another two months.

✞

'No, I'm not having anything to drink this evening,' John said.

'Is that because of your *régime*?' Sir Christopher asked.

'Would that it were, but the truth of the matter is that I need to keep my wits about me this evening, as, right after dinner, I am going to have to root about in your study in order to find the Alberti lecture.'

'You *still* haven't found it?' Sir Christopher said in a tone that sounded more accusatory than interrogative.

'No.'

'And I was hoping that we might listen to that new recording of *Rienzi* after dinner.'

'I'll put it on for you, of course,' John said, 'but I really want to find that blasted lecture first, if only so that I don't have to waste any more of my time over so *trivial* a matter.'

'It's a pity you'll miss *Rienzi*,' Sir Christopher said.

'I read not long ago that it was one of the Führer's favourite works; apparently the party rallies in Nuremberg invariably began with the overture from *Rienzi*,' John continued in a challenging tone of voice.

'Did they *now*?' Sir Christopher, refusing to rise to the bait, asked coolly.

When, later in the evening, he was standing on the library ladder, methodically scouring one shelf after another, John listened to the distant strains of the music wafting up from the room a few steps below. He did not actively dislike what he heard, but he could not shake off the idea that, in comparison to the virginal purity of a piano sonata, there was something inherently meretricious in opera as an art form. Forced to choose between the two – which he was not, but he didn't realise that – John would always opt for Schumann over Wagner, not to mention Donizetti. Nor did he care to admit that, whereas Schumann left him free to dream, Wagner forced him to concentrate on the matter at hand, and his self-indulgent, if not exactly lazy, mind always preferred reverie to application. This evening, however, he very much needed to apply himself.

By the time the second disc of the opera came to a close, he was seriously irritated by the amount of time he was forced to lavish on this seemingly fruitless search; when the third one ended, and he turned round, seeing Sir Christopher posed on the threshold of his own study, John felt closer to despair.

'Well?' Sir Christopher, his arms crossed behind his back, asked.

'Well *what?*' John asked.

'Have you found the Alberti lecture?'

'Obviously I wouldn't still be looking for it if I *had* found it?' John testily shot back.

'Obviously,' Sir Christopher said in his most inscrutable manner.

'But I will find it,' John said with unconvincing assurance.

'You had *better* find it,' Sir Christopher said in what, to John, seemed an overtly menacing fashion.

Find it or what? Or bloody well what? What will you do? Throw me out in the stree— John shouted to himself, interrupting his inner tirade in horror of its implication. Aloud, he said, 'Right you are. Why don't you get ready for bed – do your teeth and so on. It's quite late after all that music. I'll be there in a minute to lay out your things.'

John did prepare Sir Christopher for bed as usual – the nightshirt, the handkerchief, the pills, the turned-down bed – but he did not, for the first time ever, kiss him goodnight. As soon as he could unobtrusively absent himself, he closed the door to Sir Christopher's bedroom and crept off to the darkened drawing room, where, with a particularly fine bottle of Pauillac for company, he piled more wood on the grate, slumped into his regular armchair and lit a cigarette, something he had never before dared to do in this room. By the time he had uncorked the wine and sipped but a few drops, he was gazing deep into a brilliant fire, whose wildly rampageous flames seemed exactly to mirror the accusations and assaults that flickered and flared and crackled through his own mind.

John was honest enough with himself to admit that, in the past, he had often been afraid of Sir Christopher – dreading the flush of temper or the silent scorn – but he had never before been willing, or indeed able, to acknowledge just how tenuous his foothold was in his master's realm. Tonight, however, he realised the ease, the perfect legal right, with which Sir Christopher could expel him, cast him right out in the street. With but a twitch upon the thread, Sir Christopher could sunder their attachment forever. It was true, he reminded himself, that Sir Christopher had recently changed his will, naming him, John, as sole beneficiary, but it was equally true that there was nothing to prevent him from changing his will yet again, from irrevocably dis-inheriting him, simply because he failed to find a lecture on Leon Battista Alberti that had been written well before he was even born.

Though John had long thought that Dr Faustus's famulus had spoken prophetically, when he said: *I think my Master means to die shortly. He has made his will and given me his wealth.* John was equally sure that *his* master did not mean to die for years, during which time he might redraft his will many times over.

Gasping at the fragility of his own position, John took a large gulp of wine, vowing all the while never to divulge the slight-est glimmer of his trepidation to Sir Christopher. He would adopt *enforced ceremony*, cloaking his fear and resentment in *smiles and affa-bility*, but the truth, such as he knew it, would remain a province all his own, his very own mental reservation of private murmuring and unvoiced longing. Henceforth, he would unhesitatingly equiv-ocate, swearing *in both the scales against either scale.*

He was perfectly aware that the rigid bachelor of Königsberg put a prohibition on lying under *any* circumstance, even if the lie might save an innocent person; to John, such an interdiction had long seemed perfectly laughable, not even worth discussion. The more flexible (and more widely entertained) belief, as argued by the slave of Madame de Staël, that one is duty-bound to tell the truth only to someone who has a moral right to it, might once have seemed logical to John, but now, with his convictions shaken and his *amour-propre* deeply wounded, he preferred to ally himself with the tenets of the supreme poetic dandy. He was, tonight, convinced that no one can bear to know, know truly, what another – espe-cially, perhaps above all, his beloved – thinks of him, thus is it that lying and deceit form the fundamental basis of all human relations: *Si, par Malheur, on se comprenait, on ne pourrait jamais s'accorder.*

But barricade his thoughts though he might behind a shield of lies, John realised, albeit reluctantly, that he was not strong enough to stench the stirrings of his own heart, and so it was that, even as he pledged allegiance to a cynical *dandysme*, he involuntarily began to wonder if Sir Christopher had actually noticed the withheld kiss this evening, or if, more damning yet, he had been relieved to be spared the attention. And wonder John did, as he continued to stare at the hypnotically hysterical dance of flames until sleep overcame him.

✝

'There you are,' Sir Christopher said, standing at the doorway to the drawing room in his nightshirt and black velvet slippers, as he flicked on the blinding overhead light.

'Oh, I must, uh, I must have fallen asleep,' John stammered, jumping up nervously from his chair.

'Little wonder,' Sir Christopher said, pointing to the empty wine bottle on the table before the smouldering fire. 'You might have set the whole house alight. And it positively reeks of cigarette smoke in here.'

'Ah, that, I can, uh, explain.'

'Your explanations are of no interest to one. Indeed, the only thing about you of the slightest interest is to know have you, or have you not, found the Alberti lecture?' Sir Christopher asked, crossing his arms, inquisitor-style, over his chest.

'Well, not yet, but I'm sure that I—'

'That's enough. I've already rung up Rita. She's found a replacement for you. You can leave forthwith. Here's five hundred dollars,' Sir Christopher said, extracting the money from the breast pocket of his nightshirt and flinging it at John. 'Now, get out!' he finished, obdurately pointing to the door.

'Rita? Rita? What does Rita have to do with this?' John asked desperately, as he bent down to gather the scattered banknotes.

'She was on to you from the beginning. She knew you stole the repeater. We both knew it. We just wanted to see if you would confess or not. We never thought you would actually frame her.'

'I didn't frame her. It was you who accused her, not me. You must just give me one more chance,' John puled.

'No, it's too late for that,' Sir Christopher said in his most adamantine fashion. 'Rita has produced a charming young man to replace you: he's clever and scholarly and handsome and well born and, to boot, he's thin. I'm sure that he won't lose lectures and fall into a drunken stupor before an open fire. You've had your chance, and you squandered it; now you have to make way for those on the way up. I'm finished with you.'

'But I, uh, I—' John whispered, falling to his knees.

'You what?' Sir Christopher asked, looking down at John with withering contempt.

'I love you...'

✟

I love you, John heard himself say out loud as his head banged against the low table, jolting him awake in the pitch dark. Startled and confused, he twisted round on the floor, not sure where he was, till he saw one last flame sparkle, splutter and expire in the mountain of ash constellated in the fireplace. He assumed that, when asleep, he must have slithered out of his armchair onto the floor, where he had been assailed over and over again, or so it seemed to him, by the same terrifying nightmare.

With difficulty, he heaved himself up, turned on a light and looked at his watch. It was half past four. With great deliberation, he inched round the drawing room, straightened cushions, unrucked the carpet and tidied the grate. Finally, and most important, he removed all incriminating traces of his presence: the empty bottle, the glass, the corkscrew, the dirty ashtray.

As he teetered toward his bedroom, John was aware of his head pounding with a force that, he felt sure, no consumption of alcohol, alone, could have induced. Several times, both in the front hall and in the smaller passageway parallel to the via de' Bardi, he felt obliged to stop, pressing against the wall for support. A few steps before he would have reached the door to his bedroom, he lurched forward, scraped his head against the wall, drawing blood, and flailed about. Frantically, he latched on to a wooden panel covering a shallow niche in the wall, yanked it open and leant both his arms on it.

When he had first arrived in this apartment, John thought this niche a rather useless and, even worse, æsthetically unpleasing thing, but he had soon changed his mind, finding it the perfect place to store hundreds of Sir Christopher's discarded thrillers, well out of view, behind a closed panel. Now, in the dark hours of the morning, he thought the presence of this niche a positive benediction.

Panting, he crossed both arms over the top of the open wooden panel – roughly the height of his shoulders – and pushed his blood-stained forehead down heavily on the back of his hands, thereby yanking the door off its hinges and knocking himself, as well as most of the books in the niche, to the floor. He lay there, face down on the hall floor, books all about him, even *on* him, worried more about the havoc he had wreaked than the injury he had suffered.

'At least Leonard Bast,' John cried hysterically, 'was killed by an avalanche of, presumably, *decent* literature, not this trash that engulfs one.'

After not more than a few minutes, he brushed the books off himself and, with difficulty, worked himself up into a sitting position, his back propped against the wall. Drowning in a sea of despised thrillers – he cared less than ever who had killed Roger Ackroyd – his eye fell on a hardcover book that he had given to Sir Christopher last Christmas, *The School for Illiteracy* by one Guinevere Grasemann. He remembered how much Sir Christopher had adored this book – reading it in a single go on Christmas night, and then again on Boxing Day – thanking him repeatedly, as he never did for any of his other, more expensive, more carefully pondered presents.

John picked up the book, making no attempt to protect it from his sweaty, bloody grasp. Thinking that he might fling the book right down the hall and, along with it, all of his own murderous frustration, he tugged at it viciously, when out tumbled thirty-three folded sheets of the palest blue tissue-fine paper.

CHAPTER III

Identity Theft

'I NEVER FOR a moment doubted that you would find it,' Sir Christopher said, looking up from the *International Herald Tribune* at breakfast on Wednesday morning, as John handed him the soiled copy of *The School for Illiteracy*, with the Alberti lecture tucked inside.

'No, of course not,' John whispered.

'Though I must say that I do think it frightfully clever of you to have looked inside this book. What led you to do that?' Sir Christopher asked.

'I simply can't *imagine*,' John said, his voice rising. 'We should just be grateful that you didn't throw that old thriller in the wastepaper basket – with the lecture inside – as you've done with so many other of those dreadful books you read.'

'Goodness, what a drama there would have been then!' Sir Christopher said with a laugh.

'One shudders to think,' John said.

'You mustn't forget that I did tell you at the time, when you gave me the book at Christmas, that it was one of the best thrillers one has ever read – a masterpiece of the genre – and that it should definitely be saved. You really ought to read it yourself,' Sir Christopher said, sliding the book across the porphyry tabletop toward John. 'I don't see how one could fail to like it.'

'*On verra*,' John said, recoiling from the blood-stained object with a horror akin to that which, he imagined, Herod must have felt when Salome presented him with the charger containing the severed head of the Baptist. 'For now,' John continued, 'I have to think about this absurd luncheon that you've got us embroiled in today, mingling Milton Isner and the dreaded Casey with Virginia Stewart Lambert and her young son.'

'What are you planning to give us to eat?'

'I haven't exactly had much time to think about it,' John said.

'I am sure that, whatever you arrange, it will be beautiful. But who on earth,' Sir Christopher asked, looking up, 'can be ringing the front doorbell at this hour of the morning?'

'I had better go and see,' John said, 'because Annunziata is already doing the beds, and Lord knows what that new cook, Drusilla, is up to.'

'And?' Sir Christopher asked, when John returned.

'It was just something from DHL,' John said, brandishing a cardboard folder.

'Here,' Sir Christopher said, extending his hand.

'Actually,' John said, with no little degree of satisfaction, 'it's for me.'

'Oh,' Sir Christopher said, more surprised than indignant, though John interpreted the tone of his voice otherwise.

'It's from Permelia Hollingsworth,' John said, ripping open a tissue-lined envelope.

'You do seem to have her eating out of the *palm* of your hand,' Sir Christopher said.

'Hmm...' John said. 'It would appear,' he continued, after having read on, 'that, though she is ostensibly writing to thank one – as well she might – for having taken her round Florence, she really wants something else. It's all about renting the Villa Reale di Montalto for that ball she wants to give for her daughter in the middle of August, at which, she specifies, we are both expected.'

'Oh, goodness,' Sir Christopher said, 'I can see already that that party is going to be the most chthonic nuisance. We'll have to make sure to be away at the time. I think the Bach festival in Leipzig is already over in August, but it might be just the time to go to Bayreuth.'

Torn as he was by wide-eyed curiosity about attending such a grand fête and gnawing fear of putting a foot wrong in such treacherous terrain, John did not know how to reply to Permelia Hollingsworth. Strange though it might seem, it was not the idea of mingling with a throng of Italian nobles on the opulent grounds of a royal villa that alarmed John, but, rather, that of being confronted by the ruling class of his own country. After nearly six years in Florence, John was perfectly aware that most aristocratic Italians tended to lump all vaguely well-mannered Americans together: they made no distinction between colonial families and post-industrial ones – any such lineage as there was in America seemed pathetically recent to people who claimed kinship with the likes of the Consul Fabius Maximus or St Zenobius; nor did they ask any probing questions about schools or clubs – it was all the same to them if you attended Williams College or Wayne State College; and they saw no difference between the Knickerbocker Club and the Harmonie Club.

John's own countrymen could not, however, be so easily duped. He knew that it was easier for an American of the second rank to be accepted by European nobility, even royalty, than by the keepers of the gates in Philadelphia or Boston or New York. And what of an American of *no* rank, such as himself? How would he answer, how would he evade, the probing lances of inquisitorial Hollingsworths or Biddles?

At least, John said to himself, *I now have a deadline for my* régime: *I must fit into my dinner jacket by the middle of August!* To Sir Christopher, he said, trying to sound light-hearted, 'I don't think Dodo will let you off the hook *that* easily.'

'That's precisely,' Sir Christopher said firmly, 'why we must know the exact date of this absurd entertainment, so as to be sufficiently forearmed. Does Mrs Hollingsworth mention it in her letter?'

'No, she doesn't. But she does say that her son – she mentioned him at luncheon the other day – who works at Morgan's in Paris, is coming here this very weekend "to tie up loose ends", as she not so eloquently puts it, with Patsy de' Pazzi – though, what *she* has to do with it, I have no idea. Here, you can read it yourself,' John said, proffering three thick sheets of Nile blue paper, streaked with large, childish writing.

'To judge from this rather illiterate missive,' Sir Christopher said after a quick glance, 'I'd guess that Ludovica Bonamici is demanding an exorbitant sum – in cash, it would appear – as down payment for the rental of the Villa Reale di Montalto and that the Hollingsworth son is being used as a go-between to funnel the money into the rapacious hands of Patsy de' Pazzi.'

'But I thought Montalto was owned by the three Piccolomini-Brown sisters,' John said.

'It *is*,' Sir Christopher said, buttering but one side of his toast. 'Ludovica Bonamici is the eldest of the three sisters – she was born to one papal title and married to another – and she controls everything. She's tough as nails, you know. It wouldn't in the least surprise one if she has kept her two really charming sisters – Carlotta and Viola – completely in the dark about the whole scheme of renting Montalto to the Hollingsworths, while surreptitiously diverting the money to her dreadful daughter, Patsy de' Pazzi.'

'I didn't know that Patsy de' Pazzi was the daughter of Princess Bonamici,' John said.

'But *of course*,' Sir Christopher replied in a shocked tone of voice, one with which John had become all too familiar over the years. *Any* subject, John realised, with which Christopher Noble-Nolan was himself intimately acquainted – whether it be the Köchel number of the *Jupiter Symphony*, his friendship with Andrew Bruntisfield, the author of *Maria Stuart* or the genealogy of the Piccolomini-Brown family – was deemed a most basic tenet of common knowledge, and ignorance thereof would, invariably, be greeted by a freshet of intellectual, indeed moral, indignation on Sir Christopher's part, whereas a subject in which he was *not* well versed – oriental art, contemporary music, film or the stock exchange – was haughtily dismissed as just so much dreary dust, quite unworthy of his attention.

'Hmm,' John replied sheepishly.

'Anyway,' Sir Christopher continued, 'it looks as though Mrs Hollingsworth is expecting us to do something for her son when he passes through Florence this weekend.'

'We really don't have time for that – what with all the entertaining we've had to do lately,' John groaned, thinking of the *régime* he had dreamt of starting.

'We'll see. So long as Dodo doesn't get on to one personally, I think we can get the boy down to a drink,' Sir Christopher said, turning back to his newspaper.

'*Signor* John,' Annunziata said, tapping on the door of the dining room, '*c'è un fax per lei nell' archivio.*'

'*Grazie. Grazie mille,*' John said politely. He disliked being addressed as '*Signor* John' – he thought it made him sound like a child – though he did not blame the maid, so much as the circumstances, for the usage. 'I'll bet' – he turned to Sir Christopher, as he stood up – 'that that's a fax from Dodo in London – something about her grandson. If so, we're *really* in for it then.'

✟

As they sat in front of the fire after dinner that night – listening to yet three more versions of the *Kinderszenen* – John replayed to himself the events of today's dreaded luncheon with Milton Isner. So terrified had he been of being ensnared by his past mistakes – the self-satisfied pride and the misplaced ambition – that he had hardly dared to speak during the meal. He feared, above all, that his former dissertation adviser might be tempted to compare him with his coevals, all of whom had, by dint of single-minded application and routine drudgery, far outstripped him. John had only to recall the names of those fellow graduate students – Butterworth, Klinefeld, Russo and, not least, Casey – to whom he had once adopted so undisguisedly a condescending attitude, for the full threat of Professor Isner's potentially severe judgment, his unsheathed sword of Choler, to dangle menacingly before him.

It was, therefore, in defiance of all expectation that John felt Professor Isner tap him avuncularly on the shoulder, as they said goodbye at the front door – Sir Christopher not having bothered to get up – and tell John that, should he ever want to return to New York, he would always have a place in graduate school, no need even to ask. But John knew that he never would go back, never *could* go back. He was forever tethered to his master. And yet, though the memory of that dream last night, that which had stirred piteous fear in the lake of his heart – *nel lago del cor* – had somewhat abated, such calm as he now experienced only served to incite flagitious thoughts of revenge for the shabby treatment that he felt he had been subjected to over the missing lecture.

Why don't you just die? he repeated to himself over and over, as, after dinner, he looked across the room at Sir Christopher, dozing in his armchair by the fire. *Yes, just die, that way you won't ever be able to threaten me again. Never will I have to worry about being cast out in the cold, disinherited, despised and rejected. Die, die, DIE!*

As if to inflame his own ire, he went back to reading *The School for Illiteracy*, the thriller of which Sir Christopher thought so highly. He had picked the book up before dinner with the deliberate intention of throwing it down in disgust in front of Sir Christopher later in the evening – hoping, thereby, to demonstrate the superiority of his own tastes and the delicacy of his sentiments – and yet, in spite of what John thought of the book's psychology (obtuse), its language (clichéd) and its plot (contrived), he found himself swept up by its monstrous awfulness.

The central conceit of the novel – the senseless murder of an upper-middle-class English family at their country house by their illiterate housekeeper and her wily accomplice, a former prostitute turned religious fanatic – was of no interest to John, but he *was* fascinated, more than he liked to admit, by the description of the early lives of these two repulsive women in the squalor of south London suburbs. There seemed no measure that either one of them would not resort to – without so much as a flicker of conscience – to ensure that no importunity, even a trifling one, should incommode her: the trollop thought herself perfectly justified in lacing her mother-in-law's tea with tranquillizers, so as to have the old woman off her hands; and the moron did not bat an eyelash over suffocating her sickly father with a pillow, for he *had* requested, one time too often, to be pushed in his chair up to the common. So excited, so distraught did these tales of perfidy make John feel that he suddenly jumped up, tossed the book aside and yelled, 'Utter rubbish, it is!'

'Oh, you didn't like it?' Sir Christopher, waking up, asked in a disappointed voice.

'It's *too* squalid,' John said. 'I don't know how you can go on with this trash.'

'It says here, in the *New York Review of Books*,' Sir Christopher said, pointing to the paper crumpled in his lap, 'that Wittgenstein adored thrillers.'

'That explains a jolly lot about the *Tractatus*, I dare say. Now, I think it really is time for bed. I, for one, am exhausted, as I hardly slept last night, what with searching for that old lecture unto the wee hours. Come,' John said.

'I suppose that one *is* tired,' Sir Christopher said. 'One did, after all, have quite a busy day. And I didn't think old Milton Isner too bad. Though one did have rather to restrain oneself, when he started to go on about the mindset – I mean mindset! – that inspired the *Lamentation* hanging above the piano in my study. It was on the tip of my tongue to say, "But, my dear Milton, I believe that works of art are made, not by mindsets, but by things called *hands*, which is why I know, positively know, as you might not, that that picture is a perfectly authentic, indisputable Giovanni Agostino da Lodi." '

'Of course,' John mechanically agreed, all the while thinking that now, unlike the person who had first arrived in Palazzo Vespucci six years ago, he couldn't care less about the attribution of this picture. The only thing that, today, interested him about this panel – and, indeed, it obsessed him – was its deeply ambiguous depiction of the bond between Christ and the disciple whom He loved. As he had, over the years, scrupulously studied this image of St John the Evangelist clutching the throat of his unusually young and handsome Saviour, John often asked himself, *Does the disciple want to succour or to strangle his master?*

'And you do see what one means about the peculiar way old Milton Isner wears his trousers? Right up his chest, they go.'

'Professor Teufelsdröckh he's not,' John said, 'but I found Milton Isner very nice today, nicer than I'd ever before given him credit for. I did, however think that his little research assistant, that Casey, was deeply out of his depth. Did you notice the way – quite indecent way – he fawned upon Virginia's young son? I thought Casey's manner wholly inappropriate. I'm sure Virginia was miffed,' John, who had tried to pass himself off during luncheon as an old and cherished friend of Mrs Lambert's – she, whom he barely knew – insisted. Vincent Casey was the same age, the same height, the same religion, the same sexuality, the same class and the same milieu – Hartford rather than Providence – as John Forde, and the latter despised him, even *hated* him, for the mirror image he presented of himself. When John had been obliged to show his contemporary the nineteen Francesco Vanni drawings in Sir Christopher's bedroom after luncheon, he stood guard silently and haughtily, as if to underscore the difference in social standing that he liked to think now separated them.

'At least,' Sir Christopher said, 'there are no other engagements for the rest of the week, so that we really can get down to Leonardo.'

'On the contrary,' John said, extending his hand to help Sir Christopher out of his chair, 'we have Dodo's grandson for luncheon on Saturday.'

'Oh goodness, I'd forgotten all about that.'

'Well, you're the one who got us into it.'

'Had it been anyone *but* Dodo, one would have resisted – what with all the interruption to one's work of late – but she really did seem to expect us to invite the poor lost boy to a meal.'

'I would hardly call him a "poor lost boy". He is, after all, an investment banker at Morgan's in Paris,' John said, trying to curb the asperity he already felt toward this young man – he who, John imagined, enjoyed every advantage, every port of access that had been denied to himself.

'What's his name, again?' Sir Christopher asked, oblivious to anything but his own difficulty in rising from the chair.

'Zeb Hollingsworth,' John said dryly, squiring Sir Christopher toward the front hall.

'Zeb. Zeb? Zeb! I do call that *highly* eccentric,' Sir Christopher exclaimed, stopping in his tracks.

'Well, that's how Dodo referred to him in her fax, and it's how he signed himself in the one he sent this afternoon to confirm luncheon on Saturday.'

'How extraordinary.'

'I assume,' John said, as he tried to glide Sir Christopher back into motion, 'that it must be short for Zebulon. And to judge from what I've been able to dig up on the Hollingsworth family, so far from being eccentric, it's really quite a traditional given name amongst that clan. The boy's father, Permelia's husband, is actually called Levi, another one of their long-standing names, ever since they were granted about one third of modern Pennsylvania by William Penn himself.'

'I thought he was called Biddle, Permelia's husband. She's forever saying "Biddle" this and "Biddle" that.'

'She does rather go on that way, I admit, but that's his middle name. According to his entry in *Who's Who*, the ambassador's full name is Levi Biddle Cadwalader Hollingsworth,' John said, as he turned on the bedroom lights.

'How extraordinary not to have so much as *one* Christian name.

Anyway, I hope that we can find something to talk about to the boy.'

'That's why I invited Alice,' John said.

'I wonder if that was wise? We don't want her making a scene — the way she did at Tommy Tornabuoni's on Passion Sunday.'

'I'm sure that she'll be a great asset,' John, who was counting on Alice to animate the conversation, said.

'*Do* try to keep her off my mother's food, will you?' Sir Christopher asked.

John laughed. 'I'll do my best, though I doubt that I'll be able to quash the subject of the ball that Leopold Kline supposedly gave in her honour in Newport before the war.'

'Oh dear, that old ball,' Sir Christopher said.

'The most important thing is that the dreaded Trixie has gone back to her people in the north, so we don't have to worry about any more screaming matches.'

'Thank God for that,' Sir Christopher said drowsily, as John tucked him into bed. 'And oh,' he added, contorting his voice markedly, 'I was thinking, back when we were fiddling with all those different versions of the *Kinderszenen*, that it would be a very good thing — really indispensable — if we were to have an index, not just an index, but a proper catalogue of all the compact discs.'

'Yes, quite indispensable that would be,' John said softly, all the while thinking regretfully of Diaghilev's advice to Boris Kochno, which he had read years ago, back when he first arrived in Florence, in an essay by Jefferson Birstein: *Il faut qu'un secrétaire sache se rendre indispensable.*

Yes, he sighed to himself, *I have made myself the indispensable secretary, whereas I should have sought to become, as Gide had exhorted Nathanaël, the most* irremplaçable *of beings.*

After he had put Sir Christopher to bed (*and* kissed him on the forehead), John went into the kitchen and opened the refrigerator in search of the white wine — just one glass, he promised himself — but, before he could touch the bottle, his eyes alighted upon a red-and-white cardboard box with black lettering, containing the albumin he had gone to fetch at Careggi on Monday. John removed the box of medicine from the refrigerator and placed it in the centre of the kitchen table. Ever since Sir Christopher had had the trouble with his liver four years ago, Dr Werner came to Palazzo Vespucci every Friday morning to give him an albumin drip, and it was the responsibility of John, naturally, to see that they always possessed a full supply of this globular protein. As no local chemist carried the substance, which cost the rough equivalent of one hundred dollars per phial, he generally went once a month to the hospital at Careggi – sometimes by bus, more often by taxi – to stock up. It had been impressed on him, both by Dr Werner and the nurses in the *casa di cura* where Sir Christopher had first been treated, that the albumin must always be kept well refrigerated, for heat denaturation, to which it was extremely sensitive, would entirely deprive it of its curative value.

John sat down and, recalling those two lunatic ministering angels of death in *The School for Illiteracy*, stared at the innocuous box of medicine and said to himself, *What if? What if I...?* No longer tempted by the wine – not even *one* glass – he went off to his bedroom with the box of albumin under his arm, taking great care to hide it in a warm spot at the back of his clothes press.

The following morning, Thursday, after a deep, dreamless sleep, he awoke early. As if propelled by a force outside himself, he got up, bathed, dressed and went off to Santa Croce before the bells struck seven. Though he knew that Mass would be celebrated in the vernacular, he still brought his Tridentine missal with him, more as a crutch to lean on than as a prop to flourish. If asked, he would have found it exceedingly difficult to say why he had made this pilgrimage; he expected no guidance, sought no forgiveness. He would have welcomed deliverance, deliverance from himself, but he did not believe that attainable in this life, and he lacked the courage, at this stage, *to rush into the secret house of death* – not for many years to come, years of unbearable solitude, would he dare to take that irreversible step. For now, all that he could really hope for, he thought, as he sat in a side chapel and vaguely listened to the litany of saints, was to be shrouded in a warm, oblivion-inducing fog, and this he would not have found if he had stayed at home and lain awake in bed.

John had thought for some time that one of the great advantages of *not* being a native speaker is the ease with which one can block out the chirping tongues round one. And so it was that, this morning, he paid not the slightest attention to the chanting friar but calmly let his eyes flit back and forth through his anachronistic missal, till he landed on the Collect of the Day. He was familiar with (and fond of) the appointed Gospel, from St Luke, in which Christ asks Simon: if a creditor were to forgive equally and absolutely two debtors, one of whom owed him fifty pence and the other of whom owed him five hundred pence, which of the two would love him more? To which Simon replies that he supposed the man who was forgiven more would, in return, love more. Jesus answers that his disciple has rightly judged, whilst John told himself that he also would have decided the same. As he read on, however, he came upon a coda – that he had entirely forgotten and that quite stopped his heart – in which Jesus warns: *but to whom little is forgiven, the same loveth little.*

My God, my God, John cried to himself in horror, *he who is forgiven less, loves less!* At that moment, with devastating purity, he realised that, as he had never been forgiven for his own treachery – for it was unknown to Sir Christopher and so never *could* be forgiven – that it was he, John Forde, not Christopher Noble-Nolan, as he had long assumed, who loved less. Now, with the admonition of St Luke ringing in his ears, he understood how misguided his application was, how false his identification. It was he who loved less, he who should seek forgiveness. Convulsed with remorse, John jumped up, ran home and threw the denatured phials of albumin on the rubbish heap.

✠

John found it difficult, even painful, to look at the scion of Hollingsworth. Though he thought Zeb Hollingsworth staggeringly, indeed devastatingly, handsome – his very tall frame, muscular build, light blue eyes and thick hair, the colour of old gold, were everything that John venerated, everything that he was not himself – it was not the young man's pulchritude, per se, that unsettled him; rather, it was his aura of absolute ease and unblinking confidence (without any trace of arrogance) that deranged all of John's senses. Never before had he witnessed someone engulfed in such an all-consuming cloud of entitlement.

From the snippets of conversation he had been able to register, John worked out that Zeb Hollingsworth was about four years younger than himself – the same generation, by any normal reckoning – and yet they seemed, to him, utterly antipodean. Zeb Hollingsworth, like his father, and Lord knows how many generations of Hollingsworths before *him*, had graduated from St Paul's and Princeton, with a 'gap year' thrown in somewhere along the way; he worked for two years for an investment bank in New York and had, since September of last year, been at Morgan's in Paris. John thanked God that he had had the foresight to ask Alice to lunch, as he now felt in desperate need of her to keep the conversation afloat.

'Speaking of balls, your grandfather gave the most magnificent ball in my honour, when, just before the war, my book on Cleopatra came out and was a *runaway* success,' Alice prattled on.

'Which war was that?' Zeb Hollingsworth asked guilelessly.

'It certainly wasn't the Great War!' Alice exclaimed.

'When I was growing up,' Zeb Hollingsworth said, 'the "war" meant Vietnam.'

'Well, I was referring to *the* war, the Second World War, if you like. The ball took place in the summer of '39. *Too* lovely that ball was that your grandfather gave for one in his magnificent house in Newport, overlooking the bay,' Alice unashamedly repeated herself.

'I think you must mean my *great*-grandfather,' Zeb Hollingsworth said with a smile.

'Yes, Leopold Kline, Dodo's father, would be your great-grandfather, wouldn't he? I remember being taken to see his pictures in Newport, when I was still a boy, and frightfully impressive they were, above all *The Young Knight in a Landscape* by Carpaccio,' Sir Christopher said.

John noted, if not the deference, at least the solicitous interest that Sir Christopher showed in addressing this young man, the offspring of privilege – an effort such as he never made when speaking to a young art historian of obscure origin – but, though he twitched inwardly, said nothing.

'Your *great*-grandfather? That doesn't seem possible. Goodness, how young you must be,' Alice said.

'Actually, I turned twenty-six last week,' Zeb Hollingsworth said.

So, I did calculate correctly, John said to himself, but he realised that the mathematical score mattered nought. It was the perception that counted, and he suddenly grasped, from the flirtatious manner that Alice had adopted, that she viewed the new arrival as existing on quite a different plane, in quite another time period, to himself. John knew that he had many secrets, but he now understood, as he never had before, that his own youth was the best kept of them all. *Secretum meum mihi* kept ringing in his ears as he glanced round the table, for he saw that, even those who knew his actual age, perhaps especially those who knew it, did not think of him as young, and they certainly didn't treat him that way. No octogenarian ever explained to *him* what he or she meant to say by 'the war'. Unlike Lambert Strether, John *could* explain why he missed his own youth and why, after all these years, he should care: to be young had, to John, meant to be vulnerable and, above all, to be ashamed – both ashamed of what he *was* and ashamed of what he was *not* – so that when he found himself confronted by the likes of Zeb Hollingsworth, who so clearly revelled in his own youth, his regret was overwhelmingly bitter.

'Twenty-six! What a lovely age to be,' Alice continued, 'but still not so young as to be free from amorous intrigue. I'll bet all the pretty young girls are after you, trying to get you to tie the knot. Is there anyone in particular?'

Zeb Hollingsworth smiled. 'I'm just playing the field for now.'

Playing the field, John said scornfully to himself, wondering if such a vulgar expression endeared Zeb Hollingsworth to the aged Alice. *Is that what she considers 'masculine'?* he asked himself, not failing to note that, in all the years he had known Alice, she had never once asked him if he had a girlfriend. Of course, she never asked him if he had a boyfriend either, but it was always just tacitly assumed that he was like 'that' – an assumption about his most private persona in which he seemed to have no voice whatsoever. In a similar vein, he remembered that the last time he had ever seen his parents, the weekend of his twenty-fourth birthday in May of 1983, he noticed that his mother had recently had a photograph of him framed – the only one of himself on view in their house in Providence – at a dreaded high-school prom, when he was seventeen years old, clutching the arm of the sister of one of his classmates. Espying that image, he had been filled with a visceral desire to smash it to bits. Ironically, he had genuinely liked the girl pictured next to him – a fragile creature, infinitely superior to his parents in intelligence and sensitivity – but he could not abide that his mother should think that, by displaying a picture of him in heterosexual masquerade, she, like Alice, was free to determine his identity according to her own lights.

'Ever the gay young bachelor you are,' Alice, reaching out to clutch Zeb Hollingsworth's hand, said.

The young man roared with laughter. 'You might say that.'

The muscular shall lounge in bars; the puny shall keep diaries in classical Greek, John, feeling very much ignored, quoted to himself.

'Still, I imagine that you're hiding some Parisian beauty, of ancient lineage of course, up your sleeve,' Alice persisted.

'To tell you the truth,' Zeb Hollingsworth said, 'I don't really know too many French girls – they're not exactly the friendliest people in the world – but my two Cadwalader cousins, Sarah and Elizabeth, are living in Paris, and they introduce me to lots of American and English girls.'

'I can see that it must be rather off-putting actually to *live* amongst the French,' Sir Christopher said.

'Better than living in this manless town: Florence! A twisted knot of bachelors, such as exists nowhere else on God's good earth,' Alice snarled, casting an accusatory glance at John and Sir Christopher. Like many an embittered spinster, Alice looked upon homosexuality as a personal affront to her femininity; to her, every faggot was a blackguard who had spurned her ineffable charm, someone who, by attaching himself to another of his own sex, had both snatched a potential suitor from her clutches and, coward-like, turned his back on his rightful duty, thus making him personally responsible for her solitary state.

Though John was genuinely fond of Alice – she was the first person in Florence to have accepted his presence as an inalienable fact, always inviting him along with Sir Christopher, and he had spent many a cosy Sunday afternoon alone with her, listening to her stories, luxuriating in the sense of belonging – he thought her dreadfully unjust on the subject of homosexuality. *Where,* he asked himself this afternoon, *would poor old Alice be without her fag friends? Only the fags will put up with her. I don't see many straight men lining up*

*to invite old Alice to lunch or dinner. Once a woman is no longer 'bedable',
she might as well be dead, so far as most cynical male heteros are concerned.*

'I suppose,' Zeb Hollingsworth, who was utterly oblivious to the
undercurrent, gabbled on, 'that I'd like Paris more if my French
were a bit better. But I'm afraid that, in spite of all those French
governesses Mummy was always plying us with, I've never quite
mastered the language. But I also have to admit that I had my heart
set on going to London. I mean, I know so many more people there
– my Gaylord cousins, and Grandmamma of course, not to mention
all my pals from Henley.'

'Why *didn't* you go to London then?' Alice asked.

'I had a job all lined up with Slatkin Brothers in the City, at
what turned out to be the worst possible moment. It was just then
that the president of the company in New York, John Cornflower,
was indicted for insider trading, and the whole company risked
going under, right at the moment that they were transitioning from
private partnership to Wall Street's first public corporation. In any
event, Daddy didn't want me to have anything to do with that firm
– said it would be a terrible blot on my CV – and that's when the job
at Morgan's turned up.'

And how did the job at Morgan's just turn up? John fleered to himself,
all the while noting that the rich and entitled generally referred to
'Mummy and Daddy', even sometimes to 'Mamma and Papa', but
rarely ever, as he did himself, to 'my mother and my father', and
never – God forbid! – to 'Mom and Dad'. In the present discourse,
John felt ever more cast aside, even repudiated, by the company.

'Cornflower was in touch with one a few years ago,' Sir Christopher said. 'He had ambitions to put together a collection of old
masters. He'd already made some quite decent purchases on his
own. He even appeared in Florence seeking advice – about what, I
don't quite remember. Do you, John?'

'Ah, um, yes, it was about that putative Botticelli portrait that had
been floating round the market for ages,' John replied softly. 'You
said that you thought it was entirely workshop.'

'Yes, that's quite true.' Sir Christopher chuckled. 'One did render
the picture perfectly worthless. I advised Cornflower against it, and
he followed one's advice. In fact, he seemed like rather a shrewd
man. I'm surprised that he was stupid enough to get caught.'

'He can't, Cornflower, have been so shrewd as all that, because he lied – lied under oath. And there's *never* any reason to lie,' Zeb Hollingsworth gushed.

Never any reason to lie? Never any reason to lie! John shouted to himself. *No,* never *any reason to lie – provided that you're rich and handsome and well born. No reason at all to lie, when you already have everything! I am sure that you, dear Zeb, would never even think of lying, but that is only because you don't need to lie. Just please do be aware that there is no virtue in resisting a sin by which one is* not *tempted. And by the way, your looks won't last. You've got no character in your face. You're not much better, I'd guess – even if you're taller – than Montgomery Woodstoke was at your age. You're certainly no Bindo Altoviti. You might as well be a pasteboard cut-out. Utterly banal, you are,* he went on ranting to himself.

'There's still time for you to move to London,' Alice said. 'Who knows? You might wind up there in a year or two.'

'Actually, I'm moving back to Philadelphia in September, to go to law school at Penn. Daddy insists that it's the best path to follow. And he should know, as that's exactly what he did.'

'Leaving lovely old Europe already? That seems a pity,' Alice said, as though genuinely aggrieved.

'Yep,' Zeb Hollingsworth belted out, 'it's back to the good ole US of A. I'm actually really looking forward to it, as I've hardly ever lived in Philadelphia – what with following Daddy's postings around the world and being away at school so much – and it seems silly to have the kind of name I do and *not* know the City of Brotherly Love.'

'As a matter of fact,' Sir Christopher said, 'John told me that the rather unusual – if I may say so – given names that both you and your father bear are actually typical Philadelphia Hollingsworth names. He said your proper name must be Zebulon.'

'However did you know *that*?' Zeb Hollingsworth, looking at John with a broad smile, asked.

'Oh, just something one read,' John said, trying not to blush. 'I suppose it must have been in a book by that Philadelphia historian who coined the term WASP.'

'I know who you mean,' Zeb Hollingsworth said, snapping his fingers. 'I just can't think of his name.'

'Nor can I,' John lied, desperate to be done with the subject, one which left him feeling perilously exposed, as though making clear to the world the subservient admiration he felt for his social superiors. Turning away from both the conversation and his interlocutor, he repeated the word 'banal' over and over to himself, before inclining his head toward Alice and asking, 'Do you want more asparagus? Annunziata will help you.'

'Well, I can't resist. *Grazie. Grazie tanto*,' Alice said in her execrable accent, taking an enormous second helping from the serving girl who had been standing silently at her side for five minutes. 'So sweet of you to make them specially for one. You know how one adores them.'

John made a point of repeating exactly the same menu that he had given to Professor Isner and Mrs Lambert on Wednesday, but, whereas he had had, three days ago, to enlist all of his willpower in order to resist the temptation to indulge, today – so hideous and decrepit did he feel himself to be in contrast to the aggressively healthy young man at his side – he could hardly swallow a bite without becoming sick, each repellent morsel choking his throat in a near-suffocating hold.

Whilst John was assaulted by imaginary glimpses of a hulking Zeb Hollingsworth gliding his single scull, in all his Apollonian splendour, across a sheet of vitreous water, he imagined that he himself *look'd not like the ruins of his youth / But like the ruins of those ruins*. Despondently, he glanced down at his plate and said, 'I am glad you like the asparagus, Alice.'

'Your *sauce maltaise* is absolutely delicious – infinitely superior to the ordinary hollandaise – just the sort of *recherché* thing your mother would have served, Christopher. But then she did, Dame Sophia, always have *the* most delicious food, even during wartime. I am afraid that I would never be able to get my old Judita to replicate this lovely concoction,' Alice said, dowsing yet another spear in the glossy orange-coloured compound. 'Though I must say that I will never understand why Americans insist on peeling their asparagus – it removes *all* the taste!'

'I thought I was the only American here?' Zeb Hollingsworth asked.

'I'm American also,' John whispered.

'*You*? American?' Zeb Hollingsworth, looking straight at John, asked with unconcealed astonishment.

'Yes. In fact, I'm probably more American than you, as your mother is English, or half English, anyway,' John dared to say. In truth, he thought it inconceivable that anyone could be *more* American than Zebulon Biddle Cadwalader Hollingsworth. Curiously, but typically, John's knowledge of this young man's mixed background – the Kline/Delfington heritage – only added to his conviction that he represented the most perfect flowering of a uniquely American phenomenon: the seamless union of individual achievement and distinguished ancestry, fortified, rather than compromised, by the introduction of alien elements, for John would not admit so much as a whiff of European *fin de race* degeneracy to becloud his ideal of the American ascendancy.

Casting a covert glance round the table, John was consumed by a vertiginous onrush of envy and contempt, knowing ashamedly that he would, without hesitation, swap his own unblemished (but thoroughly proletarian) blood for just a drop of Zeb Hollingsworth's tainted (but perfectly lordly) blood, that he would give anything to be the grandson of Dorothy Kline Delfington rather than that of Dolores Norah O'Donnell. 'I was born *and* raised,' he continued, altering his voice in an unnatural fashion, 'in New England. Providence, Rhode Island.'

'So you just pretend to be English?' Zeb Hollingsworth asked.

'I don't *pretend* to be anything. I simply choose to speak this way,' John snapped, cringing at the fatuity of his own words. Whereas it could once have seemed natural for Americans abroad, cut off from their family and homeland, gradually to acquire a continental accent, John realised that, in this present era of easy travel and instant communication, any such mutation was highly suspect. It might have been acceptable, *just*, for T.S. Eliot to style himself an English gentleman – this was viewed as poetic metamorphosis, not bogus impersonation – but for himself, the obscure John Forde, there was no such excuse, or so Zeb Hollingsworth's outburst of incredulity seemed to imply.

John suddenly saw that an affected voice such as his own was, nowadays, likely to be construed as regret of one's origins – more a betrayal of the subject's dubious background than proof of his international sophistication – and Zeb Hollingsworth, he was sure, would, like Amory Blaine's mother before him, think that only very vulgar people *regret* being American. In the nearly six years he had been living in Europe, John thought much more than he ever had before about what it means to be American, and, though he had never openly spurned his national allegiance, he could not deny that he had often sought to camouflage it. He had consciously adopted a mask in the hope of fashioning a new self. Nietzsche, whom John was fond of quoting, but whom he in no wise resembled, wrote that every genius wears a mask; but not every masked figure, John was forced to concede, is a genius. Challenged by the unparalleled specimen of authentic American manhood that was Zeb Hollingsworth, John feared that he had accomplished not the transformation but the surrender of his own identity. Never before had he felt so deeply, so dirtily phoney.

'No, I didn't mean anything. After all, look at the way Grandmamma Delfington speaks – nobody could sound more English than she does – and she also was born in Rhode Island, just like you. And as for only Americans peeling their asparagus, I can only tell you, Miss Varrow,' Zeb Hollingsworth said, trying, in his most diplomatic fashion, to smooth things over, 'that when my paternal grandmamma was in Paris last week she took me to dine, twice, at the Grand Véfour, where the bottom quarter of the asparagus were all peeled, just like this. Hmm, delicious!' He smiled, as, with a flourish, he picked up a thick stalk and dropped it gracefully in his beckoning mouth.

'Dodo *would* take you to the Véfour. She's mad on luxury, your grandmother,' Alice said.

'Actually, I was referring to my Grandmamma Hollingsworth. And she's usually mad on austerity, being a Philadelphia Quaker. She was born a Strawbridge, you know.'

As if anyone should *know,* John said to himself. And yet, ironically, he had to admit that it was he, alone of the company, who did know; he who was impressed; he who had gone to the trouble of looking up the history of the Hollingsworth family; he who could reel off the names of the Biddle uncles and Cadwalader cousins and Strawbridge strays. How curious, really fantastically surreal, John thought it must be to feel free, as Zeb Hollingsworth so transparently did, to regale a party of strangers with a roll call of one's relations. Though he enjoyed no such privileged *droit d'aînesse*, he knew that it was, on the other hand, acceptable for a man who has risen to the top of the heap from humble beginnings to recount the squalor from which he sprang – what more amusing after-dinner conversation? – but that it was greatly frowned upon for one such as himself, he who had accomplished nothing, to parade his far from glorious background in public. And so was it that he had sedulously avoided, in these last years, alluding to *any* blood relation. In this time of self-imposed silence, he had often, as a source of consolation, quoted to himself the words generally misattributed to Napoleon: '*Moi, je suis un ancêtre.*' Today, however, he felt this was precisely the problem: he *was* his own ancestor.

'But your grandmother Delfington must surely come to Paris quite often, doesn't she?' Sir Christopher asked with the same (to John, irritating) solicitude.

'Oh yeah, she does,' Zeb Hollingsworth said. 'She's always popping over to Paris, taking me around exhibitions – you know how Grandmamma Delfington *loves* art – and pushing obscure books about Paris on me. As a matter of fact, she gave me an inscribed first-edition of *The Autobiography of Alice B. Toklas* for my birthday last week. She said that it would help me to understand life in Paris better, though I can't claim that I've gotten very far with it yet.'

'How extraordinary of Dodo to think that a handsome young man like yourself would have any time for a fat old lesbian like Gertrude Stein. You'd be much better off,' Alice said, 'reading one of my lovely biographies. The Empress Sisi is just the subject for you. So pretty, she was. I would give you a copy, except that I don't have any left. Wild success the book was – don't you know – they couldn't *keep* it on the shelves!'

'That old empress hardly has much to do with Paris,' Sir Christopher said, as if taking sides. 'I think it is merely another proof – not that proof be needed – of how frightfully clever Dodo is just to have *thought* of giving you *The Autobiography of Alice B. Toklas.*'

'I consider it one of the cruellest books that I've ever read,' John said with unexpected vehemence.

'How so?' Zeb Hollingsworth asked with wide-eyed curiosity.

'It's the only instance I know of – in art, if not in life – of someone completely and irreversibly appropriating the life of another, appropriating it to the point of annihilation. And the way Miss

Stein left poor old Alice, who had sacrificed her entire existence to her, penniless, all the pictures going to the grasping Stein heirs. There's a frightfully clever American in Paris who is meant to be publishing something about the disgusting way Alice was treated by Miss Stein – I do hope he sets the record straight – and her last, miserable years in utter penury. And as for Miss Stein's actual writing – if *that* is what it is called – it's atrociously, indeed laughably, bad. She was just jolly lucky to have been a woman – propped up and promoted by the feminist mafia. No *man* could ever get away with publishing such rubbish as *The Making of Americans* and have people take it seriously. I think she was a perfectly revolting creature, Gertrude Stein: an obese, conceited, despotic, talentless, ardent fascist, Nazi-sympathising pig.'

'But I thought she was *Jewish*!' Zeb Hollingsworth said in his best Daisy Miller simulacrum.

'And so she was,' John said, gaining animation, 'that repulsively fat Hebrew dyke. But it didn't stop her from lobbying for Hitler to receive the Nobel Peace Prize in 1934, by which time Dachau was already up and open for business – oh, but that was "ironic", the feminists say – nor from devoting years to a translation of Maréchal Pétain's speeches into English. Wagner's anti-Semitism was nothing, mere child's play, in comparison to Gertrude's. And when you think that neither she nor Picasso – her communist alter ego – lifted a finger to help Max Jacob to escape, leaving him to die at Drancy, the French narthex to the gas chambers, whilst she went out of her way, after the war, to aid that despicable collaborationist, Bernard Faÿ.'

'Bernard who?' Zeb Hollingsworth asked.

'Faÿ, Bernard Faÿ,' John repeated himself.

'How is that spelt?'

'F-A-Ÿ, with a diæresis over the Ÿ.'

'Is that like an umlaut?'

'Yes. Why?' John asked.

'It's just, um, ah,' Zeb Hollingsworth said, seeming for the first time at a loss for words, 'that I think the copy of Gertrude Stein's book that Grandmamma Delfington gave me was inscribed to him. In fact, I'm sure that it's lovingly inscribed to Bernard Faÿ. I thought he must be German. Who was he exactly?'

'His politics were German,' John said, 'but he himself was French, irredeemably French. The worst sort of collaborator, worse even than that filthy *collabo* pig, Mitterrand. Bernard Faÿ had the poor head of the Bibliothèque Nationale ousted and sent to Buchenwald, whilst gleefully taking over his position, for which he was eminently unqualified. Once he seized power, he reported directly to Maréchal Pétain in Vichy, to whom he dedicated an exhibition and whom he put in contact with Miss Stein, who was comfortably ensconced with Alice – they were not in the least in "hiding" – in Savoy for the duration of the war. He even saw to it that the Maréchal should have coal – not the only substance they were responsible for burning up – delivered to the far from fragile Gertrude in 1941. And when not sucking up to Pétain, Faÿ was busy compiling thousands of documents to prove that a Jewish-Freemason conspiracy was responsible for reducing France to the second- (some might say third-) rate power she is today. It is impossible to estimate how many people he sent to their deaths, but it is a *fact* that he was directly responsible for the deportation of thousands, including a whole trainload of Jewish Children from Culoz, the village where old Gertrude was installed, straight to Auschwitz – a fact that Miss Stein *must* have been aware of. After the war, Faÿ was sentenced to a lifetime of hard labour, but, coward that he was, escaped to Switzerland. He also managed to safeguard Miss Stein's precious picture collection in Paris during the war, and, mean, greedy materialist that she was, she surely felt forever in his debt. She even wrote to the authorities after the war, defending his atrocities. I dare say, it's one thing to lose Max Jacob, but quite another to misplace one of her possessions. As Hemingway so rightly later said of Gertrud Stein: *a bitch is a bitch is a bitch.*'

'Gosh,' Zeb Hollingsworth said, rubbing his forehead, 'I don't know what I should do with the book now.'

'You should burn it. Burn it in honour of all the Jews that Faÿ and his beloved *cochonne*, Miss Stein, helped to send up in flames.'

'Burn it! Are you mad?' Alice interjected. 'It's probably worth a fortune.'

'I suppose you ought really to read the book first, to see how truly awful it is. And if you persist, you'll then come across an explanation, somewhere near the end, as to why I speak the way I do,' John said with mounting aggression.

'I don't understand,' Zeb Hollingsworth said.

'Old Gertrude writes, in her most *méchante* manner, that they were all terribly impressed by Glenway Wescott's English accent, which, she claims, he acquired on graduation from the University of Chicago. Wescott was,' John explained in answer to Zeb Hollingsworth's blank stare, 'an American writer, quite a good one – infinitely better than Gertrude, which wouldn't take much – who floated round Europe in the late twenties and early thirties. In any event, Hemingway, who despised Wescott – not because of his mores, but because he had the guts *not* to hide them – explains to Gertrude in *The Autobiography* that when you matriculate at the University of Chicago you write down just what accent you would like – modern, Elizabethan, whatever you fancy – and they give it you at graduation. That's how I got my accent – just as Glenway Wescott got his.'

'Does that mean you went to the University of Chicago?' Zeb Hollingsworth asked, utterly bewildered.

'Yes, it does,' John answered.

'That's a good school,' Zeb Hollingsworth said in a pathetically well-intentioned spirit.

A good SCHOOL! he shouted to himself. John Forde had gone to the University of Chicago: first, because he had not been accepted at Princeton, the American university which most closely conformed to his fantasy of a halcyon refuge for the *happy few*, where one could lounge about in eating clubs and study in the shade of gargoyled turrets; second, because of the other places to which he had been admitted *and* offered a scholarship – Brown and Georgetown – Chicago was the farthest away from his childhood home of Providence; and third, because he had some idea (mistaken, he soon learnt) that it was a sort of American version of Cambridge.

Having read in a college prospectus that one could study 'Greats' at the University of Chicago, he conjured up visions of *The Longest Journey*, in which undergraduates would lie about on the floor, lost in philosophical discussion, whilst running their fingers through one another's hair. Though he did find a good deal of lying about and a certain amount of discussion, such encounters invariably revolved round the triple axes of politics, sex and drugs, none of which subjects John felt comfortable with. There had, however, been no idle fingers running through *his* hair during his undergraduate years. The 'cow' was not there, and John had been more than eager to return to the east coast for graduate school, so that it positively enraged him to find himself now in the position of defending his alma mater to this young philistine who had, with his lordly ancestry, John imagined, simply sauntered into Princeton.

'What year did you graduate?' Zeb Hollingsworth, with almost painful simplicity, persisted.

'1981,' John, who did not know if he wanted to rage against or to cower before Zeb Hollingsworth, replied in an undertone.

'*Really?*' Zeb Hollingsworth, who had obviously pegged John as being about twenty years older than himself, said with transparent surprise. 'I guess,' he added tactfully, 'that means we're just about exact contemporaries, as I graduated from Princeton in 1986 – it would have been '85, but for my gap year. Anyway, I really do appreciate your offering to accompany me to see this Countess de' Pazzi after lunch. I wouldn't know what to do on my own.'

'You mean Patsy de' Pazzi? Why on earth are you going to see her?' Alice asked.

'It's all about the ball for my sister, Felicity,' Zeb Hollingsworth said evasively.

'Yes, I know,' Alice said, devouring the last of her *Sole Colbert*. 'You mentioned, when you first arrived, that your mother wants to rent the Villa Reale di Montalto this summer, but then we got diverted on to the beautiful ball your grandfather – or rather great-grandfather, as you insist – gave in one's honour in Newport before the war. But do tell one, why aren't you dealing with the Piccolomini-Brown sisters direct, instead of with that dreadful Patsy de' Pazzi? And more to the point, why are *you* entangled in all this? It sounds to me like the work for a lot of old ladies, not for a dashing young banker such as yourself.'

'Well,' Zeb Hollingsworth said, looking collusively at John, 'I guess we can tell her?'

'Tell me what? I hope that you haven't been keeping secrets from one, John,' Alice, who couldn't bear *not* to be *au fait*, said.

'It has nothing to do with me,' John said.

'No, I was the one who was all uptight about it,' Zeb Hollings-worth said, blessedly unaware of how alien his vocabulary seemed to those seated round the table. 'But I suppose there's no harm in telling you. You see, in order to secure the rental of the Villa Reale di Montalto for one week in August, Princess Bonamici insisted that they receive a down payment, *this* week, of fifty thousand dollars in cash, delivered to her daughter in Florence, or the deal was off. The rest can be paid later on.'

'The *rest*!' Alice shrieked. 'And do you mean to say that you've got fifty thousand dollars, fifty thousand dollars in cash, on you right now?'

'Yep,' the young man said. 'My pockets are simply bulging with it. I didn't really want to do it, but Mummy begged me and promised that I would have a diplomatic pouch, through Daddy, to transport the money. I certainly wouldn't want to do anything illegal. Anyway, Mummy's at a summit meeting now with Daddy in Moscow, and Felicity is still at Bryn Mawr, so there was really no one else to do it. And just to complicate matters, I have to go to Hong Kong for the bank tomorrow, so I flew here this morning, will deliver the money this afternoon, then take the train to Rome, sleep there tonight, fly off to Hong Kong first thing in the morning and then head straight back to work in Paris on Wednesday.'

'Just the *idea* of all that travelling makes one exhausted,' Alice said, helping herself to a massive slab of insolently ripe Stracchino.

To John, the thought of such a charged *emploi du temps* inspired, not exhaustion, but envy. How pathetically servile, he lamented to himself, his own position seemed in comparison. No one needed *him* to jet round the world.

'I know what you mean,' Zeb Hollingsworth answered Alice Varrow. 'But Princess Bonamici didn't leave us much choice.'

'They are extraordinary, those Piccolomini-Brown sisters. Don't you think, Christopher?' Alice asked.

'Quite,' Sir Christopher replied absently.

'So brash! And to think of the airs they put on now. You know' – Alice turned to Zeb Hollingsworth – 'they may go on as much as they like about the grandeur of their papal titles, but all the money comes from the "Brown" part of their name. And that was originally Braunstein, till they conveniently changed it. They're nothing but Alsatian Jews who struck it rich with a cement factory in Argentina. And as for Ludovica Bonamici's daughter, Patsy de' Pazzi, you'd better be *really* careful of her. It's a wonder they ever let that family back into Florence after the Conspiracy.'

'What conspiracy was that?' Zeb Hollingsworth asked innocently.

'It was a foiled plot to kill the Medici in 1478, known as the Pazzi Conspiracy, after which the family were, for years, banished and their property confiscated,' John explained, looking at Sir Christopher, from whom he tried (unsuccessfully) to elicit a raised eyebrow.

'Believe me, she's a menace, that Patsy de' Pazzi. And the *size* of her now! Have you seen how perfectly enormous she's become, Christopher? Some people even say she's a murderess.'

'I do think that's rather an exaggeration, dear Alice,' Sir Christopher said.

'*Se non è vero, è ben trovato*,' Alice said solemnly.

'What does that mean?' Zeb Hollingsworth asked, completely unembarrassed by his own ignorance.

'Even if it's not true, it *should* be,' John translated for Zeb Hollingsworth, thinking to himself that a more useful epigram might be: 'Even if it is true, it should*n't* be.'

'One thing that I can promise you *is* true,' Alice said excitedly, 'gospel truth – Lulu recounted it all to one, in vivid detail, the other day – is that Patsy de' Pazzi is a confirmed, *sick* kleptomaniac. She might have to be committed. Lulu was actually present, lunching at Palazzo Canigiani, when it all came to a head. Some people feel sorry for Patsy, say that she only steals in order to attract the attention of her husband, who has installed his mistress, a little shop girl, right under her nose, there in the palace. But however the Florentines might pity Patsy, none of them will ever again invite her – you know how jealously they guard *their* possessions – not since she was found a fortnight ago, found red-handed, rooting about in Kitty Canigiani's jewel case, her pockets already stuffed with Kitty's famous emeralds, the *entire* parure.'

'Yes, she is perfectly dreadful,' John, who knew nothing of the allegations of kleptomania, concurred. He had, however, his own private reasons for disliking this woman. Nearly two years ago, on a beautiful summer night, he had been invited along with Sir Christopher to an elaborate dinner given by Daisy Cavalcanti at her villa in Greve in Chianti. Though the guests were evenly divided, seven male and seven female, John could not help noting that all the men were unmarried – including the infamous 'Whores of Virtue', whose very existence Sir Christopher refused to acknowledge – whilst all the women, though married, were unaccompanied by their husbands, all of whom were, presumably, off philandering.

At the end of the evening, he found himself seated on the terrace next to Contessa de' Pazzi, who, by her belligerent muteness, made it painfully clear that she thought this scabrous assortment of unmarried men nothing short of an insult to her feminine charms. John had met her two or three times before, but she obviously had no idea who he was and even less desire to be reminded. After several abortive stabs at conversation, John mentioned that, the other day in the Boboli Gardens, he had run into her daughter, Laudomia – one of the few younger Florentines with whom he had a nodding acquaintance – who was pushing her infant son about. In an instant, the subject of her grandson transformed Patsy de' Pazzi from silent succubus into frenzied haruspex: she seemed to think that there was no iniquity from which this child might not deliver the corrupt Florentines, no division he might not mend, no magical powers of healing he did not possess, the very saviour of his race.

Flabbergasted by this torrid outburst, John looked off into the distance and, after a pause, said, 'Well, anyway, he seemed a sweet boy, your little grandson, when I saw him in the park with Laudomia.'

To which the rotund Contessa de' Pazzi growled back, 'Actually, he's a very, very *masculine* boy.' Whereupon, she shoved a cigarette in her mouth, turned her back on John and relapsed into her taciturn, disapproving self. Undoubtedly, she had long since forgotten the exchange, but to John the snub had only grown over time, rankling and rotting, till, in his mind, it achieved perfectly grandiose proportions.

'In fact,' he added today, 'I think Patsy de' Pazzi is the only truly and inherently *evil* person whom I've ever met in my life.'

'You see, young man,' Alice said to Zeb Hollingsworth, as she smothered her *fraises des bois* in clotted cream, 'I told you that you'll have to watch out for that Patsy de' Pazzi. Keep that money close to your chest.'

'As I'm actually *delivering* the money to Countess de' Pazzi, I think that I'll be safe, though, after all I've heard, I am certainly grateful that John has agreed to go with me,' Zeb Hollingsworth said with a conspiratorial wink. 'Anyway, Mummy said that I should tell you guys that she's counting on all of you for the big night of the ball.'

'I'll need someone to drive me, of course,' Alice said, already fretting about being left behind.

'Can't you get a lift with John and Sir Christopher?' Zeb Hollingsworth asked.

'But he doesn't drive,' Alice said, looking dismissively at John. 'So peculiar, particularly for an American.'

'You don't know how to *drive?*' Zeb Hollingsworth asked, shocked.

'I *do* know how to drive. I just no longer have a valid licence,' John said. The truth of the matter, which he had never even explained to Sir Christopher, was that, though he had, like most middle-class Americans, obtained a driving licence at the age of sixteen, he could not renew his Rhode Island permit, as he no longer had any contact with his family. And when he learnt of his master's antipathy to driving, he decided, as in so many a domain, to imitate him, hoping, thereby, to share in the sense of honour that accrued to Sir Christopher for *not* driving: chauffeurs drove; gentlemen were driven. But today, he realised that what might appear grand in a distinguished elderly scholar merely looked suspect in someone of his age and murky origins.

What is your background? Maybe not even middle-class, but pure prole? Zeb Hollingsworth's look of astonishment seemed to say.

'When exactly is this grand entertainment to take place?' Sir Christopher, to John's immense relief, broke in, thus disposing of the subject of John's driving skills or lack thereof.

'We're taking the Villa from Monday, the fourteenth of August through the following Monday, the twenty-first. Of course, there will be lots of parties and dinners during the week, but the big night of the ball is Saturday, the nineteenth.'

'Just over *ferragosto,*' Sir Christopher said, '*such* a pity.'

'What's *ferragosto?* And please,' the young man said coaxingly, '*don't* tell me you won't be here.'

'*Ferragosto* marks the solemnity of the Assumption of the Virgin, on the fifteenth of August, when everything in Italy closes and most people go away for at least a fortnight. In fact, the Italian tradition of holidaying during the month of August goes all the way back to the Emperor Augustus, who initiated *the feriae augusti* in order to grant workers a respite from their labours,' John explained.

'We were already planning on Bayreuth for that week. There's what promises to be a frightfully good new *Parsifal*,' Sir Christopher added.

'Oh really, Christopher, you can surely forgo that bloody old opera of yours for once,' Alice said. 'You're constantly at the opera, but how often do you have the chance to go to a beautiful, gay coming-out ball?'

'We'll see, Alice. We shall see,' Sir Christopher said with a knowing smirk.

'And what *we* should see to,' John said to Zeb Hollingsworth, 'is ringing up for a taxi, as soon as we've had coffee. We don't want to be late for Patsy de' Pazzi. And even more, I don't think you want to go careening about the streets of Florence with all that money on you.'

'You might drop me at the same time,' Alice said, granting John more attention than she had throughout most of luncheon.

'It's hardly on the way, dear Alice,' he replied.

Alice laughed. 'Oh, everything's more or less on the way in Florence.'

In this manless *town*, John scoffed to himself. Aloud, he simply said, 'Fine, fine.'

'Before we go, could I just ask you to take me up to that loggia you pointed out? It must have a great view of the river,' Zeb Hollingsworth asked as he went over to the French window in the dining room and looked to the right.

'Of course,' John answered. 'I don't imagine that you, dear Alice, want to go up there, as you know it so well,' John said tactfully to the lame old woman, who could hardly have managed the steps.

'No, I think I can live without another view of Christopher's rare, *non*-flowering plants,' Alice, to John's immense delight, said.

'We'll have coffee in the drawing room,' Sir Christopher, immune to Alice's sarcasm, said placidly.

'Good. I'll just escort our visitor upstairs then,' John said, leading the way back to the front hall, through the darkened *cabinet de dessins* and on to the door leading to the loggia. Climbing the steep stairs *behind* Zeb Hollingsworth, John felt free to gape in wonder at the broad shoulders, tapering back, thin waist, powerful thighs and callipygian perfection striding forth before him. As soon as he arrived on the small upper landing, however, and found himself standing agonisingly close to the young man who once again towered over him, John immediately cast his eyes to the ground and unbolted the door to the loggia.

'God, this is fantastic!' Zeb Hollingsworth lurched forward.

'Yes, it *is* nicely positioned,' John said for what seemed to him the millionth time.

'You can say that again. I just love this river. The Arno, you said?'

'That's right.'

'It reminds me of Lake Carnegie at Princeton,' Zeb Hollingsworth said, leaning over the edge of the loggia. 'I used to spend all my time rowing and sculling there. Do you ever do that here, on the Arno?'

'People do. There's even a boathouse along the Arno.'

'What about you?' Zeb Hollingsworth asked.

'Me? *Me* personally?' John asked warily.

'Yeah. Why not? You'd be good at it.'

'Now you're making fun of one. Fun of *me*,' John, embarrassed by his own affectation, corrected himself.

'Believe me, that's the last thing I would want to do,' Zeb Hollingsworth said, placing his hand on John's shoulder. 'Actually, the reason I asked you to bring me up here was because I wanted to be alone with you, so that I could apologise for saying that stupid thing about your *pretending* to be English. I certainly didn't mean to offend you. In fact, I think it's great the way you speak. I wish I could talk like that,' he continued with heartbreaking sincerity. 'And then, you're so knowledgeable. I really admire that. Obviously, I should be more careful of what I say. Mummy's always telling me that I speak without thinking and that one day my big mouth's going to get me into terrible trouble.'

'I rather doubt that,' John said, daring to look straight up into Zeb Hollingsworth's eyes for the first time. Though he had taken solace throughout luncheon in telling himself, telling himself repeatedly, that there was something pathetically banal in this paragon of blond-haired, blue-eyed American beauty, John, if honest, would be forced to acknowledge that it was precisely this young man's 'banality' that exerted such a powerfully seductive hold over him. Devoid of all affectation or anxiety or bile, Zeb Hollingsworth was balanced and sound and gladsome, existing in perfect harmony with the laws of God *and* man.

Oh, for the blessing of such blissful banality! John mourned to himself. Aloud, he said, 'And now I suppose we must be off to deliver that money to Lady Macbeth herself.'

'Yeah.' Zeb Hollingsworth smiled. 'But believe me, I meant it. You *would* make a good oarsman. It's really all about concentration. And you seem so focused, so calm.'

'Hmm,' John said with a woeful smile.

'Sometime, when I come back, maybe in the summer, we'll take a two-man scull out together. I'll break you in, buddy,' he said, squeezing John's shoulder.

'*Sometime*,' John said, shrugging the hand of devastation off his shoulder.

✠

John Forde stood at the south foot of Ponte Amerigo Vespucci and, with a hopeless sense of loss, watched the long silhouette of his compatriot vanish in the direction of the train station. He shook his head and murmured to himself, 'It's no use. It would never have worked.' He was not so deluded as to be voicing regret over a missed romantic adventure with the transparently unobtainable Zeb Hollingsworth, but, rather, he was acknowledging the impossibility of his ever fitting into a world such as the one that this young man inhabited. Still, he wondered what would have happened if he himself had gone to law school? Stayed in his native land? Got a normal job? Married a placid girl? [regular]

'It's no use. It would *never* have worked,' he repeated to himself, for he knew that, even if he had managed, for a time, to integrate himself with the normal, the cheerful, the elect – to follow the strait and narrow – that he, like Tonio Kröger before him, would eventually have gone astray, that he would ultimately have forsaken

La Porte étroite for the wide gate and the broad way, leading to his own destruction. And so, resignedly, did he turn his back on the bridge and begin to make his way home.

With no particular pattern and no set intention, he wandered through the district of San Frediano toward Santo Spirito, thinking along the way how strange it was that there should be so many a grand church in Florence lacking a proper façade – San Lorenzo, Santa Maria del Carmine, Santo Spirito itself. He stopped in front of the latter but preferred, today – so unlike the impassioned young man he had been a mere six years ago – not to enter the church. This afternoon, in the reproachful shadow of Zeb Hollingsworth's unerring completeness, he felt himself to be the very antithesis of all these unfinished Florentine monuments: he was all exterior, but no glowing interior. And so he pushed on, wending his way aimlessly through a warren of little streets, plotting all the while to settle down seriously to *The Disciple* and, thereby, to fill the void within.

Lost in such thought, he came face to face with Lulu de' Portinari. Cramped though the *vicolo* in which he found himself was, he felt sure that he could avoid this waspish old woman, who appeared entirely consumed by her yapping little dog. Nonetheless, after the assaults to his ego this afternoon, he defiantly stopped, as if to assert his own existence, and said, 'Good afternoon, Duchessa. How lovely to see you.'

'Oh, yes, lovely to see you also,' she said in her flawless English, looking up with a blank stare.

Over the years, John had seen Duchessa de' Portinari at Alice's overpopulated gatherings more times than he could count, as well as at any other number of scattered Florentine entertainments. She had even once come to dine in Palazzo Vespucci, and Sir Christopher had, in return, been invited, *alone*, to lunch at her palace in via de' Serragli. She was never overtly rude to John, but she seemed unable, or unwilling, to register him, particularly if he were on his own. He was perfectly aware that, just as one might patronise the same restaurant for years but fail to recognise a faithful waiter from that establishment if one crossed him in the street – the restaurant itself being an indissoluble part of his identity – so too did Duchessa de' Portinari find it difficult to place him, unless he were standing in the immediate shadow of his master. Nonetheless, he intrepidly continued, 'Perfect day for a *passeggiata*, isn't it? I can see that Marzocco thinks so.'

'Does he not?' She smiled broadly at the mention of her scrappy dog's name. 'We must profit from this glorious weather, whilst we can.'

'I quite agree. Actually, I'm now walking all the way back from the train station,' John exaggerated, 'in order to do just that.'

'Oh, have you been away?' she asked in a confused voice.

'No, I was seeing off an old *childhood* friend of mine – Zebulon Biddle Cadwalader Hollingsworth. Perhaps you know him? We actually had Alice to lunch with him this afternoon. She was on great form, singing your praises to no end, I might add.'

'Oh, of course, I see now,' Lulu de' Portinari patted John's hand, as if to say that she finally realised who he was. 'But Alice told me that Tommy isn't at all well. I was frightfully worried. What can one do for him?'

'I really don't know,' John said.

'Well, when you see him, will you please give him my love? Are you on your way there now?'

'Where?' John asked with trepidation.

'Why, back home, to Palazzo Tornabuoni,' she said.

'But I, um, I,' John said, recoiling in horror from the old duchessa, 'I live in via de' Bardi, with Sir Christopher Noble-Nolan.'

'Oh, but of course you do,' Lulu de' Portinari said with a laugh. 'I'm afraid that I had you confused with that other one. What's his name? Woodstock or Woodstoke, is it? But now I see. You're Christopher Noble-Nolan's "friend". Anyway, I really must be getting Marzocco home for his supper. So particular, this little...'

John turned and, without a trace of valediction, began to run home. Once hidden behind the locked door of his room, he threw himself face down on his bed and, though not crying, began to exhale choked, stentorian gasps of breath. That he should be confused with the sleazy, uneducated Montgomery Woodstoke, twenty-one years older than himself, was galling enough, but to be dismissed as Christopher Noble-Nolan's 'friend' – heterospeak for faggot – was positively wounding, all the more so as he felt the anonymity in which he floundered was born of his own passive devising. For the first time, he saw that, because he had never had the courage to forge his own homosexual identity amongst family, friends or associates, he was forced to accept that which was foisted upon him, and so would he remain forever hostage to others' perceptions and prejudices. Whether that identity be parental denial (a perjuring prom photo), Alice's silence (neither a girlfriend nor a boyfriend have), Duchessa de' Portinari's dismissal (the fungible 'friend') or Zeb Hollingsworth's beautiful banality (the oarsman cometh) was of no matter; the fact remained that, in each instance, his identity had been fashioned for him not *by* him. The untouchable Christopher Noble-Nolan remained, as always, the elusive element in the equation. How exactly, he wondered, did Sir Christopher identify him? He had no idea.

The following morning, however, John saw a new picture of himself: he weighed himself, and utterly horrified he was. He estimated that he must have gained over fifty pounds in the not quite six years that he had known Sir Christopher. He stared at his swollen, defaced face in the bathroom mirror. Cringing at what he feared was an exact reflexion of the disfigured state of his very own soul, he forced himself to within an inch of the glass and, fusing verses, chanted: NON SUM QUALIS ERAM. *Look in my face; my name is Might-have-been; I am also called No-more, Too-late, Farewell.*

CHAPTER IV

But the Angels Didn't

IN THE NEXT weeks, John had little thought for anything but his thirtieth birthday at the end of May. So alarmed was he by the prospect of this milestone, so terrified that this decennial change would come crashing down on him like a cudgel, smashing all those illusions he still harboured of refashioning his life, of transforming himself into a worthy, productive individual, that he did manage, in the upcoming two months, to adhere, with *some* regularity, to his new literary project, *The Disciple*, in the hope that its realisation would validate him in the eyes of the world and, above all, verify to himself his very being, the existence of which he doubted more than ever. But though he did jot down a great many notes for his intended novel, make several detailed character sketches, collate a bountiful (but refractory) selection of quotations and fill an entire notebook with variant first sentences, he had not, by the time of his thirtieth birthday, finished one complete chapter.

And he was no closer to his goal when his next birthday came round, nor the birthday after that, nor the one after *that*. It was not simply that the tenacity demanded of such a long-term project was alien to John's nature, but, more important, that he lacked the fortitude and the self-confidence to face the disappointments, even quite minor ones, that life so relentlessly metes out, and for one so umbrageous as himself – one to whom every slight, every snub, every criticism was of monumental, never-to-be-forgotten, significance – this was a debilitating handicap. Confronted by a harsh word from Sir Christopher, a blank stare from a society grande dame or a mild phonetic correction from anyone, John would slink into a black mood, escape from which he could engineer only through the mind-blotting vapour of alcohol. Like Zeno, who chose to blame his faults – his incompetence, his idleness, his constant shilly-shallying – on his addiction to cigarettes, for failure is so much easier to endure if one can graft it on to someone or something *else*, John could, so long as he limped along on the crutch of alcohol, indulge himself in dreams of unrealised literary glory.

As if to ensure that he would never be forced to test the limits of his imagined talent, he set himself impossible goals, thereby guaranteeing his own failure. On any given day, he might plan to go on a diet, give up drink, stop smoking *and* write five pages a day of his novel – all at the same time; and as soon as he faltered in one domain, as he inevitably did, the others quickly followed suit. He was even deluded enough to think, after having read (and believed) the more than improbable claim that Stendhal had written all of *La Chartreuse de Parme* in fifty-two days, that he might write his own book in the same span of time.

Equally unrealistic plans followed, tumbling one upon another, as he continued all the while to minister unsparingly to Sir Christopher. Finally, the endless tergiversation – Ossianic ambition, but no resolve – began to take its toll on John, so much so that he sought, as a perverse gesture of punishment, to document his own demise. Over and over, he photographed himself in the long bathroom mirror, a cigarette dangling from his mouth, whilst striking intentionally unflattering poses. And the more corrupted did his image appear, the more did he give way to that deadliest of sins: sloth. To mediæval churchmen, most notably Aquinas, acedia was an unpardonable offense because the hopelessness it engendered implied a loss of faith, whilst to the Renaissance humanist its tragedy entailed a collapse of creativity; to John, who pictured himself, like one of those emblematically obese figures lolling about on an ass, this counsel of *ignoble ease, and peaceful sloth, / Not peace* – most decidedly *not* peace – was born of the despair he felt at witnessing the fabric of his life fray, fiercely and frantically fray, from every possible edge. Here he now was, set to turn thirty-four years old in little more than a month, by which time most men have already begun to construct a career with a discernible pattern and a definite outline, still perilously poised on the threshold, without accomplishment and without prospect. Whichever way he flew was *Hell*; himself was *Hell*.

It was not until he found Sir Christopher in a second coma, on

Epiphany of 1993, that John was able to come to a truce with himself. Looking down at Sir Christopher's inert body, he had coldly said to himself, My *life will start, when* his *ends. For now, I am in limbo.* And from that moment forth, he regulated his drinking, stopped smoking (for a time) and lost some weight. He did not, however, even pretend to write. 'The book will have to wait, wait till...' he went on deluding himself.

Today, as he laid out Sir Christopher's clothes in preparation for Palm Sunday Mass, his mind drifted back to that January morning, three months ago. Unlike the coma Sir Christopher had fallen into eight years before, this recent one appeared, to John, to be life-threatening, and he had not hesitated for an instant to call an ambulance. Though Sir Christopher did manage once again fully to regain his mental faculties, his physical strength, after the recent coma, now appeared permanently diminished: he was terribly unsteady on his feet; his hands shook more violently than ever; and he seemed always to be cold. But as if inspired by such challenges to his authority, Sir Christopher continued to work and to write, undaunted, at the same rigorous pace, whilst John breathlessly panted after him: the monograph on Leonardo was soon to reach proof stage; an article on Michelangelo's correspondence appeared last week in the *TLS*; and the writing of an autobiography had even been undertaken.

The biggest and, to John, least agreeable upheaval brought about by Sir Christopher's recent coma was their exchange of bedrooms. On his return from the clinic, Sir Christopher had moved into John's bedroom, so as to avoid the set of five pietra serena steps leading up to his own room, whilst John installed himself in the spare room. Though this reversal had been urged on by John, he had intended it to be a temporary arrangement; it soon, however, became painfully clear to him that Sir Christopher particularly liked the new disposition, as, with the enfilade of three inter-connecting rooms along the via de' Bardi, he could leave his door open and shout out for John at any moment of the day or night. Though he was humbled to witness Sir Christopher's fear of being alone and touched to see to what degree Sir Christopher depended on him, John could not but regret the loss of autonomy. For nearly ten years, those three rooms along the via de' Bardi had been his private fiefdom, territory that Sir Christopher could rarely be bothered to penetrate.

Where am I to hide my heart now? he asked himself this morning, as he heard Sir Christopher shouting his name from the bathroom.

'I'm right here,' John said, tapping on the door before entering. Finding Sir Christopher, not for the first time, lacking the strength in his arms to push himself up from the bath, he leant over from behind and, putting his arms under Sir Christopher's, went to heave him up but, as he did so, felt him slither away, his face gliding right under the water. 'My God,' John shouted, as, in his thoughts, he left Sir Christopher to drown; in truth, he plunged his own upper body – shirt, links, tie and all – right into the water to retrieve him. 'You could have died that way.'

'Thank goodness you were there to save one,' Sir Christopher said in a water-logged voice.

'Here, put this on,' John said, dragging Sir Christopher from his bath, as he swaddled him in Peter Mason's towel dressing gown – a frightfully functional garment, he was *now* willing to concede. 'Why don't you sit on this *chauffeuse.*'

'It's a good thing this bathroom is so large. You never would have been able to manage that manœuvre in the tiny little one attached to my old bedroom,' Sir Christopher said.

'Hmm,' John mumbled laconically, for he did not like to say anything that might be construed to encourage the permanence of their change of bedrooms.

After he dried himself, yanked his own tie off and rolled up his sleeves, he then sprinkled Sir Christopher with Robert's talcum powder and splashed him with Trumper's eau de Portugal. Curiously, John, who was squeamishly modest by nature – he had absolutely *hated* being obliged to share a bedroom with two of his brothers during childhood – was not in the least repulsed by Sir Christopher's exposed state. As he glanced at the trembling mass of sagging flesh that was now Sir Christopher's body, he thought of Ribera's depiction of the penitent old St Jerome in the desert. Keeping in mind this vision of the revered scholar-saint's wizened frame, John leant down and, with deep and genuine affection, kissed the back of Sir Christopher's neck.

'Thank you for looking after one so beautifully. It must be a terrific bore for you,' Sir Christopher said humbly.

'No, I don't mind, and I wouldn't want anyone else to do it,' John said truthfully. But still, he would have preferred to be valued for devotion that went *beyond* the physical.

'You've no idea how perfectly god-awful it was to have all those female nurses mauling one over in the clinic.'

John did not know if this was just old-fashioned misogyny on Sir Christopher's part, or a true predilection for himself, and so merely said, 'Here's your stick. Now, let's go to the bedroom and choose a suit for you.'

'Speaking of the bedroom,' Sir Christopher said more assertively, 'I think it would be nice to have all the Francesco Vanni drawings brought down from my old room and hung up here. One might as well be surrounded by beautiful things so long as one can.'

'All right,' John muttered, seeing no end in sight. 'But it's going to be a big job. There are nineteen drawings in your old room. I'll have to hang a lot of prints in place of the drawings in order to cover the holes – one cannot just leave the walls bare. And one shouldn't forget that my room – well, *this* one – gets much more sun than your old room. And light is the archenemy of drawings.'

'I don't think that much matters,' Sir Christopher said with a dismissive flick of the wrist.

'As you like,' John said, reflecting that, contrary to common assumption, it was he – he who had been raised amidst ghastly Formica and faux panelling – who was much more attentive to protecting textiles, books and drawings from the elements than Sir Christopher – he who had lived all his life surrounded by works of art.

'Now,' he changed the subject, 'do you want a black suit or simply a dark one, with an understated stripe?'

'Oh, I think a solid black one. After all, it *is* Palm Sunday,' Sir Christopher said.

'And then, almost directly Mass is over – as the Mass does go on today – we have the lunch party for Tommy Tornabuoni's ninetieth birthday,' John said.

'I do call it highly eccentric to have one's birthday, one's ninetieth birthday, on a Sunday. But to have it on *Palm* Sunday, well I think that is really beyond the pale,' Sir Christopher said.

'Old Tommy can hardly help that. I mean, there's an awful lot I don't understand about him – such as why he's gone from reviling me to naming me his literary executor – but I don't really think one can hold him accountable for what day of the week his birthday falls on,' John said with a laugh, whilst inserting links in Sir Christopher's cuffs.

'I wouldn't be so sure. I do think it makes one look rather careless – one's birthday on a Sunday, on *Palm* Sunday! And as for your being Tommy's literary executor, I suppose that he just woke up – saw what a disaster it would be to allow Mr Woodstoke to stick his finger in the pie. I imagine it also gave him a certain pleasure to think he could lure you away from one. But then, with all he has, Tommy has never been content, always thinks himself worthy of more recognition, more honours, more praise.'

'That's quite true,' John said, realising that one of Sir Christopher's strengths, perhaps his *greatest* strength, was clear knowledge of his own limitations. John knew of other art historians who, having reached a certain peak, sometimes a very elevated one, longed to scale higher, even if it meant turning their backs on their own accomplishments. He had read of one great expert on Italian drawings who repudiated his best work as a misguided descent into pedantry, believing that he should have devoted himself to the higher calling of æsthetics, transforming himself into a modern Goethe – a rôle for which he was eminently unsuited. Then, there was another one he came across, who had cast aside decades of serious work, labouring under the delusion that he was now meant to be the Ruskin of the television generation. Sir Christopher, on the other hand, had never deviated from his childhood ambition to be an eximious connoisseur and pain-staking scholar; he had no pretensions to being a 'thinker' or someone who would, in any way, shape his own historical period.

As he continued to dress Sir Christopher, John looked at him and felt a great surge of pride in his master's sense of self-knowledge: to him, there was dignity and disinterest and not a little disdain engraved on that noble brow. *If only*, he said to himself, *I could share in that accomplishment.* Aloud, he repeated himself, saying, 'Yes, quite true. Tommy never is content. But I guess that is what spurs him on, even at the age of ninety, always imagining, indeed believing, that he should be revered, that he should be honoured. And to think that, just a year ago, he gave me an inscribed copy of Steven

Spanday's collected poems at Christmas, as a deliberate slap in the face, and now, here he is, having his solicitor send one papers to sign about his literary estate.'

'It is curious, I admit. One never knows what old Tommy will get up to, nor what his motives are. Do we have any idea who will be there today?' Sir Christopher asked.

'Alice told me yesterday on the telephone that it's to be a very small, subdued gathering – just eight of us. Pretty much the usual suspects: Tommy and Alice, and you and I, of course; then the dreaded Lulu de' Portinari; and, finally, the two imports, Dodo Delfington and Clementine, Countess of Arden. I must say that I don't understand the fascination that the latter seems to hold for everyone.'

'Well, Clementine was very beautiful – in an *ice*-cold sort of way – when she was younger. Crystal, as you know, was quite besotted with her.'

'When I mentioned something to her yesterday about those two works your brother dedicated to her, she cut one off – cut one off quite sharply – saying that she could hardly remember those early books and had never bothered with any of the later ones. Once their friendship had, as she so generously put it, *soured*, she gave up reading him altogether. And what's more, it's one thing for Crystal to have had an *amitié amoureuse* with the then Clementine Chamberlain nearly fifty years ago and quite another for old Tommy to be playing up to her in 1993. He even has her staying with him in Palazzo Tornabuoni. And no one, to my knowledge, is ever invited to stay in the Palace.'

'One mustn't forget,' Sir Christopher said, 'that she was the niece of one prime minister and the wife of another. That's exactly the sort of thing that would appeal to Tommy's snobbish instinct.'

'Even so, I must say that Lady Arden *can* be ungracious. Not a word of thanks did I get for escorting her round Florence all of yesterday, and Dodo told me that she barely acknowledged the lift she gave her out here on her æroplane.

'Which tie do you want?' John asked, whilst helping Sir Christopher to button his trousers.

'The silver Charvet. But you must understand that someone like Clementine, someone who's spent her whole life in the public domain, has a tremendous sense of entitlement. She honestly believes that people *should* be honoured to invite her everywhere or to chauffeur her about. And then, Clementine has always had so little money herself, so that she demands more than most people in a similar situation. She was, poor thing, completely disinherited by her wildly rich, fanatically Catholic mother for marrying the divorced Anthony Arden, or Anthony Paradise as he was back then, before being raised to the earldom. Apparently, Clementine's mother wrote to her that Golgotha was a lonelier, more deserted place since her defection to "paradise" – after which she never spoke to her daughter again. But that only makes seven people for luncheon. There must be another man. Is that Woodstoke going to be present?' Sir Christopher asked.

'No, according to Alice, he's not,' John said. 'She claims that he is off sulking in Rome – he's taken up with a girl, you know.'

'That *type* always does, in the end,' Sir Christopher said jubilantly.

'Alice told me that Woodstoke is to be replaced by Count de' Pazzi,' John said.

'You mean old Pansy de' Pazzi?'

'I believe that Alice said he's called Pazzino de' Pazzi, which is quite bad enough,' John said.

'Pazzino may be his proper name, but he's always been known as "Pansy", an epithet that suits him *right* down to the ground,' Sir Christopher said, laughing loudly.

'What relation is he to the vile Patsy de' Pazzi?' John asked as he knotted Sir Christopher's tie.

'I suppose he must be her father-in-law,' Sir Christopher said.

'I'll have to look him up in the *Libro d'Oro*,' John said, referring to the Italian version of *Debrett's*.

'Yes, I am quite sure, now, that that's who he is,' Sir Christopher said. 'I believe that he's a cousin of the Tornabuoni, somehow, but then they're all related to one another, these grand Florentines. I haven't seen him for æons – he was in hiding, in one South American country or another, for decades after the war. To be fair, one must admit that he has had the decency rarely to show his face in public, ever since he was allowed to return to this country twenty or so years ago, but I remember him quite well now, back in the 1930s. The two things one could never understand about him are how so outrageously an effeminate creature could have fathered such an aggressively virile son as Patsy's husband, Piero de' Pazzi, and how, even more, he himself could have been such a wildly ardent fascist, engaged in the most gruesome of combats in the North African theatre. One would have thought he would faint straightway at the sight of blood. But thick as thieves he was with Tommy's elder brother, Bibi – what with their shared fascist passion. I believe that Pansy was even condemned to death in absentia. Lord, what a luncheon we are in for. Now, could you help me with this one lace?' Sir Christopher asked.

'Yes, of course,' John said, kneeling down to tie Sir Christopher's right shoe and, not failing, as he did so, to repent the severely swollen state of Sir Christopher's feet, so characteristic of someone with a liver ailment and so deeply *un*characteristic of his *raffiné* master.

'I wonder if you'll put this in a book someday?' Sir Christopher said, leaning over to stroke John's hair.

'No, never,' John sputtered, jumping up, alarmed that Sir Christopher might realise anything of his literary plans, all of which he had jealously guarded over the years. 'You know, in spite of what the great Symbolist poet might have said, not *everything* in the world exists so as to end up in a beautiful book.'

'*There* one couldn't agree with you more,' Sir Christopher said. 'Entirely too much is divulged today, and frightfully unhealthy it is. That's why we have to think, think so carefully, about this question of the autobiography. I'm really quite enjoying the writing of it – though it will obviously have to take a back seat once the Leonardo proofs arrive – but still, I've decided that it should be like an officially commissioned royal biography, just the outlines of one's life. Certainly nothing *personal*. Now, if only we could think of a title,' Sir Christopher said.

'What about *Ex Cathedra?*' John said with more than a hint of derision.

'Now that *is* rather a clever idea, really frightfully clever,' Sir Christopher said.

'Hmm,' John said, displeased to see that his intended slight was favourably received. 'Now please, do just turn round, whilst I attach your braces in the back. They're going to have to be tightened.'

'I do hope that one is not going to start losing a lot of weight. That would be an infernal nuisance,' Sir Christopher said.

'Not a lot of weight. Just a bit, which is quite normal after all you've been through,' John said. He could not help reflecting on the irony of Sir Christopher, who, he estimated, had lost at least twenty-five to thirty pounds in the last three months, worrying about being too thin, whilst he himself continued to fret over the gain of every ounce.

'Well, it seems quite a lot of weight to one,' Sir Christopher said agitatedly. 'This suit will really have to be altered. One doesn't want to go about looking like old Milton Isner. Yes, I wouldn't be surprised if one has lost an entire stone. But so long as the Leonardo book is finished, it doesn't really matter. One's work will be complete, so much so that I don't want you to wake one, if it happens again.'

'If *what* happens again?' John asked, thinking that he knew exactly what Sir Christopher meant.

'If one falls into a coma, just leave one be. But do promise that you will let one die here, at home, and not in some god-awful hospital,' Sir Christopher said.

'Well, I absolutely promise about the part of keeping you at home. That, you need not worry about. As for the other bit, I don't know.'

'It's quite true. I don't want to be woken up again,' Sir Christopher said tranquilly.

'How could one just leave you?' John, who, like the Sage of Weimar, had never heard of a crime of which he did *not* deem himself capable, asked.

'Now, here's your coat,' he continued nervously. 'Just stand still, whilst I brush you off, and then we can go into breakfast. Thank God we've got that new servant to come in on Sundays to take care of things. I don't see how I could possibly cope on my own anymore, what with so many other things piled up.'

'I quite agreed with you from the beginning, when you suggested adding someone else to the staff. It was getting to be too much. And now that we've sold the Guido Reni, we don't really have to worry about things,' Sir Christopher said, referring to the last truly important Baroque picture from his collection. 'But still, one does worry,' he said in a different, pensive register, as he sat down on the edge of the bed.

'What is there to be worried *about*?' John asked.

'Obviously, the Guido Reni money will see me through, but I wanted there to be enough for you also. And though the other works of art may be quite nice – especially the Vanni drawings – they're not really all that valuable, nothing like the Bolognese Baroque pictures, which have nearly all been sold off now,' Sir Christopher said, looking down.

'Maybe,' John whispered, 'I'll be forced to write that *beautiful* book yet.'

Overcome with guilt that he had underestimated Sir Christopher's concern for him, he extended his hand and, continuing in the same low tone of voice, said, 'Come, let us go and breakfast and then head off to have our palms blessed.'

✟

John looked about the *cabinet de porcelaine*, the chosen site for Tommy Tornabuoni's sumptuously arranged birthday luncheon – there was nothing so bourgeois as a 'dining room' in Palazzo Tornabuoni – which was a veritable monument to the local eighteenth-century Doccia factory: porcelain flowers, plates, ewers, birds and candlesticks adorned every wall, ledge and table; even the chandelier and chimney-piece were fashioned in ceramic.

Though John would never allow himself to become jaded to the magnificence of such surroundings – the inexpugnable memory of his relentlessly middle, middle-class childhood in Providence (all those scrunched-up paper napkins!) precluded any such amnesia – he was, today, much more preoccupied with the guests than with the *mise en scène*. With his hands hidden, he tried to calculate the average age of the assembled party on the tips of his fingers. Over and over he counted, but he thought his wobbly sum-making must be at fault. Incredulous, he covertly glanced round the oval table again. In descending order, he enumerated them: Count Pazzino de' Pazzi was ninety-three years old – John *had* looked him up in the *Libro d'Oro della Nobilità Italiana*; next was Dodo Delfington, clocking in at ninety-two years of age; then, Tommy Tornabuoni himself, ninety years old this very day; followed by Alice, who claimed to be eighty-two, but who was, as John knew from having recently snuck a look at her passport, eighty-eight; then Lulu de' Portinari, who looked, John was happy to note, every inch her eighty-five years; followed by the immaculately, but severely, presented Lady Arden at eighty-one; Sir Christopher was, at seventy-nine, the Benjamin of the group; whilst, at thirty-three years of age, John Forde lagged farcically behind. Collectively, he came up with the count of six hundred forty-one years for the members of the party, which, divided by eight, made the average age of those present (including himself) just over eighty years old. *Eighty*! he shrieked inwardly.

So accustomed was John to having ransomed his youth that he did not normally take exception to being the youngest – sometimes by decades – at Florentine gatherings, but he thought today's concentration of geriatric horrors worthy of a very Juvenal's fustigation. Disease and deformity of every kind danced round him: one (poor Alice) was bloated and arthritic, barely able to hobble; a second (old Lulu de' Portinari) was almost blind, hardly capable of spearing her food, half of which dribbled down her pendulous cheeks; here was another (the still alert, but nonetheless diminished, Dodo) increasingly deaf, smiling blankly, as isolation overtook her; and yet one more (the intransigent Lady Arden), with her face made, not of skin, but of vilest leather, her upper and lower lips, wrinkled out of all recognition, scratching at her mouth like an old she-ape, hiding herself in the shady Thabarcan woods; whilst the host (Tommy Tornabuoni), with his shiny bald pate and assortment of stray hairs rambunctiously sprouting from nose and ears and knuckles, slobbered over a repast that he could neither taste nor smell; finally, and worst of all, there was the witless fool (Pansy de' Pazzi) who could not recognise the friend with whom he dined last night nor remember that his wife, whom he had buried twenty years ago, was not still in his midst.

Surely, it is better to die before the misfortunes of age overtake one. And why do all these repulsively tabescent creatures go on frantically clinging to life? They complain of the infirmities of old age and claim *they are tired of living, but let death come close, and they mount a violent fight. All they do is occupy space. Why won't they just give UP*? John screamed to himself.

And then, there was Sir Christopher, frail but still *la distinction même* in comparison to this gallery of decrepitude. But he was not yet eighty, a mere child. *And what would happen*, John asked himself, horror-struck, *if Sir Christopher were to live to be ninety-three like that old man there? Or even ninety-six? Or ninety-eight? Or one hundred and two? It's been known to happen. One's heard of it.*

To begin with, John was sure that, if Sir Christopher were to live another fifteen, even ten, years that the money would run out, as they lived – thanks to John's unreasoning extravagance and Sir Christopher's wilful oblivion – wildly beyond their means; but, before that dreadful day should come, he knew that he himself could not hold on another decade, let alone more. He was simply too exhausted. He would abandon the struggle. Just as he was wondering how many more years – even *months*, he dared to think – Sir Christopher could live, he turned to listen to Dodo Delfington's question.

'I don't suppose – what with Christopher being so ill – that there's any hope of the two of you coming to Glyndebourne with me in June?' Dodo whispered in John's ear, as she looked worriedly across the table at Sir Christopher.

'It's rather hard for me to say. To tell you the truth, I would have thought it better to plan on something for the end of summer – maybe Salzburg again – by which time Christopher might well have built up his strength,' John said.

'Unfortunately, that's the one thing I can't do. My only American grandson is getting married in Philadelphia in the first week of September. And I really must be there, from mid-August on, as he is *quite* one's favourite grandchild. Have you ever met him?'

'I don't know. What's his name?' John, who never let a day pass without summoning up a vision of Zeb Hollingsworth's banal beauty, asked.

'Zebulon Biddle Cadwalader Hollingsworth,' she said proudly. 'He's known as Zeb.'

'Oh, yes, I think one did meet him. Not quite sure. Is he rather a tall young man?'

'Wonderfully so,' Dodo said proudly.

'As a matter of fact, I now remember that I actually accompanied him three or four years ago to deliver the money, in cash, for the rental of the villa for your granddaughter's ball to this,' John said, leaning in and nodding his head toward Count de' Pazzi, 'man's *dreadful* daughter-in-law.'

'Yes, of course, I'd forgotten all about that,' Dodo said. 'Anyway,

I'm so happy that you and Christopher were able to be present at that lovely ball at the Villa Reale di Montalto.'

'Yes, the sort of ball one's always dreamt about,' John spoke truthfully of the party he had *not* attended, whilst thinking regretfully of being locked in the stifling theatre at Bayreuth during an endless *Parsifal.*

'Particularly happy you were at the ball, that is, as it does not look,' she said, casting another nervous look at Sir Christopher, 'as if you will be able to make it to any wedding in Philadelphia, though you will, of course, both be invited.'

'I would have thought it highly unlikely that we'll be able to come. But tell me,' John, who could not control his curiosity, asked, 'whom is he to marry, your grandson? Another proper Philadelphian, I assume.'

'No. She's English. And yet, ironically, though she *is* perfectly English, a Cadbury-Fry,' Dodo said, 'her given name is Philadelphia. Philadelphia Cadbury-Fry – it almost seems like destiny. And believe me, they look like brother and sister: so tall, so blond, so beautifully blue-eyed, they both are. No relation, of course, but it will prove a wonderful uniting of English and American Quaker families.'

'I do regret that we are unlikely to be present for the occasion. Christopher is just not up to such travel,' he said vaguely, as he was suddenly, and rancorously, reminded of the marriage, a few years back, between Vincent Casey and Virginia Stewart Lambert, the latter of whom was ten years older – and many million times richer – than John's former fellow graduate student.

How dare people claim that that little creep, Casey, is bisexual. He is *nothing but a fag, a fag who occasionally sleeps with women,* rich *women!* John snarled to himself.

'How long has Christopher been like this? I mean, he looks so painfully thin,' Dodo said, calling John back to the present.

'Ah, um,' John faltered, 'ever since that coma in January, three months ago.'

'Is there nowhere you can take him? Some cure that might not put things right? Bressanone or Baden-Baden?' Dodo asked.

'As a matter of fact, we're going to Glion, right after Easter, for three, maybe even four, weeks,' he answered, brushing aside the flaming fish that the butler proffered, *following* an oyster and champagne risotto, thinking all the while how much more refined was the understated food that he himself arranged to have served in Palazzo Vespucci.

'Glion? Where's that?'

'It's overlooking Lac Léman, in the hills above Montreux,' John explained. 'We're staying at a place called the Hôtel Victoria. As a boy, Christopher stayed there with his mother, Dame Sophia, in 1926, whilst she was being treated in the clinic next door at Valmont, where Rilke was also a patient.'

'Let us hope that it produces some results,' Dodo said.

'Well, it's all Christopher's idea. And he seems to be convinced that it will be very therapeutic, just breathing in the mountain air and reading at leisure. He wants me to bring the complete works of Sir Walter Scott with us, though how I am going to manage *that* I cannot quite fathom. Anyway, I am sure that the change will do him good,' John said.

'The difference is quite unbelievable,' Dodo, moving in yet closer to John, awkwardly persisted, in a way she would not have done even a year ago. 'It's not much more than six months since we all last saw one another. And then, we were marching across bridge after bridge in Venice. Now, even with a stick, he can hardly walk. If he didn't have you to lean on, I don't know what he would do. You're really like a son to him.'

John had often heard this comparison before and always thought it unjust, for a true son, he believed, would do less for his father than he did for Sir Christopher but expect more in return. The sons of myth and religion rise up in rebellion against their fathers, killing them, as Oedipus did Laius, or, at the very least, dethroning them, as Christ did His Father, transforming Himself into the figure of primary importance in His eponymous faith. The sons of history may be less violent, but they are no less assertive. Thus will they, who are convinced that they were born to take over from their fathers, not shrink from underscoring the infirmities of their elders, gleefully point out their errors and forcefully push them into a position of submission, till they can completely snatch the reins out of the incompetent old hands.

John doubted that Count de' Pazzi was granted more than an hour or two a week of his son's time – out of sufferance more than affection – but was sure that no one would question his son's absolute right to inherit from, indeed to replace, his father, whereas John, who devoted his every waking moment to Sir Christopher, felt himself viewed under a sempiternal cloud of suspicion. Even Sir Christopher's (*normally* gentle) confessor, Father Hennessy, had had the presumption, not long ago, to ask – with what, to John, seemed an accusatory glint in his eyes – what would happen to all of Sir Christopher's possessions after his death. No priest, he was sure, would ever have dreamt of posing such a question to a 'true' son. The blind and decrepit Oedipus had the loving arm of his daughter on whom to lean his old body, but his sons, engaged in internecine struggle to wrest their father's kingdom from him, were nowhere to be found in his hour of need. *No*, John said to himself, *I am nothing like a son to him; I am much too faithful.*

'And is Christopher still able to write?' Dodo asked, taking hold of John's arm.

'That he *can* do,' John said, making a conscious effort not to voice the embitterment he felt at being so utterly overwhelmed by the demands of Sir Christopher's scholarly work. 'As a matter of fact, we should have the proofs of his Leonardo book in not much more than a month's time, and just last week he published the lead article in the *TLS*, called "Michelangelo and the Angels", about a new two-volume edition of Michelangelo's correspondence, edited by one E.H. Ramsgate.'

'Why "Michelangelo and the Angels", if it's about his correspondence?' Dodo asked.

'Well, the article really concerns the warring factions of dæmon and angel in Michelangelo's life, the struggle between the prosaic, money-grubbing, mean-spirited, malevolent side of his nature – as all too demonstrably evinced in his correspondence – and the purity of his artistic ambitions. In the end, of course, it is the angel who wins. Christopher finishes the article by recounting a charming story in which Michelangelo complained to the painter Signorelli that he felt so unwell and so tired that he could not work. "Do not worry," replied Signorelli, "the angels will come down from heaven, they will hold your arms and help you." As a perfect, final flourish to his article, Christopher concluded, "And the Angels did." I'll leave a copy of it for you at your *hôtel*. It really is, I think, one of the best short things he has ever written,' he said truthfully. John had long hoped that, one day, someone might comment upon the fluent evolution of Sir Christopher's writing style under *his* disciple's watch, but no such observation had yet been forthcoming, nor did he now think it ever would.

'You two are looking thick as thieves,' Alice, obviously bored, said from the other side of the table, as she helped herself to a turkey, stained beautifully pink and stuffed with foie gras and cream – the presentation of which (if not the taste) filled John with floods of envy.

As was so often the case in Palazzo Tornabuoni, John thought, the seating seemed to have been expressly arranged both to thwart conversation *and* to offend the guests. Today, at the magnificently dressed oval table, Tommy Tornabuoni had, inexplicably, put to his right Lulu de' Portinari, who, even if a duchess, did not take precedence over a foreign countess. On his left, he put an obviously *very* dissatisfied Lady Arden, who, immediately she was installed, proceeded to sneeze violently, thereby destroying the artful arrangement of rose petals that traced the design of the damask tablecloth. Throughout luncheon, John half heard her tell endless stories of protocol mayhem, whilst vehemently insisting, on three separate occasions, that the French never use the word *placement* but always *place à table*. She spoke only to Sir Christopher on her left; he listened attentively but commented sparsely. On his left was Alice Varrow, who, regardless of whether anyone were listening, spoke incessantly. Presiding at the far end of the table was the near-incoherent and, as Sir Christopher had forewarned, wildly effeminate, Count de' Pazzi, who could barely make himself understood by Dodo Delfington on his left. Completing the oval was John, sandwiched between Dodo and Duchessa de' Portinari. Obviously, he made no attempt to speak to the latter.

Trying to include Alice, John leant forward and said, 'I was telling Dodo about a beautiful article Christopher's just published in the *TLS*. You really should read it yourself, Al—'

'Now tell me,' Alice cut John off heatedly, 'is it really true that Christopher is going to write his autobiography? I don't think it a good idea, not a good idea at *all*.'

'Well, as he's already started, it's a bit late for that,' John said, casting a knowing glance at Alice, as if to remind her that she was actually seated *next* to Sir Christopher.

'He's just entirely too buttoned-up, not at all the right temper-ament for writing a lively, gay memoir,' Alice obstinately dug her heels in. 'Now, if one wanted to write *oneself* about all the suitors one has had, and the beautiful, gay parties one has attended – not least the magnificent ball your father gave in one's honour at New-port, right before the war, Dodo – that would be one thing, but Christopher, no, that's not his sort of thing. So much better for him to stick to his art studies – stitching together all those dismembered polyptychs from San Gimignano and so on.'

'You'd better be careful, Alice, because some of your *less* than kind comments have already begun to be repeated back to Christo-pher,' John, who was starting to feel exasperated, said untruthfully.

'What! Who? *Who* has been talking against one? Trying to stir up animosity toward one?' Alice seethed, lowering her voice to a threatening snarl.

'I couldn't very well name names,' John said.

'Names? Names! You mean there's more than one person talking against me. Oh, I can't believe it, simply cannot believe it. But then I shouldn't be surprised. This is a problem I've had my whole life, my *entire* life,' Alice said, burying her face in her scarf and collaps-ing back in her chair.

Afraid that Alice was about to burst into tears and make some embarrassing pronouncement about her own envious nature, John reached out to pat her arm and said, 'I wouldn't take it to heart, dear Alice, but maybe it's just best if we drop the subject, for now, at least.'

'No, I *must* talk about it,' Alice said, dropping the scarf from her perfectly dry eyes. 'It is, as I said, a problem I've had my whole life, from the time I was a young girl. This jealousy, this constant jeal—'

'I don't know, Alice, that this is really the ideal time for a public confession,' John interrupted, out of what he thought was a show of charity.

'Confession? Confession!' Alice screeched incredulously. 'I am only telling you what has *happened*, this constant jealously that has dogged one through one's entire life. I can understand that people, particularly other girls, should have been wildly jealous of one when one was sixteen and so lovely to look at, but those days are rather gone. And, Lord knows, it's not as though I hold an impor-tant position or have any money or property, or even possessions, for people to be envious of,' she continued. 'And, you know, I'm not really, not really all *that* famous.'

'Not famous?' Tommy Tornabuoni shouted from his end of the table. 'You, dear Alice, *not* famous? Why, your praises are sung, your portrait bedecked with flowers and lovingly venerated, throughout the civilised world.'

'Now, don't exaggerate, Tommy,' Alice said, lapping up the mockery as greedily as she did a second helping of turkey and foie gras.

'Just the other day,' Tommy Tornabuoni continued tauntingly, 'I read a very admiring reference to your great work on warrior queens in a new historical novel on Queen Zenobia by that American – what *is* his name?'

'Oh, you mean Tore Auchinleck – not his real name, I might add. He was born Eugene Vidali. He pinched both his given name and his surname from his mother's *second* husband,' Alice said. 'Just as he pinched, I dare say, half his information on Zenobia direct from one. He does churn out those historical novels, old Tore Auchinleck, from Julian the Apostate right up to Henry Adams.'

'The Waverley novels apart, I think it an inherently vulgar genre, the historical novel,' Sir Christopher intervened firmly.

'I must confess,' Lady Arden spoke up for the first time, 'that I've always been rather fond of that French novel about the Emperor Hadrian by that woman – I can't remember her name.'

'Marguerite Yourcenar,' John offered.

'Yes, that's it,' Lady Arden said with a prim smile.

'Oh, but that is too marvellous, I agree,' Sir Christopher said. 'And on *quite* a different level to anything poor old Tore Auchinleck could ever write.'

'*Quite* a different level,' John concurred.

'It's so funny, *so* funny,' Lulu de' Portinari began to cackle uncontrollably, as she turned toward John, 'how you repeat everything Christopher says. Now your voice is even beginning to sound like his.'

Aside from the fact that he found it wildly unjust that he – he who had first brought *Mémoires d'Hadrien* to Sir Christopher's attention – should, in this instance, be accused of parroting his master, John thought old Duchessa de' Portinari the most loathsome creature whom he had ever had the misfortune to encounter. With very little effort, and *no* remorse, he could easily have picked up the carving knife that accompanied the pink turkey and plunged it deep into her wrinkled neck. Instead, he violently kicked the sleeping little dog at her feet and pointedly turned his back on her. In an attempt to unite the far end of the table, he said in a loud voice, 'As I was saying, or *trying* to say, before being so rudely interrupted, you, Alice, should really read Christopher's new article in the *TLS*, "Michelangelo and the Angels".

'And I could leave a copy for you also, Signor il Conte, if it should interest you,' John addressed the drooling old man who stared blankly at his fellow guests.

'Angels? Angels? I love angels. Yes, of course, and it is the angels who will guide the dove, our own Holy Ghost, whom we send forth next Sunday, when he is set alight with the flint that my ancestor, yet another Pazzino de' Pazzi, brought back to Florence on his return from the Crusades. The flint is kept at Santi Apostoli. But I own the cart. I OWN the cart!' Count de' Pazzi shouted in heavily accented, nearly incomprehensible slurs. He was, in fact, the only aristocratic Florentine whom John had ever met who did *not* speak perfect English.

'I'm afraid that I don't quite follow,' Dodo said, looking helplessly at John.

'Perhaps, Signor il Conte, I might explain to our visitor, Lady Charles, about the hallowed ceremony to which you refer?' John asked with exaggerated deference.

'Oh yes, explain, explain,' Pansy de' Pazzi said, laughing uncontrollably.

'You see, Dodo, every year on Easter Sunday, a rocket in the shape of a dove is set alight on the high altar of the Duomo, with flint relics *said* to have been brought back from the Holy Sepulchre in Jerusalem by Count de' Pazzi's ancestor, also Pazzino de' Pazzi, following the first Crusade at the end of the eleventh century. The dove flies down a wire from the sanctuary to a cart, loaded with fireworks, outside in the piazza. If the cart explodes and the dove manages to fly back to the altar, this is thought to be a good omen for the next harvest, and so it is known as the *Scoppio del Carro,* the explosion of the cart. And the cart itself, *il Brindellone,* as it is called because of its flying pennants, is kept by Count de' Pazzi in its very own house in via il Prato.'

'Oh, but how well you tell the story, *giovanotto*. "*Giovinezza, giovinezza, / Primavera di belleza*",' the aged count began to sing, tears streaming down his face in a fit of emotional incontinence so typical of the very old.

'Really, Pansy, there's no need to cry,' Alice scolded, whilst attacking the *coeur à la crème* with raspberries. 'And I hardly think this is the time or place to be bursting into Fascist song – what with the fate of Tommy's brother, Bibi.'

'Oh, but, Trixie,' Count de' Pazzi said, clasping Alice's hand, 'just think how, before the war, on summer evenings at Forte, we all used to sit in a circle – you and Pifi and Costanza and I – and sing those lovely songs for hours and hou—'

'I am not Trixie,' Alice growled, retracting her hand. 'I am her sister, her much *younger* sister. Trixie's been dead for over two years now – Lord, how I miss her.'

'But Costanza just told me that she—'

'For God's sake, Pansy, your wife has been dead for almost twenty years! Don't you remember that it was *because* she was dying that you were allowed back in this country?'

'"*Il valor dei tuoi guerrieri, / La virtù dei tuoi pionieri / La vision dell'Alighieri / Oggi brilla in tutti i cuor / Giovinezza, giovinezza / Primavera di bellezza*",' Count de' Pazzi continued to chant in a low, moronic hum. '"*Giovinezza, giovinezza...*"'

✞

The vision of Alighieri? I mean really! John said to himself, shaking his head in disbelief, as, later in the afternoon, he sat alone on the terrace of Caffè Rivoire, sipping a Campari and wondering how that old Florentine Fascist could have dared to invoke the name of the sacred Dante. So right the poet had been, John thought, to rejoice that, over land and sea, the name of Florence was spread through hell and to describe the Florentines as a 'thankless, malignant people ... avaricious, envious and proud'. Overcome by contempt for that old, demented Fascist count and outright hatred for Lulu de' Portinari, John felt a spring of revolt welling up within him toward all Florentines, even toward the city itself.

Looking up at the hulking mass that was Palazzo Vecchio, John beheld not a monument to civic liberty but rather the site of Hitler's triumphant 1938 visit to Florence, where Mussolini had prophetically inscribed the city's *livre d'or* with the words, *'Firenze Fascistissima'*.

Glancing round the Piazza della Signoria, which he *thought* he knew by heart, John was for the first time struck that almost all of the statues in this square celebrated violence and war: Perseus dangling the severed head of Medusa; Hercules battling the centaur, Nessus; Judith brandishing her sword over the vanquished Holofernes; Menelaus clutching the corpse of the slain Patroclus; Hercules wielding his club over the writhing Cacus; the rape of the Sabine women; the rape of Polyxena; and, most famous of all, the lone David, poised to kill.

How very *Florentine: death and destruction on every visage*, John said to himself as he looked about, seeing no longer the city of his dreams but, rather, a leviathan of traffic, noise, heat, dirt, fortifications, crenellations and harsh, aggressive, cyclopean rustication. When Dante wrote that 'There is a place in Hell called Malebolge, all of stone, which is the colour of iron', John thought he might well have been describing Florence itself.

I'll leave this accursed place as soon as he *dies*, John said to himself, wondering if, at the same time, he had not even begun to dislike the fine arts. He used to be troubled that he had never once been reduced to tears by a painting or a sculpture – let alone a work of architecture – whereas he had, on more than one occasion, cried furiously over a novel, a poem or a sonata. Today, however, he felt curiously vindicated to be *un*moved by the sight before himself, thus confirming him, or so he thought, in the belief of his literary vocation.

'If it isn't Mr Forde,' John heard a voice pulling him back from his hysterical invective. 'I see that you are going about with *the* review.'

'Oh, um, yes, Miss Ramsgate,' John said, standing up to behold a woman dressed in a fine Savile Row suit – even if not *quite* Huntsman – along with a Jermyn Street shirt and tie and a St James's Street hat. He had often heard it said in Florence that Miss Ramsgate's greatest joy in life was to have a priest tell her to remove her hat in church, at which she sniped, 'But, Father, I am a *woman!*'

'How faithful you are to your master to promenade in public with his literary offspring,' Miss Ramsgate said, pointing to the copy of the *TLS* that John had absently left on the *caffè* table.

'Actually, I was just about to leave Sir Christopher's review of your new edition of the Michelangelo correspondence for a great friend, Lady Charles Delfington, at her *hôtel*. I hope you were pleased with the article,' John said, still trying to collect himself.

'Quite,' Miss Ramsgate, who maintained extremely frosty relations with Sir Christopher, ever since he had published a wickedly condescending review of a guidebook to Florence that she wrote thirty years ago, said. 'Though I must say that I didn't like that last sentence – about the angels. I think Michelangelo himself would have found it hostile to the Florentines.'

'*Hostile?*' John said indignantly. 'On the contrary. After all, you yourself published that famous letter of Michelangelo's in which he says that he never had to do with a more ungrateful and arrogant people than the Florentines. I think he would have been quite flattered by the reference to the angels.'

'Perhaps,' Miss Ramsgate, evidently pleased to have riled John, said. 'May I introduce you to my colleague, Lady Una Crotchwell?' she continued, nodding toward a bejewelled, blue-haired woman, entirely covered in pink tulle, with shoes, hat and bag to match.

'Hello. How nice to meet you, Lady Una,' John said, extending his hand. He could not fail but to be struck by the contrast between the two women – one so feminine and flouncy, the other so masculine and meticulous – thinking that they fit right into the skewered Florentine landscape. Here, the foreign art historians – a bizarre assemblage of humourless German professors, diesel dykes, flamboyant fags, deeply corrupt Balkans and Jewish atheists – were as unattractive as the local fascist inhabitants. There was even a former vacuum cleaner salesman from Kansas City, turned mediæval manuscript expert, who numbered amongst the art historical elite.

'Too, too lovely,' Lady Una Crotchwell cooed.

'We should be on our way, then,' Miss Ramsgate said. 'And as for Rilke,' she added in her butchest, most disapproving, voice, as she indicated the little book that John was clutching, 'I hope that you won't mind my saying that I think it most peculiar, almost indecent, that you should be reading his beautiful German in a *French* translation.'

'I always think that Rilke loses something in the original,' John had the presence of mind to reply.

Looking stumped, Miss Ramsgate said nothing and, turning to go, tipped her hat.

Alone again, he sat down and opened the copy of Rilke's *Journal florentin*. Though he had bought this slim volume at the French bookshop in Piazza Ognissanti in anticipation of the upcoming Swiss trip, he read it now as a kind of prophetic vision:

> *Je me souviens d'abord du premier soir qui me paraît assez significa-tif...je pénétrai tout à fait par hazard sur la place de la Seigneurie. Le Palazzo Vecchio se dresse devant moi, oppressant par sa masse abrupte et compacte, et je crois sentir sur moi son ombre grise et lourde... Florence ne s'ouvre pas comme Venise à l'hôte de passage. Là les palais clairs et gais sont tellement confiants et bavards!... A Florence, il en va tout autrement; c'est presque en ennemis que les palais dressent leurs fronts muets en face de l'étranger, et un méfiant orgueil s'attache autours des sombres niches et des portails...*

With intense concentration, he read on, enchanted by this portrait of a dark, mysterious, utterly unwelcoming Florence – not a city of flowers but a valley of stone, *presque en ennemis* – when, after twenty pages more, he was deeply disconcerted by one sentence. He reread these few lines repeatedly, translating them to himself with great attention. Finally, he took a small Moleskine out of his pocket and jotted down:

> *Whoever is noble and serious does not imitate the small gestures/man-nerisms of a distinguished man (?*un homme de valeur*) – but rather his broad style – which, in all great artists, is: the solitary path to himself.*
>
> –RILKE, FLORENCE 1898

Trembling at the idea that he himself had spent years simply copying the superficial traits of Sir Christopher – the accent, the syntax, the pronunciation, the clothing, the violent likes and dis-likes – without in any way emulating the quiddity of his character, his unwavering devotion to work and to thought, John closed his notebook dejectedly, doubtful that Rilke would number *him* amongst the 'noble and serious'.

Perhaps, he said to himself, *old Lulu de' Portinari had been right to make fun of one after all?*

Looking round the art-filled square, with tears in his eyes, he was grateful that they were to leave for Switzerland in little more than a week, thinking that there, hidden away in the mountains and inspired by the lake – and, above all, far from Florence, the scene of his own corruption – he might set seriously to work on *The Disciple*.

☩

Sir Christopher sat in the back of the car with a handkerchief carefully positioned on his head. From what John could gather, this was meant to protect the unusually silent Sir Christopher from the sun, though John could not help believing that this little patch of white cloth was perfectly inutile; moreover, he thought, but did not dare say, that Sir Christopher looked, most improbably, as though he were wearing a yarmulke. They had now been together in the car for over ten hours, having twice briefly stopped, on both of which occasions Sir Christopher had resolutely refused to budge.

When, yesterday morning, John had proposed that they leave Switzerland after only five nights, Sir Christopher had leapt at the suggestion, for their alpine retreat had proved an unmitigated disaster. They had arrived easily enough in Geneva, flying (at John's insistence) direct from the æroport at Peretola on the Tuesday of Easter week, but, just as John scrambled to find a taxi to take them (and their mountain of luggage) to the *hôtel* at Glion, Sir Christopher had, in his habitual impatience, tripped over his own stick and fallen – fallen hard – on the corner of a revolving metal luggage ramp, gashing his eyebrow and drawing quantities of blood. So rattled did Sir Christopher appear by this incident that he lost control of his bladder in the taxi, leaving John with the delicate task, on their arrival at the Hôtel Victoria, of escorting his urine-soaked, blood-splattered master, past a throng of gaping Swiss burghers and eye-averting *hôtel* staff, straight to his room.

After he had washed and dressed Sir Christopher, John went back to the front hall, only to find that the trunk of books he had sent by special courier on Holy Saturday, containing complete sets of the Waverley novels and *The Decline and Fall of the Roman Empire* – Scott and Gibbon being Sir Christopher's preferred authors, with Ed McBain coming in a *very* close third – had been returned to Florence by the Swiss customs office.

Sitting alone in the *hôtel* dining room that first night, when he ordered a sublimely rich *émincé de veau*, John had no alternative but to devote himself to the paperback copy of *Mansfield Park* that he had hastily bought that very morning in via de' Tornabuoni – the only literary accompaniment he had with him, save for his endless notes for *The Disciple*. By nature, neither John nor Sir Christopher was a Janeite. Each, for quite different reasons, mistrusted Miss Austen – Sir Christopher thought her entirely too sensitive and feminine, whereas John found her unswerving inclination to reward the good and punish the evil hopelessly naïf – but, for the first few days of their would-be Swiss idyll, she remained their only literary diversion.

When Sir Christopher awoke the next morning, John found him better and stronger than he ever would have imagined after their harrowing arrival. Following a long Swiss breakfast in bed and an even longer *levée*, Sir Christopher was conducted to the front hall, where he sat down to listen to John read aloud from *Mansfield Park*. That day, and the two following ones, Thursday and Friday, involved a fairly placid recounting of the travails of Fanny Price – the poor cousin stranded amongst her rich and selfish relations – though they were punctuated by several more, but not disastrous, falls for Sir Christopher. Early on Saturday morning, however, John found Sir Christopher crucified to the footboard of his bed, the same affected eyebrow perilously close to being impaled on a finial. Blood was everywhere.

'One would rather die than lose one's eyesight,' Sir Christopher said, as John heaved him off the end of the bed. 'Imagine a *blind* art historian.'

'There's no question of your going blind. Don't even mention such a thing,' John said, trying to sound authoritative. 'Now, tell me, would you like to go back to Florence? We'll do whatever you want.'

'Yes, please, get one out of this hell. I want to be at *home*, with you in the adjoining room,' Sir Christopher cried.

'Fine,' John said. 'But I think that we'll have to get a car and driver to take us back. I don't see how we can go through that labyrinth of an æroport again.'

'Yes,' Sir Christopher agreed, 'we obviously must be driven.'

But when John came back to Sir Christopher's room later in the morning to announce proudly that he had managed to secure arrangements for their return to Florence tomorrow, Low Sunday, Sir Christopher seemed far from pleased. 'I want to leave *now*,' he shouted.

'That's impossible,' John said.

'But you promised!'

'Listen,' John, sitting on the edge of the bed, said patiently, 'it's already a quarter past eleven. You have to wash and dress; I have to pack for both of us; you would need some sort of luncheon, and we have to check out. We couldn't possibly leave here before two or three and that is much too late to be setting off. It's a ten- or twelve-hour drive to Florence. Plus, I've already reserved a car to pick us up tomorrow morning at nine o'clock. I think we were jolly lucky to find a driver on a Sunday at all. I was afraid that we might have to wait till Monday to leave. Why don't you get up, and I'll help you to dress? Then we can go down to the hall, and I'll continue reading to you.'

Now, as the cupola of the Duomo loomed in the distance, the spoiled inhabitants of Mansfield Park seemed far behind, though the account of Fanny Price's banishment to the squalor of her native Portsmouth – punishment for her refusal to marry a rich suitor, as well as reminder of the polluted waters from which she sprang and to which she might, at any moment, be cast back – remained vivid to John, remained, in fact, one of his favourite scenes in literature for the rest of his life. In reading and rereading it in years to come, he often trembled at the idea of being expelled from Florence himself and sent back to *his* native Providence.

'If you like,' John said, 'tonight – once I've got us settled – we can take up again with *Mansfield Park*.'

'Hmm,' Sir Christopher grunted.

But even before they got out of the car, John saw that they were not likely to get much reading done tonight. He had instructed the driver to go round by the entrance along the Arno, as he feared that the impatient traffic of the via de' Bardi would leave him little time to unpack the unwieldy luggage and the ever more intractable Sir Christopher. After the portress opened the gate along Lungarno Torrigiani and the car had driven up to the back portal of Palazzo Vespucci, John could still not get Sir Christopher out of the car. He was not at all sure that Sir Christopher was even able to stand.

Assailed by what he thought a brilliant idea, he dashed up to the apartment, went to the *archivio*, where he found the only chair on wheels in the house, and dragged it downstairs. Realising that Sir Christopher's resistance was motivated more by fear than by hostility, John carefully placed him in the chair and pushed him across the courtyard to the lift. Once they reached the second floor, they were obliged, with the utmost difficulty, to mount on foot the four pietra serena steps leading to the apartment. Leaving Sir Christopher seated in the office chair, alone, in the front hall, John ran back downstairs, paid the driver his exorbitant fee and unloaded the luggage. It was not till after nine o'clock in the evening that he was able to uncork a bottle of wine and sit down in the drawing room with his newly beloved authoress.

He felt utterly exhausted from lugging Sir Christopher about – his weight was no mere metaphor – but also greatly reassured to have safely and properly installed him in the swan bed, so much so that he couldn't even be bothered to finish the bottle of wine he had opened and retired himself at half past ten. It was, therefore, with a mixture of resentment and anxiety that he heard his simple Christian name being twisted into a four-syllable threnody at two o'clock in the morning. 'JOHNNNNNN,' Sir Christopher's unmistakable voice rang out.

'What is it?' John called, as, dashing into the room, he turned on the lights and found Sir Christopher sprawled on the floor, the contents of the overturned night table scattered all about him. 'What happened?' he continued gently, as he knelt down to comfort Sir Christopher.

'Where *were* you? Why did you forsake one?' Sir Christopher asked him.

'But I was just in the bedroom next door,' John defended himself. 'It's two o'clock in the morning. What do you expect? I was asleep. I certainly didn't *forsake* you.'

'Well, now that you are here, we must go, must go at once,' Sir Christopher said, trying to sit up.

'What do you mean go? Go *where*?' John asked.

'Back to Florence. You promised you would take one back, away from this hell.'

'But we are *back*, back in Florence, at home in the via de' Bardi, in Palazzo Vespucci, everything in its proper place. Just glance around you. Look, this is your icon, the one that belonged to your mother and that you always have on your night table,' John said, as he knelt down to pick the brass object off the floor.

'That should really be polished. It looks terribly scruffy,' Sir Christopher said. 'And I also think the piano needs to be tuned and, while you're at it, we might have some of the marmalade cake. It's been simply ages since we've had that.'

'Yes, of course,' John sighed, feeling, as the ever *in*constant Benjamin Constant did toward Madame de Staël: *always necessary but never adequate.* 'And now that we have returned to Florence, I can attend to all those things.'

'It's no use making excuses. We must leave for Florence, leave at once,' Sir Christopher said as John heaved him back onto the bed and put right the overturned night table, not failing, as he did so, to regret the smashing of the Ming vase, mounted as a lamp.

'I'm not making *excuses*,' John said. 'I was just pointing out old friends. You see, here is the beautiful swan bed, and there are the nineteen Vanni drawings, each in its rightful place.'

'I don't think there will be any difficulty in getting them through customs. The Swiss don't know a thing about Francesco Vanni,' Sir Christopher said.

'Please be reasonable,' John said, clasping Sir Christopher's hands as he laid him back in bed. 'Now, just let me go and get you a new carafe of water and a dustpan, so that I can sweep up this mess, and then I will come back and sit with you for a while. We could even read for a bit from Miss Austen if you want.'

But before he could finish in the kitchen, John heard Sir Christopher once again clambering about. He ran back to the bedroom only to find him dangling from the dangerously high bed, tugging furiously at his nightshirt. 'But what are you doing?' John asked worriedly.

'I told you that I want to go. Go *now*. And one must obviously be dressed for that.'

'But we are home, home in Florence. Where do you want to go *to?*'

Sir Christopher thought for a moment and then said staunchly, 'I want to go to Mansfield Park. Now please, get one's clothes.'

Realising, as he hadn't yet done, that Sir Christopher was now seriously delusional, John thought it best to humour him, in the hope of tiring him out, and so said, 'Right you are. Do you want a striped shirt or a white one?'

'Oh, I think one must have a *white* shirt, if one is to cross the border,' Sir Christopher said.

John spent the next forty-five minutes laboriously dressing Sir Christopher in full regalia – suit, tie, braces, links – in the hope that he might then put him back in the archive chair and wheel him round the whole apartment, thereby making him see that they were, in fact, 'home'. But even once he had placed Sir Christopher in front of one of the French windows in the drawing room, pointing out the spire of the Palazzo Vecchio and the cupola of the Duomo, Sir Christopher refused to be convinced, saying, 'When does the car come to take us back to Florence?'

'Shortly, very shortly. Why don't you take these, whilst we're waiting,' John said, proffering three sleeping pills and a glass of water. 'Dr Werner prescribed them to control your bladder.'

He then wheeled Sir Christopher back to his bedroom, where he had already put his mattress on the floor. Knowing that Sir Christopher could climb out of the dangerously high swan bed and hurt himself, John thought that placing his master on the ground was the best, perhaps the *only*, way to protect him, for he would, in such a position, be physically incapable of hoisting himself up. John had not, however, counted on the fact that Sir Christopher *was* capable of wrestling with him until the breaking of the day, even wounding the hollow of his thigh. Through the rest of that night, John prayed that the angels would come down from heaven, hold his arms and help him. But the angels didn't.

CHAPTER V

Passiontide

IN THE EARLY morning hours of Thursday, 27 May – not quite
six weeks after their return from Switzerland – as John was blow-
ing smoke out one of the French windows in the drawing room,
he heard a tremendous explosion coming from the other side of
the river. He extinguished his cigarette on the silver waiter that
he had appropriated as his covert ashtray and leant heavily on the
elaborate *crémone*, trying to work out what had happened. Though
he soon heard the whirr of countless sirens – a not unfamiliar
sound in Florence – he saw neither flame, nor spark, nor vapour.
Shortly before three o'clock – after he ran a half-finished packet
of cigarettes under the kitchen tap and vowed, once again, to stop
smoking – he went to bed, thinking that there must have been a
gas leak somewhere in the city.

It was not until eight o'clock the following morning, when Dodo
Delfington rang up from London, saying that she had just heard
on the BBC that a bomb had been set off in the Uffizi and wanted
to make sure they were both all right, that John understood the
origin of last night's noise. As the next few days unfolded, it became
clear that the hand of the Mafia had been at work, but, though the
damage to the building had been significant – shattered glass was
everywhere and all the surrounding streets were to be cordoned off
for weeks to come – only three pictures had been utterly destroyed.

'I've been reading about the ongoing investigation in the *Herald
Tribune*,' Sir Christopher said on the following Monday morning
as John laid a tray before him – since their return from Switzerland there had been no question of Sir Christopher's getting up
for breakfast. 'It's an absolute tragedy,' he continued, 'about that
beautiful picture by Sebastiano del Piombo.'

'Not to mention,' John, in a misplaced humanitarian gesture, said, 'the five people who were killed – that guardian and all his family – and the forty-eight who were seriously wounded.'

'Yes,' Sir Christopher said, as he generously buttered both sides of his toast, 'that was most unfortunate. But one must be honest and admit that the guardian and his little family at the Accademia dei Georgofili who lost their lives will, in some sense, carry on – they *are* just the sort of people to have heaps of relatives – whilst a great work like *The Death of Adonis* is utterly irreplaceable. An absolute masterpiece of High Renaissance painting it is.'

'It's written here,' John said, pointing to a national Italian news-paper, folded into the side compartment of the breakfast tray, 'that, though severely damaged – apparently a great shard of glass has sliced the canvas horizontally in two – the Sebastiano *can* be restored.'

'One only prays so,' Sir Christopher said.

'What's more,' John continued, 'there's also a notice in the same paper saying that Richter is giving a concert in Florence at the end of this week – at the Accademia, of all places – as a gesture of solidarity with Florence and the loss she has suffered.'

'I do think that's good of him to give a concert for Florence,' Sir Christopher said. 'Shows what a true artist he is, Richter – that he should feel for this loss.'

'Quite,' John said, not knowing how else to reply, for he still felt more than a lingering sense of that same ambiguity and hostility toward Florence and her patrimony that had possessed him when, a few weeks back, he was seated in Piazza della Signoria on Palm Sunday. He had not, of course, been reduced to the sort of philistin-ism that would welcome destruction, nor had his utter antipathy to all manifestations of violence diminished in the least. It was simply that now, in these tensile days with Sir Christopher, he saw nothing but cold marble or varnished paint when he visited a museum or church, whereas, formerly, the deeper his melancholy the greater had been the consolation that he drew from the fine arts. But since they had come back from Switzerland, John could hardly bear to look at a work of art – a difficult proposition in Florence, of all places – feeling as though the triumph of the æsthetic was a direct challenge to his own corrupt nature.

To John's surprise and, he had to admit, to his chagrin, Sir Christopher had recomposed himself miraculously well after their hellish first night home from Glion, of which he appeared to remember nothing. At about six in the morning, following the night of their return, John had escaped from the stranglehold of Sir Christopher's grasp on the bedroom floor and, with great effort, undressed his drugged master; with even greater effort, he wriggled him into a nightshirt, rolled him onto a carpet, replaced the mattress and then heaved him back into the swan bed, as if to make out that that dark night of the soul had never been. When, at about eleven that morning, Annunziata brought in breakfast and John stood guard, he knew that his hopes of freedom were dashed, as he heard Sir Christopher, looking down at the tray, forcefully intone, 'Is there not more butter than that? Lent, after all, *is* over.' In the days that followed, as Sir Christopher regained his strength (and his exaction) with alarming rapidity, John had often said to himself, *Lent may be over, but* my *Passion has just begun.*

When, a fortnight ago, the behemoth of Sir Christopher's Leonardo proofs arrived, John felt, like David of the *Psalms*, ready to halt, his sorrow continually before him; unlike David, he could not (not yet) declare his own iniquity, nor be sorry for his sin.

'Obviously,' Sir Christopher said, 'we must go to the Richter concert. I should think you had better go to fetch the tickets first thing this morning – as it is bound to sell out quickly – whilst I continue with the proofs of the next chapter.'

'Fine. But I'll have to get you installed in your study before I go,' John said to Sir Christopher, who was now incapable of managing the mere five steps up to that room. Sir Christopher could not, in fact, walk more than a few paces without leaning on John, insisting, nonetheless, as he did so, that he never overtly grasp him but, rather, that John should extend his right forearm, parallel to the ground, like a sort of neutral bar, on which Sir Christopher was to lean. Even when Sir Christopher communicated on Sundays – a ritual from which John still obstinately refrained – his disciple was expected seamlessly to guide his master to the altar rail, arm held woodenly aloft.

'Right you are,' Sir Christopher said. 'We can go over whatever corrections I might have to the proofs after luncheon.'

✝

John looked about the 'Hall of Prisoners' with no little awe, some restive longing and a devouring sense of repentance. At his suggestion, they had taken seats, all of which were unnumbered, at the very back of the beautifully lit main room of the Accademia, thus providing them with a panoramic view of Michelangelo's celebrated unfinished sculptures – the four slaves intended for the *Tomb of Pope Julius II* and the *St Matthew* for the Duomo – on up to the Tribune where the original *David* reigned and at whose feet Sviatoslav Richter was in the midst of performing a programme composed entirely of late Beethoven. It was, John thought, the most moving union of image and sound that he had ever known.

He glanced over at the *Awakening Slave* – within touching distance, on his left – and felt how belligerent he had been ever to doubt the transformative power of great art, and how jejune, even obtuse, he had been to think one could argue the superiority of one art form over another. Literature, music, the fine arts, they complemented (and sometimes inspired) one another; they did not, however, vie each with the other. *Art is not a competitive sport*, he contritely admitted to himself. Rail though he might at his own enslavement to Sir Christopher, he knew, as his eyes darted round the room, soaking up this unique assemblage of tortured masterpieces, that he did not, for once, agree with his revered near-namesake: *Art can find comfort for a broken heart*, he said to himself.

As if to atone for his æsthetic apostasy, John spent the next few days rambling round Florence in order to pay obeisance to those works of art he most particularly loved. From gallery, to palace, to chapel, to convent he went, gently inclining himself before those old friends whose pardon he sought.

A week after the Richter concert, his quest ended, close to home, when he walked into the church of Santa Felicita and beheld, just on his right, Pontormo's *Deposition*. Trembling, John stared at this icon of Mannerist genius. Stript of all vestige of religious allegory – neither ladder, nor cross, nor tomb being present – the large altarpiece is magically brought to life by nearly unimaginable hues of burnished turquoise (melting into pale plumbago) and creamed strawberry (shying away from frothy pink), all shot through with violent streaks of puce, emerald and sage. It seemed to John that the colour itself was an actor, a major actor, in the drama.

He pushed at the grille, which, miraculously, opened and stepped into the minuscule Capponi Chapel, bowing before the swooning Virgin and the limp Saviour, both of whom were supported by a chorus of startlingly androgynous attendants. Humbly, John acknowledged that the art of painting, at this level, where the marriage of technical perfection and imaginative daring belonged to a sui generis realm, was one of the unparalleled instruments for exploring the entire range of human thought *and* emotion.

How could one ever *have doubted*? he asked himself as he knelt down and kissed the drooping right hand of Christ. It was almost as if, in a final gesture of expiation, John hoped to choke himself on the blood of our Saviour's nail wound.

When he arrived home that afternoon, just before five, he was greeted by news that restored his faith to its former ardour – a faith not just in the fine arts, but in Florence and, indeed, the Florentines themselves.

'Would you look at this?' Sir Christopher asked, holding up a sheet of cream-coloured writing-paper with a large red *giglio* embossed at the top. 'It was delivered by hand this afternoon, right after you left for the German Institute.'

'Goodness, it's from the *sindaco* of Florence,' John said, gingerly taking up the missive.

'So it is,' Sir Christopher said. 'Just read it. You'll see that they are proposing to make one an honorary citizen of Florence.'

'That's a tremendous distinction – the freedom of the city,' John said, bending down to kiss Sir Christopher on the forehead.

'Is it not?' Sir Christopher said with a smile. 'Much grander than all those old honorary degrees.'

'It would appear from the mayor's letter,' John said, 'that they were planning to decorate you on the twenty-third of June but that, in light of the recent turmoil, they are going to put it off till the autumn. A pity that, as it would have been so wonderfully symbolic to have the ceremony take place on the Vigil of the Baptist, the very day I first laid eyes on you, exactly ten years ago.'

'Actually,' Sir Christopher, who shared none of John's sentimental attachment to dates and anniversaries, said, 'it's just as well, as one will have to write a very carefully scripted speech and have it translated into Italian, and we do not want any interruptions at the moment, now that the Leonardo proofs are upon us.'

'Of course not,' John said blankly.

'I must say that I am frightfully happy with the way the Leonardo book has turned out,' Sir Christopher continued, 'so much so that I think it deserves a dedication.'

'*Really?*' John asked in amazement, for he knew that Sir Christopher's many books had borne only sporadic dedications and that those few testimonials – with the exception of that to Andrew Bruntisfield in his 1965 monograph on Piero – had invariably been granted to professional, extremely well-placed colleagues. Otherwise, no emotional attachment or even family member had ever snuck between the austere covers of a work by Christopher Noble-Nolan. His first book, on Taddeo Gaddi, back in 1937, had – with rather *too* naked ambition, John thought – been dedicated to the then Director of the National Gallery, whom the young author barely knew, whilst his three most recent volumes, all on Botticelli, carried no dedications whatsoever. John held his breath, wondering if he himself were finally to receive the public acknowledgement he had so long craved.

'Yes,' Sir Christopher said, 'as it is likely to be, if not one's last book, at least one's last full-scale monograph, I thought it would be nice to dedicate it to the memory of Mamma. It was, after all, she who set one on one's path so many years ago.'

'I think,' John said, trying to choke back his disappointment, 'that that would be highly appropriate, though I can't help saying that it might have been nicer if you had dedicated a book to her when she was actually *alive*. She might have appreciated that,' he added bitingly.

'Oh no, Mamma expressly forbade one – and Crystal also – from ever dedicating a book to her. She was very level-headed about the matter – said that dedications were springboards and should serve some useful purpose for a young writer's career. And jolly well right she was, but now, of course, that doesn't apply. One of the strange things about getting old is that one no longer has anyone to look up *to*. One might put something about that in the autobiography. Would you make a note of it?'

'Yes,' John respired heavily.

'I say, what a busy summer – even autumn – it is going to be. Certainly no time for dashing off to Salzburg or Bayreuth.'

'No,' John concurred, gaping at Sir Christopher's ability to mask his infirmity as a manifestation of strength. And in the work-clogged, sweat-stained months that followed, John continued to marvel at (and to despair of) his master's fortitude: the Leonardo proofs were rigorously corrected, the speech written and the autobiography resumed. As the strain of ministering to an imperative invalid mounted, so too did John's admiration for, resentment of and devotion to Sir Christopher intensify, reaching a peak on the October day when he stood in Palazzo Vecchio and watched the mayor of Florence grant the freedom of the city to Sir Christopher, who, in that hallowed setting – Vasari frescoes blazing all about and Michelangelo's *Genius of Victory* looming in the distance – looked every inch the great humanist, the highest calling, John thought, known to civilisation.

That day, John Forde's cunctative conversion from presumption to confession was made complete, for, as he positioned himself discreetly to one side and beheld the decoration of the, to him, still beautiful, but painfully frail old man, he admitted to himself, as he had never quite dared to do before, that the disciple he had consciously set out to become ten years ago was fated to remain forever in the shadows. In his ignorance, he had, when he was twenty-four years old, honestly believed that he would one day stand shoulder to shoulder with Sir Christopher as his equally distinguished companion, but today he was reluctantly forced to admit that not even by taking thought could he *add one cubit unto his stature.*

John had long realised that, had Sir Christopher not already been immensely accomplished when they first met, that he, John, would not ever have fallen in love with him, but he only now saw that it was this very accomplishment that ensured his own failure. *Every successful man is more or less a selfish man. The devoted fail,* John quoted the Wessex novelist to himself, as, with tear-stained eyes, he looked up at the dais and felt overcome by the heavy (but unshakeable) burden of his own devotion. Never had he loved Sir Christopher more; never had he valued himself less.

As the autumn wore on and Sir Christopher's demands increased in inverse proportion to his deteriorating health, John comforted himself with the delusion that *one* day he would set to work on *The Disciple* and, in so doing, claim the position that he felt was due to him. It was, therefore, with a great sense of disquietude that, sitting alone before the fire on 10 November – the eve of Sir Christopher's eightieth birthday – whilst reading an article about the correspondence of Henry James in the *TLS*, he learnt that, little more than one hundred years ago, Paul Bourget had published a novel entitled *Le Disciple*. Registering the pre-emptive use of 'his' title, John gasped for breath, feeling that he had been robbed, mutilated, even eviscerated.

From his reading about Henry James and Edith Wharton, John knew the name of Paul Bourget – a once fashionable novelist who, even in his native France, had since fallen into the utmost oblivion – but little more than that. He stayed up most of the night, scouring his library, in the hope of uncovering the mystery of Bourget; wildly, he grasped at the merest hint of dispraise with which to tarnish this 'interloper', as he immediately came to think of him.

He was delighted to learn that Bourget was not just a vociferous anti-Dreyfusard, but a particularly nasty, all-round anti-Semite – a typical, John thought, right-wing, closeted homosexual, which it suited him to believe the married, but childless, Bourget was – and he was positively overjoyed to learn that, whilst Bourget had had the temerity publicly to declare himself Henry James's 'disciple', the master himself had nothing but contempt for the Frenchman's work and, even more, for his person.

With ever increasing pleasure, John read over and over again that night an 1893 letter from Henry James to his older brother:

About Bourget himself I never had any delusions. He has, I think, a distinctly charming and affectionate side, but it loses itself in an abyss of corruption and in a sort of personal avidity … Oh yes, you are right in saying in a manner he has got much more out of me than I out of him – and yet you are wrong. I have got out of him that I know him as if I had made him – his nature, his culture, his race, his type, his mœurs, his mixture – whereas he knows (as a consequence of his own attitude) next to nothing about me. An individual so capable as I am of the uncanniest self-effacement in the active exercise of the passion of observation, always exposes himself a little to looking like a dupe – and he doesn't care a hang! And yet I like Bourget…

To what extent, John asked himself repeatedly, did this letter mirror his own relations with Sir Christopher? John wanted to think that, maugre Sir Christopher's sudden (and sometimes unpredictable) changes of mood, he knew everything there was to know about him – not simply his background or his worldly accomplishments, but his temperament, his beliefs, his prejudices, his weaknesses, even his self-possession – and he was equally convinced that Sir Christopher knew nothing of him, not his spurned past or his imagined future, neither his twisted motivations nor his grandiose aspirations and that he certainly had not the least conception of the depth of his love nor the extent of his hatred. Feeling, as did the poet from Verona, that the indissoluble union of love and hate – the one remorselessly inspiring the other – was as torturous as it was ineluctable, John glanced at his watch and quoted to himself, *Odi et amo: quare id faciam, fortasse requiris. / Nescio, sed fieri sentio et excrucior.* It was eleven minutes past five in the morning, exactly the hour at which Christopher Noble-Nolan had been born eighty years ago.

✝

'How perfectly scrumptious!' Sir Christopher, who had insisted that the *one* thing he wanted to eat on his eightieth birthday was a beautiful (and completely out of season) Cavaillon melon, exclaimed.

'Yes,' John said brightly as he put down the breakfast tray. 'You see,' he continued, lifting the top off a small, pale pistachio-coloured fruit with dark, vertical sutures – so unlike the commonplace cantaloupe, with its unattractively webbed rind – 'it is perfectly ripe, as one can tell, not only from the wonderful perfume but, even more, from the fact that it has ten stripes down the sides; if it has nine, or eleven stripes, it is either not yet ready or past its prime. I had to buy an entire crate of them – at a perfectly usurious rate, I might add – from that shady vendor at the Mercato di San Lorenzo. I insist, therefore, that each one be absolutely ripe – exactly ten stripes down the side – before we cut into it.'

'Too, too delicious,' Sir Christopher said, without having yet tasted a morsel.

'I read in the *Larousse gastronomique*,' John said, 'that in 1864 Alexandre Dumas was asked by the city of Cavaillon to contribute some of his works to the local library and replied that he would be delighted to donate *hundreds* of volumes, on the condition that he be granted a life annuity of twelve Cavaillon melons a year, one per month.'

'And one can well understand Dumas's demand,' Sir Christopher said as he tucked in.

'Apparently, they've been cultivating the Charentais melon in Cavaillon ever since Charles VIII brought back the seeds from Cantelupo in 1495.'

'Perhaps,' Sir Christopher said, after he had scooped out the last sliver of brilliant orange flesh, 'we should try sending a copy of my book on Leonardo, when it comes out in January, to the library in Cavaillon and see if it inspires any such similar offering.'

John laughed. 'Perhaps. Now, here is my birthday gift to you,' he continued, producing a small, elaborately wrapped package.

'How lovely,' Sir Christopher said, disfiguring the ribbon and tearing the paper to shreds. 'Oh,' he continued, with noticeably less enthusiasm, as he opened an antique leather box, 'it's another gold repeater watch.'

'Not just *any* gold repeater,' John said. 'Have you read the Greek inscription on the dial-plate? It's exactly the same one that both Dr Johnson and your mother had on their watches. I thought it seemed *too* perfectly providential, when one stumbled upon it in Switzerland, back in the spring. Infinitely more distinguished than a watch with someone else's initials on it – initials encircled with diamonds *en plus* – like that of Dodo's father.'

'Very nice it is,' Sir Christopher said as he returned the watch to its box.

'Now look, we must make way for the eggs Benedict,' John said, as Annunziata stepped meekly into the room.

'A birthday breakfast of dreams,' Sir Christopher said, pushing his present aside.

'It *is* what you asked for,' John said mordantly.

As he handed the desecrated melon to the maid and centred the new, piping hot plate on the tray, he could not fail to note that Sir Christopher seemed more pleased with the food than with the much pondered gift, a gift whose inscription he had had, contrary to what he implied, added himself.

'You know, I was thinking last night, when I went on reading till quite late,' Sir Christopher said as he leant over to pick up a book from his *table de chevet*, nearly falling out of bed in the process, 'how *un*like the characters in *Daniel Deronda* you are.'

'Whatever do you mean by that?' John asked in a slightly worried tone of voice as he jumped up to steady the breakfast tray and reposition the worn paperback he had bought in via de' Tornabuoni that first summer he had arrived in Florence. 'I read that book years ago and don't remember much about the characters, except for Mordecai and Daniel himself, both of whom I thought exemplary.'

'Oh no,' Sir Christopher said, 'I don't mean *them*. One always skips all the Jewish bits in *Daniel Deronda* – frightfully boring they are. I was referring to Mallinger Grandcourt and Gwendolen Harleth. Last night, I reread that scene at Genoa, quite extraordinary scene really, when she coolly stands in the boat and watches her husband drown. He was a brute, of course. But still, I mean, they both – *she* was no saint – did everything to make each other's lives miserable. All so unlike you, taking such trouble to arrange one's birthday breakfast and, just generally, looking after one so beautifully.'

You have no idea, you know nothing about me – not my nature, my culture, my race, my type, my mœurs, my mixture – nothing, John, appropriating the master's verdict on the detestable Bourget, said to himself. Aloud, he said, 'I only want you to be happy.'

'And unimaginably happy you make one,' Sir Christopher said as he pierced both yolks and unleashed an eruption of perfectly composed, velvety yellow liquid.

'Actually,' he continued, 'you can take that book away now. I think I've read as much of it as I want. One certainly doesn't want to get bogged down in Daniel and that Jewish singer running off to the Holy Land.'

'That prig Leavis, you know, proposed a *judenrein* version of the book,' John said, purposefully employing the Nazi terminology. 'He thought it should be cleansed of all trace of Daniel Deronda and his mysterious Hebrew ancestry and simply retitled "Gwendolen Harleth".'

'Not a bad idea, not a bad idea at all.'

'I don't know,' John, who considered Leavis the archetypal hetero-academic bully, said pensively as he fingered the book, stopping at a passage he remembered having heavily underscored ten years ago, thinking it, back then, an auspicious portent of the devotion that he imagined Sir Christopher sought from him: 'You must,' the ailing Mordecai implored Daniel, his devoted young follower, 'be not only a hand to me, but a soul – believing my belief, being moved by my reasons, hoping my hope, seeing the vision I point to, beholding a glory where I behold it!' But such fusion, he sadly now felt, was not what Sir Christopher had envisaged.

'Where does the drowning scene take place?' John asked.

'It's toward the end. Book seven, I think it is.'

'I'll have a look at it.'

'Yes,' Sir Christopher said, 'by all means do. And you might bring me *Kenilworth* as a replacement. And then, it seems to me that one really should go to look at a transcendently great work of art today, of all days, one's eightieth birthday. I think the Masaccio *Trinity* in Santa Maria Novella would fit the bill nicely.'

'If you like,' John, who dreaded the time *and* effort that such an excursion would entail, agreed, 'but we shall really have to go in the morning, as I will be wildly busy all afternoon with preparations for your birthday dinner.'

'This morning it is then,' Sir Christopher said. 'And that way, I can work on the last chapter of the autobiography in the afternoon.'

'All right,' John, who thought Sir Christopher's nearly completed autobiography all *wrong*, said. It was not merely that he found that this work remained perilously close to the surface – the very antithesis of Augustinian interiority – but, even more, that it unwittingly presented a self-portrait of emotional hebetude, the spectacle of which John had no desire for the world at large to behold, even less to exploit. In recounting his own life, Sir Christopher eschewed any hint of familial devotion, sexual identity or romantic attachment: his father was brushed off as a 'failure'; his mother was lauded for possessing a 'masculine mind'; Andrew Bruntisfield was described as a 'tremendous friend'; John himself was mentioned, once, as 'my secretary'.

Furthermore, in describing his professional life – much the longest part of a not very long book – Sir Christopher did not hesitate to claim that he 'enjoyed' sacking people, nor to shrink from labelling one fellow art historian as 'insufficiently ruthless' and another as 'pathetically loyal', while in a chapter recording the works of art in his own collection, including every stick of furniture in his apartment, he went so far as to write: 'I prefer objects to people. Objects are more constant than people; they never change their nature, and they do not pall.'

Most alarming of all, to John, was the eerily cold detachment with which Christopher Noble-Nolan described the brutal murder of his own brother: 'One was taken to identify the body at Chelsea Coroner's Court, and, when the trolley was wheeled out and the sheet over his face turned down, one was struck by the dissolute, almost evil, expression on his face. One might have been participating in some unwritten Jacobean tragedy.'

On reading this, John thought immediately of Lord Henry Wotton's heartless advice to a devastated Dorian Gray, when he learnt of the suicide of his working-class mistress: 'You must think of that lonely death in the tawdry dressing room as a strange lurid fragment from some Jacobean tragedy, as a wonderful scene from Webster, or Ford, or Cyril Tourneur.'

John knew that it was pointless to imagine that he might convince Sir Christopher to write something more self-revelatory, but he did harbour the hope that he might encourage him to cut some of the less attractive passages of sentimental paralysis. John's apprehension was, therefore, redoubled when, two days after the birthday dinner, he was handed the finished manuscript of the autobiography, including a dedication that Sir Christopher himself had typed in that very afternoon: *To John Forde, without whose help this book could not have been produced.*

'And now,' Sir Christopher said, as John stared in disbelief at his own name, 'I trust that no one who reads this book will learn a thing about one – *nothing.*'

And no one ever did learn anything about Sir Christopher Noble-Nolan from his autobiography, for John saw to it that it was never published.

☦

The night after John had been presented with the unexpected dedication, Sir Christopher rolled out of the high swan bed and, thudding to the floor, broke his right ankle. Whilst in hospital to have the fracture set, Sir Christopher had fallen into another coma – one which, Dr Werner had warned, was liable to be fatal. And though this was not the case, John was only too glad that the lapse had not occurred under *his* responsible watch. Contrary to all prognostication, he managed to get Sir Christopher home by the feast of St Ambrose, the traditional opening of La Scala, which they had often attended in the past, but the memory of which now seemed, to John, like some bizarre ritual from a remote culture, for, in a matter of weeks, the tenor of life in Palazzo Vespucci had changed forever: ramps, a wheelchair, a hospital bed and a succession of nurses now disfigured the landscape.

Hopefully, John looked each morning for signs, not of improvement, but of deterioration, and yet there was no consistency, either forward or backward, to the changes he noted. Some days, Sir Christopher rallied – reading for long stretches at a time on his own, either in bed or seated in a wheelchair in the drawing room before the fire, the warmth of which he craved desperately. Other days, he fussed terribly – tossing relentlessly in bed, rejecting all succour, utterly inconsolable. A few times, he hallucinated – once insisting that the night nurse should be let go for having tried to hang a fake Duccio in his room: 'It would be hard enough to sleep with a real Duccio in the room, but a *fake* one!' he had thundered. Most days, he simply slept.

But no matter what his state of mind, even when delusional, his character – arch, exigent, confident – remained inviolable. Today, Christmas, the first time they had been completely alone since Sir Christopher's return from hospital on 7 December, John found his master brightly cheered by the elaborate breakfast he had prepared – including the last of the Cavaillon melons – and the pile of gifts, all of which had been acquired at the penultimate moment, as John had doubted that Sir Christopher would ever live to see the holiday in. But as the day wore on, Sir Christopher's mercurial temperament got the upper hand. At luncheon – consisting of a barely acknowledged soufflé *renversé aux truffes* and a single, superb and strictly forbidden glass of Pomerol – Sir Christopher was petulantly taciturn; at teatime, he was drowsy and affectionately compliant; by dinnertime, he appeared overtly hostile.

'Do let this blasted thing down,' Sir Christopher barked, violently rattling the guardrail of the hospital bed, as John entered the room shortly before eight. 'I can't abide being penned in.'

'I only raised it,' John explained, lowering the barrier, 'as you fell so soundly asleep right after tea. And we don't want you tumbling out of bed again.'

'Well one is wide awake now,' Sir Christopher said. 'And do tell me,' he continued, 'you've never said what happened, whilst I was in hospital, with the autobiography. Did you send the manuscript off to the publisher, as we had agreed?'

'Yes,' John lied.

'And they still haven't replied?' Sir Christopher asked.

'Oh, but I showed you a reply – that very nice fax,' John said truthfully, 'when you were still in hospital. Perhaps you don't remember? I can go and get it for you right now, if you like.'

'Yes, please do.'

'Here you are,' John said as he returned in a matter of minutes, brandishing a forgery.

When Sir Christopher had been in hospital, John wrote to the publisher in London to say that, due to illness, the delivery of the autobiography was to be indefinitely delayed, but, so as not to arouse Sir Christopher's suspicion, he fabricated a reply from the commissioning editor, acknowledging receipt of the manuscript. The wonderful invention of the fax rendered this an easy task: he simply photocopied the masthead of the firm in question from an old letter on to a blank sheet of paper, upon which he typed a message of acceptance (delighted acceptance) and a list of prospective publishing dates; he then took the sham document to an *hôtel* in Borgo San Jacopo and had it faxed back to Palazzo Vespucci, leaving him in possession of a perfectly credible transaction.

On the one hand, John was keen to suppress publication of the autobiography because he thought it left Sir Christopher vulnerable to the sting of his own vituperative pen: the many Neville Pounders of the art historical establishment, those who had been the victims of Sir Christopher's wildly unfavourable reviews over the years, would, John imagined, be only too happy to pounce on these stilted, often thrasonical, recollections. On the other hand, John was even more desirous of protecting *himself*.

All the while Sir Christopher was in hospital, he had repeatedly asked himself what would happen if Sir Christopher were to die before publication. Who would believe the dedication when the book did come out? Surely everyone — Professor Isner, his fellow graduate students, Casey above all, even Lulu de' Portinari — he feared, would whisper that he had smuggled his own name into a narrative from which he ought forcibly to have been excluded. He dreaded that he might be compared to one of those maligned literary heirs — an Anton Schindler or a Robert Craft — accused of falsifying conversation books or of fabricating diary entries, but, fragile egotist that he was, he also longed for official recognition. John did not want Sir Christopher's memoirs to appear without the dedication to himself, but he did not believe that such attestation would be granted credence. Concealment was his only solution.

'As you can see, they are planning,' John said, as he handed over the faux fax to Sir Christopher, 'on publication for Christmas of next year.'

'A whole year we have to wait,' Sir Christopher said, pushing the fax away without having read it.

'Apparently,' John, greatly encouraged by Sir Christopher's lack of interest, said. 'It looks,' he continued lying, 'as if they're planning to produce a quite handsome edition, with lots of photos. I imagine that it will arouse a good deal of interest — maybe even encourage someone to write about you.'

'But I don't *want* anyone to write about me,' Sir Christopher cried. 'You must promise me that you will stop anyone from snooping about. Put up every obstacle. And *you* certainly must never yourself write anything about me.'

'But of course,' John said sarcastically.

'I mean it,' Sir Christopher said fiercely.

'I hardly think anyone would be interested in *my* memoirs,' John said, regretfully realising, as he did so, that he had just convinced Sir Christopher of his future silence, not on account of his loyalty but because of his own insignificance. At the same time, he could not help recalling Sir Christopher saying to him on Palm Sunday, little more than six months ago, when he had knelt down to tie his shoes, 'I wonder if you'll put this in a book someday?' *Which of these,* he asked himself, *represent my master's true intention? Probably both,* he replied to his own question.. Aloud, he resumed, 'Now, just let me fetch your dinner — there's some beautifully clarified bouillon and a bit of smoked salmon — and then I thought we might try that new portable CD player that I got you for Christmas.'

'Why don't you give me the catalogue of the discs? I can choose something whilst you are getting dinner,' Sir Christopher said.

But when he returned shortly, bearing a tray specially decorated for Christmas, John found Sir Christopher actually standing up, clutching the end of the bed and rooting about in the bedclothes with his stick.

'*Whatever* are you doing?' John demanded, placing the tray on the floor as he ran over to steady Sir Christopher.

'My circle fell down there,' Sir Christopher said distractedly.

'Your "circle"?' John asked, wrapping his arms round Sir Christopher's back.

'How is one meant to read without them?'

'You mean your spectacles? You've lost your spectacles?' John asked, worried by Sir Christopher's confusion.

'Yes, of course,' Sir Christopher said exasperatedly.

'Please, *please* get back into bed. Then I'll find them for you. And look, here they are, right next to you, on the night table.'

'So they are,' Sir Christopher said unapologetically as John guided him back to bed.

'Now, just eat this,' John said, placing the tray in front of Sir Christopher, 'and then we can listen to some music.'

'I need a new timetable,' Sir Christopher said in between sips of bouillon. 'This one I have here is hopelessly out of date.'

'We have a current Italian train schedule, the *Orario generale*, in the archive upstairs. I'll get it for—'

'No, no, no,' Sir Christopher interrupted, 'I need an *international* timetable. Only *Thomas Cook* will do. I'd like to calculate exactly how long it would take to travel from Caracas to Buenos Aires and how many stops one would be obliged to make along the way.'

'Right you are,' John said as he sat down to calm his fraying nerves. Though he could not deny that he had always known Sir Christopher to be attracted by the minutiæ of railway schedules, plotting any number of hypothetical journeys round the world with the same obsessive concentration that he devoted to reassembling the predella panels of dispersed altarpieces, the absurdity of someone who was unlikely ever again to leave his apartment – leave it whilst alive – demanding a timetable was not lost on him. Nonetheless, he patiently continued, 'I'll buy you a new one tomorrow.'

'Tomorrow? *Tomorrow?*' Sir Christopher asked irascibly.

'Well, I can hardly go out and track one down on Christmas night, now, can I?' John said, gritting his teeth.

'That's true,' Sir Christopher agreed sullenly. 'But please don't forget. And whilst you're out tomorrow you might get some other cake for tea. I'm quite bored by the marmalade cake; we've had it *so* often. And I need a new ribbon for my typewriter. And I think that icon wants polishing again. And a whole stack of new thrillers would not be out of place. And then, I'd also like—'

'Please, for God's sake, that's enough. You'll drive one insane,' John shouted, shouted quite loud, as he jumped up and whisked the tray away from a startled Sir Christopher.

How could I have stooped so low, so low as to show my emotions like that? Show him what I really feel about him? The very opposite of Henry James's mastery of Bourget, John berated himself in the kitchen. Quaking at the thought of a reprise of that delusional night when they returned from Switzerland, he took an enormous gulp of vodka and plunged three sleeping pills in a cup of steaming camomile.

'Why don't you drink this up?' he said in a strained voice, offering Sir Christopher the tisane on returning to the bedroom. 'Then we can listen to some music.'

'I should have thought the Berlioz *L'Enfance du Christ* would be the correct choice,' Sir Christopher replied as he sipped his drugged tea.

I would have thought the Victoria Requiem *infinitely more appropriate,* John said to himself. Aloud, he said, 'Whatever you like.'

Once the music began, John retreated to an armchair in the corner of the room and sunk his head in his hands. After a time, a rather long time, of futilely attempting to blot out all thought, he looked over at his drowsy master and then opened *Daniel Deronda*, rereading, for the fifth or sixth time in as many weeks, the scene of Gwendolen Harleth watching her husband drown in the bay of Genoa. Gwendolen hadn't pushed Grandcourt from the boat – he fell through his own clumsiness – but nor did she make any effort to save him: she impassively watched him drown, refusing to throw him the rope for which he begged.

John looked now at the sleeping Sir Christopher and wondered if he himself were not just as culpable as Gwendolen, standing idly by and watching his master fade right before him. Quivering, he read yet again Gwendolen Harleth's confession to Daniel Deronda. Like her, John felt as if he were two contradictory creatures, each trapped in the secret hollows of a moral conscience incessantly in conflict with itself. He knew that he was, at times, guilty of wanting Sir Christopher to die. And it was not simply that the burden of looking after him had become crushingly heavy, but, more incriminating, that he sought to avenge himself on him by whom he felt betrayed. A part of him longed for freedom, whilst another, equally strong, part knew, knew instinctively, that Sir Christopher's death would deprive his own life of *all* meaning. And so it was, as the music came to a conclusion, that he walked over to the bed and, with remorse and rancour beating simultaneously in his breast, bent over to kiss the sleeping Sir Christopher on the forehead.

'I know that you hate me,' Sir Christopher, without opening his eyes, whispered.

'*What?*' John asked, as he recoiled in horror and made to turn off the lights on a once again somnolent Sir Christopher.

✝

John spent the rest of Christmas night, alone, morosely sipping vast quantities of champagne – Sir Christopher's most despised libation – in front of the drawing room fire. Repeatedly, he asked himself if Sir Christopher had actually uttered those six fatal words – *I know that you hate me* – or if, in his agitated state, he had not simply imagined the whole scene. He would never know for sure.

A large marbled notebook mourned from his lap, whilst a capped fountain pen sat mutely on the table beside him, but the motions of his mind and the heaviness of his heart were not, tonight, to be committed to paper. In the more than ten years that he had lived in Florence, he had bought (and filled) over thirty volumes from a small shop, Il Torchio, located right in via de' Bardi. It had long seemed to him that this picturesque outpost had been expressly invented for his diaristic passion. Ever since that summer of 1983, when he had been seduced by the journals of Jo Leigh-Fiennes, John had felt inspired, almost obliged, to catalogue every derailment to his plans, to decorticate every slight to his ego, to justify every proposal to his aspirations, and yet he was now incapable of recording so much as a line about what seemed to him the most traumatic event of his life with Sir Christopher. Instead, he calmly got up and went back and forth to his study several times, hauling out all the earlier volumes of his diary, which he stacked on the low table in the drawing room. Thirty-four, he counted – exactly his own age.

He would have liked to find it tragic, but he knew it was merely bathetic, that, in all the years he had spent religiously detailing his obsession with his master, he had never once thought to hide these volumes, so painfully confident was he of Sir Christopher's unremitting *in*curiosity.

Shivering, he then added to this assemblage all of his papers for *The Disciple* – a farrago of notebooks, loose-leaf sheets, even index cards – along with a meticulously transcribed commonplace book, which began with a quotation from St Paul to the Galatians: *But let every man prove his own work, and then shall he have rejoicing in himself alone, and not in another.* Finally, he added all copies of his correspondence, including the first (and *only*) letter he had ever written to Sir Christopher, on 24 June 1983. And therein, he imagined, as he surveyed the landscape, lay the key to his heart, a heart Sir Christopher would never know.

Henry James, John thought, might well have taken pleasure in the art of self-effacement – but then he *liked* Bourget – whereas he himself loved Sir Christopher. Thus did it wound John unbearably to see, in this mountain of papers, his own secrets, crowding round him like the Instruments of the Passion – cross, lance, sponge, crown, chalice, veil, dice, thirty pieces of silver. And yet... and yet, he was sure that to have made known the confidences locked within these pages would have secured him not deliverance but expulsion. And so it was that, with great deliberation, he stood for hours before the blazing fire and burnt page after page *after* page, all the while quoting to himself from the sombrous son of Salem: *What a trustful guardian of secret matters fire is! What should we do without Fire and Death?*

The following morning, when he went out to buy a *Thomas Cook* timetable, along with the many other things Sir Christopher had demanded – and even some he had not – John returned to the Accademia. Gingerly, he wended his way through the crowds and stepped into the 'Hall of Prisoners'. In the cold light of day, these unfinished sculptures looked even more anguished than they had, under romantic shadowing, on the night of the Richter concert six months ago. He inspected the grooves and notches, the mallet and chisel marks, with utmost attention – the ultimate manifestation of the *non-finito* – before standing back to take in all four slaves at once. Not only were they miraculous illustrations of the artist's difficulty in liberating the figure from the block of marble – Michelangelo's lifelong obsession – but they represented, to John, the very embodiment of man's struggle, his fruitless struggle, to effect his own manumission from the shackles of imprisoning matter. Similarly, John saw that, writhe and rebel though he might, he could never escape the suffocating shell that was his pitiable self. That day, for the first and *only* time in his life, he cried before a work of art.

✞

One by one, like the candles of Tenebræ, the lights round John were, with remarkable chronological precision, extinguished, till there was but one central flame burning bright, Christopher Noble-Nolan himself – *Quomodo sedet solo civitas...*

Dodo Delfington was the first to go, expiring in her sleep, in late January of 1994, at home in London, at the age of ninety-three. With consummate grace, she departed with no sign of struggle, leaving strict instructions that she was to be cremated without ceremony; a memorial service at St James's Piccadilly was to follow six months later. Her vast fortune was to be equally divided between her two daughters, save for a handsome legacy to Zeb Hollingsworth, who, alone of her grandchildren, was singled out; there were no bequests to charity.

In the middle of February, Tommy Tornabuoni succumbed to a violent bout of pneumonia – his 'weak' heart strong until the end – at the age of ninety. His funeral, which seemed to John to speak more of professional ambition than artistic dedication, was celebrated with great pomp and no intimacy in, not surprisingly, the Tornabuoni chapel in Santa Maria Novella. There wasn't a wet eye in the church. As expected, he left his entire estate to the city of Florence to provide for the upkeep of his palace and its collections;

less expectedly, he kept his word about naming John as his literary executor.

Alice Varrow, who was hoping for, at least, a life annuity from the noble baron, was not mentioned in his will, but then she would not have had much time to squander any such longed for inheritance, as she herself died, whilst shouting out for her maid, in the first week of March at the age of eighty-nine, furiously battling her infirmities till the end. Her sparsely attended funeral, at the dingy little Anglican church in via Maggio, left John deeply saddened. Not only did he think she deserved a better send-off – he was sure that he had seen more people crammed into her little house at Bellosguardo at any one time than were present for her obsequies – but, more important, he realised that her passing would leave a very real gap in the diurnal cycle of his life. For years now, he had spoken to her every single day on the telephone and saw her several times a week. Forever grateful for the welcome, nay the acceptance, she had shown him on his arrival in Florence, he had come to feel overtly protective of this impossibly demanding, maddeningly opinionated and perversely charming old woman. True to form, she left debts all round, including nine different bank accounts – five in Italy and four in England – all of which were *seriously* overdrawn. She also bequeathed her library to John – much of which duplicated his own, but all of which he cherished.

Advancing upon the *infandum dolorem* of years, in which, as the most celebrated convert of the Oxford Movement put it, *the stars of this lower heaven were, one by one, going out,* John's greatest regret was that, even if his literary ambitions were one day to be realised, all of these people – people whom he had longed to impress, even to be loved by – would only ever have known him as an unaccomplished, fat, faggy, non-entity of a secretary.

And so there remained but one – the only One – to magnify.

At the onset of the new year of 1994, Sir Christopher's strength, and in turn his spirits, had improved considerably. First, he was encouraged by the removal of the plaster from his ankle in the second week of January, leading him to believe, mistakenly John thought but did not dare to say, that he would be able to walk freely again. They did take a few hazardous turns round the apartment – Sir Christopher leaning heavily on his stick with his right hand, whilst pushing John away with his left – though the idea of testing the outside waters was never broached.

The great boon to Sir Christopher's morale came, however, in the appearance of his Leonardo monograph at the end of the month. For day after day, a transformed, perfectly alert, immaculately dressed Sir Christopher sat before the fire in his wheelchair, perusing his own work. With the most minute attention, he scoured not just the long text but every caption, every footnote, every bibliographic citation; he even found a mistake in the index that he told John, with breathtaking confidence, should be corrected in *future* editions. He was wonderfully, even humbly, grateful that he had lived long enough to see the publication of what, he must have known, would surely be his last book – a large, lavishly produced tome, more than worthy to stand side by side with his other works.

But as January rolled into February, even the charms of his own writing could not prevent the obnubilation of Sir Christopher's faculties. Gradually, but irretrievably, he started to lose his sense of time and place; and he had increasing difficulty in finding the right word – saying 'turn off the book', when he obviously meant 'turn off the light'. He then began to address the startled Italian servants in French – much better French than John had ever before heard him speak – till one day, in early March, he simply stopped speaking altogether.

It was, therefore, with a certain relief, bathed in remorse, that John watched Sir Christopher slip into a coma on the afternoon of 21 March, the Monday of Passion week. He immediately called Dr Werner, insisting that he wanted to keep Sir Christopher at home, as he had promised him he would do.

Upon arrival, later that afternoon, Dr Werner agreed that it was pointless to send Sir Christopher to hospital; the end, he said, was only a matter of days, maybe even hours. And yet, though Sir Christopher unmistakably bore about him *the mark of death, the sign of his own sin* – he had received extreme unction from Father Hennessy for what was now the fifth time – he would not embrace the end.

For twelve days, John watched, amidst an ever-changing round of nurses, as Sir Christopher languished. Except as a will to struggle, he could hardly be said to have been alive. John decided, therefore, that this evening, Good Friday, he could, without risk, venture out to the celebration of Tenebræ, which was to begin at nine o'clock, in their habitual chapel in Piazza Santissima Annunziata. He knew, however, that he had to be home in just over two hours, as there was a break in the nurses' schedule from eleven to twelve, when Sir Christopher would be unattended.

As he entered the chapel, John was happy that he had made the effort to come out on this chilly night. Though he regretted not having been able to attend the Pedilavium of Maundy Thursday or the Good Friday Mass of the Presanctified, it was the rite of Tenebræ that meant the most to him. He could vividly remember the awe he had felt at his first Tenebræ in the spring of 1984 – a service of which he had been wholly ignorant, in spite of, or perhaps *because* of, all his years of Catholic education in America – and the gratitude he would forever bear to Sir Christopher for introducing him to its beauty, whose inspired music, not to mention gravity, had long left him speechless.

Tonight, he glanced at the altar, already stript and the tabernacle, bare, though most of his attention was focused on the triangular-shaped Tenebræ candlestick, known as a 'hearse'. After the solemn chanting of each psalm, he watched as a solitary candle was extinguished, one after another – seven up each sloping side – in what seemed an inexorable march forward into darkness, till only the candle at the apex, the Christ candle, remained alight. The six altar candles were then put out during the Benedictus, as the Christ candle was hidden, leaving the church in total darkness, when the priest began violently to pound the floor with a mallet and slam a pew with his breviary, bringing forth the *strepitus* or 'great noise', symbolising how the earth did quake and the rocks did rent at the hour of Christ's death. Finally, the sole remaining illumination, the Christ candle, was meant to be shown to the congregation and then extinguished, at which all would depart in silence, but John was so overcome by foreboding at the thunderous sound of the *strepitus* that he dashed out of the chapel before the last candle was snuffed out and ran home to Sir Christopher.

As soon as he entered the bedroom, John could see that, during his brief absence, there had been a marked change. Sir Christopher's body was now absolutely rigid, and he was breathing with great difficulty. After the nurse left, John sat in the stygian darkness next to the bed, clutching Sir Christopher's glacial hand. Soon, a series of eldritch moans began to emanate from Sir Christopher, the sound of which seemed to push John – no matter how tightly he clung – further and further away from his master, deep into an intractable *region of unlikeness*. He knew that it was normal, maybe even admirable, that he should pray for deliverance for Sir Christopher, but the closer the final moment came, the more unfaithful did John feel. He feared that such thoughts would condemn him to freeze forever in Judecca, the innermost ring of the bottom pit of Cocytus, entombed in ice – 'like straw in glass', *come festuca in vetro* – keeping silent company for all eternity with the Treacherous to their Masters. Shortly before midnight, Sir Christopher let out a final, devastating wail – louder than the *strepitus* itself – and, bowing his head, gave up the ghost. John was filled with a terror that cannot be told.

That night, John Forde did not die himself, but nor did he live. Sundered from his Master, the disciple was deprived of life *and* death.

AUTHOR'S NOTE

I am not he; he is not I.
He is not he; she is not she.
They *are* they.

M. M.